MW01167137

ESCAPE
TO THE SKY

ESCAPE
TO THE SKY

Enjoy the read!

Cheers,

Don Fink

12/13/2012

DONALD E. FINK

LIBRARY OF CONGRESS CONTROL NUMBER:		2012917801
ISBN:	HARDCOVER	978-1-4797-2242-6
	SOFTCOVER	978-1-4797-2241-9
	EBOOK	978-1-4797-2243-3

This book was printed in the United States of America.

To order additional copies of this book, contact:
Xlibris Corporation
1-888-795-4274
www.Xlibris.com
Orders@Xlibris.com
120936

Dedication

To my late brother, Conrad, whose famous red pen sharpened the focus and finely tuned a manuscript into a readable novel; to my pilot friend Chris Wheal, for adding the English touch; to my writer's club and book club friends for their encouragement and help; and finally, to Carolyn for her thorough final edit and her love, support, and understanding of my need to spend hours on the computer.

So it was that the war in the air began. Men rode upon the whirlwind that night and slew and fell like archangels. The sky rained heroes upon the astonished earth. Surely the last fights of mankind were the best. What was the heavy pounding of your Homeric swordsmen, what was the creaking charge of chariots, besides this swift rush, this crash, this giddy triumph, this headlong sweep to death?

—H. G. Wells, *The World Set Free*

Chapter 1

SPAIN, SPRING 1938

Ben and Reggie spotted the enemy airplanes at the same time; two German Condor Legion fighters sliced overhead from left to right and rolled into a diving attack from behind. Ben, flying as Reggie's wingman, twisted in the seat of his open-cockpit Russian fighter to track them.

"Omigod!" he shouted. "Messerschmitts! Bf 109s! We're sittin' ducks!"

Reggie signaled "break" and slammed his Polikarpov I-16 fighter into a tight climbing turn to the right, arcing back toward the enemy airplanes. Ben swept into a wider right turn, opening space between his airplane and Reggie's.

They were volunteer pilots in Spain's bloody civil war, flying reconnaissance patrol for the Spanish Republican Air Force over Nationalist army enemy positions along the Ebro River, west of Barcelona. When the German Condor Legion fighters supporting the Nationalist rebel forces jumped them, Reggie led Ben into a maneuver they had briefed earlier—if attacked from above and behind, separate and take on the enemy airplanes individually. Don't stay in close formation and present a big target.

Ben shot another quick look over his right shoulder. The German fighters also separated; one dived on Reggie's fighter, and the other came after him. Ben pulled his airplane into a tighter turn. G-forces crammed him into the seat, shoving his goggles down on his nose. He heard his combat instructor's voice: "Always turn into the arc of the enemy's turn. Make him pull tighter and tighter. If you roll outside, he'll roll in behind ya and cut ya off at the pass."

Turbulent air slapped Ben's leather helmet as he hunched behind the windscreen. The staccato chopping of the Bf 109's guns cut through the roar of his airplane's radial engine. He grunted under the high g-load. Tracers flashed past his left wing. Ben pulled the stick to tighten his turn. A quick look in his rearview mirror showed the German pilot pulling even harder, bringing his guns to bear on Ben's tail.

Ben slammed the control stick farther right and pulled. The I-16 reared its nose into a high-speed aerodynamic stall. The left wing lost lift first, and the Polikarpov rolled violently to the left, whipping into a snap roll. The nose pitched up again as he rolled upright in one of the sloppiest maneuvers he had ever flown.

"Shit! Shit! Shit!" Ben yelled.

His I-16 seemed to slam into an invisible brick wall and shuddered on the edge of another high-speed stall. Ben shoved the stick forward to get the nose down and regain airspeed. To his amazement, the Bf 109 slashed past his right wing. The sudden change in relative speed made the German pilot overshoot.

Ben rammed the I-16's nose farther down and saw the enemy airplane ahead of him and slightly to the right. He kicked right rudder and punched the trigger button. Four 7.62 mm machine guns—two in the nose and one in each wing—spat bullets, shredding the tail of the Bf 109. Pieces of aluminum and fabric streamed past Ben's airplane.

"Whoa!" Ben yelled, and pulled into a right-climbing turn to avoid ramming the stricken German fighter. Rolling wings level, Ben looked down to his left and saw the Bf 109 dive and flip inverted. The canopy flew off. The German pilot tumbled out of the cockpit and was snatched away in the slipstream.

The small drogue chute popped out of the German's parachute pack, snaking out the main chute, which blossomed and jerked the pilot upright as he drifted away. Ben rolled left again to watch the German plane dive like a lawn dart into the ground, exploding in a ball of fire and smoke.

The fight seemed to have lasted an eternity. Ben realized it had taken only seconds. He quickly scanned the sky. His instructor had stressed staying alert. "Don't focus on one thing too long," he had said. "Don't fly straight and level for more than a couple seconds. Keep your head on a swivel. Watch your tail!"

Ben searched for Reggie and the other German fighter. He spotted Reggie high above him, waggling his wings, and he climbed to join him. Ben shook from head to toe. Bile burned his throat.

"God, don't let me barf," Ben pleaded, swallowing hard. Tremors wracked his body as he slid his fighter into position off Reggie's left wing. Reggie waved and pumped his right fist in a triumphant Republican salute. Ben returned a halfhearted wave and concentrated on keeping the vomit from welling up in his throat.

Ben's mind whirled. *Where's the other 109? Did Reggie shoot him down?*

Ben raised two fingers and shrugged. They used hand signals because their Russian fighters had no radios. Reggie pointed downward to a second smoke plume rising from a hillside.

This was Spain, 1938; and Ben Findlay, a nineteen-year-old American pilot, had scored his first aerial kill. He was a new volunteer pursuit pilot, flying for the Spanish Republican government in the civil war against the Nationalist rebels led by Gen. Francisco Franco. Reggie, Lt. Reginald Percy, was his flight leader. A Brit, he was one of thousands of volunteers who flocked to Spain to help the Republican Loyalists fight Franco's rebel forces, which were backed by Nazi Germany and Fascist Italy.

The Polikarpov I-16 fighters Ben and Reggie flew were basic single-wing, open-cockpit designs, but they were effective in the hands of experienced pilots. They were almost crude flying machines compared to the Bf 109s that German Chancellor Adolph Hitler had sent to Spain, with a variety of other aircraft, as part of the Condor Legion, in support of Franco's drive to make Spain a Fascist state. The Spanish civil war also provided an excellent proving ground for the new Luftwaffe that Germany had been rebuilding secretly since the early 1930s. Mussolini's Fascist government also sent fighter and bomber units to support the Nationalist rebels. Soviet dictator Josef Stalin responded by sending the Polikarpov squadrons to Spain to bolster the Republicans' ragtag air force.

Reggie waved urgently and pointed inside at the instrument panel. He chopped a hand across his throat. Ben got the message and checked his fuel gauge. The needle was dropping toward empty! He stayed on Reggie's wing as they swung into a wide 180-degree turn and headed back to Zaragoza Aerodrome, their home base.

"What a stupid mistake!" Ben snarled. "Shoot down your first enemy airplane by sheer dumb luck and then run outta gas!"

Reggie rolled level and signaled straight ahead. Ben concentrated on maintaining position with Reggie's airplane, risking quick peeks inside to check his fuel status. It was going to be close. Finally, he spotted familiar landmarks around Zaragoza and relaxed. *Airfield's just over the next ridge!*

Reggie pointed down and made a sweeping motion with his left hand. They would fly a left circling pattern to landing. Ben cranked the landing gear down, pushed the propeller control to fine pitch, and started the arcing descent to the field. Coming over the fence, he kept well left of Reggie's airplane, chopped the throttle, flared, and let the I-16 settle. It dropped smoothly onto the grass field in one of his better three-point landings. Remembering that the brakes on the I-16 were about as effective as dragging his feet, Ben let the fighter run straight on until the speed bled off. Then he S-taxied back to the flight line, weaving from side to side so he could see around the I-16's bulbous nose.

The two fighters bumped across the field, and the pilots pivoted them into their tie-down spots with bursts of power and differential braking. A ground crewman clung to each inner wingtip to aid the turn. Ben pulled the mixture control and shut off the fuel selector. The engine coughed, backfired, and clanked to a stop. He cut the master switch and slumped in his seat as the cooling engine crackled and pinged, and the instrument gyros whined to a halt.

Bile erupted into his gullet. Ben swallowed hard and yawned, working his jaw to clear his tortured ears. Russian ground crewmen stepped up on the left wings to help the pilots unbuckle their safety harnesses. Ben's crew chief extended a hand to help him out of the seat. Ben waved him off.

Reggie hopped out of his cockpit and bounded over to Ben's airplane. Clambering up on the wing, he cuffed Ben on the side his head. "I say, Benjamin, old lad, one hell of a fight!" he shouted. "Your first kill! Four more and you're a bloody ace!"

9

He peered at Ben's white face and saw his Adam's apple bobbing as Ben struggled to keep the contents of his stomach in his stomach. "Steady on, old man," Reggie said. "You hit? Wounded?"

Ben shook his head, unable to speak.

"I say, we haven't pissed ourselves, have we?" Reggie asked with a sly grin.

"No, I haven't pissed myself!" Ben finally croaked. "I'm tryin' not to throw up. And my legs feel like wet noodles."

"Right-ho," Reggie said. "Catch a few deep breaths. What you need is brandy."

Ben stifled a sour belch as Reggie helped him out of the cockpit and steadied him. "In we go, m'lad," he said. "We'll give our Russian friends a quick debrief and find that brandy."

Ben, fresh off a farm in Michigan, and Reggie, a member of the English aristocracy, made a curious pair of volunteers, the only non-Russian pilots in Russian Volunteer Squadron 27. They had been assigned as replacements for pilots killed in the fierce air combat that had raged over the Barcelona sector.

Ben stared dumbly as Reggie used a combination of English, Russian, Spanish, and hand signals to recount their clash with the German fighters to the Russian squadron intelligence officer. Their double victories were significant. Germany had sent its elite fighter and bomber squadrons to Spain, and the German pilots were highly motivated. The two sides had been evenly matched, but as the Condor Legion pilots gained experience, they began to turn the tide in Franco's favor. Hitler also sent advanced versions of the Bf 109 fighter to Spain, increasing the odds against the Republicans. Reggie's description of the fight and their double victories earned both pilots congratulatory thumps on the back.

Reggie led Ben to their cramped room, eased him into a chair, and poured a large brandy. "Drink this, m'lad, and you'll feel the world of difference," he said.

Ben protested he didn't drink alcohol, and then took a sip. He choked as the brandy burned his throat. "God!" he sputtered. "How can anyone get hooked on this stuff?" Ben finally emptied the glass. He blinked through tears as Reggie poured him a second. He quaffed it as well, remarking on how the fumes curled out of his nose.

Ben awoke, sprawled fully clothed across his bunk. Someone had removed his boots. His leather flight helmet, goggles, and gloves lay on the floor. He had no idea what time it was or, for that matter, where he was. His mouth felt puckered, and fur coated his tongue.

Reggie burst into the room. "You've missed dinner in the mess, old chap, but I've brought you this bit."

Ben's stomach churned as he tried to sit up.

"Here you are, Benjamin. Have a go at this." Reggie shoved a plate of sausages and potatoes under his nose. Ben recoiled and slumped back in his bed. Reggie pursued him, insisting that he eat something.

"Sorry for the meager offering, old bean," he said. "But our Russian friends don't put much stock in haute cuisine. Look, we're on the roster for tomorrow morning's patrol, and you need something in the old tummy."

Ben sat up and, once started, wolfed down the entire plateful. He even chugged a glass of raw Spanish red wine. "Reggie," he said. "I feel terrible. Why am I so whacked?"

"Nervous reaction to your first combat, old cock," Reggie replied. "Adrenalin response, don'tcha know. You didn't half shoot the works today. Used up a bloody month's supply, I shouldn't think. Not a wonder you're all played out. I say, quite an afternoon, eh? You've become quite the fighter pilot!"

Ben frowned as Reggie prattled on. *Damn Englishman! How can he be so cheery after what we've just been through?*

Ben shrugged off his flying gear, had a long pee, and washed his face in the cold-water basin. He made a pass at brushing his teeth and peered into the mirror. "Couldn't wait to get into the Spanish civil war, eh? Well, hayseed, here ya are."

Ben flopped into bed. Wild images of the dogfight flashed through his mind. As sleep overtook him, his thoughts turned to home, the farm in Michigan. *Sittin' high up on that windmill platform, I couldn't wait to see what was out there over that horizon. I had no idea!*

Chapter 2

MICHIGAN, BAKER AIRPORT, SPRING 1936

Morning chores took longer than usual that Saturday, and Ben was late for his job as ramp monkey at Baker Airport. He ducked out of the barn to avoid another nasty encounter with his father. Skipping breakfast, he jumped on his bike and zoomed out of the yard. Gravel ricocheted from the worn tires of his Schwinn Flyer bicycle. He strained his lanky farm-boy frame as he pedaled down the country road leading to the airport. Butch and Bertha, his two faithful cocker spaniels, scrambled after him, ears and tongues flapping.

Ben skidded to a stop. "Hey, you two," he yelled. "You can't come with me! Get back home!" They slunk back to the driveway, tails drooping. Life on the farm was getting to be a bitch, with the old man getting meaner every day. "Still, shouldn't take it out on the pups," Ben muttered.

Ben wished he could stand up to the old man like his older brother, Joe, but what would that get him? Out of the family, living with relatives, trying like Joe to get into college? Ben still had another year plus of high school and had to keep his head down to slip by without a big bust-up with the old man.

He focused his anger and frustration on the pedals. Mr. Simpson was gonna be pissed off at him for being late. The old guy was okay. The new owner of Baker's Flying Service, Al Simpson, worried about keeping the business afloat. Nobody had much money, and Simpson needed every customer he could get just to cover expenses. The gas pumps opened before seven a.m., when the few weekend flyers who could afford it wandered in.

Straining over the handlebars, Ben recalled his first visit to Baker Airport. One Saturday afternoon a year ago, following another row with the old man, Ben hopped on his bicycle and pedaled away. Wasn't sure how he ended up at Baker Airport, but there he was, wandering along the flight line.

Ben's early boyhood fantasy had been to drive big race cars at the Indianapolis Motor Speedway, the famous two-and-a-half-mile brick track where intrepid drivers thrilled spectators with such races as the 500 Mile Classic. Charles Lindbergh and his daring solo flight from New York to Paris in 1927, briefly captured Ben's interest. But then Louis Meyer, who had won twice at Indianapolis, and Wilbur Shaw, his feisty competitor, became Ben's heroes. He pinned newspaper photos and stories of the Indianapolis drivers on his bedroom wall.

This all changed one spring afternoon when Ben gaped as a high-wing monoplane, its engine sputtering and backfiring, sideslipped to a landing on the level pasture at the rear of the farm. Ben and the dogs sprinted toward the airplane as it rolled to a stop. The engine coughed a cloud of smoke from the exhaust and quit. By the time Ben and his hounds reached the airplane, the pilot was standing on a wooden box alongside the nose, cursing the oil-streaked engine.

"Hey, Mister!" Ben panted. "You okay? Need help?"

"Huh? Ah, naw, kid. Thanks," the pilot replied. "Oil line come loose. Hadda land before she blew all the oil. That'd a ruined the motor for sure."

"Ya need some oil?" Ben asked, eyeing the pilot's leather flying jacket, jodhpurs, and laced high-top boots. "We got some in the toolshed."

"Thanks, kid. I carry extra. Soon's I get this line tightened, I'll top her off and be on my way."

"What kinda airplane is this?" Ben asked.

"Travel Air 6000," the pilot said. "She'll carry six. I was headin' for Baker Airport to pick up a charter when the oil line blew."

Repairs completed and oil tank refilled, the pilot gave Ben a wave and climbed back into the cabin. "Stand back, kid!" he yelled. "When I get her started, I'm gonna taxi down to the end of the field and take off in that direction. You an' yer dogs get over there and keep outta the way."

Butch and Bertha cowered when the Travel Air's radial engine roared into life, and the airplane trundled down to the end of the field. Ben's spine tingled as the airplane turned and roared past. The pilot flicked him a quick wave, and the airplane soared over the trees and was gone.

"Wow! Would I love to be able to do that!" Ben shouted. "Baker Airport! I can get there on my bike. Sure would like to see what's goin' on there."

On his first visit, Ben watched a bright yellow open-cockpit biplane pull up to the gas pumps. As soon as the propeller stopped, a burly man levered himself out of the front cockpit, stomped back to the rear cockpit, and waved his arms as he shouted at the other pilot. He slammed his leather helmet and goggles on the ground. When he wound down, the hapless occupant of the rear cockpit unhooked his safety harness and scuttled off to a nearby wooden building. A sign above the door announced, "Baker's Flying Service—Under New Management."

The pilot muttered as he kicked wooden chocks against the airplane's balloon tires. He dragged a stepladder from the gas pumps, hoisted the hose up to the top wing, and began filling the airplane's fuel tank.

"'Scuse me, sir," Ben said.

"Yeah, whaddaya want?"

"Well, sir, I thought I'd—"

"Don't call me *sir*! Name's Brice," the man interrupted without looking around. "What can I do for ya?"

"Well, sir, umm, I mean, Mr. Brice, I wonder if I could get a job here. I could do what you're doin'. . . gassin' up airplanes, mebbe checkin' the oil. I think workin' here would be really swell."

"So ya wanna be a ramp monkey, eh?"

Ben had no idea what a ramp monkey was, but if it meant working around airplanes, that would be swell! "Yeah, uh, I guess so. I'm really interested in aviation."

"What's yer name?" Brice demanded and, before Ben could answer, he added, "My name ain't Mr. Brice, by the way. It's just plain Brice. Who're you?"

"Ben, sir, er, 'scuse me, Brice. Benjamin Findlay. I live on a farm 'bout four miles from here."

Brice turned and regarded a slim, broad-shouldered lad who had yet to fill out his six-foot frame. His blond crew cut was closely cropped. Blue eyes stared unblinking from his boyish face. He wore a blue-and-red flannel shirt trucked into a nondescript pair of work pants and a pair of oversized boots. He held an equally nondescript cap, which had seen better days, scrunched in his large farm-boy hands.

"Now here's a human canvas waitin' to be painted on," Brice muttered. "Like the son I never had." Ben blinked and started to ask what Brice had said, but Brice interrupted. "What makes ya think ya can do this job, kid?"

"I'm a hard worker an', an' dependable," Ben said. "I pretty much run our farm. My old, uh, my dad works in the city and isn't around much, so I do all the chores and things. A neighbor works the fields, but I do everything else all by myself since Joe—he's my older brother—since Joe left."

"Hard worker and dependable, eh!" Brice tightened the gas cap and clambered down from the ladder. "Far as I'm concerned, we damn well need a ramp monkey here, but that's up to Al Simpson in there." He pointed to the Baker's Flying Service building. "He's the boss. I'm just his flyin' instructor. Need ta convince him."

Ben thanked Brice and headed up the steps to Baker's Flying Service, swallowing to control his nervousness. A musty fragrance flavored with engine oil, gasoline fumes, and old leather wafted through the room. Al Simpson looked up from his desk.

"Can I do something for you, young feller?" he asked, regarding Ben over half-glasses.

Ben cleared his throat. "Umm, yessir, I hope ya can. I was talkin' to Mr.—umm, to Brice—out there at the gas pumps, an' he said you need a ramp monkey to work weekends and durin' the summer when things get real busy. I can do that job. Would really like to work in the flyin' business."

Simpson pushed back in his chair. "Worked airport ramps before? Know what the job is all about?"

"No, sir, but I'm a quick learner an' dependable. I could sure do what, ah, Brice is doin' to that biplane. An', an' more!"

"You still in school?" Ben nodded. "So you can work weekends till school's out and then work a full week, including weekends?" Ben nodded again.

"Can't pay you much," Simpson said. "But you'd get good experience. And maybe ole Brice could arrange to give ya flyin' lessons. That sound good to ya?"

"Yessir!" Ben almost shouted. "I'd really like that."

They discussed Ben's salary and settled on the hours. Ben walked out the door as the new part-time ramp monkey for Baker's Flying Service. He wallowed in the sights, sounds, and smells of aviation. He loved every minute, a dream come true for a fifteen-year-old clodhopper. Ben roamed the airport, making friends wherever he went. One pilot described him as an "open-faced kid, kinda like Lindbergh." He had the gangling walk of a boy whose coordination hadn't caught up with his six-foot frame or his size 12 shoes. His ready smile and bright blue eyes disarmed people, as did his habit of running his large hands through his crew cut.

"I'm gonna spend the rest of my life in aviation," he often said. "Isn't anything else I wanna do."

Ben's Schwinn Flyer wobbled over a rut, rousing him from his reverie. He rocketed onto the airport grounds, threaded down a dusty road between small single-airplane hangars, and skidded to a stop behind Baker's Flying Service.

"Hope I scraped all the manure off my boots," he muttered, checking his soles.

He greeted Simpson with a cheerful, "Mornin', chief."

Simpson eyed the clock and grunted. "Mornin'. You're runnin' late! Get your butt out to the pumps. We got customers waiting."

"Yessir!" Ben bolted out the door.

The day flashed past in a flurry of pumping aviation gas, checking oil levels and tire pressures, wiping cockpit windshields, swinging the props on airplanes that didn't have starters, and pulling wheel chocks. Lunch was a greasy hamburger wolfed down at the Fly Inn lunch counter, chased by a bottle of Vernors Ginger Ale.

"Michigan's famous Vernors Ginger Ale," Brice once proclaimed. "A great drink, made better only with a little Irish added."

In the early 1920s, Baker Airport had been an open grass field, little more than a level cow pasture with a few rickety buildings as hangars and an office shack. A colonial-style brick terminal was completed in 1934. It had become an established municipal airfield by 1936, serving nearby Flint. It boasted a paved five-thousand-foot main runway and a two thousand, five hundred-foot intersecting strip. Departing passengers checked in at the terminal for American Airlines' two daily flights, and then walked out across the ramp and up portable stairs into the airplanes.

A glass control tower sat on the roof of the terminal, topped with a rotating beacon that flashed white and green, the signal for a civilian airfield. Many of the original wooden structures had been replaced by two metal hangars and other newly constructed wooden buildings. Baker's Flying Service was housed in one of the refurbished original buildings.

An American Airlines Douglas DC-3 arrived at nine a.m. from Detroit, then continued west to Grand Rapids and across Lake Michigan to Milwaukee. In the afternoon, the return flight flew the reverse of that route. Other airplane traffic at Baker consisted mainly of local flyers, sport aviators, training flights, air charter services, and the occasional crop duster.

Ben wondered what it must be like to be an airline pilot. They must have a great life, flying all across the country. Ben had become a pilot himself, under Brice's guidance. Brice was a flyer of early vintage, "older than God or dirt," another instructor joked during a hangar flying chat with Ben. Behind his back, they called him the Ancient Pelican. To his face, by his demand, he was Brice.

"One hell of a pilot," the instructor told Ben. "He flew wood-and-canvas crates in the Great War. He's an ace—shot down five German airplanes!"

Brice was in his midtwenties when the U.S. Army shipped him to France in 1917 with minimal training. He slogged through the trenches as an infantryman for several months, watching U.S. Army Air Corps planes zooming overhead.

"I applied for transfer to the Air Corps. Learning to fly was my great escape," Brice told Ben. "Anything was better than livin' like a rat in the mud of eastern France, waitin' to clamber out of the trenches and run through machine-gun fire. Guess I was born to fly. Spent the rest of the war swooping over the carnage below. Wouldn't have lasted long in those trenches."

Brice said he was happiest when soaring among the clouds. After the war, he barnstormed across America, risking his neck daily in various "old flying crocks."

"Got more flight experience than any flyer 'cept the angel Gabriel," he boasted. "And walked away from a lotta crashes. Never quit flying the damn airplane 'til all the pieces come to a dead stop."

Ben worshipped the man. He had no idea how old he was—maybe fifty. Some mornings, he looked closer to a hundred! Ben coveted the man's long, leather flying jacket; his sweat-stained helmet with its fur-trimmed goggles; and his archaic leather flying gloves. He tried to imitate Brice's walk but managed only a ridiculous parody of the man's peculiar rolling gait. Brice's rusty red hair, flecked with gray, usually was mashed flat from wearing the tight-fitting leather helmet. He was husky, once over six feet tall. Now he walked with hunched shoulders, bent forward at the waist, belly spilling over his belt.

"Shortened the old spine with too many hard landings," he joked.

Long exposure to sun and wind left his face weather-beaten. The skin around his eyes, considerably whiter where the goggles fitted, was crinkled permanently from hours of squinting into the sun and laughing at his own raucous jokes. His light blue eyes became piercing if his dander was up. More often, especially when he had a cup or two of his favorite coffee with a little Irish in it, they twinkled like a leprechaun enjoying a practical joke. Joking and savoring the Irish came easily to Brice when he wasn't flying. But he was dead serious about flying.

Brice never mentioned a wife or family. Word was his wife left him years ago while he zoomed around the barnstorming circuit. Ben treasured the flying lessons Brice gave him in return for maintaining his open-cockpit Stearman trainer, an early Model 73 version. Brice had been a test pilot for Stearman in the early 1930s.

"I got along great with the Stearman folks," Brice said. "They sold me this Model 73 for a good price. She was fitted with the original 210-hp Continental engine, but I had her upgraded with a 245-hp Jacobs R-755. The bigger engine gives her much better performance."

The Stearman biplane was not a graceful flying machine with its double wings, long-legged taildragger stance, blunt radial engine, and enormous wooden propeller. But to Ben, it was a beautiful bird that opened new vistas for him. The Stearman was unofficially known as the Yellow Peril because of its bright yellow fabric-covered wings and fuselage. The name suited the aggressive way Brice flew it. Ben kept it spotless and gassed up. With Brice at the controls, the airplane performed amazing maneuvers.

"She turns so tight you can fly her up your own arse if you want to," Brice joked. "Keep the revs up, as we used to say in the Great War. Don't let her skid in the turns and stay at least ten knots above stallin' speed and you can fly her to hell and back!"

With that, he'd launch into lurid accounts of his many escapades in the war and barnstorming in the 1920s and 1930s with the Flying Flivvers. Once in the cockpit of the Yellow Peril though, the jokes stopped. Flying was serious business. Brice taught Ben the Yellow Peril's systems and the basic rules of flight.

His first flying lesson started with Brice leading him on a walk-around inspection of the airplane. "Put your parachute on the lower wing. *Gently!* That's fabric covering," Brice said. "Start your inspection here on the left side. You'll fly from the backseat, and I'll sit up in the front hole and try to keep you from killing me! When you go solo, you'll fly from the back cockpit. That's how the Stearman's center of gravity is rigged. Now lemme show you the controls and gauges."

The instrument panel had only an engine tachometer, engine temperature gauge, airspeed indicator, altimeter, oil pressure and fuel gauges, compass, and turn and bank indicator. "Real pilot doesn't need anything more," Brice muttered.

He then described how moving the control stick side to side raised and lowered the ailerons on each bottom wing, to make the airplane roll left or right. Moving the stick back or forward raised and lowered the elevator on the tail. This pitched the nose up or down.

"When ya wanta climb, ya don't just haul back on the stick," Brice said. "That'll slow you down real quick an' maybe lead to a stall. To climb, you increase the power by pushing the throttle lever here. Opposite is true for descending. Pull the throttle lever back, and you'll slow down and the nose'll drop. Remember, pull back on the stick too much without addin' power and you'll stall and maybe spin!"

Brice indicated the two large pedals on the floor, which moved the rudder on the vertical fin right or left, causing the nose to move laterally. They also controlled the wheel brakes. "Put your heels in those stirrups on the pedals," he said. "They keep your feet on the pedals when you're maneuvering in the air. To stop when you're on the ground, press on the top part of the pedals with your toes. Use differential braking—one pedal at a time—to turn while taxiing.

"First thing you do for the preflight check is unlock the controls." He released the swing arm that held the stick and rudder pedals in place. "Then you make sure the fuel valve is closed and the magneto switch is off."

Ben peered inside, noting each control and switch as Brice pointed them out.

"This switch controls the dual magnetos. They provide current to the spark plugs. The switch has four positions: off, left, right, and both. After engine start and before takeoff, you cycle that switch to left, back to both, then right, and back to both again, to make sure both magnetos are working. If one fails in the air, the engine'll still run, but rougher. Switch it off and on to see if it comes back online. But never take off on only one magneto."

Too much to remember!

"Now we'll do the walk-around inspection," Brice said.

He led Ben around the airplane, inspecting the wings and all attachment points, checking the oil and gas levels, moving the control surfaces on the wings and tail, and giving the entire fabric-covered fuselage a close look. Back at the left side of the cockpit, Brice described the start-up sequence.

"Once you're strapped in the cockpit, our mechanic inserts a crank into that opening on the left side of the nose just behind the engine," he said. "He'll use that to wind up an inertia wheel that stores energy to turn over the engine.

"Before he starts cranking, he'll call to you, 'Fuel on, switch off!' And you double-check and call the same back," Brice said. "You then ease the throttle open about an inch and move the fuel mixture lever to the full rich position. When he gets the wheel spinning, he'll call, 'Fuel on, switch on.' And when you respond, he'll engage the inertia wheel that'll turn the engine over. You then hit the booster switch to fire her up."

The Stearman had no radio or intercom, Brice explained, so he'd communicate with Ben by yelling into the mouthpiece of a Gosport Tube attached by smaller tubes to earpieces in Ben's leather flying helmet.

"Gosport Tube," Ben exclaimed. "What's a Gosport Tube?"

"It's a gadget invented by a Brit flyer in Gosport, England, near Portsmouth, I think," Brice said. "It's crude, but works great. You can hear me, but ya can't talk back. I like that part."

Ben shivered with excitement as he strapped into the Stearman's rear cockpit, savoring the aroma, a mixture of leather, oil, and gas, seasoned with a hint of sweat. He listened as Brice recited the prestart checklist. A tingle shot up his spine as the big radial engine's 245 horses roared into life with snorts, bangs, and a cloud of smoke. Brice then ran through the engine checks, including cycling the magnetos to ensure both were working.

Taxiing to the runway required a series of S turns because the Stearman's long main landing gear legs, needed to keep the huge wooden propeller clear of the ground, and its taildragger stance blocked forward visibility over the radial engine. On takeoff, when the tail lifted, Ben could see over the nose.

Brice told Ben to keep his hands lightly on the stick and follow along on the pedal controls as they taxied onto the runway. Brice kept up a running commentary to his student in the rear cockpit.

Brice raised his right hand and signaled *go!* Ben clung to the controls. His stomach lurched as the Yellow Peril accelerated down the runway and leaped into the air.

"Wow!" he yelled. "This is great! Hooowee!"

Once over the practice area, Brice leveled the airplane and gave the trim wheel a couple of turns to reduce pressure on the stick.

"Lemme show you how to do this," he yelled into the Gosport. "I'll demonstrate the maneuver twice. Follow through on the controls, and then you do it. When ya turn, use the stick and rudder pedals in unison to roll and get the nose comin' around . . . *No, not like that*! . . . *Like this*!" Brice snatched the controls and precisely demonstrated the maneuver.

"Ease your grip on the stick!" he yelled. "Don't strangle the goddamned thing! Use your fingertips! Keep a light touch! Find the groove. Find the bloody groove! Let her do the flying!"

Hour after hour, Brice yelled at Ben from the front cockpit. Ben relished it.

"Feel the airplane through your ass!" Brice yelled. In more polite circles, it was called flying by the seat of your pants. "The airplane wants to fly streamlined. If you're cross-controllin', slippin', or skiddin', you'll feel the side pressure on your butt!"

As the propeller wash swirled around his head, Ben shifted back in the seat, relaxed, and let the Peril do the flying. Several hours into their training, he felt the Peril responding to his lighter touch.

He soon could make the Peril do what he wanted in the air, but low and slow on final landing approach, he was persistently late with the flare. The airplane bounced on its stiff main gear and ballooned back into the air. Brice always caught her and eased her down.

"Don't try ta drill her into the ground!" he shouted. "Look out over the left side. Ease her down. When she stalls, suck the stick back in your gut. Let her settle!"

Months passed, and Ben struggled to balance his farm chores and unhappy home life with his golden moments at Baker Airport, flying with Brice. One Saturday morning in early autumn, Ben found the landing groove. The Peril responded to his every command. There was an uncanny silence from the front cockpit. Brice signaled Ben to pull off onto the taxiway and stop.

Chapter 3

A FLYER IS BORN

"I gotta pee!" Brice shouted from the front cockpit. He stepped out onto the lower wing. Ben, scrunched down in the rear cockpit, didn't notice Brice fasten his safety harness across the empty seat. He missed the signal that Brice wasn't getting back into the airplane.

Brice dropped to the ground, shifted his parachute harness over one shoulder, and scowled at Ben, who blinked back. "Okay, Brice!" Ben called over the rumble of the idling engine. "I'll wait here."

Brice pulled off his leather helmet and scratched his matted thatch of hair. Ben frowned at the man's questioning look.

"You wanna be a flyer or what?" Brice shouted.

"Yeah, of course."

"Then while I'm in there doin' my business, why don't you go out and do three takeoffs and landings, 'stead of sittin' there like a damn fool!"

"*Solo*? Uh, I can go solo?" Ben gaped.

"Yeah, *solo*!" Brice shouted, mimicking his student. "That means goin' alone. You're ready. So get your ass out there and do it!" Brice stepped away from the airplane. "And don't crash my goddamned airplane! Yellow Peril is all I got." He wheeled and stumped toward the operations shack.

Ben swallowed twice, his mind whirling. "Guess this is it," he mumbled. "*Boy*, it sure looks empty up there without Brice in the front cockpit! Who's gonna yell at me or grab the controls if I make a mess of this? Damn. I need to pee too, but I better get going."

He clutched the stick and reached for the throttle lever. Brice's instructions echoed in his mind. *"Don't strangle the stick! Keep a light touch! Look out to the left during the landing flare. Don't mess it up!"*

Ben jockeyed the throttle and taxied back to the runway. The Peril seemed unusually sprightly. Of course! Brice's two hundred-plus pounds were no longer onboard.

"Didn't tell me to adjust the trim," Ben wondered. "I guess he expects me to figure that out for myself."

He sucked his dry tongue and turned the elevator trim wheel to compensate for the shift in the Peril's center of gravity. He concentrated. *Watch for nose-up pitch changes on the takeoff and especially on the landing flare.*

Ben pushed the throttle forward. The airplane leaped into the air. "Wow!" he yelled. The Peril weighed just under two thousand pounds, and without Brice's bulk, she was eager to fly.

Ben climbed the Peril into a knee-knocking circuit around the airport, following the standard left-hand rectangular traffic pattern. Near the end of the downwind leg, flying parallel to the runway, he pulled on the carburetor heat, closed the throttle, and started a descending left turn toward the final approach leg. He sensed the airspeed, not wanting to chance even a quick look inside at the airspeed indicator, and peered over the left side of the cockpit. He turned onto the final approach leg.

"Airspeed feels okay, wings level, and I'm lined up with the runway," he coached himself. "Let her descend, flare, hold it, hold it . . . Stick back! Let her stall!"

The Peril plopped solidly onto the runway. Great! Not a bad three-point landing on his first solo try. As he lifted off on his second run around the traffic pattern, Ben's spirits soared.

He yelled into the slipstream, "*Heeeyoo!* I'm flyin' the Peril all by myself. *Yeowee!*"

The second landing went well, and Ben decided to try a tail-high wheel landing. This was where he encountered the most problems, bouncing the stiff main gear legs off the runway. But he hit the groove again, and the Peril rolled smoothly onto the runway, dropping her tail to the three-point stance as she slowed to taxi speed.

"*Solo!* Hot damn. I'm a pilot!" Ben yelled. "Best day of my life." He taxied back to the ramp. Brice was nowhere in sight. *Guess he wasn't worried much about me breaking ole Peril.*

Ben shut down the Peril's engine, hopped out of the cockpit, and set the wheel chocks. He strode into the operations shack, grinning. Al Simpson, who had watched Ben's solo flight, extended a beefy right hand and crushed Ben's.

"Way to go, sport!" he shouted and slapped him on the back.

Brice emerged from the men's room rubbing his hands. Ben looked at him openmouthed. *That was a long pee.*

"So how'd it go?" Brice growled, covering the fact that he had crouched behind the gas pumps, watching every second of Ben's flight. "I was busy here. Did ya bring my airplane back in one piece, or are they draggin' the wreckage over now?"

Deflated, Ben pointed outside to the parked Yellow Peril to prove his solo had gone okay. Inside he was yelling, "*Yeowee!* I'm a flyer!"

"Ahright," Brice growled, "now we're gonna concentrate on makin' you a *real* aviator. Let's get started!" He strode out to the airplane. "We got a lot of work ahead of us!"

They spent the next hour working on aerial maneuvers and shooting touch-and-go landings. Other than telling Ben which maneuver to perform next, Brice said little from the front cockpit. Ben sensed he didn't touch the controls once. *Here I am, first solo and back in the air with ole Brice. Puts on his tough guy act, but he's one swell fella an' a great instructor.*

After the fifth landing, Brice told Ben to return to the airport ramp. They shut down the Peril and secured the aircraft.

"We might make a pilot outta you yet," Brice said, and walked toward the operations shack. "See ya tomorrow."

Ben stood next to the Stearman, listening to the ticking and pinging of its cooling engine. Summer sure had zipped by! It hadn't been easy, balancing his farm chores and problems with his increasingly abusive father against his time at Baker Airport. On the rare times when he was around, the old man bitched about the time Ben spent flying. Other than that, he took little interest in Ben; he ignored him. But Ben stuck it out.

"Today I hit the groove!" he exulted. "Gonna be the best flyer ole Brice has ever trained!"

Chapter 4

THE FAMILY

At the dinner table that night, Ben didn't mention he had soloed. It would only trigger another argument with the old man about wasting time and money on this "flying foolishness." His mother, who thought flying was dangerous, didn't want to hear anything about it.

Ben sighed. *That's my happy family circle. Dunno if I can stick this out till I graduate.*

That night he lay awake wondering how it had all gone so wrong. His father was self-absorbed and self-indulgent, a dour man who never smiled much, at least not around home. His deep-set blue eyes were cold and calculating. Ben rarely made eye contact. His father was short and powerfully built, and took excessive pride in how he dressed.

Ben's relationship with the old man was getting worse. He never offered Ben advice or encouragement. When he did take notice, it was to criticize. His father had left school at an early age and was extremely sensitive about his lack of formal education. But he had attended a technical school and held a full-time engineering job in Flint. A neighbor farmer did the major fieldwork on a crop-sharing deal, and Ben and Joe handled the morning and evening chores. Now Ben had sole responsibility for them.

His father was a part-time parent at best, preferring his circle of friends. Sometimes he didn't even come home at night. This drove Joe up the wall and led to the big blowup that had prompted Joe to leave home. As the older brother, he had borne the brunt of the old man's bizarre behavior and resented the effect it had on their mother, who tried vainly to pacify everyone.

As Ben stared into the shadows on the ceiling, he struggled with the thought that he also was failing his mother. She was a warmhearted, loving person who tried to avoid confrontations at all costs, which explained why she had continued to endure the many slights and indignities from the old man.

Ben's earliest memories of his mother welled up in his mind. She was the product of a close-knit family of three sisters, each of whom had graduated college with teaching degrees. She had been slim and shapely, with thick brown hair and soft brown eyes, and stood erect. She had a sly sense of humor and laughed easily. Motherhood suited her; she could not resist cuddling any baby she could reach. Ben remembered savoring her warm hugs as a child. Now the years of marital stress had worn her down. She had neglected herself, put on weight in all the wrong places, and stood in the sloped-shoulder, stooped posture of one who had lost her zest for life.

"How could this have happened? How could I have let this happen?" Ben snarled to the ceiling.

Ben rose feeling stale and unrefreshed from another restless night. But his family worries disappeared, brushed aside actually, by the time he reached the airport. Ben hustled through the routine on the ramp until Brice signaled it was time for another instruction flight.

"Okay, we got you through your solo, but that's only the start," Brice said. "There won't be any slackin' off. Resting on your laurels is a quick way to get a big head and a fat ass. Either one can earn you a smokin' hole in the ground. Becoming a good flyer takes work!"

And work they did. As Ben mastered basic maneuvers, Brice introduced him to aerobatics.

"You need to spend some time upside down, what the theoretical flyers call unusual attitudes," he said to Ben's delight. "We'll pull some g's, both positive and negative."

What came next were tight turns, loops, hammerhead stalls, snap rolls, chandelles, and spins. As they pulled out from the first loop, g-forces tugged Ben's chin to his chest, and his hand slipped off the control stick. His goggles pinched his nose, and he felt like an elephant was sitting on his chest. He had forgotten Brice's advice to tighten his gut muscles and grunt, to counter the g's.

Wow! That was somethin' else! I guess I can get used to this, but woof!

Brice also showed him the falling-leaf maneuver, stalling the airplane and allowing it to slide off on one wing to the left, and then holding the stall to the right and back to the left. The airplane rocked like a leaf falling from side to side to the ground.

"This teaches ya how to control the airplane even after she stalls," Brice shouted down the Gosport. "Someday it might save your ass! Now lemme show ya some aerobatics."

Brice demonstrated each maneuver with precision, and Ben endured shouts and curses as he tried to duplicate them. He worked fiercely to find the groove and after several hours of instruction, began to perform the maneuvers with consistent precision.

"Okay, now we're gonna string all these maneuvers together in an aerobatic routine like you might do at an air fair," Brice announced one day. "Pull your safety harness real tight, and follow through with a light touch on the controls. Any time ya want me to stop, waggle the stick real hard."

Brice zoomed the Peril up to three thousand feet over the airport. He had told the tower he'd waggle his wings to signal he wanted to perform aerobatics over the airfield. A green light flashed from the tower. Permission granted. He yelled down the Gosport, "We're gonna use the runway intersection as a reference point. We'll dive down over the field from the east, pretendin' that the crowd is along the taxiway parallelin' the runway."

Ben peered over the side of the cockpit as they flew an arc away from the airport and then turned back toward midfield.

"Hang on," Brice yelled. "I'm gonna chop the throttle so they won't hear us comin' down behind 'em."

Ben's stomach lurched as Brice cut the throttle and pushed Peril's nose over into a steep dive. As they rocketed toward the taxiway, Ben grimaced.

"Hey, we're gettin' awful low!" he yelled. "Don't drill us into the ground!"

"Now we'll give her full throttle about time we're over their heads, and they won't know where the hell we've come from!" Brice shouted as he pulled back on the stick and shoved the throttle lever forward. The Jacobs engine roared to life, and the Peril thrust her nose up into a swooping climb.

Ben was caught unprepared for the sudden onset of g-forces. His chin snapped to his chest as his hand again slipped off the stick. He grunted and tried to tighten his gut muscles. "Gawdalmighty!" he gasped. "Think I lost my stomach!"

"Now . . . we pull up into a loop . . . over the center of the field," Brice grunted down the Gosport. He too was fighting the g-forces. "See, we're coming outta the loop running away from the crowd line, so we snap it into a maximum bank turn to the left," he said. The g-forces continued to shove Ben toward the floor.

"You okay back there, kid?" Brice yelled, looking for Ben in the rearview mirror. "Still with us?" Ben struggled to nod. "Good, 'cause we're gonna roll into a max turn to the right and complete a horizontal figure eight back at the intersection."

Ben tried to visualize the track they were following before sagging again under the increasing g-forces.

"Through the final turn," Brice yelled. "Now airspeed's kinda low, outta energy, so we need ta build up some speed." He leveled the Peril's wings and pushed the throttle wide open. As the airspeed increased, Brice swung the airplane into a wide turn back toward the runway intersection.

"Here we go!" he yelled as he pulled up into a steep climb. "We'll stand her on her tail and let her stall, kick left rudder as the airspeed drops off, and bingo—a hammerhead stall!"

The Peril cartwheeled to the left as the nose dropped. Brice recovered, dived along the runway line to regain airspeed, and pulled up for a second hammerhead stall to the right.

"Now we'll recover goin' back the other direction along the runway line. Build up speed an' pull into a second loop," he said. "Watch as we come out inverted from the top of the loop and start downhill. I'll roll upright like this . . . dive an' . . . pull into a second loop."

Ben's vision blurred. His stomach churned. "Not gonna throw up," he said through clenched teeth.

"Then we roll upright on the second downward leg. That's a Cuban eight," Brice yelled, clearly enjoying himself.

Ben grimaced in concentration. Ground his teeth. "Not gonna waggle the stick!"

"Now we use the speed to pull a tight chandelle turn to the left, dive, and give 'em three snap rolls as we fly back along the runway," Brice grunted. "We need ta build up more airspeed again, turn back along the runway, and zoom back up to three thousand feet."

As the Peril lost airspeed, she seemed to momentarily stand on her tail, engine roaring. "Close the throttle, pull back on the stick, and as she stalls, slap in full left aileron and full right rudder," Brice yelled. "An' we roll into a vertical spin! . . . Let her turn three turns, center the stick, shove it forward to break the stall, and kick left rudder to stop the spin." The Peril swung wings level in a steep dive.

"Then we dive back along the runway. By this time, we got 'em wettin' their pants," Brice chortled. "Then we use the extra airspeed to pull a tight turn back up the field and give 'em a four-point roll, one, two, three, four, like this!"

Ben's head swirled, his stomach lurched. "They aren't the only ones wettin' their pants," he grunted.

"Now we roll level, pull into a circling approach, and touch down on the numbers, keepin' her rolling along on the main gear till we're in front of the grandstand. A piece of cake and a real crowd-pleaser," Brice rumbled as the Peril touched down, dropped to the three-point stance, and rolled off onto the taxiway.

"Piece of cake?" Ben yelled as they taxied to the ramp. "Where'd that come from?"

"Huh? Oh, that's what my Brit friends said after a tough mission. I was an exchange pilot with a Royal Flying Corps squadron in France during the war. Our squadron commander 'volunteered' me. Guess he figured since I was the newest pilot in the outfit, I was probably the most expendable."

"Another war story?" Ben asked ruefully as they rolled up to the gas pumps.

Brice shut down the Peril's engine and levered himself out of the front cockpit. He peered at Ben and ignored his sour expression. "How'd ya like the little demonstration?"

"Great!" Ben said, forcing a smile. His stomach continued to boil and rumble. "Now what's this about a piece of cake?"

"Well, as I was sayin', off I went to fly de Havilland tubs with the limeys, while the guys in my squadron got to fly the French Spads. I didn't think it was such a good deal."

Brice scratched his two-day stubble with a sausagelike thumb. "But you know, most of those Brits were nice guys. Some of 'em strutted around like they had a swagger stick up their arse, but there were a couple I really liked. I remember one in particular who—"

"Here we go," Ben muttered, rolling his eyes.

"Pay attention, dammit! This is important! Name was Percy, Reginald M. Percy. A 'Leftenant,' as the Brits called the rank. I flew on his wing, and he taught me how to stay alive. 'Any fool can fly an aeroplane,' he used to say, 'but it takes a special sort of person to effectively fight with one.' Sounds kind of prissy, but you know, old Percy was one hell of a pursuit pilot. He was one of the few from his squadron to survive the war. He was responsible for me stayin' alive and becomin' an ace.

"Asked me to stay in touch after the war, and I did for a while," Brice added. "But I was a barnstormin' bum with no fixed address, so it wasn't easy. I think old Percy ended up some kind of a bigwig in the Brits' Air Ministry." Rousing from his reverie, Brice scowled at Ben. "Now where the hell were we goin'?" he demanded. "What were we talkin' about before you got me distracted?"

"You were telling me about 'piece of cake,' I think," Ben said.

"Yeah, piece of cake," Brice growled. "If you remember half of what I teach you so's you're well prepared and look at every flight as a piece of cake, 'stead of some god-awful impossible task, you'll do okay."

Two days later, Brice signaled Ben it was time for another lesson.

"Let's strap our butts in the Peril and see if you can show me how to fly a full aerobatic routine like I showed ya! I'll tell ya what maneuvers I want."

And Ben did, to his surprise and Brice's obvious delight. A couple of maneuvers were a little ragged, but the overall effect was pretty good.

"You keep that up, and you'll be ready for the air fair circuit," Brice joked. Uncommon praise!

Ben wore a foolish grin for the rest of the day. At home that night, he ventured to share his good news at the supper table.

"It'd help if you'd spend more time around the farm and less at the airport with that flying bum," his father snapped. "So you've learned how to fly an airplane. What good does that do to any of us?"

Ben excused himself and stepped out into the night. *Why'd I even bother?*

Chapter 5

THE BOY/MAN, AUTUMN 1936

School started after Labor Day, his last year of high school. Ben now had his own car, a solid old jalopy he named Excalibur. Not much to look at, but dependable. He could zip over to Baker Airport any time he had a couple of spare hours. Weekends, after chores were done, were dedicated totally to the airport and flying.

Ben had changed over the summer, no longer a boy, not yet a man. He still was gangly, but farm chores and high school sports had toned his body. He carried his 165 pounds on a muscular frame. He kept his blond hair short—it made showering easier after practice and games—and shaved every day.

His face had become angular but otherwise unremarkable. He tried to achieve Brice's aviator look by squinting to develop those distinctive wrinkles around his eyes. Ben reluctantly returned to school for his senior year. The football coach regarded him with interest, noting how his frame had filled out over the summer. Everyone was saying this was the team's year to take the conference championship, maybe even make a run at the state playoffs. Exciting stuff, but something was missing for Ben.

"Football isn't that much fun anymore," he told one of his buddies. "I just can't get fired up about it."

Flying was bigger, more challenging, and exciting. He held a B plus average in his classes and still had fun with his buddies. But weekends at the airport meant he was seeing less of them. Ben was drifting away from his circle of friends, but he didn't know what to do about it; he wasn't even sure he minded it.

Once into the season, Ben put his heart into the game, trained well, and worked hard in practice. He made a solid contribution, played left tackle on offense, linebacker on defense, and kicked the extra points and field goals. He notched a record number of quarterback sacks. The team was undefeated, nailing the conference championship with a thirty-one to seven blowout of their archrivals. They squeaked through the district championship round, winning the final game on Ben's field goal in the closing seconds. Their fortunes turned in the first round of the state championship playoffs, and

Ben was the cause. He missed a point after touchdown kick and a field goal attempt. They lost by four points, his points. None of his teammates blamed Ben, but he could see in their eyes that they felt he had let them down.

Ben sat sulking in the locker room when their coach sat next to him.

"Big lesson learned tonight, Ben," he said quietly. "Life doesn't always play out the way we'd like it to. Don't blame yourself. Winchester outplayed us. It was a team loss, not just your missing a couple of kicks. The important thing now is how you respond to this. I expect you to pull up your socks and get on with your life."

Ben nodded. "Not that easy, Coach. I really let the other fellas down."

Ben recovered from his humbling experience and got back into the swing of high school life. He dated occasionally, but had no steady girlfriend. He attracted friends who looked to him as a leader. He had never made it with a girl, unlike some of his buddies who, if their locker-room stories were believable, had sex with every girl they took out. His mind focused more and more on flying, and he couldn't carry on much of a conversation with girls. They all were excited about him being a pilot, but they couldn't appreciate any of the finer points of flying. Nor could his buddies.

Special treats for Ben were brief solo flights in the Yellow Peril or ground flying with Brice at the Fly Inn lunch counter. He developed a mature pilot's skill for a farm boy not yet eighteen.

When autumn slipped toward winter, he bundled several sweaters under his leather flight jacket, pulled his helmet straps tightly, and flew over the Michigan countryside ablaze with fall colors. His cares and worries swirled away in the Yellow Peril's prop wash. Home, family problems, farm chores, school, sports, his buddies, and even girls were forgotten. He particularly liked flying in late afternoon, when dusk came early on shortened winter days. Whatever wind was blowing whispered into a light breeze as the sun slipped toward the horizon. The amber afterglow blazed ragged red and orange streaks in the sky and cast exaggerated shadows on the snow-covered ground.

Ben hummed softly, trying vainly to carry a tune, as he floated the Peril in for a landing late one December afternoon with just enough daylight for him to see the runway.

"Flare, flare," he coached himself and pulled back smoothly on the stick. The Peril slipped obediently onto the concrete in a perfect three-point landing.

"Wow!" he shouted. "Can understand how Brice liked the air fair circuit!"

Unfortunately this was almost 1937, and the golden age of barnstorming had passed. Ben satisfied himself with the thought that maybe something else would come up. Meanwhile he had his flying, and that was enough!

Chapter 6

MR. SMITH, SPRING 1937

Mr. Smith appeared at the airport one Saturday afternoon in late spring. A tall, serious-looking man, his black hair was slicked down with hair oil. A thin Clark Gable mustache accented his upper lip. He wore a white shirt, a dark tie, and an expensive-looking double-breasted suit that fit his lean frame closely. A foreign correspondent-style trench coat draped over his shoulders. His wing tip shoes were highly polished. Ben always kept his best shoes well shined—his everyday boots were usually caked with mud or manure—so he noticed other people's shoes.

Ben found the man waiting in the operations shack. As well-dressed as he was, he had a rumpled look. *He's been traveling. I'll bet, sleepin' in coach cars on a lotta night trains.*

"Can I help you, sir?" Ben asked.

"Yes. I'm looking for a Mr. Brice, Curtis Brice. Do you know him?"

"Sure," Ben said. The man's penetrating gaze made him uneasy. *Are those outlines of flying goggles around his eyes? His cheekbones have the same sun crinkles Brice has. Must be a flyer.*

"That's him out there in the pattern in the Yellow, umm, in that yellow Stearman. He's trying to teach the Johnson fella how to make a landing they can both walk away from." His clumsy attempt at humor seemed lost on the man. The stranger's expression didn't change.

"I'm Mr. Smith, Adam Smith," he said. "I'd like to talk with Mr. Brice about a local flight to check out some property around here."

"Mr. Brice ought to be back in about fifteen minutes, unless they crash. Then it'll be sooner." Ben bit his tongue. Why was he trying to be a comedian?

"Mr. Simpson—he owns Baker's Flying Service—isn't here right now," Ben stammered. "Like a cup of coffee?"

"Black, please," Mr. Smith said.

Those eyes. How do you get a look like that? Gotta practice gettin' that look. Has to be a flyer.

"You work here?" Mr. Smith asked.

"Yessir. Name's Ben Findlay. I'm the ramp monkey. Uh, I run the ramp here—pump gas, check the oil, check tire pressures, pull the chocks, that sort of thing." Why did this man unnerve him?

"You're a pilot?" the man asked, indicating Ben's leather jacket.

"Yessir. Up to advanced aerobatics now. Brice has been teaching me basic aerial dogfighting maneuvers. He was in the U.S. Army Air Corps during the war. Flew with the Royal Flying Corps as an exchange pilot. He's an ace. Shot down five German planes. After the war, he spent more'n ten years barnstorming on the air fair circuit."

He took a deep breath and gave Mr. Smith a blank look.

"I know about Mr. Brice's accomplishments and his reputation, which is why I came to see him," Mr. Smith said, eyeing Ben thoughtfully. "We know quite a bit about him."

We! Omigod. Is this fella from the Bureau of Air Commerce? Is Brice in some kinda trouble? Have I said too much about him?

"Well, yeah, I guess anybody in aviation would know about Brice," Ben stammered. "You a flyer, Mr. Smith?"

"I am. I'm also an instructor. How is Mr. Brice as an instructor?"

"Just great!" Ben gushed. "Growls and barks a lot, but he hasn't bitten me yet. Taught me everything he knows, and he's one great pilot who—"

Brice stormed through the door. "Damned fool! That Johnson kid is gonna kill me someday," he snarled. "That is *if* I don't kill him first! The Peril's still in one piece, but just barely."

Ben jumped in. "Brice, this is Mr. Smith. Mr. Smith, this is Curtis Brice. Mr. Smith wants to see you about a flight—"

Brice cut him off with a wave of his hand. "Gas up the Peril, sport. Another student's due in about half an hour." He turned to Mr. Smith. "How can I help you?"

Ben shuffled outside, dying to know what the two of them were talking about. Half an hour later, Mr. Smith walked out of the operations shack, gave Ben a wave, and strode off. When Brice came out, Ben was all over him. "Who's Mr. Smith? Is that his real name? I don't think it is, do you? What'd he want? He isn't from the BAC, is he? You aren't in some kinda trouble, are you?"

"Down, boy!" Brice yelled. "You're droolin'. Mr. Smith—and no, that ain't his real name—just wants to charter a local flight over some property he's interested in."

"Why'd he need you to fly him?" Ben demanded. "He said he's a pilot. Why wouldn't he just rent the Peril or some other airplane and fly himself?"

"Maybe he wants someone to do the flyin' while he does the lookin'," Brice snapped. "It's a charter flight, boy, maybe an hour or so on a little cross-country. Easy couple of extra bucks. No big deal! You got the Peril gassed up? Here comes my next student."

Ben watched Brice fire up the Peril, and he and the student were gone in a cloud of exhaust smoke and dust.

Mr. Smith returned the next morning, dressed in flying gear. Ben gaped. *Sure looks like a flyer.*

Smith and Brice huddled over a map spread on the lower wing as Ben pretended to polish the windshield, straining to eavesdrop. Brice frowned and waved him away from the Peril. The two men climbed into the airplane, Brice in the rear cockpit and Smith up front. They took off and headed east.

A little over an hour later, the Peril came thrumming back. No other planes were in the pattern, and Ben gazed in wonder. Brice was lining up for his aerobatic routine!

For the next fifteen minutes, Brice put the Peril through the whole sequence, hitting the crossover point precisely after each maneuver and finishing with two crisp four-point rolls before circling for a landing. As they taxied in, Mr. Smith was shaking his head and grinning broadly. He stepped out of the cockpit and pumped Brice's hand.

"Wonderful flight," he said. "Thank you very much, Brice. Great aerobatic routine!"

Brice told Ben to refuel the Peril. "Mr. Smith wants to buy me a cup of coffee at the greasy spoon."

An hour later, the two men emerged. Brice stumped over to Ben. "Peril ready?"

Ben nodded, looking over Brice's shoulder at the other man.

"He wants to fly with you," Brice mumbled. "By the way, real name is Frank Silverman. Also wants to buy ya lunch at the greasy spoon tomorrow. That all right?"

Ben nodded dumbly. "Why would he want to fly with me?"

"How the hell do I know!" Brice snarled. "Ask him, 'stead of standin' there with ya bare face hanging out!"

Ben approached Mr. Smith, a.k.a. Silverman. "Brice says you want to take a short hop with me in the Peril. We can go now, if you want."

"Did you say 'peril'?" Silverman asked.

"Yeah, Brice's Stearman. It's called the Yellow Peril."

Another penetrating look. "Why don't you just show me what you can do with the, uh, Peril?" Silverman said. "Half an hour ought to do it. I'll just sit up front and enjoy the flight."

They took off into the soft light of the late spring afternoon. Ben left the pattern, climbed to the practice area, and put the Peril through her paces with every maneuver he could think of. Silverman gave him a thumbs-up signal and pointed back to the airfield. Back at the gas pumps, Silverman held out his right hand.

"Nice flight," he said. "How about lunch tomorrow?"

Ben nodded.

"Good. See you tomorrow." Silverman turned to leave.

"Before you go," Ben pressed. "Mr. Simpson wants to meet you. Can you come into the operations shack?"

Ben left the two men and backed toward the door. He hopped down the steps looking for Brice, but the Ancient Pelican already was taxiing out with another student.

"Damn!" Ben muttered. "Got a million questions for him."

Ben didn't get a chance to speak with Brice until the sun slipped into a blazing pool of yellow, orange, and red on the horizon. Brice saw him coming and raised a hand.

"Tomorrow morning, sport. Right now I need a couple of Irish coffees. God, what a day! Days like this make me think I need to get out of this crazy business."

Chapter 7

THE OFFER

Ben steered his jalopy home, his mind swirling. He ran through the evening chores like a robot, ate dinner without tasting it, and said little. He tossed fitfully most of that night. He squinted sleepily as the morning dawned cool and blustery, the sky spitting a light drizzle. *Wind's outta the west, means a strong crosswind. Overcast rolling in. Won't be any flying today.*

Ben found Brice huddled with Simpson in the cramped office. Brice gave a quick nod toward the Fly Inn.

"I told Ben I'd buy him breakfast and discuss yesterday's flight," Brice said. "I'll check back with ya later."

Settled in Brice's favorite back booth, Ben studied the older man's face. Brice hadn't shaved and looked like he hadn't slept either.

"Just black coffee for me," Brice told the waitress. "What's for you, Ben?"

Ben ordered scrambled eggs, sausages, toast, tomato juice, and coffee. Brice winced.

"Brice, what's going on?" Ben pressed.

Brice said Silverman was a recruiter looking for pilots. "Silverman needs pilots for a special job, a special job overseas. Spain, to be precise. You know where Spain is, and what's happenin' there?"

Brice could see Ben wasn't sure. "There's a civil war goin' on there," Brice said. "Whole thing came to a head last year when a bunch of army officers led by Generalissimo Francisco Franco—call themselves the Spanish Nationalists—staged a coup against the Loyalist Popular Front government of the Spanish Republic. Popular Front's made up of a lot of liberals an' left-wingers, including Communists, Socialists, and other loonies. But it's the legitimately elected government."

Brice continued. "Didn't take long before both sides were goin' at each other in an all-out civil war. Franco's got most of the Spanish army high command behind him.

Now it could turn into somethin' much bigger'n a civil war, threatening to spread all over Europe."

"Why would it spread to the rest of Europe?" Ben interrupted.

"See, Hitler in Germany and the Italian dictator Mussolini support General Franco's Nationalist movement. They want a Fascist government in Spain that'll join their Axis Pact. Don't know for sure what those two bastards are up to, but you can bet it isn't gonna be in anybody's best interests but their own. They're doin' a lot of terrible things, especially to the Jews in Germany."

"Hey!" Ben said excitedly. "We studied that in our current events class. The Nazis want to drive the Jews out of Germany and maybe all of Europe, and the Italian Fascists have joined with them."

"Are you tellin' the story, or am I?" Brice grumped. "What's happening now in Spain is the last round of political shenanigans that've been going on there since the turn of the century," he said. "Spain had a king named Alfonso XII who pissed everybody off. He was forced to allow democratic elections, and the second Spanish Republic was formed by politicians and people opposed to the Fascists, who also were trying to gain power.

"There were a lotta general strikes all across Spain, and street fightin' broke out . . . factory workers and farmers against the right-wing conservatives and the Spanish army. After a bunch of government crises, another election was held in February of '36. The leftist Popular Front government won."

Ben started to interrupt again but was stopped by a glare from Brice. "The result is the Socialists, Communists and other left-wingers in Spain support the Republican Popular Front, or the Loyalists, as they're also called," Brice continued. "And the right-wingers and half the Spanish army support the Nationalist rebels trying to boot out the Republicans.

"The Nationalist and Republican armies have the country pretty well divided and are knocking the hell out of each other and anybody who gets in the way. At the moment, the Nationalists are knocking more hell out of the Loyalists than vice versa. The only clear thing is that the real losers are the Spanish people. They're gettin' beaten up and killed by both sides."

Ben frowned, but sat back. *Better not interrupt again.*

"The Nazis and Italian Fascists are sending military support to the Nationalists. And a lot of liberal groups around the world, including Socialist and Communist parties—some from America—are supportin' the Republicans," Brice continued.

"You've heard of the Lincoln Brigade from America. They joined with the International Brigade to fight for the Republicans. Germany sent in the Condor Legion, from their 'nonexistent' Luftwaffe, to support the Nationalists. Italy sent in the Aviazione Legionaria."

"Not sure I can keep all this straight," Ben muttered.

"A lot of people who aren't Communists, or even Socialists, think Spain is the place to make a stand against the Nazis and Fascists," Brice said. "That's why so many fellas volunteered to fight for the Republic. Oh, some of 'em are just in it for the adventure, but I guess many see this as some kinda holy crusade to stop the Fascists. They think that crazy bunch eventually will threaten the rest of Europe."

"Interesting," Ben said. "But how does Mr. Smith, uh, Silverman fit in the picture?"

"I told you, he's recruitin' combat pilots to fly in Spain! Now does he look like some Nazi or Fascist bastard?"

Ben shook his head.

"Naw, Silverman's involved with the Loyalists," Brice said. "Not sure what's drivin' him. Maybe it's what the Nazis are doing to his people in Europe."

"His people?" Ben asked.

"Well, yeah, the Jews," Brice said quietly. "Silverman is Jewish, an' as you know, the Nazis have been treatin' the Jews pretty bad since Herr Hitler came to power."

Ben nodded. "What's this got to do with us? Uh, I guess Silverman wants you to go fly for the Republican air force, right?"

"Not me, kiddo," Brice said. "You."

Ben recoiled. "*Me!*"

"Yeah, you. Silverman offered me a deal, said I'd be mainly trainin' pilots," Brice said. "I told him I was too old. Had my time in the Great War. Told him to talk to you."

"But I haven't even finished high school! I'm only seventeen!"

"Soon to be eighteen," Brice corrected, "and you look at least eighteen to me, mebbe more."

Ben rocked back again, stunned. "You think I could do this?" he squawked. "I'd never get the old man to agree, even if I was eighteen. And he sure as hell won't sign any paper saying *I am* eighteen! Jeeze, Brice. I dunno. I mean, even if I wanted to—and I'm not sure I do—I don't think I could swing it. Dad would knock me silly for even mentioning it. And poor Mom, she'd faint on the spot."

"Up to you, Ben. Your decision. But if I was thirty years younger, I'd sign up in a flash!"

"If you were thirty years younger, how old would you be?"

"Eighteen."

Ben rubbed his face with both hands. "Brice, I need to think about this before . . . before I meet Silverman."

"Yeah, 'spect you would," Brice said. He paid the check and stumped out the door.

Ben slumped forward, holding his head in his hands. What to do now? *Need to get out of the trap I'm in, but Spain? Can I really go over there and fly for the Republicans?*

He walked through the mist rising from the flight line. "If I tell the old man what I wanna do, he'll blow his stack," he muttered. "Call me a Communist, or an idiot. Probably throw me out of the house. Mom would faint, maybe have a heart attack. She's been hurt enough. Can I really do this to her?"

He rubbed his face and glanced at his watch. *Couple of hours before I meet Silverman. Wish I could take the Peril out for a spin and air out my brain.*

Ben squinted at the heavy gray clouds scudding over the airport as rain lashed across the tarmac. No flying today. He ran to the operations shack and headed for the storeroom. He flopped into a weather-beaten leather chair shoved into one corner and fell asleep.

Chapter 8

ESCAPE!

Ben snorted awake and squinted at his watch.

"Damn!"

It was afternoon. He slipped into the men's room, had a long pee, and washed his hands and face. Looking into the mirror, he tried to put on his serious flyer's look.

"Forget it," he told his reflection. "Don't try to fool Silverman. He'd see through you in a second." He tucked in his shirt, hitched up his pants, and headed for the door. "Remember, don't babble," he mumbled. "Let Silverman do the talkin'."

He found the man sitting in the Fly Inn's back booth.

"Afternoon, Ben. Glad you could join me."

"Not much happening on the ramp," Ben said.

"I guess not. What looks good to you?" he asked, handing Ben a menu. Ben knew the menu by heart.

"Their special is a great meat loaf dinner. Mashed potatoes, green beans, and a salad," he said.

"Two specials," Silverman told the waitress.

"I think you know why I'm here and why I want to talk with you," Silverman said. "I've talked with Brice about my search for pilots to fly for the Republican Air Force in Spain. I assume you're familiar with the situation there."

Ben nodded. *Thank God for Brice's quick history lesson this morning.*

"I'll get right to it. I asked Brice to join us as an instructor, not as a combat pilot. But he said he's too old. Had his shot in the Great War. Suggested I talk to you."

"I understand." *Wait him out.*

"How old are you, Ben?" Silverman slipped the question in so smoothly, it almost caught him off guard.

"Eighteen, last birthday," Ben replied, astonished at how easily the lie rolled off his tongue.

"Eighteen," Silverman said, fixing Ben with his level stare.

He knows I'm lying.

"How's everything at home?"

Again, a smooth question. Ben almost flubbed it. "Oh, ah, it's all right. My dad and I don't get along, but life on the farm's okay."

"And your mother?"

"Ah, Mom's great, a handwringer, always worried about me, whether it's flying or playing sports. But she means well. She's okay." "Okay" was figuring heavily in his description of his home life.

"Have about three months before you graduate?" Silverman added. "You'd be willing to leave before completing that?"

Ben hadn't seen that question coming. "Yeah, ah, I guess so," he stammered. "I'm fed up with school. Flying has changed my whole outlook on life." *Am I laying it on too thick?*

Their food arrived, and they ate quietly, exchanging innocuous comments about the meat loaf and the lousy weather. Their empty plates cleared, Silverman leaned back.

"Let's talk some specifics," he said. "And let's leave the bullshit aside."

Ben flinched as if he'd been slapped.

"We need pilots badly, Ben. The Condor Legion is pounding our army's positions pretty hard. They've launched bombing raids all over the Republican part of Spain, killing lots of civilians in the process. We need pilots to help stop them. With a little more training, you'd have those skills. Now how old are you really?"

"I'll be eighteen in a little while," Ben responded.

"And you say it doesn't matter if you don't complete high school?"

Ben hesitated. *Better give it to him straight.* "It doesn't mean that much to me. I'm not getting anything out of school anymore. Not even from sports."

"And your parents? Can you get their permission to do this?"

"I'll do my best," Ben said. *Not a chance, but maybe Brice can help.* Surprised, Ben realized he'd already made his decision. *Spain!*

"Okay," Silverman said. "Now what's motivating you to even consider my offer? What's in it for you? Do you believe in our cause?"

Ben sat back stunned and tried to organize his thoughts. *What's motivating me? I love to fly. I wanna get away from the old man . . . an', an', what? Jeeze, I can't just say that.*

"Umm, ah, I guess I hafta say I dunno for sure," Ben stammered. "This is all happenin' so fast. Sure sounds like a swell adventure, an', an' I love to fly. I talked with Brice about what's goin' on in Spain. I know about the civil war, but I'm not sure I know what you mean about your cause."

"Honest answer," Silverman said. "Our cause? The Fascists, with a lot of help from the Nazis, are persecuting a lot of innocent people. They're an evil bunch—"

"Because of what they're doin' to the Jews?" Ben interrupted.

Silverman gave him a long look. "Yes, the Jews and a lot of other people,' he said. "The Nazis have a dangerous ideology concerning the supremacy of the Aryan Race. They're using it to justify purifying the population of Germany. It already has affected what's happening in Spain, and we see it eventually spreading all across Europe, maybe the world."

"When you say 'we,' who do you mean?" Ben asked. "I mean, is the Spanish Republican government behind all this? Are they puttin' up the money?"

"Several international organizations are financing our efforts," Silverman said. "I can't give you all the details. We're getting support from a lot of reputable people who're concerned about how the Nazis and Fascists would benefit from a Nationalist victory in Spain. They have to be stopped, Ben. And Spain is where we have to make that stand."

"Is it mainly because you're Jewish?" Ben asked.

Silverman paused. "That's part of the reason," he said quietly. "But I'd feel this strongly about it, no matter what my ethnic background was. Does any of this trouble you?"

Ben sat silently for a moment, then shook his head. "No, I guess not," he said. "But I'm not sure I understand all of it."

"We can sort this out later," Silverman said. "Right now, let's get to the point. We need pursuit pilots. What you've shown me in the air and the way you talk makes me think that with a little more training, you could handle that quite well."

Ben shifted in his seat. "Me, a pursuit pilot?"

Silverman gave him another long look and continued. "Here's what we can offer you, a five-hundred-dollar signing bonus, two hundred and fifty dollars when you sign up and another two hundred and fifty when you board the boat for Spain."

Ben gulped. "Five hundred dollars!"

"And you'd get fifty dollars a month. It may not seem like much. But we pay for room, board, and uniforms," Silverman said. "You'd be on contract for a minimum of one year or the duration of the war."

"I . . . I have to think about this," was all Ben could stammer. "Can I talk to you or call you tomorrow?"

"Sure," Silverman said. "You need to think this through. You also need to decide whether you want to fight the Nationalists because of what they represent."

"Ah, I'm still not sure," Ben said. "I suppose a lot of fellas are volunteering for that reason. But I hafta say I don't really know." *Dope! That was a dumb response.*

"Okay," Silverman said, "I accept that. Take some time to mull it over. Now how about a piece of lemon pie?"

Silverman paid the bill, and they parted outside the Fly Inn with a handshake. Silverman strode to his car, and Ben stood in the drizzle, feeling alone and confused. He found Brice snoring in the storeroom leather chair. Ben cleared his throat. Brice didn't stir. Ben cleared his throat again, a little louder.

"Do that one more time, kiddo, and I'll throw you outta the window," Brice snarled, his eyes still closed. "And there ain't a window in this room yet!"

"Brice, I gotta talk. I need to get some things straight in my head. Please!"

Brice fixed a bloodshot stare on Ben. "Awright, sit down, the doctor is in. Can't this wait until tomorrow when I get my brain back? I can hear what you're saying, but I'm not sure I can make any sense of it."

Guess he's had more than a couple of Irishes. "Brice, you gotta help me," Ben pleaded. "Silverman made me an offer. He wants an answer tomorrow. And I gotta get home for evening chores."

"So what've I got, five minutes to counsel you on a decision that'll change your life?" Brice grumbled. "Right now I can't even think about thinkin'. Let's take this up tomorrow."

"Brice, tomorrow is Monday. I have to go to school."

"School! You're talkin' about sneakin' off to fight in the Spanish civil war, with or without your folks' permission, and you're worried about school?"

"Okay, okay!" Ben exclaimed. "Forget school. Do I answer Silverman tomorrow?"

"That's up to you, kiddo. Are you happy enough at home to stay there until you can thumb your nose at the old man and walk out? Or do you want to leap outta the nest now?"

Ben was silent. He was on the brink of taking a big step forward to a better future or making the worst mistake of his young life.

One part of his brain was urging, *Go! Make the break—I'll never have another chance like this.* The other part was equally adamant. *Am I old enough? Don't do anything stupid. Don't care about the old man, but what about Mom? Will I be abandoning her?*

Brice locked eyes with him. "Ben, you need to decide why you'd want to do this. Do ya have some kinda high-falutin' idea, like you'd be doin' your part to help save the world from the Fascists, or does this just sound like a neat and excitin' adventure?"

Ben looked at his shoes. "I dunno. Haven't given it that much thought."

"Well, you better," Brice snapped. "This isn't some lark you can run off on and then come sneakin' back home if you don't like it."

Brice sat in silence for what Ben felt was an eternity.

"I guess I can help," Brice said finally. "What I see is you need a letter sayin' you have permission to do this, right? You think you can get that from the old man?"

Ben shook his head. *Not a chance.*

"Well, lemme see," Brice said thoughtfully. "Maybe I can work up a letter for you and sign it. Save him the trouble," he added with a leer. "Angie has a notary stamp."

Angie, the Baker's Flying Service much-put-upon secretary, housemaid, nursemaid, and the real power in the organization, was under Brice's spell. She'd do anything for the old goat. Well, almost anything.

"I'll bet I can convince her it'd be a good idea to type up a letter I'll compose and to notarize the thing for you."

"Would you do that for me, Brice?"

"I'll work it with Angie. Now go home and milk your damn cows and let me sleep."

"Brice, I—"

"Go! See ya tomorrow."

Chapter 9

THE CONFRONTATION

Ben's spirits soared as he sped home. He ran upstairs, changed into his work clothes, and sprinted to the barn, giving his mom a quick hug as he flew past her in the kitchen. He came crashing to earth when he encountered his father.

"Where the hell have you been?" he snarled. "Am I going to get any work out of you, or do I have to hire someone? I can get a hired hand who'll do some real work around here. And for less than it costs to feed you."

"I'll do the milking," Ben muttered, brushing past him. "I always do. And I'll shovel out the shit and put down fresh straw, feed the cows and the pigs and—"

"Don't give me any of your stupid back talk!" his father roared. "You wouldn't do anything around here if I didn't stay on you. What you need is a good boot in the ass!"

Ben whirled, face taut, fists clenched. His father squared his muscular frame and sneered. "You gonna get physical?

Ben stiffened, and then relaxed. "It'd be a waste of time," he snapped, and reached for the milk pail.

Ben fumed through the evening, milking at a record pace, but took time to twist the occasional teat and squirt warm milk toward the gaggle of barn cats lined up behind the cows.

"Here you go, you worthless bums," he muttered, arching streams of warm milk into their upturned mouths.

Ben strained the milk into large metal cans. He banged their covers in place and lugged the cans to the cooling tank where icy water from the farm's deep well swirled around them. The truck driver from the co-op dairy would collect them in the morning.

Butch and Bertha scrambled to keep pace as he worked off his anger with the heavy labor. He trembled as he scooped the manure-sodden straw from behind the cows. Was it anger, excitement, or anxiety? How much longer could he resist? The old man was pushing him away, and Spain was pulling him on.

"Just can't stay on the farm anymore," he fumed. "But can I run off to Spain?"

Ben thrashed the bed all night and watched bleary-eyed as the sun rose. He rushed through the morning milking, no doubt leaving the poor cows wondering what they had done to deserve such jerking on their udders. He skipped breakfast over his mother's objections, saying he had to get to school early. Instead, he headed for the airport.

Brice was rummaging through papers in the office. "Mornin', sport," he said. "You look like hell. Didn't get much sleep last night?"

"No breakfast either," Ben said.

"Okay, let's go to the greasy spoon and put some fuel in your tank," Brice said. They ate in silence.

Brice eyed him mopping up syrup with his last bite of pancake. Ben stared dolefully back.

"What am I supposed to do?" he blurted. "Brice, you're the only person I can talk to. Never had a real talk with the old man, and Mom wouldn't understand any of this. Don't even have any close buddies. Help me, please!"

Brice swallowed hard and gave Ben a long look. "Damn," he grumbled. "If only I were eighteen again. What a pair we'd make!" He squeezed Ben's shoulder. "Okay. You gotta settle down. Think this through. You have the basic skills Silverman is lookin' for. Sure, you'll need more training, but Silverman will arrange that, probably even before you'd leave for Spain.

"I might even be able to help there. He won't ask you to clear outta here tomorrow, won't be able get you to Spain much before the end of this year, maybe early '38. Between now and then, you'll have a lot of flyin' to do and a lotta growin' up."

Ben stared at him. "You make it sound pretty and easy," he mumbled.

"I'm not sayin' it'll be easy," Brice fumed. "What I'm sayin' is, it'll take a lotta work and a lotta growin' up! I'm also sayin' you have what it takes to do this. If you *really* wanna do this, then make up your damn mind. I'll help you all I can." Brice squinted at Ben. "Really gave it to ya, eh? But I'm right. It's time to grow up or continue wallowing in this rut you're in. Let's see what you're made of!"

Ben stared at his plate. "Okay," he said, lifting his head. "I guess that's like gettin' thrown in at the deep end. You think I can do this. Now I gotta convince myself."

"I think I can help you do that, Ben. Let's work on a plan."

Brice said he knew someone who had access to a North American BT-9 basic trainer, a low-wing monoplane powered by a 400-hp, seven-cylinder Wright radial engine. It was bigger than the Stearman, double its weight at slightly over four thousand pounds. And it had a tandem cockpit that was enclosed by a greenhouse canopy. Its fixed landing gear had a taildragger stance like the Stearman, but it had wing flaps and a variable pitch propeller, which added to the challenge of flying it.

Ben said he wouldn't be able to afford flight time in a BT-9. Brice waved him off. "No problem. I'll finance it, and you can pay me back when you get your advance from Silverman."

Ben had made up his mind. He'd tell Silverman that afternoon he wanted in on the deal. *Now how in hell am I gonna pull it off?*

Chapter 10

The Commitment

Silverman wasn't in when Ben called after lunch. He left the phone number at the airport and prowled like a caged animal. The phone rang shortly after three p.m. It was Silverman.

They chatted amicably, and then Ben heard himself say, "Mr. Silverman, I want to go to Spain."

Hanging up the phone, Ben went looking for Brice. He found him in the Fly Inn.

"Welcome to my office," Brice said. "Sit down. I can tell by your face what answer you gave Silverman."

"Brice, I did it! I told him I'd go to Spain. Dunno if it's the smartest thing I've ever done or the dumbest."

"You won't know that until it's too late to change your mind," Brice said somberly.

They spent an hour looking at all possibilities and working out how Brice could forge a letter from the old man. They agreed Ben had to go back to school for the rest of the school year and resume a normal routine.

At home, he told his mother he wasn't feeling well and needed a nap. He waved off her concern and the proffered thermometer, then stretched out on his bed. The enormity of his commitment swirled through his brain. *Well, I've come this far, and there's no looking back now.*

He performed the evening chores automatically. His father didn't come home for dinner. Ben and his mother ate in silence.

"Where does it hurt, Ben?" she asked. "Should you see a doctor or at least the school nurse?"

Ben stared into his plate. "Naw, Mom, I'm just tired."

He was at the chores by daybreak. At breakfast, his mother's red and swollen eyes shocked Ben. It was as though he was seeing her for the first time. She seemed to have shriveled into an old woman. Her once-erect frame was hunched, her rich brown hair mousy and flecked with gray. Her soft brown eyes were glazed and sunken. The old man hadn't come home last night, and she probably sat by the window watching for him into the wee hours. Ben's stomach churned. He clenched his fists in anger. *I'll have no problem turning my back on him. But how do I leave Mom behind?*

He gave her a special hug as he left for school. "See you this afternoon," was all he could manage. He didn't know how to console her, and walked out with a storm of emotions swirling through his brain.

He parked Excalibur behind the gym, not certain how he arrived at school, and headed for his first class. His mind was not on school. The math teacher, guessing he had caught Ben daydreaming, posed a question to the class about two drivers traveling at the same speed along the same route from point A to point B. The first driver took an hour and a half to make the trip and the other ninety minutes.

"What's the difference?" he asked, calling on Ben.

Ben responded with a "Huh?" Then, "Ah, I don't know."

His classmates jeered. The rest of the day passed in a fog. His homeroom teacher and baseball coach accepted his made-up excuse for missing school and practice the day before. *Gotta be more careful for the next couple of weeks.*

Home bristled with tension that evening. His mother was white-faced and withdrawn. The old man, finally home with no explanation, put on his pugnacious act when she inquired where he had been. "None of your business," he snapped.

Ben couldn't look at him. He quickly ate in silence, then excused himself as soon as possible. Flopping across his bed, he began to work out how he would leave. Should he pack his suitcase and sneak out after dark, slip over the porch roof, and drop to the ground? Or should he face the old man and say he was leaving home, like Joe did? Another open question was timing. *I'll give it a couple of weeks to work things out with Silverman, and then I'm gone.*

Sleep did not come that night. Ben watched another dawn through bleary eyes.

Chapter 11

THE COUNTDOWN

"I got a letter for you," Brice smirked as they huddled in his back booth "office" in the Fly Inn. "It looks so legal I can't believe it," he said, shoving the letter into Ben's hand. "To whom it may concern, etc., signed, sealed, and delivered. Nice-looking notary stamp, ain't it?"

"Brice, you and Angie can get into trouble over this! If the old man comes looking for me, won't the two of you be responsible for helping me disappear?"

"Naw! You and Silverman will be long gone before he comes around. And I won't have any idea where you've gone because you're not gonna tell me."

Ben shifted uneasily in his seat.

"Silverman may or may not need this letter," Brice said. "It might be good insurance, in case you get stopped somewhere along the line, but that isn't gonna happen! He is gonna have to get you a passport though, so you'll need your birth certificate.

"Remember! I don't wanna know where you're goin' or how you're gettin' there. After you arrive wherever, drop me a note."

"Tell me again that I'm doing the right thing," Ben said.

"Only you can decide that, sport. Better decide it soon. Silverman's due within the hour. Now get back to your gas pumps. Got some flyin' to do."

Silverman was sipping coffee in the Fly Inn when Ben joined him. Silverman noted the stress lines etched in his young face. "Everything okay? You look a little uptight. Didn't sleep much last night?"

"I'm fine," Ben mumbled. "I'm ready to talk about the details."

Ben ordered a burger and a chocolate malt, and Silverman, a pastrami sandwich and coffee.

"I have a letter for you," Ben said, sliding the paper across the table as though he didn't want to touch it. "I think that covers everything."

Silverman read it carefully, then a second time.

"From your father?" he asked.

"Yes. It's even notarized."

"I see that, by Angie, Simpson's secretary. Does your father come out to the airport often?"

"Ah no, he doesn't. But she notarized it anyway."

"It must be wonderful to have friends like Brice and Angie," Silverman chuckled.

Ben sat hunched, looking at his folded hands.

"Look, Ben, if we're going to make this work, we have to be up-front and honest with each other, right?" Silverman said evenly.

Ben nodded.

"I think you want this very badly, and I want you to do this just as badly. But this letter," he snapped the page with his finger, "doesn't fool me and won't fool anyone else either."

Ben slumped back in his seat.

"May not even be needed," Silverman continued. "We probably won't get you signed up and off to training until after your birthday. But I'm going to keep this letter in your file until you are eighteen. Then I'm going to tear it up. Who knows, if a situation arises before then, this might keep both of us out of trouble. Now let's get down to business. And remember, no more bullshit!"

As they ate, Silverman outlined the plan. It would be another four to six weeks before he could get all the arrangements in place. He would mail Ben a bus ticket to Detroit, where he'd meet Silverman and five other pilots before boarding a train for New York.

"We have three trainer aircraft stationed at an airfield in rural New Jersey," he said. "We'll spend several weeks of intensive flight instruction. Those who pass will return to New York City with me. Then we head for Brooklyn and board a freighter for Barcelona. Ah, that's the capital of Catalonia in northeastern Spain."

The name exploded in Ben's brain. *Barcelona! Must be some kinda swell place.*

"In Barcelona, you'll be sworn in as a volunteer pilot, probably a sergeant pilot, in the Republican Air Force," Silverman continued. "I hope to recruit enough pilots to make an American squadron. If not, you'll be assigned to whatever unit needs replacement pilots."

"This sounds too good to be true!" Ben blurted, then started to mumble an apology.

"Never mind," Silverman said easily. "This all must sound pretty exciting now. Better be prepared though for some tough going. I think we'll be attached to one of the Russian air force units Stalin has sent to support the Republicans. In that case, you'll receive advanced training in two Russian airplanes, the Polikarpov UTI-4 two-seat trainer and the I-16, a single-seat fighter version of the same airplane."

Ben gaped. *Am I hearing right, or is this all a dream?*

"Now I need your signature on a real document," Silverman said, slipping two sheets of paper across to Ben. "Here's your contract. Read it carefully. I don't want you signing anything you don't understand."

Ben's commitment was for a minimum of one year or the duration of the war. A $500 signing bonus. Hearing it was one thing, seeing it on a contract was another! His pay was $50 a month. *I'd do this just for room and board.*

Ben put his shaky signature on the document. Silverman handed him a second copy for signature.

"Congratulations, Ben, you'll soon be a volunteer member of the Spanish Republican Air Force! Now all you have to do is complete the advanced flight training."

Ben flashed a weak smile, vigorously pumping Silverman's hand. "Thanks," he gulped.

"All right," Silverman said. "That's it, except for one thing. You'll need to get your birth certificate, or a notarized copy of it, so we can get you a passport in New York."

Might be able to dig it out of the family metal box. But I don't want to go behind Mom's back. Just have to ask her for it. "Okay," he said finally. "I'll have it when we meet in Detroit."

Silverman rose to leave. "I have other contracts to get signed," he smiled. "You'll get an advance of one hundred dollars on your signing bonus when we meet at the train station in Detroit. Need any money now?"

Ben shook his head. "I've saved some of my money from the ramp job."

"All right. I'll mail your bus ticket in care of Baker's Flying Service."

"Before you go," Ben said. "Brice has arranged for me to get some flying time in a North American BT-9 basic trainer. Thought it'd help if I got some experience in a more advanced airplane than the Stearman before I went off to war . . ."

"War" stuck in his throat.

"A BT-9, eh?" Silverman said with a tight smile. "Brice is a versatile man. Handles it all, from notarized letters to the latest in basic trainers. Won't ask where or how he got the airplane. Really sorry I couldn't convince him to join me. Sure could use someone with his talents."

Chapter 12

FINAL PREPARATIONS

A pilot flew the BT-9 into Baker Airport next Friday evening. Brice called Ben to come out for a look. Ben didn't see the pilot, and Brice didn't explain where he was.

"We've got this bird until Sunday afternoon," he announced. "Supposed to be on a cross-country flight, but as you can see, it ain't. We'll get started tomorrow morning soon as you're through jerkin' the tits on your beloved cows."

Ben was up before dawn. He sailed through the morning chores and was roaring down the road for Baker Airport as the sun peeked over the horizon.

Brice had the BT-9 ready to go. It was a low-wing monoplane trainer with a tandem cockpit. Its sliding greenhouse canopy made it look like a serious flying machine. It was larger than the Stearman, its control surfaces fabric-covered, as were portions of the fuselage. The airframe was aluminum and steel. No wood like in the Stearman.

Brice guided Ben through a walk-around check of its inspection points, wing flap system, and variable pitch propeller. He explained the blades were set in fine pitch for takeoff, then adjusted to coarse pitch for better efficiency in cruise.

"You'll fly solo from the front hole, so get up there," Brice said.

Ben felt small in the cavernous cockpit, gigantic compared to the Peril's cozy open cockpit. Brice said to leave the canopy open during takeoffs and landings. "Once we're up and away, slide it shut."

The cockpit briefing took half an hour. "Here's the flap handle," Brice said. "We'll use five degrees of flap for takeoff and retract them slowly when airborne. On landing approach, extend the flaps in stages to the full position before touchdown. The gear is fixed, like on the Stearman. But after takeoff, I want you to pretend you're reaching for the gear crank and say out loud, 'Gear coming up.' Get into that habit. You'll soon be flying airplanes with retractable gear."

Brice pointed out the master switch, primer, mixture control, the propeller control, the navigation instruments, carburetor heat to prevent icing in the carburetor throat during reduced power flying, and the radio. "Radio!" Ben smiled. "No more yelling down a Gosport Tube."

Pre-startup checklist completed, they fired up the 400-hp, Wright R-975 radial engine. Its seven cylinders burst into life with a throaty roar that made the Stearman's engine seem puny. Brice talked him through the engine and flight control checks, telling Ben to cycle the propeller from fine to coarse pitch and back to fine.

"Set five degrees of flap and taxi out into takeoff position on the runway. When we're cleared for takeoff, hold the brakes, and advance the throttle. When you feel her straining, release the brakes and slowly give her full throttle—not too fast, or the prop torque'll run you off the left side of the runway. You'll need more right rudder on the takeoff roll than on the Stearman."

Ben tensed. Excitement clenched his gut.

"The tail's gonna come up fast, be prepared," Brice continued. "She'll lift off at seventy knots. Let her fly. Once you see a positive rate of climb, pretend you're raisin' the gear."

Ben clutched the stick and opened the throttle. He was amazed at how quickly they were airborne.

"Gear comin' up," he said, reaching for the imaginary gear crank.

Heeding Brice's command to not strangle the stick, he kept a light touch on the controls. The BT-9 responded sprightly to all inputs, handling like a much smaller airplane.

"Now raise the flaps and adjust the prop," Brice said from the backseat.

Ben flipped the flap switch up and shifted the propeller to coarse pitch. The airplane smoothed out considerably. They headed for a practice area. Brice told him to level at an altitude of five thousand feet and roll the airplane through gentle turns and basic maneuvers.

"Now gimme a power-off stall," Brice said.

Ben was surprised at the BT-9's gentle stall characteristics. Aileron control was good throughout the maneuver. At the break, the airplane didn't tend to roll off on either wing. Wingovers and chandelle turns followed, with Brice coaching him through each maneuver.

"Lemme see max bank angle turns to the left and right," Brice instructed.

Ben pulled the airplane into the first tight turn. The nose dropped and airspeed rose.

"You need more throttle and back pressure in the turns," Brice said. "This beast has a big engine out front. Tight turns, especially to the left, can turn into a spiral if you ain't careful."

Ben corrected and hit the groove on subsequent turns.

"Okay!" Brice chortled. "Let's do a loop."

Ben pushed the stick forward, let the airspeed build, and pulled up smoothly almost to the vertical position. He was late with the application of full power on the pull up, and the BT-9 shuddered as the airspeed dropped dramatically. The airplane stalled, and they tumbled out of the loop and flipped into a spin. It happened so quickly, Ben was disoriented and struggled to regain control. He slammed the throttle back and worked the stick and rudders. He recovered in a steep dive, pulled the airplane level, and eased in the throttle. They had dropped one thousand feet.

"Do that closer to the ground, and you're dead," Brice said quietly into his earphones. "Climb back to five thousand, and try another loop. Watch your entry speed, pull back smoothly on the stick, nothing abrupt, and keep the power up until you're over the top and starting down the other side. Keep lookin' up and back to catch the horizon as soon as you're over the top."

Something was different about this flight. Brice was coaching him, not bellowing at him for being ham-fisted on the controls. Maybe it's because they were communicating by radio and Brice wasn't shouting down the Gosport.

For Brice, it was time to guide Ben through refinement of his already considerable piloting skills with as little intervention as possible. The second loop went smoothly. Ben pulled the aircraft through the vertical, keeping plenty of power on, and pulled the power back on the inverted downhill leg to recover in level flight.

"Nice," Ben heard in his earphones. *Wow! Is this really Brice I'm flyin' with?*

Brice directed him through more maneuvers, including spins, and then said, "Let's head back to the field and shoot some touch-and-go landings. Don't forget prop, gear, and flaps."

Descending toward the pattern, Ben pulled on carb heat, rolled onto the downwind leg, and set the prop on fine. He lowered the landing gear and selected initial flaps as he turned onto the base leg. On final, he selected full flaps and closed the throttle. He flared too high on the first approach, and the airplane slammed onto the runway. But it stayed down and didn't balloon back into the air.

"Don't drill her into the ground!" Brice grunted. "Sneak a peek out to the left side like in the Stearman. Check your height before suckin' the stick back."

The next three landings went well. Brice called the tower and said their final two landings would be made from an overhead break.

"For an overhead, fly the final at a higher altitude and speed than normal," Brice said. "Over the end of the runway, roll into a tight 360-degree left turn, bleeding off speed and altitude. This is where you drop flaps and gear. Comin' out of the turn, roll level on the runway heading and land."

He added, "That's the way modern pursuit pilots make their approaches. I'll do the first one. You follow through on the controls and then fly the next one."

Brice flew the first overhead approach with precision, simulated lowering the landing gear in the turn, and hit the runway numbers with a smooth touchdown. Ben flew the second approach and rolled out high and fast as they descended toward the runway.

"She slips nicely," Brice said quietly into his earphones.

Ben cross-controlled with left stick and right rudder, and the BT-9 dropped smoothly into a sideslip. As the airspeed bled off, Ben rolled the airplane level, glanced out the left side to gauge his height, and sucked back the stick. The airplane slid down to a smooth three-point landing.

They flew again early the next morning, and Ben quickly developed a feel for the BT-9. His aerial maneuvers were smooth, and he nailed two overhead break approaches, touching down on the runway numbers both times. After the flight, he fueled the airplane, checked the oil, and polished the windshield. Brice's elusive pilot friend appeared, strapped into the cockpit without acknowledging Ben, and started the engine. He taxied to the runway and was gone. Brice flashed Ben a big wink.

Later that afternoon, Ben intercepted Brice following his last instruction flight. "Brice, I gotta get going," he said.

"I know! You've got forty-eight tits to jerk before sundown. Meet me in my office."

Settled in the Fly Inn's booth, Ben sipped a Vernors while Brice nursed a black coffee.

The old boy looks pretty relaxed. Am I doin' okay with this BT-9 beast?

"You did well today, Ben," Brice said evenly. "Still a few rough spots, but I like how quickly you got the feel of the bigger airplane. Tell ya what, next weekend we'll concentrate on aerial work an' do some combat maneuvering. My friend'll join us in the Peril, and we'll do some dogfightin'. That sound okay?"

"Okay!" Ben yelled.

Brice handed him a BT-9 pilot's manual.

"Memorize this," he grumbled. "And in your free time, think about flying the BT-9. Fantasy flying can be a big help in developin' the right habits and reactions."

"As if I need to be told to fantasize about flying!" Ben grinned.

Chapter 13

THE BREAKING POINT

Roaring home in Excalibur, Ben mentally flew the BT-9, reaching out for the imaginary landing gear handle, flaps, and propeller control. He nearly missed the turn onto the road home.

"Keep your mind on driving," he muttered. "After a day of flying like this, it'd be real dumb to kill yourself drivin' home!"

His father scowled as he steered Excalibur into the driveway.

"Looks like he's spoiling for a fight," Ben mumbled.

The old man lashed out even before he was out of the car, following him to the house, ranting about how little work he was getting out of Ben, and telling him he could get a hired hand for less than it costs to feed him. Ben had heard enough. He whirled on his father.

"Why don't you just do that?" he said, surprised at how calm he sounded. "Yeah, go ahead. Hire someone to replace me, and I'm out of here. I'll give ya a month's notice."

His father flinched. Veins bulged on his neck. He blinked twice. His face blossomed crimson, then purple. He bunched his fists and leaned toward Ben with a growl.

"Go on, swing at me!" Ben taunted. "And when you do, I'll knock ya on your ass!"

The old man stared openmouthed. "Okay," he snarled. "That's the way you want it. Fine with me! The sooner you're out of here, the better. And don't bother to come back!"

He pushed past Ben, snapped at Ben's mother, and stormed into their bedroom. Ben whirled and saw a stricken look on his mother's face. He wasn't aware she had seen and heard everything. She had a hand over her mouth, tears welled in her eyes.

"Mom, I'm sorry," Ben said. "I . . ."

His father stormed back past them. Ben watched him get in his car, back around the pump house, and speed out of the driveway, leaving a shower of gravel in his wake.

He won't be home tonight. Ben turned to his mother, who stood like a statue, hand covering her mouth. "I can't take this anymore, Mom," he said quietly. "I have to move out, or I'll go nuts."

"Ben, nooo," his mother moaned. "First Joe and now you. Why can't you try to get along with him? He's under a lot of pressure at work, and he worries about keeping the farm going."

"Mom, please! I'm keeping up my end of the bargain. I get the chores done every morning and night. I'm also doing a lot of other work around here. He just can't stand it that I'm having such a good time flying with Brice an' learning so much. He's never cared about anything I do."

Afraid you haven't really, either. But can't say that.

"I can't talk with the old . . . with Dad. All he ever does is rant at me!"

Ben wanted to tell his mother he was angry about the way his father treated her. But he didn't know how. Instead, he stared at her in silence. She stifled a sob and gave him a quick hug.

"Did you mean what you said? Are you really leaving home?"

"Yes, Mom. I have to get away."

"What will you do? Where will you go? Up to Aunt Vivian's, like Joe?"

"I dunno, Mom. I think I've found a flying job. You know, instructing, that sort of thing." He hated the lie, but the truth would destroy her.

His mother turned, saying she was going to lie down for a while.

"She'll be up all night, waiting for the old man," Ben muttered.

After evening chores, he walked to the pump house. When younger, he climbed to the small wooden platform just below the large windmill blades. From there he would scan the far horizon and wonder what interesting and wonderful places lay beyond it. He clambered up the ladder and sat on the platform, dangling his legs over the edge.

"Amazing," he mused, looking at the horizon a couple of miles away. "Back then, I really thought I could see forever."

A soft breeze swirled around his head, wafting scents of early summer lilacs mixed with apple blossoms from the orchard behind the house. He remembered the fun he and Joe had ramming around the farm. His hand went instinctively to his left cheek, tracing the scar that extended from just below his eye. His older brother had nearly poked out his eye as they played pirates with wooden swords. *Good thing he didn't get me in the eye. Not much future for a one-eyed pilot.*

Memories of hunting the fields around the farm with Joe and neighbor kids swarmed into Ben's mind. Pheasant hunting was great, especially with Butch and Bertha working out in front of them. Watching the two cocker spaniels bound out of the tall grass with ears flapping for a quick look around had always made them hoot with laughter. Fishing for bullheads in Swanson's "crick" was special, as were their forays into nearby woods and the mock war games they played in the back pasture.

Joe was two-and-a-half years older than Ben and always had assumed the role of protector for his younger sibling. He considered Ben as the kid. *Probably always would*, Ben mused. They had different builds; Joe was shorter and more stoutly built, like their father. He had inherited dark brown hair and brown eyes from their mother, and was serious-minded beyond his years. But he had strong sense of adventure and knew how to have fun. "Talk about bein' happy-go-lucky, bare-ass, and free," Ben chuckled.

The sky reddened into a fiery sunset. Tentacles of orange clouds stretched across the sky as the solar disc slipped out of sight. Peeper frogs began their evening song in the cattle pond. The cows puffed and grunted as they settled in the barnyard, placidly chewing their cuds. Butch and Bertha hunkered in the driveway below, occasionally cocking their heads upward and giving him tentative tail wags and quizzical looks. *What a beautiful place this is. Part of me'll always stay here.*

The shouting match with his father swarmed into his mind, and anger clutched at his throat. "Dammit!" he shouted into the gathering dusk. "Why does the old man have to spoil all this? He doesn't give a damn about anything I do!"

At dark, he clambered down, fed the dogs, and made a last check of the barn and chicken house. He and his mother ate a late supper in silence. Neither had an appetite. She picked at her food. He ate sparingly. There wasn't much more to say. How could he explain to his mother what he wanted to—no, had to do? His heart sank as he saw how distraught she was.

"Mom," he said, getting up and putting his arms around her. "It's going to be okay. Things will settle down after I leave. You'll see. I'll stay in touch. Anyway, I won't be leaving until school's out next month."

She sobbed silently, her shoulders heaving.

Ben knew things would never settle down. The old man would probably make her life a living hell, but that had to be her battle. He had his life to live, and had to get on with it.

"Now Mom, I have studying to do," he said. He didn't tell her he would be studying the BT-9 manual, not schoolbooks.

"All right, dear," she sniffed. "I'll clean up here. You get to your studies."

"Ah, one more thing," Ben said quietly. "I'll need my birth certificate or a notarized copy of it. The flying service I'm applying to needs it for insurance."

"Insurance?" she asked, worried. "Is what you're going to be doing dangerous?"

"No," he smiled. "It won't be dangerous. Just a formality." Half-truths and outright lies flowed too easily.

"All right, dear, I'll have it for you when you're ready to leave," she replied, choking on the word "leave."

He kissed her on the cheek and slipped up to his room. He buried his nose in the BT-9 manual. It was nearly midnight when he came up for air. He tiptoed to the stairs and heard his mother moving around in the kitchen.

"Mom, I'm turning in," he called. "See you in the morning. G'night!"

"Good night, dear," she called in a small voice.

Nightmares plagued his sleep. He snorted awake from a particularly bizarre dream in which he zoomed away on some kind of a conveyance, leaving a wailing woman in the dust. Drenched in sweat, he rose and paced the room to cool off.

Days and weeks melded together, as he strove to maintain a facade of normalcy. Only Brice, Silverman, and Mr. Simpson knew his plans. How could he tell anyone else he'd be leaving soon, maybe even before graduation?

Ben and Brice had three more flights in the BT-9. Brice's pilot friend joined them for the final air combat session, flying the Yellow Peril. Brice briefed Ben.

"We'll fly out to the practice area and climb to three thousand feet, see. My buddy will fly out ahead a couple of miles, and we'll circle while he gets set up. Remember, he doesn't have a radio in the Stearman. Then we'll fly toward each other, offset about two hundred yards. When we pass, we'll both whip toward each other in maximum bank turns and try to get on the other's tail for a simulated shot."

The dogfight would continue until one pilot achieved firing position. Brice, riding in the rear cockpit of Ben's airplane, would be the judge of whether a kill had been scored. To break off the engagement, Brice would wave his arms over his head, yell "break off" to Ben, and the pilots would roll away from each other and then have another go.

The first engagement was uneventful. Both pilots tentatively probed each other's capabilities and reactions. Brice gave them the wave-off, and they positioned for another go.

"Get aggressive," Brice growled in his headset. "Muscle this thing around, get on his six o'clock position. Get a quick shot."

As the airplanes passed, Ben pulled the BT-9 into a climbing turn, rolling it on the left wingtip. His adversary was also turning tightly to the left, and they ended up staring at each other across the diameter of the circle they were making in the sky.

"Now you gotta cut across the circle!" Brice barked. "Pull up, roll right, and snap back into a diving turn to the left. Slice into him!"

Ben wrenched the BT-9 to the right, then left.

"That's right! You're bringing your nose to bear on him! Do that again, and you'll be in position to kick some left rudder and get a deflection shot! Careful you don't skid in the turn and fall into a spin!"

Ben rolled through several more right/left maneuvers and sliced the BT-9's nose around toward the Stearman. He kicked in left rudder, and the BT-9 shuddered into a skidding turn, verging on a high-speed stall. But the nose was now pointing at the Stearman's tail.

"Ratatatat!" Brice yelled. "Bingo! You blew his tail off! I call that a kill! Break right! Fight's over!"

Ben rolled right, and Brice waved his arms. The Stearman pilot headed away to position himself for another engagement.

"That maneuver I just showed you is one way to break a standoff," Brice said. "Sometimes it's better to roll outta the circle and quit the fight, but you gotta have an escape route. Don't let the other guy dive on your tail."

They ran through several dogfighting engagements, setting up differently to work on procedures for countering crossover interceptions, overhead attacks from the rear, as well as head-on encounters.

"Whatever you do, keep maneuverin'," Brice shouted. "If you're jumped from behind and you're rollin' right, flick left and then back right. Never quit trying to shake the enemy off your tail!"

Sweat drenched Ben's shirt and dripped from his leather helmet by the time Brice gave the final wave-off signal and pointed back to the airport.

"Let the Stearman go in first, and then give me an overhead-break approach," he said.

Ben taxied in and shut down the engine. He sat limp in the cockpit for a few minutes, regaining his strength and reviewing what he'd learned.

"Meet me in my greasy spoon office in ten minutes, and I'll buy ya a cup of coffee," Brice said.

Ben already was munching a Danish pastry and sipping his coffee by the time Brice joined him.

"Couldn't wait for me?" Brice said as he slid into the booth.

"Sorry, Brice, but I was starved," Ben mumbled through a mouthful of crumbs. "Hey, that was swell today! Is that really what aerial combat is like?"

"Yeah . . . except when the other guy is shootin' real bullets at ya, the intensity level is a little higher." Brice studied Ben for a moment.

"You know," he said finally, "you've got good reactions, and you're a good flyer. I can't stress enough about keepin' your head on a swivel. You gotta be lookin' all around you, especially back to your six o'clock position. Don't let anybody sneak up behind you. And the saying from the war, 'Watch for the Hun comin' outta the sun,' is still good advice. Always expect to be jumped out of the sun, and you'll never be caught with your drawers down.

"And always turn into the arc of the enemy's turn. Make him pull tighter and tighter. If you roll outside, he'll roll in behind ya and cut ya off at the pass. So keep him guessin'. Start a roll an' then flick back the other way."

Brice's hands simulated one airplane chasing another. "Not sure what you'll be flyin' for the Republicans, but find out real quick whether it has a tighter turning radius than the Messerschmitt Bf 109. That's probably the toughest fighter you'll face.

"I've taught you just about everything I know. Just be careful your first few times out. That'll be the most dangerous time. Stick close to your flight leader until you figure out what it's all about."

Chapter 14

No Turning Back, July 1937

Tension crackled around the farm during Ben's last weeks at home. School was almost over, but he decided to skip graduation. His father, probably his mother as well, wouldn't have attended anyway. He concentrated on completing unfinished jobs around the farm.

The envelope with the bus ticket arrived at Baker's Flying Service on Saturday, two weeks before school ended.

"This is it," Ben choked as he tore open the envelope. The departure time, three p.m. on the following Monday. His stomach lurched. That was two days from now. No turning back. "Whatever, I guess I'm on my way," he whispered.

PART 2

THE ODYSSEY BEGINS

Chapter 15

THE JOURNEY BEGINS

Ben leaned his forehead against the grimy window of the Greyhound bus as it rumbled south toward Detroit. He cringed, thinking of his leave-taking from home and Baker Airport, and the image of his mother slumped inconsolably as he packed his suitcase and small duffel bag.

"Here's your birth certificate, Ben," she had said in a quavering voice. "I wish you wouldn't do this, dear. Can't we try to work it out with Dad?"

"Mom, we've been through this too many times already!" He clutched her shaking hands, unable to look her in the eyes. "It just won't work."

"But you aren't even waiting to graduate . . ."

She doesn't seem to think that's such a big deal. An' 'course the old man doesn't care.

"I know, but I can't wait just to get the diploma, Mom. They want me at the flight training school right away."

He waited until the old man left for work before loading his gear into Excalibur, avoiding yet another confrontation. Butch and Bertha wriggled up to him in the driveway as he finished packing the car, hoping to go along for a ride.

"You can't come along this time," he said quietly, ruffling their ears.

Turning to his mother, he searched for words, then simply mumbled, "Don't worry, Mom, I'll be okay. I'll write as soon as I can. An' . . . an' I'll remember to eat my vegetables."

Totally worthless good-bye! Didn't make her feel any better!

Ben's mother wept as he embraced her, kissed her on the cheek, and slid into his car. He watched in the rearview mirror as she stood stoop-shouldered in the driveway, arms wrapped around her midsection in a mournful hug. She didn't return his wave as he sped down the road. Tears stung his eyes.

At the airport, Al Simpson said good-bye with a seriousness that left Ben feeling guilty. He pressed money on Ben. "The balance owed," he said.

"Thanks, chief, but you don't owe me anything."

Brice stood mute, his face crumpled like a mournful bloodhound. He rubbed a grimy knuckle in his eye. "Got a cinder in my eye."

Brice drove him in Excalibur to the bus terminal in Flint. Ben had sold the car to a friend for fifty bucks. Brice would deliver it.

"Keep the money, Brice. It's a down payment on what I owe you for the BT-9 lessons."

Their parting at the terminal was awkward. Ben wanted to hug his mentor but thought it would embarrass him. So they stood shaking hands, groping for words.

Finally, Brice cuffed him on the shoulder. "Remember everything I taught ya. Keep the revs up, an' watch your six o'clock."

Ben mumbled a quiet, "Thanks for everything," and strode into the bus terminal without looking back.

"Dummy!" he hissed to his reflection in the bus window. "You owed 'em all a lot more than a mumbled thanks and good-bye! Why couldn't you tell them how you really felt, especially Brice?"

Frank Silverman waited at the bus terminal information desk and led him to the lunch counter. He introduced Ben to Brad Collins and Art Rawlings, both from Iowa, and Ed Pearson from Indiana. Ted Anderson from Minnesota and Fred Jones from Illinois were due in soon.

"My midwestern contingent," Silverman said, looking them over. "Six pilots from the East Coast will join us in New Jersey."

They were among a growing number of young men from all across America volunteering to fight in Spain, some lured by adventure or money, some by the anything-goes lifestyle and thrill of war. A few, usually older and more politically sophisticated, rallied to what they thought was a cause worth defending. Whatever their motives, all were united by a love of flying.

Gathering them were shadowy men like Silverman, men who revealed little about themselves and less about who financed their recruiting efforts. Never discussed was the fact that the tide of war in Spain was turning against the Republic that Ben and his young friends could be heading into a losing fight.

When Anderson and Jones arrived, Silverman told them they'd stay overnight in the Statler Hotel and leave for New York on the 9:17 a.m. train. He handed each a large envelope.

"These contain background papers on the Republican Air Force, a Spanish/English dictionary, and five $20 bills, first part of the $250 down payment on your signing bonuses," he said. "You can use the hundred dollars for anything you need before we board the train. Just don't blow it all before we get out of town!"

At the hotel, Ben and Ted Anderson shared a double room. Brad Collins and Art Rawlings bunked in a second, and Ed Pearson and Fred Jones in a third. Ben judged the others to be older than he, probably in their early twenties. He'd find out later about their flight experience.

Ben had never been in a big city like Detroit. That night, as he drifted off to sleep, images from his life on the farm welled up in his mind. Like the times he, Joe, and a couple of friends from nearby farms hitched rides into Flint in the co-op milk truck. They perched on milk cans in the dark chilly interior of the refrigerated truck as it rumbled into Flint. They usually spent the day wandering the streets, enjoying one of the delights from the soda fountain at the Vernors Ginger Ale "castle." Sometimes, if they could pool enough loose change, they took in a movie.

Chapter 16

The Pilots

At breakfast, Silverman exuded cheerfulness, in marked contrast to his earlier stern demeanor.

"This is going well," he said. "Should have a dozen of you fellows going through advanced training by next week. That's a squadron!"

Four of the pilots standing in front of him nursed obvious hangovers. Silverman eyed them closely. "I have no problem with you boys having a good time," he said evenly. "Just keep in mind, this is serious business. Once we start flying, I don't want anyone stumbling around in the morning with a hangover."

On the train to New York, the six pilots chatted and joked.

Brad Collins and Art Rawlings were raised on Iowa farms a couple of miles apart. Both were lanky, loose-limbed men who stretched past six feet in height. Their ruddy faces showed extended exposure to sun and wind up to the hat lines. Above that, pale skin blended into blond hairlines. As do many quiet men, they responded mainly in monosyllables.

"We learned to fly with Artie's uncle," Brad finally said, after Ben pressed him for details of his flight experience. "He flew Spads in the Great War. Runs a crop-dusting service."

"Me and Brad really like flyin'," Art mumbled. "He got into a big fight with his old man, an' when Silverman came along, Brad said ta hell with it, why not go to Spain and fly for the Republicans? Sounded like a great adventure. I decided I'd tag along."

"Not sure what this Spanish war is all about," Brad added. "But I gotta say the pay is a hell of a lot better'n I was gettin' on the farm."

Ed Pearson was a polished city boy from Fort Wayne, Indiana. His easygoing manner hid a quick mind and a sharp wit. His passion was basketball, the national pastime in Indiana. He grinned when the others noted his five-foot, nine-inch frame.

"Guard's my position," he said. "Got quick feet and good hands, can dribble circles around anyone. Also got a good outside shot. Made the varsity my last three years in high school and played junior varsity at IU."

Ed said he learned to fly with the University's Flying Club, and spent most of his time hanging around the local airport. He flunked out in his sophomore year.

"I got bored with school," he said. "But I really got interested in politics and read a lot about what's goin' on in Europe, you know, what the Nazis in Germany and the Italian Fascists are doing. I agree with Silverman, we gotta fight 'em in Spain. They need to be stopped."

Ted Anderson and Ben could have been brothers, cousins at least. Ted was two years older. His frame had filled out more, but his manner and regional accent matched Ben's. He came from Scandinavian stock and looked the part, with his large frame, blond hair, and blue eyes. His oversized hands dangled from muscular arms.

"I learned to fly with the University of Minnesota Flying Club," he said, and slipped easily into a singsong parody of the Swedish accent. "Ya sir, you betcha, vee gonna get dem Yerman fellers by da neck an' boot der asses outta Spain!" he bellowed, to hoots of laughter.

He was in this for the adventure. His uncle had fought in the Great War and told Ted fascinating stories about his wild times in France.

Jones was raised in South Chicago, a city boy, the most streetwise one among them. His small frame was toned by years of training as a gymnast. His broad shoulders and muscular arms revealed weight training. His rock-hard torso tapered to a tiny waist. His short legs looked like tree stumps, and he walked with a bowlegged gait and a slight limp.

"I got into Southern Illinois College on a gymnastic scholarship," he said. "Was doing great until I wrecked my left knee on a bad landing from the high bar. Lost my scholarship, but it was a good two years. Gave me a chance to learn to fly with the college flying club. When Silverman contacted me, I jumped at the chance. I was kinda bummin' around. This looked like a great deal—flying for money and seein' the world."

Ben glossed over his flying experience, saying only that he had worked at an airport near Flint and had trained with an instructor who also was a veteran.

The train rumbled eastward. Ben glanced out the window. He'd never been this far from home. Judging from their comments, neither had the others.

Ben felt a special farm-boy affinity toward Anderson, Collins, and Rawlings. But since all five of the others had finished high school, and Anderson, Jones, and Pearson each had two years of college, Ben didn't offer details about his background. *Better not let 'em know I'm just eighteen or that I skipped high school graduation.*

He concluded from their conversation he had more flight experience than any of them, a fact he also didn't volunteer. The three college men had logged time in Piper Cubs and a couple of larger biplanes. Collins and Rawlings had flown Cubs with the Flying Farmers and had some biplane time as crop dusters.

Ben smiled. *Strange bunch to build a combat unit on. Haven't given much thought about why they're goin' to Spain either.*

They met Silverman for lunch in the dining car. Ben stared at the white starched tablecloths, linen napkins, and gleaming silverware. Silverman briefed them on the next stage of the program, collected their logbooks, and arranged to see each pilot separately.

When Ben joined him, Silverman handed him another envelope. It contained the remaining $150 from his bonus down payment, some travel papers, and a pilot's manual for the advanced trainer they would fly in New Jersey. Ben gave a start of delight at the manual's cover.

"Recognize that?" Silverman said, indicating the *North American BT-9* title on the cover. Ben grinned.

"I was impressed that Brice could get access to a BT-9 so easily," Silverman said. "We have to pay a lot to rent ours, plus something under the table. There are a lot of people eager to help our cause, for a price. How many hours did you log in the airplane?" he asked Ben.

"Ten."

"Did you solo?"

"No. Brice said I was ready, and my last two flights were supervised solos," Ben said. "I did all the flying. Brice rode along as safety pilot. He didn't touch the controls or give any advice. Said they couldn't risk lettin' me fly it alone," Ben added. "His friend was taking a big chance lettin' us use the airplane on weekends when he was supposed to be on cross-country jaunts."

"I understand," Silverman said, regarding Ben carefully. "But you're nearly qualified in the airplane, and that's a big plus. When we get to the field in New Jersey, we'll give you all a quick ground school review on both aircraft. We'll start with Stearmans as the basic trainer, but I expect you'll need only a couple of evaluation flights in it. Then you'll move up to the BT-9. You'll fly first. Brush up your skills, and let our instructors evaluate you. If you handle it well, you can go solo. That should give the rest of the boys confidence."

Ben grinned. He'd have an edge over the others in the next phase of training. But he reminded himself that he was still the kid in this outfit, and needed to take it easy and let the leadership thing work out naturally.

Silverman said they'd spend two nights in the Piccadilly Hotel, just off Broadway in midtown Manhattan. They'd have time to tour Manhattan while they waited for the six other pilots to join them. Then they'd travel by bus to Millville, New Jersey, for their flight training and evaluations.

"I'm not going to do bed checks at the hotel," Silverman said. "But don't take that as license to tear up Manhattan. You've all got a great adventure ahead of you. Don't spoil this chance by doing something stupid."

Ben's pulse quickened as the train crossed the Hudson River and headed south along the river's eastern bank toward Manhattan. Grand Central Station was overpowering.

Ben had never seen such crowds. On East Forty-second Street, all six gaped at the mass of pedestrians and vehicles. They stared at the skyscrapers and the street canyons between them.

Ben's mind whirled. *Wow! What's a farm hick from Michigan doing here?*

The Piccadilly was a modest hotel. Ben and his compatriots thought it was splendid and right around the corner from Times Square! They dumped their luggage and headed out to sample the sights. All the songs and stories Ben had heard about exotic Manhattan came true before his eyes.

Silverman directed them to an agent who sold cheap tickets to theater shows that same evening. Ben and Ted chose the musical *Babes in Arms*. The four others went their own ways.

The two new friends wandered in midtown Manhattan, ogled Rockefeller Center, and took in a movie at Radio City Theater. The biggest pipe organ they'd ever seen slid out of the sidewall with a man already playing it.

"Ever seen a movie house like this?" Ben asked, awed by the gilded pillars, broad stairway, tapestries, and chandeliers. "This looks like a palace."

"How about supper?" Ted said. "Let's have ourselves a French meal."

They descended into the dimly lit dining room of Renee's on West Forty-fifth Street. They were alone. Suppertime in the Midwest wasn't dinnertime in New York.

"Is your menu in English?" Ben whispered. "Mine's in French!"

"Look at the English translation in that small print under each menu item," Ted hissed.

The meal was excellent: grilled steaks topped by a thick mushroom sauce, and steamed vegetables perfectly cooked. They capped the meal with a creamy custard dessert, and ordered coffee.

"These are the smallest cups I've ever seen!" Ben whispered after the waiter placed a demitasse of thick aromatic coffee in front of each of them. "Woof!" he sputtered. "Strong stuff. No wonder they give ya such small cups!"

They left an enormous tip and strode out of the still-empty restaurant. The maitre d' thanked them with a slight bow and invited them to come back. Outside the two guffawed at their foray into the New York scene.

Ben bought several postcards. He wrote to Brice, thanking him for everything. He briefly described New York's unbelievable sights and told about the training field in New Jersey. Silverman gave them a post office box number that friends and family could write to. The mail would be forwarded. They'd be training at Millville Airport, Ben said, and heading for Spain in about six weeks. His mother's card was harder. He kept it light and included little solid information.

The musical that night at the Majestic Theater was stunning, overpowering them with bright costumes and lively singing and dancing. When they returned to the hotel, Silverman was reading a newspaper in the lobby.

"Not doin' a bed check, but he's sure keeping a lookout for us," Ben whispered.

The four other pilots wandered in. Silverman said they'd meet for breakfast and reminded them to bring their birth certificates so he could order passports.

"Tomorrow morning, you'll stop by Graham's Photo Studio at Sixth Avenue and Forty-fifth Street for passport photos," Silverman said. "I'll collect the photos later. I'll have passport application forms for you to sign tomorrow evening. By the way, the other six pilots arrive tomorrow around midmorning. We'll get acquainted over dinner."

Chapter 17

RUBES IN THE BIG CITY

Following breakfast, the pilots headed for the photo studio, assuring Silverman they'd meet him for dinner at 7:00 p.m. Ben and Ted then headed back to Times Square to board a red double-deck tour bus for a day trip around Manhattan. At one of the stops on Fifth Avenue, the guide led them into St. Patrick's Cathedral.

"This has to be the biggest church in the world," Ted whispered, gaping at the pillars, soaring arches, and vaulted ceilings.

Next stop was the Empire State Building, where they were let off to take a quick ride to the observation deck.

"Boy, you can *really* see forever from up here!" Ben exclaimed, remembering his windmill perch on the farm.

At a brief stop along Wall Street, they bought lunch from a street vendor. Both opted for hot dogs smothered in sauerkraut.

"When that fella asked if we wanted sauerkraut on it, I thought he was nuts," Ben said, swallowing the last bite. "But these are great! How about another one?"

Silverman waited for them in the lobby. Six other young men sat with him. He introduced Al Brewster from Brooklyn, Clarence Schenk from North Carolina, Randolph Schuller from Florida, Allan Saunders from Virginia, Rudolph Groenke from Pennsylvania, and Buford Musgrove from South Carolina.

Ben and Ted shook hands with each, sizing them up as each was obviously doing to them.

"It's great to meet you," Ben said. "I look forward to flyin' with ya." He said to Silverman, "Speaking of flying, when do we leave for New Jersey?"

"Tomorrow, right after breakfast."

That evening, Silverman led the twelve young men to his favorite restaurant on West Forty-fifth Street. Ben and Ted glanced at each other and sniggered as they headed for Renee's.

Chapter 18

MILLVILLE, NEW JERSEY

Millville, New Jersey, a small town near their new training base, was disappointing. "Not much action here," one pilot grumbled.

"Right," Silverman responded. "That's why we chose it. Won't have anybody hanging around, wondering what we're up to. And there won't be anything to distract you boys from your flying."

"Okay by me," Ben muttered to Ted. "I came here to fly and get on to Spain." "Me too," Ted agreed.

Whatever their motivations for volunteering, a sense of excitement and adventure was drawing them all toward Spain.

The Millville airport was even sparser than the town, an open grass field with three unpainted wooden hangars, a dilapidated barracks, a weathered mess hall with a sagging screen door, and a line of privies out back. A tattered windsock hung dejectedly from a pole on the main hangar. There was no control tower.

"Welcome to your new home," Silverman said with a tight smile. "This was an Army Air Corps training base during the war. Hasn't been used much since then."

Pointing to a large white frame home, he said, "That's the original farmhouse over there. The Chappells live there. He maintains the facilities, and his wife is our cook. All meals will be served in the mess hall. You boys will sleep in the barracks."

He and the other flight instructors would sleep in one of the rambling house's many bedrooms. "Now find yourselves a bunk and meet me in the mess hall in twenty minutes."

"Sheeit!" Art Rawlings yelled as they stepped inside the barracks. "Our pigs back home on the farm live better'n this!" Dust-coated cobwebs hung from open rafters like last year's Christmas decorations. In a dark corner, a pair of red eyes stared at them, blinked, and disappeared when whatever they belonged to squeezed down a hole in the floor. "Doesn't look like this place has been touched since the war," he said.

"If ma momma could see me now!" Buford Musgrove hooted. "Ah tole my people Ah was goin' off to fight the Fascists, to make the world a safer place. Didn't reckon Ah'd be startin' out ma noble crusade in a dump like this!"

"Okay! Home sweet home it ain't," Ed Pearson chimed in. "But it's where we're gonna live for the next couple of months, so let's make the best of it."

They gingerly tested the beds. Ben chose one near a dust-encrusted window. Sunlight barely penetrated the clouded panes. "At least the sheets are clean, and we have pillowcases," he said.

Silverman was in the mess hall, standing on a platform with three other men when the twelve trooped in.

"Before we get into the details of how we're going to operate here, I want to talk about why we're here," Silverman said. "When I first met each of you, I asked what motivated you to join us. You gave various reasons. Some of you needed a job. You were interested only in the money. Some were looking for adventure, and some of you just love to fly and thought this would be an exciting way to do it. I think it's fair to say none of you expressed much concern about the political or ideological issues that ignited the Spanish civil war."

The pilots shuffled their feet and glanced at each other.

"I accepted that," Silverman continued. "We need your help, whatever your motivation. The events that led to the Spanish civil war evolved over several decades, and are more complex than those that caused our civil war. I think it's fair to say the average Spaniard doesn't fully understand them either. Essentially it's a clash between the leftist and liberal—some would say Communist—ideology of Spain's Popular Front that formed the Republican government, and the conservative, right-wing, Fascist policies of the Nationalist revolutionary forces. We could spend a lot of time discussing this and still not understand what turned Spaniard against Spaniard in such a vicious civil war."

He paused to let the young men ponder his comments.

"Many of the volunteers who've gone to Spain to fight for the Republicans considered this a crusade against Fascism. They particularly hate the ideology of the Nazis, who provide considerable assistance to the Nationalists. Your main adversaries will be German aviators from the Condor Legion, a highly trained, highly motivated aviation group Germany has sent to Spain. The legion includes experienced pilots flying fighters, bombers, and supply transports. Their first-line fighter is the Messerschmitt Bf 109.

"You will be going to war. I trust you all understand that. If not, now is the time to decide you don't want to continue with this training." No one moved or spoke.

"Good," Silverman said. "A final point, if the Nationalists win, Spain becomes a Fascist state. That'll mean three major Fascist countries—Germany, Italy, and Spain—threatening the rest of Europe. The only country that really seems to understand this is the Soviet Union, which has its own concerns with Germany. Russia has sent a lot of war supplies to the Republicans, including several squadrons of pursuit airplanes. In fact, we'll probably end up flying with the Russians, but more about that later."

He paused.

"So as of now, we'll run this like a military unit. We'll use the twenty-four-hour military clock, and you'll take orders without questioning. We won't waste time marching, drilling, and saluting. But you will address the four of us as 'sir.'

"All meals will be served here in the mess hall. You'll roll out of bed at 0500 hours for thirty minutes of calisthenics. Ed Pearson and Fred Jones, our two star athletes, will take turns leading. Breakfast will be served at 0600. Ground school or flying will commence at 0700.

"These are your instructors—Luke, Rob Jamison, and Carl Owens. All three are war veterans with aerial combat experience. You'll fly with them in rotation. I'll be the flight scheduler, chief instructor, and check pilot."

"Hey, Luke," Buford called out. "Y'all look familiar. What's yore family name?"

"I go by Luke," the tall slim man responded. "But as Mr. Silverman said, you can call me sir."

His dark eyes transfixed Buford. He looked almost sinister. His thin, swarthy face was framed with black slicked-down hair and a neatly trimmed Clark Gable mustache. He wore a battered aviator's leather jacket over a white shirt and dark tie, jodhpurs, and high-top boots laced halfway to his knees.

"Better watch out for this fella," Ben whispered. "He looks like he could eat us for breakfast."

"Yeah," Buford grunted. "Only tryin' to be friendly. He looks familiar, and Ah thought maybe Ah knew his kinfolk. Besides, everybody's got a last name. Ah'm not sure I trust somebody who doesn't, or at least won't own up to it."

Rob Jamison was a study in contrast. He was dressed in stained flying coveralls. His large head, topped with an unruly mop of bright red hair, was out of proportion, even with his portly frame. Freckles spread across his round face, highlighting a snub nose and a pair of chipmunk cheeks. He wore a permanent grin that made his hazel eyes sparkle. His meat packer's hands, with thick stubby fingers, were never still.

Ted nudged Ben. "How about him?" he muttered. "He sure doesn't look like a pursuit pilot."

"Maybe," Ben ventured. "But he can probably fly circles around all of us."

Carl Owens looked like any medium-height man you'd pass on the street without noticing him. His pale face bore a bland expression, and his lids blinked rapidly over deep-set brown eyes. His brow often wrinkled into a puzzled frown, as though he was trying to remember something he had forgotten or misplaced. He periodically ran his long, thin fingers through his blond crew cut. He too wore stained flight coveralls.

"He'll be a thrill to fly with," Ted sniggered. "We'll have to do something stupid to keep him awake."

"Don't push your luck," Jonesy whispered. "I've flown with guys like him. He may look like a dummy, but I'll bet he don't miss a thing."

"All right!" Silverman snapped. "Keep it down! I have more announcements. We have two hours before lunch at 1300. When we're through here, I want you all to walk the field."

Noting their puzzled looks, he said, "Yes, walk the field! I want you to get acquainted with every hump, lump, and hole out there. We don't have runways here. Scout out the best paths to follow on takeoffs and landings. Some spots can cause trouble. Find them and memorize them.

"And walk down to the east end and look at that stand of poplars across the road. Note how tall they are, and remember what kind of altitude you need to clear them. Finally, visualize how you're going to have to sideslip to get down over them for a landing to the west without overrunning the field. Any questions?"

"Sir," Buford called out. "Wouldn't it be better to cut them poplars down and give us a safer takeoff and landin' run?"

"Could be, Musgrove, but we don't own that land," Silverman said. "And besides, where you're going, you'll be flying out of fields a lot worse than this one. Best to get used to it."

Silverman said their instructor assignments would be posted on the mess hall bulletin board, and dismissed them to walk the field.

Two hours later, they trudged back toward the mess hall, flushed, dusty, and thirsty.

"Field seems to be okay," Buford mumbled, "but I don't like the look of them poplars!"

They crowded around the assignment list. Ben felt a knot in his stomach. He was to fly next morning with Luke.

Lunch included beef stew, mashed potatoes, corn and peas, salad, and homemade bread. Coffee and lemonade were served with chocolate chip cookies, also homemade.

"Not bad grub," Ted remarked. "I might warm to this place."

After lunch, Ben sought out some of the pilots who had joined them in New York. He felt comfortable with the five fellow midwesterners and wanted to get to know the others better.

Al Brewster had an off-putting cynical air, honed on the streets of Brooklyn. He was in his early thirties, the "old man" of the group. Too young to have flown in the Great War, he joined a barnstorming troupe as a roustabout in the late 1920s, and learned to fly in a surplus Curtiss Jenny trainer.

"It wasn't a bad life," Brewster said, as he and Ben sat on the barracks porch. He was a tall, almost-skinny man who looked like he had never eaten three square meals a day. His mop of brown hair framed a thin face dominated by a sharp hawklike nose. His dark brown eyes were never still, as though he was watching for someone trying to sneak up on him.

"We bummed around a lot, kinda like circus fellas, which I guess we were," he said. "At first I was an errand boy and handyman. Then one of the pilots taught me to fly in a Jenny. After that, I got all the flying I wanted, in and out of a lot of crummy pastures and the like.

"I didn't make much money, an' what I did, I blew on booze and women. But I logged a helluva lot of flyin' hours. The barnstormin' circuit had gone to hell in the last couple of years, so when Silverman came along with his offer, I jumped at it. I don't particularly like the idea of flyin' with a bunch of Russians defendin' some Spaniards, but what the hell, the money is good."

"What do you think about the civil war in Spain?" Ben asked. "I mean, do we have a duty to help the Republicans fight the Nationalists, since the Nationalists are gettin' so much help from Germany and Italy? Brice, my instructor back in Michigan, says that if we don't stop the Fascists in Spain, they'll try to take over all of Europe."

"Lotta bullshit," Brewster snapped. "I don't give a damn about all that political stuff. I'm in this for the fun, excitement, and adventure. Besides, maybe there'll be a lot of hot little señoritas around."

Clarence Schenk strolled up. "What's this about hot little señoritas?" he asked eagerly, easing his ample buttocks onto the barracks steps. "What've I missed?"

"Nothing," Brewster snorted. "Findlay here was askin' me why I was goin' to Spain. I gave him three reasons, adventure, money, and hot little señoritas."

"Good reasons!" Schenk said. "I dunno about all the other stuff. My daddy fought in the war, and he says we can't trust the Germans. He doesn't like the Russians either, but he figures they're the better of two bad choices. Guess that's why I'm goin'."

Schenk shifted his weight to one fat cheek and loosed a thunderous fart. "Excuse me! Didn't mean to be rude, but that pretty much sums up my feelings for both sides in that there civil war."

"I think you better check your underwear," Brewster snapped. "You ain't gonna be polite company at ground school."

Ben looked at his watch. "We're due at ground school in ten minutes," he said. "I need to pee first."

"Allus go before ya go, my daddy says," Schenk chuckled. "I'll join ya."

Chapter 19

ADVANCED TRAINING

Ground school was perfunctory. Rob Jamison briefed them on the Stearman cockpit, which didn't take long, considering the spartan layout of the instrument panel. Luke described the BT-9 controls and instruments.

"Our aim is to move you up to the BT-9 as quickly as possible," he said. "But there are some basic differences between it and the Stearman that you need to be aware of. The BT-9 is a much larger airplane, more complicated and less forgiving than the Stearman. If you aren't careful, it'll rear up and bite you in the ass."

Ben smiled. *With ole Brice in the backseat, movin' up to the BT-9 wasn't all that scary. Shove your butt back in the seat, he said. Relax an' let the airplane do the flyin'. Wear the airplane. Get comfortable and take control. An' don't strangle the goddamn stick!*

Luke shared tips on the BT-9, its critical airspeeds, and what to expect under certain flight conditions. They were dismissed at 1700 hours. Dinner was scheduled for 1830.

"Let's look at the airplanes," Ben suggested.

The twelve pilots trooped to the hangar, where they met Al and Bert, the mechanic and ground crew chief. Both men, in their midfifties, had been mechanics in the Army Air Corps.

"Lived in Millville all my life. Al too," Bert said. "Been at this for 'bout thirty years, so we know how to keep these crates in flyin' shape long . . . long as you boys don't crack 'em up."

"I see you've met our mechanics," Luke said, startling the young pilots, who had not heard him approach. "It's smart to be polite to the fellas who maintain your airplane."

The pilots sat in the cockpits of all three airplanes. Ben felt comfortable in the BT-9. The others commented on how big the cockpit was, topped with its greenhouse-sliding canopy.

"At least it's got a fixed landing gear," Ted muttered. "Raising and lowering the gear is one thing we won't have to worry about."

"I have had some time in this airplane," Ben ventured. "It's not as forgiving as the Stearman, but it has plenty of power and handles well."

The others looked surprised.

"Brice, my instructor back home, told me to pretend I was raising the gear after takeoff and lowering it when entering the pattern," he added. "Said it was a good habit to get into because we'll be flying airplanes with retractable gear when we get into combat."

As they settled into the barracks routine, Ben strolled over to Randolph Schuller's bunk. "I understand you were a banner-towing pilot," he said. "What's involved in that kinda flying?"

"Pretty boring," Schuller said. "Trick is to get the thing in the air first, and then you chug around the sky, nose-high and staring at the engine temperature gauge. Biggest challenge is to keep from overheatin' the engine. It's pretty tough on engines, and you're always staggering along on the edge of a stall."

"What airplanes did you fly?"

"We had a couple of Travel Airs, a Bellanca, and later a Piper Cub. I got a lot of time in all of 'em, but it wasn't any fancy flying. We just dragged banners up and down over the Florida beaches." Schuller added that he graduated from Florida State with an engineering degree, but couldn't find a job.

"Do you think we're on some kinda crusade going off to help the Republicans in Spain?" Ben asked abruptly.

Schuller gave him a baffled look. "How'd we get from banner-towing to crusades?" he asked.

"Sorry," Ben muttered. "I'm really interested in what kind of flying you've done, but I dunno, I guess I'm worried about why we're going to Spain. You know, whether we're gonna do any good there."

"Well, it'll be a big adventure," Schuller responded. "What more do ya need?"

Chapter 20

THE CHALLENGE

Calisthenics over, Ben picked at his breakfast. The knot in his stomach grew as he thought about flying with Luke. He stood at attention next to the number one Stearman when Luke strode up at 0700 hours.

"Is your airplane preflighted and ready to fly?" Luke demanded.

"No, sir," Ben responded.

"Why not?"

"Ah, sir, I thought you'd want to watch me go through the preflight inspection, sir!"

"I expect you to know how to do that by yourself," Luke snapped. "You're the pilot in command, act like it. You will have your airplane preflighted and ready for engine start when I arrive. Is that clear?"

"Yessir." Ben scurried around the aircraft, conducting a quick but thorough inspection. "Sir, she's ready to fly," Ben said.

"Good, we'll take off to the east since we have an onshore breeze, climb to three thousand feet, and fly south about ten miles to a village called Potter's Corners. There's a small white church near the town, a water tower, and a power station with a tall brick chimney. Our practice area is over large fields just south of town.

"You'll be in command. I won't touch the controls or give advice unless it looks like whatever you're doing might get us both killed. Understand?"

"Yessir!"

"Good, let's go fly."

On takeoff, Ben guided the Stearman along the southern edge of the field where his walking inspection had shown fairly smooth turf. He leveled the airplane after liftoff, let the airspeed build, and then pulled up smoothly over the poplars across the road.

Shouldn't be any problem with the trees, unless the engine coughs or quits.

He noted an escape route. If it looked like he couldn't clear the trees, he'd roll right forty-five degrees and fly along the road. If the engine quit, he could make an emergency landing in one of several fields. As they topped three thousand feet, the engine coughed, sputtered, and quit. The propeller windmilled. Momentarily stunned, Ben realized Luke had simulated an engine failure by turning off the fuel valve.

"Stick forward, trim for best glide speed, fly the airplane, then find a field," Ben recited from his emergency briefings. "There's one over there! Now troubleshoot. Find the problem [although he knew what it was]. Line up for a dead-stick landing."

I'm high, but can sideslip, bleed off speed and altitude, and make it!

Ben focused on the field, feeling the airspeed rather than risking a look inside at the instrument panel. He rolled the Stearman into a sideslip to the left and aimed for a spot just beyond a fence that surrounded the field. Certain he could reach the field, he rolled the wings level.

Hold it . . . start the final flare now!

Cough! Blam! The engine caught, and the throttle was slammed forward. The big Wright radial engine bellowed as Luke commanded full power. Ben pulled the stick back, and they climbed out over the field. Luke raised his right hand and pointed toward the practice area.

Damn, damn! Thought I had that landing made. Where'd I mess it up?

Over the practice area, Ben flew the Stearman through every maneuver Brice had taught him. Using the crossroads south of Potter's Corners as a reference point, he ran through an abbreviated series of Brice's aerobatic routine.

"Okay," Luke said down the Gosport Tube. "Back to the field for some touch-and-go practice."

Over the field, Ben saw the wind had shifted and was blowing out of the west. This meant an approach over the poplars and a sideslip across the road to get into the short field. Concentrating on the trees, Ben executed the maneuver smoothly, rolled the wings level, and flared for a three-point landing just inside the fence. Luke signaled for a running takeoff and a second trip around the pattern.

Ben shook his head. Dummy! You forgot to pretend you were lowering the gear and flaps!

As he circled the field for the next approach, Ben studied the escape route he had mapped out in case he had problems on takeoffs to the east.

"Bet I can fly an angle approach inside the trees and swing onto a short final for a landing," he muttered. "It'll be tight, but won't have to sideslip over the road."

Turning toward the field, Ben simulated lowering the gear, extended the imaginary flaps, and started a descending turn inside the trees. He tensed. He was low and slow as he banked for the final tight turn into the field.

"Need to pull around a little tighter," he hissed through clenched teeth. The stick and rudder pedals felt sloppy. The Stearman shuddered. "Stall! Stall!" Ben yelled at himself. "You're stalling!"

The Stearman wobbled and began to roll toward the lower wing. Ben sensed it was about to spiral in nose first. Rolling wings level, he lowered the nose and slammed the throttle open. With a mighty belch, the engine roared to life, snatching the airplane forward. Ben pushed the stick, holding the nose down and desperately trying to recover airspeed.

The Stearman zoomed over the fence, barely clearing the top strand of barbed wire. They shot across the field at a forty-five-degree angle. Feeling the airspeed building, Ben raised the nose and rolled left to clear telephone lines along the north edge of the field. He had flying speed now and climbed back to the pattern altitude.

"Stupid fool!" he yelled, pounding his left thigh. "Luke's gonna wash me out!"

Ben glanced at the front cockpit. Luke was staring straight ahead. *He didn't flinch! I damn near killed us both, and he just sat there, didn't touch the controls.*

Luke's voice echoed down the Gosport Tube. "Give me a wheel landing, and make it a full stop. And this time approach over the trees. No more barnstorming bullshit!"

Ben cleared the trees and sideslipped over the fence. He set the Stearman on its front wheels, held enough forward stick to keep the tail up, and let the airplane roll to a stop as the tail dropped to the grass. He shuddered. His mouth was dry, his tongue felt wooden. Sweat oozed from under his leather helmet as he taxied onto the tie-down line and shut down the engine. He sat slumped in his seat. *Gonna catch hell for this.*

Luke stepped out of the front cockpit, dropped to the ground, and gave Ben a steady look. "Secure your airplane, and see me in the mess hall for debriefing," he said evenly.

"Yes . . . sir!" Ben stammered.

Slinking into the mess hall like a puppy that had piddled on the floor, Ben folded himself into a chair facing the table. Luke sat stony-faced.

"Let's start by you telling me how you did out there today," Luke said.

"I nearly killed us tryin' that stupid approach inside the tree line," Ben said quietly. "I thought I had enough room to make the final turn into the field."

"If we'd been in anything but a Stearman, you wouldn't have recovered," Luke said.

"Sorry, Luke, umm, sir, real sorry," Ben blurted. "Won't ever try anything like that again."

"I could wash you out for trying a stupid stunt like that," Luke snapped.

Ben bowed his head. *Here it comes.*

"But . . . I won't, because of the way you flew yourself out of trouble. Your recovery was excellent. I especially like the way you shoved the nose down to recover airspeed. Most new pilots in that situation would have hauled back on the stick and stalled!"

Ben released a puff of breath. "Thanks," he mumbled.

"You ever try anything like that again, and you're out, understand?"

Ben nodded.

"Now what else?" Luke demanded.

"I dunno," Ben replied. "I thought I handled the lost engine emergency okay, but you took the airplane away from me and—"

"I gave you back the engine because you were nicely set up for a dead-stick landing," Luke interrupted. "You'd have made the field easily. I didn't want to waste time letting you make the landing and then maneuvering on the ground and taking off from that small field. Anything else?"

"I thought my air work was okay," Ben said. "I didn't show you the full aerobatic routine, but I think I hit my crossover points okay."

"Overall your performance was good. But you'll need to watch for altitude loss during tight turns in the BT-9. It tends to tuck under, especially in left turns."

"BT-9!" Ben sagged with relief. "Won't I be flying any more in the Stearman?"

"No, you've shown me you can handle the Stearman. I'll move you up to the BT-9 tomorrow. But remember, no more wild-ass approaches inside the tree line. Dismissed!"

Ben leaped from his chair, shouted "Yessir!" and headed for the barracks.

He flopped on his bunk, sweating with relief at having avoided washing out, and sank into a twitching sleep.

At 0645 hours the next morning, Ben stood stiffly beside the cockpit of the BT-9. He had given the airplane a thorough preflight inspection. Al, the mechanic, had started and warmed the engine.

Luke strode up at precisely 0700. "Is your airplane ready to fly?" he demanded.

"Yessir! Inspected, and the engine has been started and warmed up," Ben said.

"Good. Mount up. Let's fly."

Ben aimed the airplane down the smoother south edge of the field. The BT-9's big engine soon had them airborne over the trees and en route to the practice area. He showed Luke his full aerobatic routine, his "bag of tricks," as Brice called them. He rolled the airplane into a series of tight turns to the right and left, pleased that he didn't lose altitude in either direction. Stalls also went well. He made his recoveries with minimal roll off on either wing. And he flew a series of smooth wingovers.

Luke's voice crackled in his headset. "Okay, head back to the field."

Ben was relieved to see the windsock showing the wind was still out of the east. "Won't have to slip over those trees," he muttered.

He hit the groove on two touch-and-go landings. Coming around for the final landing, he keyed the intercom. "Sir, would you like to see an overhead break for this last landing?"

"Sure."

Extending the downwind leg, Ben turned toward the field and flew the initial approach high and fast. Over the end of the field, he rolled into a tight left turn, simulated lowering the gear in the turn, notched in flaps, and continued the 360-degree spiral to line up with the runway.

Hot dog! I'm hittin' the groove on this one.

Approaching the fence, he chopped the throttle and raised the nose, and the BT-9 plopped onto the grass for a smooth three-point landing. He let the airplane roll to a stop, a grin creasing his boyish face.

"Nice," Luke said.

At the debriefing, Luke eyed him carefully. "I think you're ready to solo in the BT-9," he said. "I want you to fly with Jamison this afternoon and Owens tomorrow morning. Then we'll have Silverman fly with you and sign you off for solo."

"Yessir!" Ben shouted. "Thank you, sir!"

"A warning. You're still a student pilot. You handle the airplane well, but don't let that go to your head. You're at a critical stage in your flying. If you swagger out of here thinking you've got it made, you'll end up doing something stupid. I don't want to see you end your last flight in a smoking hole!"

Visions of Brice swirled through Ben's mind. *God, I owe him a lot.*

Ben joined the other pilots at the lunch table. He kept his head down, gobbled his lunch, and waved off all questions about, "How'd it go with Luke?"

At 1500 hours, he stood at attention next to the BT-9. Rob Jamison strolled up, still wearing his stained coveralls. His leather flight helmet was jammed on the back of his head, the earflaps and chinstrap flipped upright over his ears. He looked like the startled dog in the *Our Gang* comedy films.

He flashed Ben a bemused look. "Y'all ready to fly?"

"Yessir!" Ben responded, stiffening.

"Good. Let's cut the sir crap and go fly," Jamison said, clambering into the rear cockpit. Hurrying through the engine start and preflight checks, Ben taxied out for takeoff.

Wonder if he's awake back there?

As they soared toward the trees on takeoff, the throttle slammed shut.

"Pick a field," Jamison said laconically.

"Oh, hell!" Ben scrambled to configure the airplane for descent to a dead-stick landing. He spotted a field off to his right, started for it, and then realized it had a drainage ditch across the middle. Frantically searching, he saw a field to his left and banked toward it.

"Dammit!" he hissed. "Gettin' low and slow! Can I get over those trees?"

Skimming the trees, Ben rolled the airplane into a sideslip, leveled out, and sucked the stick back to his stomach. The main gear hit the ground, and the airplane ballooned into the air as Jamison shoved the throttle forward.

"All yours," he said. "Nice approach."

This guy's even steadier than Luke.

"Climb over the practice area, and show me some air work," Jamison said.

Ben racked the airplane into a complete aerobatic routine, including an extended spin. Pulling level, Ben rammed the throttle open and threw in a double snap roll for good measure.

"Okay," Jamison said. "Let's go home."

"I'll show the sleepy bastard," Ben sniggered.

At the field, he lined up for an overhead break approach. Coming in higher and faster than necessary, he rolled the airplane into a steeply banked left turn. Pulling on the stick to tighten the turn, he extended the flaps and rolled out on the runway heading. He quickly noted his position. "High and hot! But dammit, I'm not goin' around."

Ben racked the airplane into a left sideslip, slicing down toward the field. When he rolled level, they were lined up on the center of the field instead of the smoother southern edge. They touched down for a wheel landing about ten knots too fast. Ben saw the hammock just before they hit it. The BT-9 bounced back into the air.

Frantically working the stick and rudder pedals, Ben eased the airplane back down to a three-point landing more than halfway down the field. He hauled back on the stick and stepped hard on the brakes. They shuddered to a stop just short of the fence at the far end of the field.

Ben sat frozen, clutching the stick and throttle. His legs twitched in irregular spasms. Sweat made his gloves clammy and clouded his goggles.

"Didja leave enough room to turn around?" Jamison asked. "Or do we get out and pull her back by hand?"

"I can turn her," Ben snapped.

At the debriefing, Jamison slouched in his chair. "I thought we did okay today," he said.

We? You dozed in the backseat while I worked my ass off! And I managed to screw up again.

"Only comment I have is on your overhead break," Jamison continued. "You started too high and too hot. You should've seen that early in the break turn. If you'd expanded the circle or started your slip earlier, you'd have rolled out right on the button.

"Carl's gonna fly with you tomorrow mornin'. Show him an overhead break. But remember, adjust your descent in the first half of the turn. That way you won't need a screamin' sideslip on short final. An' stay away from the middle of the field."

Ben trudged back to the barracks, his parachute pulling like a lead weight on his hunched shoulders. He found Ted Anderson hunkered on his cot, a Stearman operator's manual propped on his knees.

"How's it goin', Ben?" Ted asked, looking up from his book.

"Okay, I guess. I just finished a flight with Jamison in the BT-9."

"How'd you do?"

"Everything went fine until I screwed up my last approach. I wanted to show Jamison a fancy overhead break, and came in high and hot. We nearly ended up in the fence on the far end of the field."

"What'd Jamison say?"

"Nothing! That's the frustrating thing. He just sat back there and let me work it out." Ben continued, "You know he and Luke must have ice water in their veins. I come close to wrapping us up in a fiery ball, and neither one of them says peep. Only difference is Luke ripped me good in the debriefing. Jamison just waved it off!"

Several other pilots drifted into the barracks. They had all heard Ben was flying the BT-9, and wanted the details.

"What happens now?" Ted asked.

"I fly with Owens tomorrow morning, and then I have a check ride with Silverman. He might sign me off for solo in the BT-9."

"Wow!" Ted exclaimed. "Solo already?"

"Yeah. Isn't that great?"

"You know," Allan Saunders interjected, "we're amazed y'all could move up so quick to the BT-9. And now they're gonna sign you off for solo?"

"Yeah," Ben said. "Uh, I had ten hours in the BT-9 before joining up. My instructor, Brice—I told some of you about him—anyway, he was able to get me some time in the airplane. My last flight with him was a supervised solo."

"Well, you're way ahead of us, right, fellas?" Saunders said. They all nodded.

"We been wondering," Fred Jones said. "How'd you get a chance to fly a BT-9? Was this through a college flying club?"

Ben blinked.

"Ah, no. I haven't been to college . . ." *Oh, what the hell. Might as well tell them everything.* "I've been flyin' with Brice for more'n a year and a half. I was the ramp monkey at Flint's municipal airport. Maintained Brice's Stearman, and he gave me flyin' lessons. Fact is, I haven't really finished high school. I left before graduation."

"Jeeze!" Rudy Groenke said. The Pennsylvania coal miner's son had just walked into the barracks. "You're still a kid! How old are ya anyway?"

"I'll be eighteen next week," Ben said quietly.

"Not even eighteen!" Rudy exclaimed. "How'd you get permission from your folks to join up?"

"I didn't. But it's a long story," Ben said, sorry he had brought it up. This caused a buzz of comments among the group. Hoping to change the subject, Ben turned to Ted. "How's it goin' for you?" he asked.

"I'm doing all right. So far, I've only flown with Owens. Tomorrow I fly with Luke, and to tell the truth, I'm scared!" None of the others had flown with Luke either.

"Lemme tell you about him," Ben said, sitting on the end of Ted's cot. The others crowded closer.

"Get out to the airplane early. Give it a thorough preflight. Ask Al to help, even to start it and warm up the engine. Luke'll arrive on the dot. Be standing at attention next to the airplane.

"When he asks if your airplane is ready to fly, shout 'Yessir' and pile your butt into the cockpit. He won't say much during the flight 'cept to tell you where he wants you to go. Oh, and be ready for him to cut the engine. He'll do it when you least expect it, so keep an eye out for an emergency field all the time. If he does it on takeoff to the east, there's an escape route south along the road. There are at least two good fields about half a mile down the road."

"Never thought of that," Ed Pearson said. "Always been concerned about gettin' over those damn trees. I've flown with Jamison and Owens. They haven't popped any emergencies on me yet."

"On takeoff is a perfect time for Luke to cut the engine," Ben said. "When you're focused on somethin' else. And speaking of those trees, don't try to impress him with fancy flyin'. I tried that in the Stearman and nearly put us in a smokin' hole."

"We heard about that," Randy Schuller said. "Been waitin' to hear your version."

"Not much to tell. Thought I'd impress Luke by turnin' inside the tree line for an angle approach. I damn near stalled trying to pull a tight turn onto short final."

"What'd Luke do?" Randy asked.

"That's just it. Not a damn thing! He sat there stiff as a cigar-store Indian. Didn't yell, didn't take the controls away from me—just let me fly outta the trap."

"Man! That took some nerve," Randy exclaimed.

"Yeah," Ben said, staring at his folded hands. "He said in the debriefing he wasn't gonna wash me out because of the way I recovered from my mistake. Then I went and did the other dumb thing, tryin' to impress Jamison with an overhead-break approach. I damn near put us in the fence at the far end of the field. But," he continued, giving them a wry smile, "I'm still here."

Chapter 21

THE FINAL TEST

"Mornin'," Carl Owens said, strolling up to the BT-9. "Ready ta fly?"

"Yessir!" Ben said, and they climbed aboard.

Ben showed Owens his full aerobatic routine, nailed the overhead break on his final landing approach, and taxied back to the flight line. Owens said not a word during their flight, didn't pull an engine emergency, and gave the appearance of someone returning from a joyride in the sky. Ben shut down the engine and secured the airplane.

"Sir, do you want to see me in the mess hall for a debrief?" Ben asked.

"Naw. Ya did real good today. I'll sign you off for your check ride. You'll take it with Silverman tomorrow morning."

Ben smiled to himself. *Damn right I did good!*

After dinner, Buford pulled Ben aside. "Me and the other guys are goin' into Millville tonight. Wanna come along?"

"You heard what Silverman said. It's off-limits," Ben said.

"Ah don't think he was serious about that," Buford responded. "Besides, we're all doing good with the flyin'. He'll cut us a little slack."

"So you're gonna walk two miles into that little burg?" Ben asked. *That didn't come out right. Me a hayseed from Michigan turning up my nose at little ole Millville. Well, I did have a big time in Manhattan. Now there's a real town.*

"Y'all are smilin'," Buford said. "Does that mean you're comin' along?"

"I might, but I'm not going to walk four miles in and back."

"Y'all won't hafta," Buford grinned. "Ole man Chappell is takin' his truck in town for supplies. We can hitch a ride."

"How about getting back?" Ben asked.

"We'll work that out," Buford said with a grin.

All twelve pilots piled into the back of Chappell's large truck. As they bumped into town, Ben thought of other truck rides he and Joe and their farm buddies used to take into Flint in the dank interior of the milk truck.

Millville's central square was dominated by a courthouse, and looked like any town in the Midwest. The marquee at the Bijou Theater announced a Charlie Chaplin movie. Buford led the group on at a fast pace, obviously looking for something specific.

"Aha!" he shouted as they turned a corner. "Success! The ole nose ain't lost it." He set off at a brisk pace for Gus's Bar and Tap. Ben hesitated at the door.

"I'm not even eighteen," he said. "They won't let me in here."

"Not a problem," Buford shouted. "Y'all get in the middle of us, an' we'll just walk in and order us some beers!"

Gus looked up as the twelve marched in the door. "Hey, fellas," he said. "What'll it be?"

"Beer all around, sir," Buford announced grandly.

Gus eyed them carefully. "You the flyers from out at the airfield?"

"Are you Gus? And if you are, how do you know about us?" Clarence Schenck demanded.

"Well, Sid Chappell comes in for a beer now an' then, and he's been tellin' me about you fellas out there doing some kind of flying training."

Buford sidled up to the bar, leaned in close to Gus, and assumed a conspiratorial tone. "Yessir," he hissed. "We're doin' somethin' real secret like, an' we can't talk about it, ya know? Now can we just have beers all around?"

Ben sipped his first beer. It wasn't bad. Fizzed like a good Vernors Ginger Ale but had a different taste. He liked it. The next one tasted just as good, and the next one even better. He didn't catch the smirks on the faces of the others when someone suggested switching to boilermakers.

"Sounds swell!" Ben exclaimed, waving off Ted Anderson, who was trying to whisper something about a boilermaker being a beer with a shot of rye whiskey added.

Ben didn't remember getting back to the airfield. He awoke the next morning with a raging thirst and a pounding headache. His tongue felt like flannel. And there was Ted, shaking his shoulder and yelling something about roll call and calisthenics in fifteen minutes.

"How'd I get to bed?" Ben wondered aloud. That is, if sprawling fully clothed across his cot can be considered getting to bed. "And where are my shoes?"

Ted urged him on, and both tumbled out of the barracks just in time for the morning routine.

By the time he finished breakfast, Ben began to feel like he was going to live. But it wasn't going to be pleasant. He considered sneaking back to the barracks for a nap.

"Damn!" he sat bolt upright. "I have my check ride with Silverman in less than an hour."

He glanced pleadingly at the sky, but there were no clouds in sight and no chance of a postponement due to rain.

When Silverman strode up to the BT-9, Ben stood stiffly, albeit a bit shakily, next to it.

Silverman's eyes lingered on Ben's pinched face and bloodshot eyes. "You feeling okay, Findlay?"

"Yessir! Didn't sleep well last night. But I'm ready to fly, sir."

As they climbed toward the poplars, Silverman's voice crackled in his earphones. "If you had engine trouble here, what would you do?"

"Sir, I'd get the nose down, turn right, and glide along that road," Ben said. "Telephone lines are on the right side, so I'd slide over to the left. There are a couple of fields off to the left."

"Good. Let's hope we don't have to use that escape route."

Silverman popped a couple of simulated emergencies on him, and despite his pounding headache, Ben reacted quickly to recover from them. His aerial work was smooth, and he nailed two good landings, the last from a precise overhead break.

As they secured the aircraft, Silverman said, "See me inside."

Ben sat stiffly in front of the briefing table. Silverman gave him another penetrating look.

"You passed your check ride," Silverman said. "You're clear to solo in the BT-9. I'll give you a training plan for each flight."

"Yessir. Thank you, sir!" Ben exclaimed.

"Now want to tell me about last night?" Silverman asked.

Ben felt like a kid caught with his hand in the cookie jar. "We hitched a ride into Millville last night," Ben stammered. "Ended up in a bar, and someone started buyin' me beers. I don't drink, but the beer tasted pretty good. Guess maybe I had too many. Don't remember how I got home."

Silverman suppressed a smile. "Did you learn anything from that experience?"

"I did, sir," Ben said sheepishly. "Don't know how to drink alcohol, so I won't. I'll also be more careful about lettin' my friends pull another trick like that on me."

"Good." Silverman said. "I'll post your solo lesson plans on the bulletin board so your friends can see the progress you're making. Dismissed!"

The next weeks passed in a flurry of activity. The other pilots moved up to the BT-9. Ben and Luke teamed up for simulated aerial combat training, Luke in one of the Stearmans and Ben in the BT-9. At first, Luke beat him badly, jumping him from out of the sun when he least expected it—the point Luke was trying to drive home. Gradually Ben learned to claw his way into position on Luke's tail for quick deflection shots.

"You nailed me good on that last fight," Luke said as they secured the airplanes in the growing dusk. "Keep your wits about you when they send you out on your first combat patrol. Stick with your flight leader, keep your head on a swivel, and you'll do all right."

Brice, the Ancient Pelican, had told him virtually the same thing.

When all twelve pilots qualified in the BT-9, they were paired off in two-pilot teams and divided into flights A and B of the "American squadron." Each pair of pilots gained experience flying as lead or wingman.

In flight A, Ben was teamed with Ted Anderson. Brad Collins and Art Rawlings, from neighboring Iowa farms, formed another team, as did Ed Pearson and Fred Jones. The two athletes from Indiana and South Chicago had become good buddies.

Flight B teamed Al Brewster of Brooklyn with Randy Schuller of Florida; Clarence Schenk of North Carolina and the Pennsylvania coal miner's son, Rudolph Groenke; and finally, Allan Saunders from Virginia and Buford Musgrove, the gregarious South Carolinian. The young men cemented solid friendships and quickly honed their skills as flying teams.

Silverman had arranged a short-term lease of a second BT-9 for the last month of air combat training at Millville. The young pilots flew the BT-9s against the four instructors in the Stearmans. At first they were outmatched by the older, more experienced flyers; but as the young men gained experience and confidence, they took great pleasure in whipping their asses.

In late November, Silverman assembled them in the mess hall. He stood on the platform flanked by Luke, Jamison, Owens, the Chappells, Bert, and Al. Silverman congratulated the twelve for successfully completing their training.

"You've qualified as volunteer sergeant pilot trainees in the Fuerzas Aereas de la Republica Española—that's the Spanish Republican Air Force," he said. "That's a mouthful, so we'll call it FARE for short. You'll be officially inducted as volunteers at our first training base near Barcelona.

"I expect to be assigned the rank of volunteer captain. And I hope we can talk the commandant into letting me form and lead the American squadron of the Republican Air Force. My Spanish contact tells me that anyone who qualifies probably will be flying the Russian Polikarpov I-16 fighter."

"The poly-poop what?" Buford blurted. "Ah don't think Ah heard that right, Captain."

"The Poli-kar-pov I-16," Silverman said slowly. "It's the Russians' frontline fighter. It's a low-wing monoplane. The airframe and wings are of mixed wood and metal construction. It has an open cockpit and a big radial engine. It's going to be one helluva airplane to fly, and you're really going to have to work to qualify in it."

"What does the *i* stand for, sir? Ted asked.

"The *i* stands for *istrebitely*—that's Russian for 'fighter.'"

"Hey, fellas," Buford burst out. "We're all gonna be 'ester-bite-lightly' Russian fighter pilots. How about that?"

"Okay, okay! Enough," Silverman said, suppressing a smile. "We'll probably start with the Polikarpov UTI-4, a two-seat trainer version of the I-16. If you can master that, fine. If not, the Russians also are flying the Polikarpov I-15. This is an earlier model biplane fighter-bomber."

"Sir?" Ben chimed in. "I thought we finished with biplanes when we graduated from the Stearman."

"The I-15 is much hotter than a Stearman," Silverman said. "It's much bigger and heavily armed, used mostly for ground attack work. But let's finish what we're doing here. We'll get into those details later."

Luke, Jamison, and Owens stepped off the platform and shook hands with each of the twelve young pilots, wishing them luck and cautioning them again to go easy on their first couple of combat missions, to stick close to their flight leaders until they get the hang of it.

"I wanted Al and Bert, who kept our airplanes in such good flying condition, and our hosts, Mr. and Mrs. Chappell, to be part of this final ceremony," Silverman said. "We owe them a lot of thanks for taking such good care of us for the past couple of months. And I'm pleased to announce that Mrs. Chappell has planned a wonderful Thanksgiving feast for us tomorrow!"

The next morning, tantalizing aromas wafted across the parade ground as the pilots completed their calisthenics. Luke, Jamison, and Owens prepared to fly out in the BT-9 and the two Stearmans. Bert and Al packed their tools, materials, and spares on a flatbed truck, and drove off to their homes in Millville.

"Sir," Buford called out. "Ah have a question. What happens to the crates, uh, I mean, the airplanes we've been flyin'? Is there another pilot group comin' along after us?"

"We don't know for sure, Buford," Silverman said grimly. "There're a couple of other recruiters working cross-country, but the news coming out of Spain isn't making it easy to attract new pilots. You fellas may be the last of the volunteers."

No one pressed him for details on the "news coming out of Spain."

Exercise over, the pilots gathered along the flight line to wave good-bye to their instructors. Luke led the two Stearmans in a V-formation takeoff. The pilots circled and swept along the field in a low-level, wing-waggling salute. Ben felt a huge lump form in his throat.

Finally, at 1600 hours, Sid Chappell rang the dinner bell. Trying not to trample each other, the young men hurried to the farmhouse and crowded into the dining room. They gaped at the extended oak table laden with an enormous roasted turkey, a soup tureen, a small mountain of mashed potatoes, and another of sweet potatoes. Two gravy boats sailed nearby. Smaller dishes held peas, beans, broccoli, cranberry sauce, and a tossed salad. Two large loaves of homemade bread sat on the sideboard, flanked by two pumpkin pies and a chocolate cake.

"Lordy, lordy!" Buford exclaimed. "We have passed through the pearly gates into heaven itself!"

The young men scrambled to find a chair. Silverman barked, "Gentlemen, stand behind your chairs until we get Mrs. Chappell seated!"

Like schoolboys, they sat with napkins in their laps. Mrs. Chappell looked at their young faces. Tears welled in her eyes, which she quickly dabbed with her napkin. "Sid?" she said quietly.

Her husband cleared his throat and mumbled a quick grace. Then he grinned at the young men. "I'll carve the bird. You fellas start with whatever's in front of ya, and we'll get the turkey platter going around in a minute."

Memories swarmed into Ben's mind of Thanksgiving dinners at home on the farm. His mother usually produced wonderful feasts of homegrown potatoes and vegetables, one of their own turkeys, and delicious pies and cakes. Even the old man seemed to mellow a bit at Thanksgiving.

Silverman tapped his glass with his fork. "Gentlemen, a toast to Mrs. Chappell for a fantastic Thanksgiving dinner. And thanks to you, Sid, for making us feel welcome here. We'll carry this memory all the way to Spain!"

By the time dessert was finished, the young men leaned back with looks of pure bliss on their flushed faces. They sat in silence, sipping the last of their drinks. Buford, group spokesman—or loudmouth, depending on the situation—turned to Mrs. Chappell.

"Ma'am," he said quietly, "after we're done with this Spain thing, I'd be honored if y'all would come on down South and meet ma family. You're so much like ma Momma, I know the two of you'd get along jus' fine."

"Why, thank you very much! What a compliment. I'd love to . . . ," she faltered and held her napkin to her mouth. Her eyes brimmed with tears.

Silverman spoke quietly. "As much as I hate an end this delightful dinner party, I have to get these lads packed. The bus departs at 0800 hours. By tomorrow night, we'll be onboard the freighter *Escobar*. She sails for Barcelona out of Brooklyn harbor sometime after midnight."

He ordered the twelve young men to line up, called them to attention, and dismissed them with a sharp salute.

That night, Ben wrote a long letter to his mother. His eyes glistened with tears as he recounted details of the Thanksgiving feast, adding how he enjoyed similar meals she had prepared. His flight training here was completed, he wrote, and he'd be moving around quite a bit. No lie there. He reminded her of the post office box number in New York. Letters sent to that address would be forwarded to him.

Ben added, "Here's a little something to help with the household budget." He slipped a ten-dollar bill into the envelope.

In letters to Brice and Al Simpson and his brother Joe, Ben detailed his flight training experiences, including his mistakes with the Stearman and the BT-9. He thanked Brice again for the lessons he had drilled into his head. He said they'd be shipping out for Spain the next night.

PART 3

SPAIN, WINTER 1937-1938

Chapter 22

DEPARTURE

Ben stared at the *Escobar*. Hardly the luxury liner he had imagined! As Silverman and the young pilots trooped up the dimly lighted gangplank, Ben saw large patches of rust had blossomed through its faded gray paint. The ship appeared to have a giant case of measles. Bulkheads, hoists, winches, and deck gear hadn't been painted in years.

The pilots bunked two together in cramped dingy cabins on the aft deck. Silverman occupied the second mate's cabin, also a dank, cell-like room with few comforts. They gathered in the officers' mess in the predawn darkness as the ship's crew scrambled to make ready to sail. The pilots stared gloomily at plates of greasy eggs, bacon, and dry toast, and wrinkled their noses at evil-smelling coffee. The captain, a tall, emaciated man with wisps of dirty gray hair, sunken cheeks, and black teeth, joined them. He wolfed down his food without a word and left.

"Not very hospitable," Silverman said. "Sorry, we couldn't afford the *Queen Mary*. But she wouldn't have taken us to Barcelona anyway. The *Escobar* is one of the few ships that can get us there."

"Why's that?" Buford asked.

"Things are pretty tense in Spain right now," Silverman said. "Regular passenger ships don't stop there anymore."

"Then how'll we get there?" Buford persisted.

"We'll run through the Strait of Gibraltar at night. The Nationalists haven't blockaded the Strait, but they have large gun batteries positioned along Spain's Atlantic and Mediterranean coasts. And they've based small attack boats and Condor Legion bombers at Traifa in the Strait."

"Ah'm not sure Ah like the sound of this," Buford muttered.

"Once we get through the strait, the captain'll steer southeast along the coast of Morocco and Algeria, and then head northeast past Majorca for Barcelona," Silverman continued.

A chill ran down Ben's spine at the exotic-sounding places.

"If we're lucky, we'll stay outside the range of the sea and air patrols until we reach Republican territory," Silverman added.

"And if we ain't lucky, sir?" Buford asked. "Ah didn't see no guns on this tub."

"There are 37 mm antiaircraft guns in the hold, along with other arms, medical supplies, food, and equipment for the Republicans," Silverman said. "They're in containers marked Construction Equipment. Once we're at sea, the crew'll set the guns up on those forward and aft deck mounts. It isn't much, but at least we won't be sitting ducks if attacked."

"Is it legal to transport arms to Spain for use in the civil war?" Ben asked.

"No," Silverman said. "But then it isn't legal to transport combat pilots there, either. That's why we boarded at night and are slipping away before dawn."

"Ah'm beginnin' to feel like an escapin' criminal," Buford blurted.

Silverman ignored him as he handed them Polikarpov I-16 pilot's manuals. "The English translation is a little rough. But they'll give you a basic feel for the I-16. The same manual serves for the UTI-4 trainer."

He added, "We're going to have a lot of free time on the crossing. I want to see your noses in your pilot's manuals and the Spanish phrase books."

Later the pilots gathered at the grease-stained rail. Harbor tugs, searchlights stabbing the darkness, nudged the *Escobar* from her berth. As the ship eased out of New York harbor, they watched silently as the December predawn highlighted the Statue of Liberty through the fog.

"We're on our way," Ben whispered to Ted. His stomach lurched, and his throat clutched. "Wonder when we'll see that lady again?"

Ben shivered in the damp air as Miss Liberty slid back into the mist. "I'm *really* leaving!"

They hit rough seas shortly after leaving New York Harbor, an ominous beginning. The captain said they were in for a stormy crossing. Asked how long the trip would be, he responded, "Whatever it takes."

His was not a happy ship; and the crew, a motley collection of misfits, did little to make the pilots feel welcome.

"Not even out of sight of land, and I'm already feeling sick," Ben muttered.

"Let's don't talk about it," Ted responded. His face had a greenish hue. The other pilots shuffled around at the railing. All appeared on the verge of losing their greasy breakfast over the rail.

The rumble of the *Escobar*'s coal-fired steam engine vibrated through the deck beneath their feet. Ben's mind flashed back to the times he and his family rode the ferry boats across the Straits of Mackinac, on trips from the farm in southern Michigan to the family homestead in the Upper Peninsula. He and Joe had wandered the big boats during those crossings, usually clambering down to the engine room to marvel at the huge piston arms driving the ship's propeller shaft.

"Let's check out the engine room," he said to Ted.

The closer they got the to *Escobar*'s innards, the more depressing the ship became. Little fresh air circulated below decks. The fetid atmosphere clung to them like a wet, sour blanket.

"I can't take any more of this," Ted blurted, his face a deeper shade of green. "I'm headin' back up to the open deck."

The engine room was what Ben imagined hell would be like. The hot yellowish-brown air felt oily and bit Ben's nostrils with each breath. The crew looked Asian, mostly Chinese. Others were darker-skinned men with Oriental features. They wore stained shorts and sandals. All were drenched in sweat, especially the collier crew. They seemed to glide across the greasy deck. A squat, sullen Chinese man thrust his chin at Ben.

"Wha' you wan' here?" he demanded. He bared jagged yellow teeth in a snarl. His sour breath made Ben recoil. "Engine loom not open fo' stranger!"

"Sorry!" Ben stammered. "Just wanted to have a look around."

"No place fo' you!" the man shouted. "You go topside!"

Ben felt his gut clutch. He didn't feel threatened by the repulsive little man, but the man's odor was more overpowering than the engine room stench. *Coming down here was a big mistake!*

He made it to the rail just in time to empty his stomach into the Atlantic Ocean.

Chapter 23

AT SEA

By the third day, the sea calmed to a rolling swell. The sky cleared, and the pilots settled into a relaxed shipboard routine. The first mate smirked that a severe winter storm awaited them in the mid-Atlantic.

"I hope we have our sea legs by the time we hit it," Ben said as he and Ted walked briskly up and down the *Escobar*'s deck. "Dunno what bothers me most, seasickness or the worry that this old tub might not make it through a really big storm."

The *Escobar* plowed eastward. Boredom numbed the young men's senses. Each day was the same, covered in dull gray mist. There was no clear line between horizon and sky. Morning calisthenics and afternoon briefings did little to break the monotony.

One afternoon, Ben spotted Allan Saunders and Rudy Groenke perched on a forward hatch cover. "Hey, fellas, mind if I join you?"

Saunders said, "Perch yourself right here [it sounded to Ben like he said 'rye-cheer']. How're ya doin', Benjamin?"

Groenke, even less vocal than the Iowa farm boys Rawlings and Person, flashed Ben a shy grin.

"You two enjoyin' the boat ride?" Ben asked.

Groenke grimaced. "Thought I was gonna die. Didn't think I could ever puke that much!" He fixed his gaze on his large rough hands, running a small knife blade under his fingernails. "Coal miners can't ever get their nails clean," he muttered self-consciously, a soulful smile creasing his craggy face.

He looks a lot older than twenty-three.

"Where'd you fellas learn to fly?" Ben asked.

"Funny you should ask," Saunders said. "Ah was just talkin' to Rudy 'bout that. We both got our first airplane ride when barnstormers flew into towns near where we lived. Got a fifteen-minute ride in a Jenny for five dollars. That was a lotta money, but Ah was hooked from the beginnin'."

Groenke nodded slowly. "Yup, me too. Spent every extra nickel I could put by on flyin' lessons. Most of my time's been in Jennies. Some in an old Travel Air."

"Wow!" Ben exclaimed. He now understood why Groenke was the last one to qualify in the flight training program at Millville. "It must have been real tough steppin' up to the Stearman and then the BT-9."

"Yup."

"Ah didn't exactly have an easy time of it either," Saunders said as he slid off the hatch cover and stretched his lanky frame.

Ben noted he seemed to be all arms and legs. "How tall are you, Al?"

"Six foot three. Ah hope Ah fit in that Russian polly-pooper airplane. Like as not ma head'll stick up over the windshield."

"You'll probably be able to see over the nose when you're taxiing," Ben said. "Won't have to S-turn like the rest of us."

Silverman gave a perfunctory afternoon briefing. The dull routine was affecting him too. He dismissed them with instructions again to "put your noses in your pilot's manuals."

Ben and Ted spent long hours on the aft deck reviewing the manual, quizzing each other on airplane systems, and studying their Spanish phrase books.

As the sea voyage dragged on, the two midwesterners talked far into the night in their cramped cabin. They speculated on what they would find when they arrived in Spain. Their love of flying cemented a deep bond between them.

One night, Ted shared an idea he had been mulling. "Ben, after we're done in Spain, wouldn't it be swell to buy an airfield somewhere back home? Some place in the Midwest maybe? What d'ya think? We could be partners, do our own instructing, fly charters, maybe some crop-dusting."

"That'd be great!" Ben said, sitting up quickly. "We could get a couple of Stearmans, find the right field, build a hangar and an operations shack. You know, Ted, that'd be a great life!"

They began working out details of their dream.

The *Escobar* slammed into the storm shortly after midnight on the tenth day out. There had been no warning before they plunged into a vicious squall line. Ben and Ted pitched out of their bunks and tumbled into each other as the ship heaved and rolled.

"What the hell?" Ted screamed. "Did we run into something?"

"I dunno," Ben gasped, trying to scramble to his feet. "What's that howling? We better get dressed and find out what's happening!"

The ship shuddered and groaned. Alarming popping noises, they learned later, came from rusted rivets breaking in the seams of the ship's superstructure. The *Escobar* breasted a huge wave and slid down the other side. They found Silverman and the other pilots in the narrow corridor, partially dressed and equally wide-eyed.

"I think we'd better get life jackets on," Silverman said, bracing his arms and legs against each side of the corridor.

Buckled into the ungainly cork-filled vests, they lurched toward the hatch leading to the outer deck. It burst open, and the first mate stumbled in, water cascading from his black rain slicker.

"Stay inside!" he yelled over the roar of the storm. "Anybody goin' out there is gonna get swept overboard. An' we ain't about to stop to pick ya up. We ran into a real corker of a storm, force 10 to 11 gale, I reckon. Nothing we can do but ride it out."

"Is the ship in danger?" Silverman sputtered as rain and spray slashed through the open hatch. "Should we keep our life jackets on?"

"We've rode out worse storms than this," the mate said, his tight smile bordering on a sneer. He was enjoying their fear. "Stay in your cabins. We'll be in this for at least another twenty-four hours, I reckon."

Ben and Ted huddled on their bunks, clutching the railings to keep from being pitched onto the deck. They looked like a pair of frightened trolls with the life jackets bunched under their chins. Neither spoke, not that they could be heard above the howling roar that tore at the ship. Tons of water slammed onto the decks. The resounding booms made their ears ring.

After what seemed an eternity, dim light filtered through the fogged porthole. Ben struggled to peer outside and was shocked. "God almighty!" he yelled. "Ted, look at this! The waves are taller'n the deck! They gotta be thirty feet high!"

"No thanks," Ted yelled, his voice quavering. "I can hear and feel it. I don't need ta see it."

There was nothing to do but hang on and hope the *Escobar* didn't capsize or split her gut and plunge beneath the waves. The howling of the wind and boom of the waves breaking over the deck nearly beat them senseless.

The first mate was right. It took two days for the *Escobar* to plow through the storm. The pilots were able to snatch drinks of water and munch biscuits, but no meals were served. The galley fire was snuffed out. Surprisingly, no one got seasick.

"Ah was too scared to even remember Ah had a stomach," Buford said later.

As the ship steamed into clear weather, the pilots emerged from their cabins, blinking in the sunlight like bears awakening from a winter's hibernation. They saw with wonder that the *Escobar* seemed generally in good shape. Seeing the rivet heads that had been sheared off in the superstructure, their thoughts went to the fasteners and welds that held the rusting hull together. The thumps of the bilge pumps proved the ship had taken on water. But she was still afloat.

The ship's bell signaled a meal in the captain's mess. Hunger overcame any concerns the pilots had about the greasy slabs of pork, tough biscuits, and lumpy mashed potatoes. They dug into their first hot meal in two days. Even the cook's vile coffee tasted good.

As the *Escobar* wallowed toward the Strait of Gibraltar, the captain slowed her so they could pass through the strait at night. Hugging the North African coast, they steamed quietly into the Mediterranean. All lights were extinguished, and deck activity stopped. Crew and passengers stood silently at the starboard rail and watched the shrouded coast of Morocco slide past.

"Never thought I'd see places like this!" Ted exclaimed. "Maybe we can stop off here on our way home. Just think . . . I'd never been outside of Minnesota before. Now here I'm talkin' about visitin' North Africa!"

"And don't forget, Spain's up ahead," Ben said, also overwhelmed by what they saw. "An' we're gonna be flying in real combat!"

Swinging northeast, the *Escobar* pointed her rusted bow toward the Balearic Islands, then turned north to run between the islands of Ibiza and Majorca. They were only hours from Barcelona. The deck crew scrambled to prepare the ship for docking.

Chapter 24

THE ARRIVAL, LATE AUTUMN 1937

Barcelona emerged from the morning fog as a harbor pilot boat churned out to meet the *Escobar*. Several tugboats waited at the narrow opening to maneuver the ship into its berth. A cacophony of shrill tugboat whistles, hooting horns, and sirens mixed with shouts from a crowd lining the quay.

Word had spread that in addition to food and armaments, there were American pursuit pilots on board. Shouts of *"Bienvenido a los pilotos Americanos!"* swelled from the crowd.

"Hadn't expected a heroes' welcome!" Ben shouted. "Hope we can live up to their expectations."

A uniformed Spaniard stood at the base of the gangplank. As Silverman reached him, he snapped to attention, bringing his leather-gloved hand to his right temple in a crisp salute. He introduced himself as Capt. Manuel Ortega de Frago.

"Me estoy dirigiendo al señor Silverman? Am I addressing Señor Silverman?" Ortega inquired.

"Yes. Capt. Frank Silverman, reporting with a contingent of twelve American pilots," Silverman said, returning Ortega's salute. "I am pleased to meet you."

Ortega remained at attention. His smartly tailored uniform closely fitted his trim frame. The leather belt and cross brace over his tunic gleamed. A prominent nose and heavy brows dominated his thin face, and dark brown eyes gave him a penetrating but friendly look. Black hair was slicked back under his forage cap, topped with a red tassel. His black leather riding boots shone.

"Bueno, maravilloso!" Ortega exulted, extending his right hand. "Good, marvelous. It is my pleasure to welcome you to España. This is a, how do you say, *esplendido*? Ah yes, a splendid moment for us. You will follow me, please?"

A phalanx of Guardia Civil, the Spanish national police, plowed a path through the crowd and led them into the terminal for passport and customs checks. Ortega hovered, waving his arms and strutting about, sometimes on tiptoes, as he gave orders to hustle the Americans through arrival formalities.

"Swish around like that back home, and people'd call ya a fairy," Ted sniggered.

Ortega soon had them ushered onto a waiting bus. Its diesel engine coughed a cloud of black smoke into the surging crowd as it chugged off to the Hotel Pelayo.

The streets of Barcelona looked forlorn, strewn with debris. Many were blocked with barricades, as if residents were prepared to defend the city street by street. Rows of stately, soot-encrusted buildings lined the broad avenues. Some were windowless, staring with the unfocused eyes of a skid-row drunk. There were few cars or trucks. Straggling bands of pedestrians scurried, heads down, along the sidewalks. Some cast furtive glances to the sky.

"Is this the beautiful Barcelona I've been reading about?" Ben exclaimed. "Where are the shops and—what are they called?—yeah, the cantinas and the flower stalls I saw in the pictures?"

Ortega said, "Barcelona has been much attacked by Nationalist bombers, the German Condor Legion, mainly. Barcelona is not yet under siege, but it may not be long in coming."

"That's why we're here," Silverman added. "Our job will be to scout out and attack the forward positions of the Nationalist army units, and to stop Condor bomber raids on the city."

The Hotel Pelayo, its elaborate facade topped with an imposing tower, was one of Barcelona's finest. But time, neglect, and the civil war had taken a toll.

The marbled lobby, impressive vaulted ceiling, and Roman columns needed cleaning and repair. A small forest of potted palms and ferns placed among the chairs and sofas needed watering and dusting. The young Americans stared at the huge stained-glass dome soaring over the lobby.

"This is more beautiful than that Radio City movie house in New York!" Ted exclaimed. "Wonder what the rooms are like?"

Ortega again took charge. He strode around the registration desk, bringing some order to the chaos, as well as adding to it.

Silverman said, "During lunch, Captain Ortega will brief us on the latest war news and give us our training assignments. We'll probably be staying here only one night. Then I expect we'll head out to their training base near Igualada, about sixty kilometers from here."

Ben and Ted marveled at the size of their room and its ceiling-to-floor windows. These opened onto a narrow balcony that gave them a panoramic view along the Plaza de Catalunya and surrounding broad boulevards. From here, Barcelona looked more like the photos Ben had studied in the library books.

"This is a beautiful place, even with the bomb damage," he said. "Wonder if we'll get a chance to look around a little?"

Silverman and Ortega were in the Catalonia room when the pilots entered. Silverman sat grim-faced, barely nodding to the group as they got settled.

"What's eatin' him?" Ben whispered.

"Welcome to this table," Ortega said with a smile. "I'm afraid this will be a modest lunch. As you see, Barcelona has been much put upon by the Nationalist enemies. Trains and ships bringing food and supplies to the city are attacked from the air, causing many damages. We are not blockaded, but all things are in shortages."

He rang a small bell, and waiters came in with platters of cold veal, rice, beans, and cabbage. Several round loaves of peasant bread were presented, and each diner tore off chunks. A rough red table wine was served in decanters.

After dessert and coffee, Silverman spoke. "Before we get into the briefing, I have an announcement," he began. "Captain Ortega has informed me that it will not be possible for us to form a separate American squadron. The Republican Air Force cannot provide the logistic support we'd require. They also need replacement pilots to rebuild squadrons that have suffered heavy losses. Therefore, as soon as you complete your transition training in the I-16, you'll be assigned to whatever squadron needs you the most, maybe singly, maybe in pairs.

"I'm not happy we'll be splitting up. I don't expect you are either. But we've come a long way to help our Republican friends fight the Nationalists, and it's up to them to decide how best we can do that. Now let's hear from Captain Ortega."

"Thank you, Captain Silverman," Ortega began, spreading a large map on the cleared table. "Tomorrow evening we travel by bus to the Aerodromo Igualada, here," he stabbed the map with a slender finger. "Road vehicles have been attacked by Condor Legion airplanes along this route, so we are to travel by dark. Igualada is a base for training. But some pursuit squadrons are kept there for—how do you say—ah, protection."

He continued, "You shall fly the Polikarpov UTI-4 two-seat trainer first."

Silverman noted that Buford didn't respond with another smart-ass comment.

"It is same as the I-16 fighter you shall fly in squadrons, but with a second cockpit for the instructor," Ortega continued. "It should take but a few flights to get you intim—umm, familiar—with this airplane. It is quite obedient in the air, but has some tricks you should learn."

Silverman interjected. "The I-16 has a better turning radius than even the Condor Legion's lead Bf 109 fighter. But overall, the 109 can outperform and outgun the I-16, so we'll fight our fight, not theirs. Oh, and one more thing . . . two, actually," Silverman said. "The propeller on the I-16 turns counterclockwise, looking from the cockpit, not clockwise like on U.S. airplanes. That means you'll need to hold left rudder to counter propeller torque on takeoff, not right rudder like you're used to. Also, the I-16 brakes are next to useless. On landing, avoid getting into a situation where you'll need heavy braking. You'd do just as well by dragging your feet."

Ortega told the pilots they'd be flying with Russian instructors, several of whom "have English." Briefings were done in Russian and Spanish, he added, but English translators were usually available. "Does anyone have questions?"

"Yessir," Fred Jones said. "Will we be inducted into the Republican Air Force before we start training in the I-16, or after we complete it? Also, what rank will we be assigned? And, ah, what's our political status? Do we have to pledge allegiance to the Republic of Spain?"

"When we arrive at the *aerodromo*, all will be made clear," Ortega said. "But to be short, you will be inducted when you arrive as volunteer sergeant pilots, with same privileges as regular sergeant pilots. But as volunteers, you do not pledge allegiance, as you say, to Republic of Spain. We do not want to make difficulties with your government."

What none of the pilots knew was that U.S. government officials were debating the status of American volunteers in the Spanish civil war. State Department conservatives demanded that the passports of all volunteers be revoked. A few insisted they lose their citizenship.

"Please to leave discussion of details for later," he said.

Silverman stepped forward. "Captain Ortega, before we dismiss the men, can you give us a brief update on the progress of the war? We haven't had any news since leaving New York."

"Ah yes . . . ," Ortega began hesitantly. "The hard part of winter approaches. So the land armies, especially in the North, will face much difficulty from cold and snow. Numerous army units, including those of the international brigades, have served Spain valiantly. But they will not have a happy Christmas. Alas, neither will we.

"The Nationalist bombers have done great damages to Madrid and Barcelona. Other cities in Republican sectors too have suffered, how do you say, hard attacks. And I have but to remind you of what Condor Legion and Italian bombers did to Guernica, with brutal bombing attacks last April that killed many of the civilian population."

Silverman interrupted. "Excuse me, Captain Ortega, can you elaborate on what happened at Guernica?"

"Guernica is a Basque town in the northern province of Biscay, on the coast of the Bay of Biscay, not far from the French border," Ortega said. "It had some . . . how would you say . . . ah, yes, some strategic importance as a Republican stronghold, protecting the city of Bilbao. And because of its bridge, bombers from the Condor Legion and the Italian Fascist Aviazione Legionaria made repeated attacks. They were Heinkel He 111s, Dornier Do 17s, the smaller Junkers Ju 52s, and Italian SM-79s. They were supported by the German Bf 109s, He 51s, and Italian Fiat Cr 32 fighters of the *Aviación Legionaria*. But there was no opposition from Republican airplanes, so after the bombings, the fighters strafed fleeing civilians. It was market day, many people were in town."

Ortega coughed and paused to regain his composure. "Ah, this I do with much difficulty. Much of Guernica was destroyed, and many hundreds of civilians were killed. Guernica was captured by the Nationalists. It has become a symbol of Nationalist brutality and how German and Italian Fascists support them."

Silverman turned to his pilots. "Guernica was a victim of the worst kind of terror bombing. The bridge, said to be the major target, wasn't even hit. This is a good example of the mentality we face when we join combat units."

Ortega added, "And I regret that we have suffered many losses of our pilots. This is why we welcome you so."

He concluded, "We think next year, 1938, will be a critical time. We must have a major victory, and we must keep the Nationalists from Madrid and Barcelona. They have beaten our Basque brothers in the North, and now we think they will drive toward the Mediterranean coast to cut the Republican sector in halves."

The Americans pondered this sobering assessment of the war's progress, and what it meant to them personally. No one had further questions.

"Now I must meet in private with Captain Silverman," Ortega said. "May I suggest you please take time to visit Barcelona? Sergeant Lopez will be your guide. Then we will meet here for dinner at 2030 hours."

Ben sputtered, "2030 hours! That's 8:30! Isn't that a little late for supper?"

Chapter 25

BARCELONA

Sergeant Lopez led the pilots to an ancient bus, acrid diesel smoke puffing from its exhaust. Lopez stood in the aisle and used a rolled-up file folder as a megaphone.

"*La bienvenida a mis amigos* Americanos. Welcome, my American friends, to my city of Barcelona, one of the most beautiful cities in the world . . . capital of Catalunya, or as you would say, Catalan."

The bus rumbled into the Las Ramblas section of the city, and Lopez pointed out the area's famous bird market. The noise was incredible.

The tour included Barcelona's Palau de la Virreina, resplendent in its eighteenth-century rococo architecture. But the damaged buildings, cluttered streets, and unsmiling pedestrians gave the city a depressed air. The bus stopped at the Monument a Colom, or the Monument to Columbus.

Lopez said, "As you know, he discovered America."

"Hey, Lopez!" Buford yelled. "Can we see a bullfight?"

"Alas, no. We are out of season. Also, the, umm, *corrida de toros*—bullring, I believe you call it—is being used as a refugee center."

The next stop on Lopez's itinerary was the Barri Gotic, the Gothic section, and the Plaza de Sant Jaume. "This is oldest sector in Barcelona," Lopez explained. "Most buildings date from fourteenth and fifteenth centuries. Next we will visit our proudest monument, La Sagrada Familia, the cathedral built by Antoni Gaudi, Barcelona's famous architect. Señor Gaudi died before it was finished. Now with the war, there is no money to complete it. But you must climb the bell tower."

Lopez did not tell the Americans that the Republican Loyalist government opposed the church and had defied the Vatican in Rome and sanctioned the killing of many priests. The Loyalists would not spend their limited funds on maintaining, much less completing, the historic cathedral.

Ben stared in wonder at the city spread out below their perch in the cathedral's spire. "Sure beats the view from the windmill back home," he wondered aloud.

"Our last stop will be the Montjuic, the large hill from which we shall be able to have a fine overview of our city," Lopez said. "The sun will set behind us and will provide many changing colors and shadows over the city."

Standing on the grand esplanade atop the Montjuic, Ben nudged Ted in the ribs. "Ever think you'd see so many wonderful sights?" he asked quietly. "When we get back home, we'll have a bunch of stories to tell, eh?"

It was 6:00 p.m., 1800 hours by their military clocks, when they returned to the hotel. They roamed the hotel like hungry wolves and were ravenous by 2030 hours. They descended on the Catalonia Room determined to eat whatever was offered. It was another simple repast, but the young men ate with gusto.

Silverman announced the schedule for the following day. "We'll gather in the garden behind the hotel for calisthenics at 0600 hours," he said. "Breakfast will be served here at 0700 hours, and at 0800 hours, we meet in the room next door for briefings from two of the Russian instructors who'll be flying with us in the UTI-4 trainers. After lunch, we'll hear from a Republican Air Force officer. He'll familiarize us with the terrain we'll fly over, the rules of engagement, and the general terms of our mission."

Ortega stood. "In the late afternoon, when the winter sun dips, we will board a bus for Aerodromo Igualada. The trip must be made in darkness with hoods on the headlamps. At Aerodromo Igualada, you will fly three sorties a day. There is not much time to master the I-16. Those who don't will be assigned to units flying the Polikarpov I-15 ground attack aircraft. We will, umm, how do you say, stand down at Christmas. But expect a new offensive early in the New Year."

Silverman dismissed the pilots, who shuffled off to their rooms.

Chapter 26

THE RUSSIANS

Silverman gathered them for the morning briefing, and they were barely settled when Captain Ortega entered, followed by three Russians, who stood stiffly beside him. The Americans eyed them curiously.

"Ah ain't never seen a Roushin before," Buford muttered. "Don't look too friendly."

Two of the men wore dull brown uniforms with loose blouselike shirts that extended over their hips. Black leather belts cinched the blouses at the waist. Their jodhpur pants were tucked into highly polished black boots. Each had a cloth forage cap folded and inserted under his left epaulet. They wore no rank or insignia. Both men were of medium height and solidly built. High cheekbones gave them a slightly oriental look.

Ben stared at their expressionless faces. "Wonder if they ever smile," he whispered.

"That one's different," Ted whispered, noting the third Russian's erect military posture and crisp uniform with a black leather jacket. "What do those red shoulder boards mean? Is he an officer?"

"Gentle . . . uh, Comrades," Ortega said. "This is Comrade Maj. Evgeny Kobzan. He is deputy commander of Training Group 21, where you will be assigned to learn the I-16. He is an intelligence officer."

The Russian offered a brief nod. "Comrades," he said, surveying the Americans with a penetrating stare, "in the name of the Soviet Socialist Republic, I welcome you to Spain, where we fight side by side with Spanish Republican comrades against Fascists." Unsmiling, he stepped back.

Kobzan was the Communist Party Commissar for Group 21, and served as deputy commander of the unit. He ensured Communist Party discipline was enforced, and was feared, more than respected.

"Bet this fella won't stand for no nonsense," Buford whispered.

"*Bueno*, ah, all right," Ortega continued. "Here are your Russian instructors, Comrade Sergei Stavoras and Comrade Yuri Golenko."

Both men stepped forward and gave curt bows.

"And these are your American colleagues," Silverman interjected. "Allow me to introduce them. When I call your name, please stand."

Each pilot stood and gave a small wave. Buford stepped forward and returned the Russians' curt bows.

"Don't expect you to remember everybody's name," Silverman continued, "so we'll all wear name tags, which will—"

"Nyet!" Kobzan said curtly. "Wear no names! In case of capture, you unnerstan'?"

Silverman said, taken aback, "Not even for training missions close to the base?"

"No use of real names for flying. Ve have Spanish war names. I suggest same for you."

The two Russian instructors unfurled a large drawing of the I-16.

"It looks like a cigar butt with wings," Brewster whispered.

Buford suggested a "dog turd with wings." He grinned, warming to the subject. "How about a Great Dane special?"

If they understood the jokes, the Russians took no notice. They described the I-16's flight controls, systems, and operating parameters. Their English was limited but understandable. When they finished, Stavoras asked, "If any questions?"

"I'd like to know why they look so glum," Buford muttered.

"Knock it off, Buford," Ben hissed. "I got a serious question."

Turning to the Russians, he asked, "Would you explain again why you do your engine run-ups and preflight checks in the chocks on the flight line, and then taxi right out for takeoff?"

The three Russians held a brief, whispered conference, and then Golenko turned to Ben. "Brakes on I-16 not strong. Cannot hold for engine tests. Remember for taxi and landing that brakes provide little anchoring."

Ben imagined heaving an anchor out of the cockpit during the landing roll. "Okay," he said. "How do they work for differential braking, to keep alignment on takeoff or for making tight turns on the ground?"

Another conference, and Silverman explained that differential braking meant applying brakes individually to help with directional control.

"For takeoff, tail, how you say, arises soon," Golenko said. "Then have large rudder that serves good for steering. On the ground, mechanics clutch wingtip to assist turning."

The Americans asked about turning radius in the air, rate of climb, airspeed restrictions, and how best to cope with the I-16's poor forward visibility on landing approaches.

"For landing," Golenko said, "left turning circular approach is best."

After the briefing, the Americans, led by Buford, crowded around the two Russians pilots. "Where're y'all from?" he asked.

The Russians exchanged puzzled looks.

"Ah think we got ourselves a communications problem," Buford puffed. "This ain't gonna be easy."

"What he asked," Ben ventured, "is where are your homes? Where were you born?"

"Ah, I unnerstan' you," Stavoras said. "Umm, I am less certain of your comrade," he added, indicating Buford.

"Buford is from the South, in America," Ben said. "He has a strong accent. Sometimes I can't understand him either."

"Vich country is his home?" Stavoras asked.

"Huh?"

"You say he is from South America. I ask vich country?"

"No, no!" Ben said quickly. "I said he is from the South. That's a region in America, ah, I mean North America. He's from South Carolina, one of the southern states in North America."

"I unnerstan'," Stavoras said. Clearly he did not.

"Give it up, Benjamin," Buford whispered. "See what I mean? We're gonna have trouble communicatin' with our Russian friends. That could cause us some problems in the air."

Buford pronounced "air" as "are." Ben understood why the Russians had problems with Buford's accent.

"You ask of our birthplace," Stavoras said. "I born Ivanovo, three hundred kilometers north and east from Moskva, you call Moscow. Comrade Golenko born Serov, village in Ural Mountains."

He glanced nervously at Major Kobzan, who stared at them stone-faced. Both were drafted into the Soviet army, Stavoras explained, and sent to English-language schools. They applied for Soviet air arm training, he added. They were sergeant pilots and had logged over one thousand and two hundred flight hours. Each had about seven hundred hours in the I-16. Both had combat experience, and each had shot down two Nationalist airplanes.

Asked how they liked the I-16, both smiled and flashed thumbs up.

"Iss good strong airplane," Golenko said. "Wery quick in turnings. Not so fast as Bf 109, but ve have tactics for handle German fighters and 'specially bombers. You vill see in training vid UTI-4. Flies much like I-16 fighter."

During lunch, Ben asked Stavoras, "What do you think about the war? Do you think the Republic is winning?"

The Russian glanced around and saw Kobzan talking with Silverman. He leaned closer. "Ve have no, umm, how you say, opinions, yes, opinions on such politics. Comrade Golenko and myself pilots. Ve talk only of flying operations."

"How's about women? Ya know, señoritas?" Buford blurted. "How long y'all been in Spain? Must be able ta tell us somethin' about the señoritas!"

Stavoras stared at him blankly.

"Buford!" Ben snapped. "Watch your mouth! Our Russian friends can't understand you in the first place. An' you ask the dumbest questions. Get serious!"

"Our Russian friends!" Buford sniffed. "Say, y'all are gettin' right cozy right quick."

"Not cozy!" Ben retorted. "We're gonna be flying with these guys, an' we need to get to know 'em. Your life might depend on it!"

Stavoras leaned in closer. "Yes, fly together. Ve talk of flying!"

The young flyers slid easily into pilot talk with much arm-waving and hand-gesturing. Absorbed in conversation, they didn't notice Major Kobzan standing behind the two Russian pilots. Stavoras gave a startled look over his shoulder and leaped to attention. Golenko followed abruptly, knocking over his chair.

"Time to end dis," Kobzan said coldly. "Return to aerodrome." He saluted and strode to the door. "Comrades!" he barked. The two pilots saluted quickly and hurried after him.

The Americans and Ortega sat, stunned by the Russians' abrupt departure.

"Ah, we have sometimes difficulties with our Russian comra—ah, friends," Ortega stammered. "Spanish high command often feels not in full control. They, ah, seem to wish to operate with much, ah, independence of direction. And their political officers, as is Major Kobzan, are much strict with Russian soldiers. They do not like, how do you say, excessive friendliness with others."

Silverman protested. "But they specifically requested that we train with them as replacement pilots for their pursuit squadrons!"

"Ah, yes, this is cause of puzzlement," Ortega said. "I believe, sad to say, they think American replacement pilots much better than Spanish ones. And they have need for replacement pilots more sooner than they can come from Russia."

Having committed to the Republican cause, for a variety of reasons, the Americans were eager to see action. That was why they had trained so hard, and why they came thousands of miles from home. But it was sobering to hear the Russians were losing pilots at a rate higher than expected.

"To move forward," Ortega said, "we will be joined soon by Capt. Leopoldo Casado, intelligence officer for Spanish Air Group 96, which controls the Igualada Aerodrome. He will give briefings on the situation around Barcelona. He also will make you familiar with terrain and landmarks. You must know these to navigate around this military sector."

Casado was as bright and personable as the Russians were dour and unfriendly. He was a slightly built man who moved with the quick grace of a bullfighter. His crisply starched uniform was tailored specifically for his trim frame. His black hair was slicked back in Spanish style, and a close-cropped mustache accentuated a sensual mouth and prominent sharp nose. Bright black eyes shone under thin brows.

He unfurled a large map and attached it to the wall. "Good day, gentlemens," he said in virtually unaccented English. "This is a map of our military sector. Igualada Aerodrome is here, about sixty kilometers west from Barcelona. We have responsibility for a large area that has as its north boundary the Pyrenees Mountains. This is the border with France. It must not be crossed."

He tapped the map with a pointer. "Here is Ebro River. It cuts across south portion of our sector, which extends about fifty kilometers beyond the river. Some of you can expect assignment to Zaragoza Aerodrome here on the Ebro. Our Russian comrades have two squadrons of I-16s based there, Squadrons 26 and 27. They also have I-15 fighters ground attack aeroplanes there, and we have two Spanish Republican squadrons on the field."

Their primary mission was to protect Barcelona from Condor Legion bombers and provide air support to ground forces opposing Nationalist army attacks from the Castile region in the northwest.

"We project a Nationalist offensive toward Valencia early in the new year," Casado said. "Our intelligence says the enemy desires to split the Republic in half. That is, to capture Valencia and separate Madrid from Barcelona. Achieving so would badly wound us and leave Barcelona vulnerable to siege from the west and the south."

He paced in front of the map and smacked the pointer on Madrid in the center of Spain. "And if Barcelona falls, Madrid will be in great dangers of being surrounded. So you see, we have very important mission to do here."

He described prominent landmarks throughout the sector and offered tips on how the Americans could use them to navigate back to base following extended missions.

"Most peoples in this sector are loyal to the Republic, so if you are shooted down, you should find friends on the ground. But do not be unconscious that not all will be friendly whom you might encounter."

He gave the pilots a somber stare. "Much hard feelings and hatred have been created by our civil war. People have been badly treated by others, and many await chances to take revenge on anyone."

"What y'all are sayin', sir, is don't get captured, right?" Buford interjected.

"What you say has much truth, I am sorry to confirm," Casado said.

The room went silent. The glamour of their "crusade" was melting away like a snowman on an unseasonably warm winter day.

Casado let the silence hang like a shroud and then concluded on a positive note. "You are much welcomed to our sector. We have much appreciation for your willingness to come to our assistance. Your Russian flying comrades will welcome you as well. Do not be discontented by their abrupt manners. They are good comrades, and they take war against the Fascists very seriously, for their own reasons."

Ortega took charge of the meeting and gave the pilots details of the swearing-in ceremony that would be conducted soon after their arrival at Igualada Aerodrome. They would be issued uniforms and assigned to barracks. Flight training operations would begin the next morning.

"We will depart hotel tonight at 1730 hours, so trip beyond Barcelona will be in the darkness," Ortega said. "The journey will take more than one hour."

Chapter 27

IGUALADA AERODROME

The bus driver clashed the gears and dropped the clutch, and they lurched into the Plaza de Catalunya. Twilight bathed Barcelona in a soft, golden glow. There was little traffic on the broad avenues and boulevards. Streetcars clanged past; and a few trucks—mostly military—trailed clouds of acrid diesel smoke. Pedestrians scurried along the sidewalks. Many moved furtively, glancing at the sky.

Outside the city, the bus's hooded headlights provided little illumination as they threaded through small, darkened villages. The bus ground up into the foothills of the Pyrenees.

"Ah tell ya, fellas, this ain't no joyride," Buford grumbled. "This seat's as uncomfortable as the hard bench pews in mah little ole Baptist church back home. Ah could no more catch some shut-eye now than I could with ole Reverend Batcher thunderin' hell's fire and brimstone from the pulpit!"

Ben peered out the streaked window. The desolate countryside depressed him. "Say, Ted," he whispered. "Ever seen such a lonely-looking place?"

"Yeah. We won't even have little old Millville to sneak into for a couple of beers," Ted sniggered. "Bail out anywhere around here, and you'll have one helluva lonely walk back to the airfield."

The thought of bailing out here, or anywhere for that matter, further depressed them.

The bus slowed as they approached a perimeter fence. Two armed guards signaled them to halt. Ortega stepped down. The guards saluted and stood stiffly as he conversed rapidly with them, showing them a list of names.

The guards stepped onboard and carefully checked everyone's passport and papers, holding the documents to dim overhead lights, and then peering into each face. Satisfied, they trooped off the bus, saluted Ortega, and raised the heavy barrier.

"I apologize for the formalities," Ortega began. "But we have to—"

"No need to apologize," Silverman interrupted. "We understand the need for security."

At what looked like headquarters, the pilots clambered off the bus and stood uncertainly in the chilly gloom.

"Inside awaits Col. Alfredo Diaz, commander of Igualada Aerodrome," Ortega said. "I will introduce you, and we will go directly to the swearing-in formalities."

An orderly in a crisp uniform and spit-polished, knee-high boots snapped to attention and saluted Ortega.

"He says we are to follow him to the briefing room where Colonel Diaz will complete the ceremonies," Ortega said. "It will be brief, and then we will pass by our supply room for uniforms and equipment."

Ortega was right; the swearing-in ceremony was brief. Colonel Diaz, a tall, thin man with a long, sad face, addressed them in English. They raised their right hands and pledged to serve honorably in the Republican Air Force as volunteer sergeants, to obey all orders, and accept assignments as given. Silverman was sworn in as a volunteer captain. Ben noted the colonel repeatedly squared his drooping shoulders, straightened his back, and ran long fingers through his thinning black hair.

Colonel Diaz gravely shook each pilot's hand, thanked them for coming to the aid of the *Fuerzas Aéreas de la República Española*, the Republic air force, and wished them well. He exchanged salutes with Ortega and Silverman, turned on his heel, and left.

"Again, welcome to the Republican Air Force," Ortega said heartily. "In that regard," he continued uneasily, "umm, since you now are in our air force, you should have saluted Colonel Diaz after he shook your hand. In Spanish military, we salute so." Ortega raised his right hand to his temple, palm forward. "Please to remember that in future, you are to salute superior officers."

"Oh god!" Buford moaned. "He must think we're a buncha hicks from the sticks!"

Silverman bent toward Ortega. "Colonel Diaz seems to be under a lot of stress."

"Ah yes," Ortega said shaking his head. "Colonel Diaz was a great pursuit pilot in the early years of our war. He destroyed ten enemy airplanes in aerial combat and many more in ground attacks. Now he has been assigned here to command the training of pilots. We have a great need to replace those we are losing in combat. These are not good times for the Republic. His is a difficult task with many challenges. And the, ah, the Russians have added to those stresses."

The young pilots listened soberly.

Issuing uniforms is the same in all military services. Disinterested supply clerks eyed each American briefly and handed out what they thought would fit. In each case, the supply clerks underestimated the height of the Americans and their shirt, jacket, and pants sizes. There was a flurry of exchanges of all items, especially pants.

As for Al Saunders, the six-foot, three-inch tobacco farmer from Virginia, awed the clerks. They finally produced the largest size uniforms they could find.

"He looks like a scarecrow," Ted sniggered as Saunders stood awkwardly with shirtsleeves two inches above his wrists and pants legs the same height above his ankles.

"For once, I'm happy about my height," joked Ed Pearson, the five-foot, nine-inch basketball player from Indiana.

"Look, Saunders," Silverman interjected. "This is the best they can do for you here. Try to make do. We'll ask them to alter a special uniform for you."

"Bet he don't fit in any of the bunks either," Buford quipped.

He was right. The bunks were barely six feet long, the room dank and gloomy.

"Looks like we have this place to ourselves," Ben said. "Wonder where the Spaniards and our Russian comrades bunk?"

"The Spanish squadrons are housed on the other side of the aerodrome," Silverman said. "We probably won't see much of them. And Major Kobzan probably will discourage any personal contact with our Russian comrades when we aren't flying."

They settled in, and Ted stretched out on the bunk next to Ben's.

"Sure has been a long day," he sighed. "Ya know, driving through that farm country back there got me to thinkin' about home. I miss my folks and the farm. Funny, isn't it? Couldn't wait to leave the place and go off on this big adventure. Now the old farm looks pretty good."

Ben's stomach lurched. Despite all the problems, tensions, and hard feelings with the old man, he too was feeling homesick.

"And with Christmas comin', I really been thinking about my family," Ted continued. "Mom always makes a big deal out of Christmas. She bakes up a whole bunch of swell Swedish breads and cakes. And we'd have a big feast on Christmas Eve with ham, meatballs, and a special potato dish. It's called Johnson's Temptation. That's some name, isn't it?"

Ben slipped into a depressed reverie, remembering how many Christmases were spoiled by the old man. Sometimes he came home drunk, having celebrated with his friends.

"And Christmas decorations," Ted continued. "Mom has a way of makin' garlands and evergreen chains that she draped all through the house. Made the whole place smell great. Then Dad and my little brothers and me would hitch old Bruce to a big stone sledge and head out to the woods beyond the back forty. We'd spend hours choosing just the right Christmas tree, chop it down, and haul it back to the house on the sledge."

"Yeah," Ben muttered. "We're all gonna miss Christmas back home."

Ted eyed him curiously, then decided Ben's sullen response was because of homesickness.

The Americans ate at a separate table in the mess hall, nodding to the Spanish and Russian pilots seated at their assigned tables. Ben gave Sergeant Stavoras a quick wave. The young Russian glanced around nervously, then nodded.

After supper, Silverman handed out flight schedules and instructor assignments. "It's going to be cold tomorrow morning, so put on an extra sweater, and wear your heavy uniform jacket. Remember, we're going to be flying in open cockpits. Now take another look at your pilot's manuals, and get a good night's sleep. Tomorrow starts a couple weeks of hard work and tough flying. Good night!"

Ben flopped across his bed and looked at his assignment sheet. "Swell!" he said. "I've been assigned to Sergeant Stavoras."

Sleep swallowed Ben and his fellow American pilots within minutes.

Chapter 28

FLYING THE POLIKARPOV

Red-faced from their morning exercise in the cold winter air, the Americans wolfed breakfast and headed for the operations room. Ben, Ted, Art Rawlings, Brad Collins, Buford, and Rudy Groenke, assigned to Sergeant Stavoras, sat on the right. Ed Pearson, Fred Jones, Al Brewster, Clarence Schenk, Randy Schuller, and Al Saunders, assigned to Sergeant Golenko, sat on the left.

"Ah-ten-*shun!*" Silverman called out as Colonel Diaz and Captain Ortega strode into the room. Colonel Diaz stepped onto the platform and told the men to be at ease. Stavoras and Golenko stood in the rear of the room with Major Kobzan.

"You are to begin your final training before joining the fight against our Fascist enemies," Diaz began. "As this year comes to its closing, we must reinforce our flying units, refresh ourselves, and prepare for an arduous year ahead. In the name of the Spanish Republic, I thank you again for coming such distances to assist us. I ask you to put much concentration on your flight training, so you may soon join one of our combat squadrons."

At "combat" the young Americans sat up and squared their shoulders.

Buford muttered, "How about we cut the speechifyin' an' get at the flyin'."

"I know you are anxious to begin flying," Diaz said, glancing at Buford. "We too want you best prepared for coming air campaigns. You will be assigned to squadrons led by our Russian comrades, who have brought us their first-line combat aircraft, the Polikarpov I-16 fighter and the I-15 ground attack aircraft. Learn them well and quickly, gentlemens! Now Major Kobzan will take charge. *Vaya con* Dios! Go with God!"

"I have no much more to say," Kobzan began. "There is great work to be done. Comrades Stavoras and Golenko will take control of you. Comrade Silverman informs me you are well knowledgeable of the UTI-4 trainer and I-16 from your studies of pilot's manuals. Becoming familiar with airplanes will continue on flight line, and then you will fly half-hour flights in turn. Comrade Silverman?"

"Right," Silverman said. "I've been informed that I will be given command of an I-15 attack squadron, so I'll focus on that airplane and not join you in the I-16 training."

The young pilots stared at him. Were they losing their leader so soon?

"That wraps it up here," Silverman said. "Now we fly," he added, looking squarely at Buford. "Let's show our Russian comrades what we can do. Dismissed!"

The pilots crowded around their instructors and followed them to the supply room to draw parachutes, helmets, and flying gloves, and trooped out to the flight line

"See what I was talking about in Millville?" Silverman asked, indicating the rough grass field. "Small rough field and trees all around. Get used to it, this is about as good a field as you'll find."

"Trees!" Buford muttered. "Them ain't poplars out there, but they're big! Why in hell locate an airfield in the middle of tree country!"

Ben's pulse jumped as they approached the two camouflage-painted UTI-4 trainers squatting on the flight line. At last, they were going to get their hands on the real thing! The stubby aircraft looked like two bumblebees. They were fat and ugly, but looked deadly. The pilots split into two groups of six and followed Stavoras and Golenko in walk-around inspections.

The Polikarpovs were basic, almost crude, airplanes. No frills, except for leather padding around the edges of the open cockpit and across the lip of the instrument panel. Small drop-down doors on each side of the cockpit eased stepping into the airplane from either the right or left wing.

"Please to put parachutes here," Stavoras said, indicating a place on the ramp tarmac. "Ve begin at cockpit. Three of you so, here on left, and three on right. Like dis all have good view. Entering of cockpit, usually done from left side."

The spacious cockpit had plenty of leg and elbow room. It was as sparse as that of the Stearman trainer they flew in New Jersey. Everything was painted light blue except for the instrument panel, which was dull black. The panel contained basic engine and flight attitude instruments the pilots were accustomed to, but not in the same layout.

"Have to work on our instrument scanning, to get used to this new arrangement," Ben said.

The monocoque wooden fuselage and the wings were covered with aluminum and fabric, Stavoras said. The thick stubby wings had a long chord that extended from the engine cowling back past the cockpit. This gave the I-16 a batwing shape and increased wing area, despite the short wingspan. The central control stick was topped with a spade handle-type handgrip, making it easy to control with either hand.

"On UTI-4, main, umm, ah, undercarriage gear legs stay fixed," Stavoras said. "Since most time spent flying trainers in airport traffic pattern, difficult gear retraction system not used. On I-16, undercarriage is raised and lowered by means of crank here on right side of cockpit wall. Needs forty turns to lift up gear legs. Dis why Russian pilots have big muscles, so!" He grinned, raised his right arm, and flexed his bicep.

"After takeoff, pilot must move left hand from throttle to stick and right hand to undercarriage crank. As turning crank, pilot must to regard angle of climb and level of vings. Most new pilots—how you say?—vobble, da, vobble much on takeoff as crank undercarriage. Care needed not to fly off-course or maybe stall. But on trainer, no need for concern this."

Stavoras directed their attention to the left side of the cockpit. "Here is throttle and mixture control lever."

"Where're the flap handle and the trim control?" Ted asked.

Ben poked him with his elbow. "That was covered in the pilot's manual," he hissed.

"Nyet! No flaps, no trim control," Stavoras said. "Dis simple airplane. Here is trim control!" Grinning again, he flexed his right bicep.

"Better keep that in mind," Ben muttered to the others. "We won't be able to trim this thing up and take pressure off the control stick. You gotta fly it all the time."

Stavoras led them around the aircraft, pointing out critical drains and attachments that needed to be checked along with the landing gear, wheels, and tires. He moved all control surfaces to verify they were not jammed, and led them back to the cockpit.

"Ground mechanics keep airplanes in good order, but good pilot always checks," he said.

Stavoras described the instrument panel layout and the simple starting sequence, and reminded the pilots to "pull left rudder pedal" to overcome torque on takeoff because propellers "turn against clock on Russian aircraft."

"Whaddaya mean, *pull* left rudder pedal?" Buford demanded. "How do ya *pull* the pedal, like this?" he asked, jerking his leg backward.

"Nyet, nyet!" Stavoras said quickly. "I mean so!" and he extended his leg.

"You mean *push* the pedal," Ben interjected. "This is *push* and this is *pull*!" he said, extending his leg and pulling it back.

"Da, da!" Stavoras said, mimicking Ben's actions. "Dis push and dis pull! Damn! English wery difficult. Makes no sense! Two vords mean opposite but spelled almost same. I mix up always! No sense!"

He pointed to Ben. "Comrade Benjamin, you fly first. Dress vid parachute and get in back cockpit. In air have simple talking tub for communicating. No radio in I-16. No need vid single pilot."

"Did y'all say talking *tub*, or what?" Buford asked.

"Da, da!" Stavoras said heatedly. "Talking tub. You see here, tub, tub, long narrow ting hollow in middle!"

Ben interceded again. "Comrade Stavoras, I think you mean *tube*. Ah, it ends with an *e*. A tub is a metal container, like one you take a bath in. It doesn't end with an *e*. A tube is like that, a long hollow thing, like a hose." He hoped Stavoras didn't think he was treating him like an idiot.

Stavoras exploded with what the pilots understood to be a Russian oath. "English!" he sputtered. "Pah! Makes no sense. Hell vid English! Ve fly!"

The M-25 engine roared to life with the cloud of smoke common to all big radial engines. Ben and Stavoras completed the pretakeoff checklist and ran up the engine while still held in the wheel chocks.

Stavoras waved the chocks away, and they taxied the UTI-4 out onto the field. They turned into the wind and accelerated on the takeoff roll. The tail lifted off the ground quickly, providing excellent forward visibility.

"Follow on controls," Stavoras shouted down the talking tube. "No flaps, so need speed over one hundred kilometers per hour for takeoff."

At that speed, the aircraft lifted off smoothly with slight back pressure on the stick.

Ben concentrated on feeling the airplane through his butt. Even with the fixed gear, it smoothed out nicely in the air. He reached for the gear handle and started counting. Before he got to thirty, Stavoras banked the airplane into a climbing left turn, to stay in the landing pattern.

"No wonder they leave the gear fixed on these trainers," Ben mumbled.

Ben concentrated on how Stavoras positioned the airplane for the final landing approach. The Russian pulled on the carburetor heat, selected fine propeller pitch prior to reducing power, and rolled into a circling left turn to line up for the landing. It was the only way to keep the landing spot in view. As they descended, Stavoras closed the throttle and used aggressive rudder inputs to keep the airplane properly aligned. As the airspeed dropped below one hundred kilometers per hour, the UTI-4 wanted to quit flying. Stavoras pulled the stick back smoothly, and the airplane dropped onto a solid three-point landing.

"You fly!" Stavoras shouted. He raised his hands to show Ben he was not going to touch the controls.

Ben pushed the throttle and felt the airplane veer right, remembering at the last minute to use the left rudder to keep them running straight. The tail came up, and they lifted off into their initial climb. Ben again reached for the gear handle to develop the right habit pattern. Sure enough, they started to "vobble," just as Stavoras said they would.

"Damn!" Ben snorted. "Gotta be careful doing this in the I-16 without losing control!"

Ben quickly developed a feel for the UTI-4 as they climbed into the left-hand traffic pattern. The stubby fighter, with its short wingspan, had a very quick roll rate, something he'd have to be careful with. It also was unstable in pitch, tending to bob like a porpoise.

"Don't overcontrol in a turn!" he reminded himself. "You can end up on your back!"

On the downwind leg, he configured the aircraft for landing and circled onto the runway heading. Misjudging the rate of descent, he began his flare early. The airplane ballooned, but he caught it, dropped the nose, and flared a second time. They banged onto the ground with a rough but acceptable landing.

"Go again!" Stavoras shouted.

Ben flew two more patterns with increasing confidence and smoothness of control. He kept the speed up on the last approach and made a tail-high wheel landing instead of stalling the airplane for a three-point touchdown. Stavoras signaled for a return to the ramp.

The five other pilots in his group crowded around as he climbed out of the cockpit.

"How'd it go?" Ted pressed. "Looked good! Easy to fly?"

"*Hooowee!*" Buford shouted. "Wheel landing, yet! How about climbin' over them trees?"

"There's plenty of room, Buford," Ben said. "Just make sure you use all of the field that's available, and make sure you have plenty of engine revs by the time you're committed for takeoff. Remember the brakes are just about useless, so if you have to abort the takeoff run, you'll probably have to ground loop to stop short of the fence.

"And if you have engine trouble right after takeoff, drop the nose, and land straight ahead. There're some small fields on both sides, just beyond the trees. They look rough, but good enough for an emergency landing."

Ted was next to fly. His first circuit around the pattern was smooth, but then Sergeant Stavoras was flying with Ted, following on the controls.

They saw Stavoras raise his hands, handing control of the airplane over to Ted. They heard the engine roar, and the stubby trainer started down the field. Suddenly it veered sharply to the right. The right wing dipped and nearly clipped the ground. Abrupt control inputs brought it back level and aligned with the takeoff run. The airplane lifted off into a wobbly climb.

"Damn!" Ben shouted. "He forgot to hold left rudder, just like I did. I hope Stavoras didn't have to take control."

Ted and Stavoras completed three more circuits of the airport pattern. The landings looked rough.

When they taxied back to the ramp, Ted clambered out of the rear cockpit looking flustered and discouraged. Stavoras hopped off the wing after him and said nothing.

"Comrade Buford. You next. Ve fly," he said. Buford strapped on his parachute and climbed into the rear cockpit, looking like a lamb going to the slaughter.

"Ted!" Ben said, as Stavoras fired up the UTI-4 engine and taxied out to the field. "What the hell happened? You were all over the sky! You're a better pilot than that!"

"I dunno, Ben," Ted said sullenly. "I just couldn't get the feel of that damn airplane! Everything seemed so different. I almost lost control on my first takeoff, and it all went wrong from there!"

Buford's first circuit of the pattern went smoothly, again with Stavoras at the controls. They bounced savagely on the second landing, obviously with Buford at the controls; then someone, probably Stavoras, fought to get the airplane under control and stopped before they ran into the fence at the far end of the field. Buford clearly would need additional dual instruction.

Stavoras then flew with Art Rawlings, Brad Collins, and Rudy Groenke. Each handled the UTI-4 all right, but as the six trudged back to the operations room with Stavoras, he shook his head.

"Most need more training before can go solo," he said. "Ve fly again this afternoon, Comrade Benjamin first." Turning to Ben, he said, "If goes vell, do aerial maneuvers tomorrow. Show me you can do good, and I clear you for solo. I need fly more vid others."

On Christmas Eve, all operations halted. The Russians "celebrated" by getting roaring drunk. The Americans joined the Spanish pilots and ground crews who gathered for Christmas Eve Mass. Afterward, Ben and Ted, overwhelmed with homesickness, trudged back to the barracks. By Christmas morning, the Russians had drunk themselves into numbed alcoholic stupor.

The air raid siren shattered the silence. *Attack! Attack!*

"Ben!" Ted yelled. "What the hell's happening?"

"We're being attacked! Dammit, Ted, we're finally in the war! Let's go!"

They sprinted to the flight line.

"All this time trainin' and trainin'! Now we're in it!" Ben exulted as they ran.

Russian pilots, some nearly too drunk to stand, grabbed parachutes and stumbled toward the flight line. Ground crews, most as drunk as the pilots, struggled to get the airplanes ready for takeoff.

Ben and Ted hesitated at the equipment room, uncertain what to do. A large hand smacked Ben in the back, shoving him aside. A tall muscular man, naked except for a pair of fleece-lined flying boots, pushed past them. He grabbed a leather helmet, jammed it sideways on his head, and shrugged a parachute onto his shoulders as he ran to one of the I-16s. He vaulted into the cockpit. The engine roared to life almost immediately.

"That guy was bare-ass naked!" Ted yelled.

Two other Russian pilots, both partially clothed, one barefoot, jumped on the same airplane, one on the left wing and one on the right. Each got one leg into the cockpit, shouting and shoving each other. The pilot on the left smashed a fist into the face of the other, who tumbled to the ground with a thud. A ground crewman dragged him out of the way as the engine roared to life, and the pilot waved the wheel chocks away. He rammed the throttle open, and the airplane trundled out for takeoff, its engine backfiring, and blowing clouds of smoke. The pilot knocked out of the cockpit rose with an animal roar and raced for an approaching two-seat UTI-4 trainer. He tumbled headfirst into the front cockpit as the airplane taxied past.

The other I-16s and two-seat UTI-4 trainers jostled onto the field, most with angrily backfiring engines. Ben and Ted stumbled out to the flight line. The chaos was mind-boggling. Airplanes milled around for mass takeoffs, every pilot seemingly unconcerned about others around him.

"They're taking off with cold engines! That's dangerous!" Ben yelled above the cacophony.

"That isn't all that's cold," Ted yelled back, pointing to the naked pilot as his aircraft raced past. "That fella's gonna freeze his balls off!"

Silverman sprinted by, followed by a gaggle of I-15 pilots.

"Captain Silverman!" Ben yelled. "What should we—?"

"No time," Silverman yelled. "Gotta get the attack squadron airborne and out of here before the bombers catch us on the ground!"

The air raid siren wailed with renewed urgency. Condor Legion bombers were approaching. The I-15s also roared into a mass takeoff run. Miraculously, there were no collisions, but one I-15 lagged behind, its engine sputtering and backfiring. The pilot finally got it running smoothly and accelerated down the field. The tail rose to takeoff position just as the first German Heinkel He 111 bombers began their attack. As the I-15 lifted off, a bomb exploded directly in front of it. The biplane was blown sideways, its left wingtip dug into the ground. The aircraft cart wheeled, flipped, and plowed to a stop upside down. Ben held his breath, waiting for the explosion. Suddenly the pilot dropped out of the inverted cockpit and crawled from under the wreckage. He limped through bomb bursts and tumbled into a nearby bomb crater. His wrecked airplane burst into flames with a loud *whump*!

On the opposite side of the field, the Spanish squadrons were struggling to get their airplanes airborne. They were not as quick as the Russians. Some pilots were taking time to warm up their engines. Several were caught by bomb blasts or destroyed in strafing attacks by Bf 109 escort fighters that snarled in behind the bombers.

"Ben! Ted!" someone yelled from behind them. "Over here, for God's sake!"

They ran to a slit trench behind the operations building just as a string of exploding bombs marched along the flight line. Two unserviceable I-16s and the hulk of a crashed UTI-4 trainer were blown to bits. But all other Russian airplanes, except for the one unfortunate I-15, escaped.

The base antiaircraft crews finally got the range on the last of the bombers sweeping overhead. Two in the trailing formation were hit. One exploded, spreading a trail of smoldering debris across the field. The second lurched and pitched up as its right engine smoked and then belched fire. The pilot swung left to avoid turning into his dying engine. This took him back across the field where several ground gunners hosed his airplane with withering fire. Flames blossomed from the left engine. The stricken bomber dived into the forest just beyond the airfield perimeter and disappeared in a giant fireball.

The escorting Bf 109s continued to sweep the field with gunfire. They wasted valuable ammunition and fuel chewing up a hangar and a few other buildings. No airplanes were left on the field. They hit the fuel truck with dramatic results and blew up a small ammunition dump, but missed the large fuel and ammo dumps concealed in the woods beyond the flight line. Worse, they became easy targets for the I-16s, which screamed down out of the sky. The escaping Russian pilots had climbed aloft, regrouped, and returned with a vengeance. Half of them targeted the retreating bombers, knocking down three. The others jumped the Bf 109s, destroying two and scattering the rest. Snarling low-level dogfights ensued, down where the I-16 held the advantage.

Two more Bf 109s were shot down. Ground mechanics and antiaircraft gun crews whooped as the Condor Legion airplanes scattered and fled back toward Nationalist lines.

"By God!" Buford yelled. "That was some kinda show! Lookit them Fascists hightail it outta here. Whoooheee! Ain't never seen anything like that!"

The I-16s swept back over the field, plopping down like giant locusts that had just stripped a grain crop. A single I-16 lagged behind, and its pilot dived for the field. He swept overhead on low-level runs, less than fifty feet above the ground. Two passes were upright, two inverted. Finally, completing a vertical victory roll with the engine sputtering, he rolled in for a landing and let the airplane run straight up to the flight line. The engine backfired and quit. His fuel tank was empty.

The Americans watched fascinated as the naked pilot hopped out of the cockpit and marched to the equipment room, looking neither left nor right. He tossed his helmet and parachute on the steps of the equipment room and strode off toward the barracks, still clad only in his boots.

Stavoras appeared, and Ben grabbed his arm. "Who the hell is he?" he demanded.

Stavoras explained that he was Ivan Ivanovich Krasnov, a Cossack from a small village on the lower Dnieper River.

"He is from long Cossack tradition," Stavoras explained. "When go on drinking voyages, they use all money for vodka. Then sell clothes to get more money. Iss something they do. Iss, how you say, hokay."

Since Ivanovich still had his boots, his drinking voyage apparently was not over.

Silverman led the I-15 squadron back for another mass formation landing. He hopped out of his aircraft, and the American pilots surrounded him as he approached.

"By God!" he exulted. "That was exciting! We got everyone, ah . . . almost everyone away safely." Indicating the smoking I-15 wreckage on the field, he asked, "How about him?"

"He survived!" Ben yelled.

"We lost one other along the way," Silverman said soberly. "One of our pilots was having engine trouble and lagged behind. A lone Bf 109 shot him down."

The Bf 109 pilot hit the trailing airplane with a long-distance burst of fire that smashed its tail surfaces, sending the Russian airplane into a rolling dive. The Russian pilot bailed out at the last minute and hit hard, but survived.

"The German then broke off his attack," Silverman said, "and turned back toward Nationalist territory. His fighter had a bright red propeller spinner."

"Ya'll missed a great show here, Captain Silverman!" Buford interjected. "This Roushin pilot come running past bare-ass naked 'cept for his flyin' boots. He grabbed a helmet and parachute and was one of the first to take off. He must've froze his you-know-whats!"

Silverman roared with laughter. "Ah, yes, that'd be Ivanovich the mad Cossack! Fantastic pursuit pilot. When on drinking binges, Cossacks often sell their clothes when they run out of money for vodka. He's from the Dnieper River region in the south of Russia. The Cossacks are Russia's professional soldiers, famous as the best cavalrymen in the world. Now they're flyers too.

"They don't hesitate to sell their clothes for drinking money. There's a rocky island out in the Dnieper River where the Russians used to take Cossacks when they'd stumble back to camp drunk and naked. They'd chain 'em to the rocks for the forty-eight hours or more it took to sober 'em up, and then take them back to their units. They'd dock their future pay for a new uniform. They're tolerated because they're damn fierce fighters."

Ivanovich had shot down two He 111 bombers, sent a Bf 109 smoking back toward Nationalist lines, and blasted a Bf 109 that had exploded dramatically over the airfield. This brought his total to seventeen kills. And he returned anatomically intact with nothing frozen.

Chapter 29

FIRST CASUALTIES

The Russians suspended flight operations through New Year's Eve as cold wet weather shrouded the field. Silverman and the Americans, depressed by the delay in completing their combat readiness, hung around the barracks as the Russians continued their drinking voyages.

A cold front blew through the first week of January, clearing the weather. Ben quickly mastered the UTI-4 trainer, flew three solo flights in quick succession, and was shifted to the single-seat I-16. His American colleagues watched with envy as he soared into the sky, a qualified pursuit pilot soon to enter the replacement pool.

On his first solo flight in the fighter, Ben struggled to crank up the landing gear. He encountered a bad case of the "vobbles," but kept the airplane upright and on course. Once airborne, he whipped the stubby fighter through tight turns and simulated combat maneuvers.

"Wow!" he yelled. "Like ole Brice used to say, feels like you could fly it up your own . . ."

Ted qualified next, still a little shaky and lacking the confidence Ben showed with the airplane. Buford was cleared for solo in the UTI-4 but got off to a bad start, veering precariously off-course before correcting and running straight down the field. He misjudged his first landing and hit the ground with a thud and two bounces.

"Omigod!" Ben yelled. "That musta knocked the fillings outta his teeth!"

Undeterred, Buford rammed the throttle open, lifted the tail, and began his second takeoff. The airplane barely cleared the trees when black smoke belched from the exhaust. A cannonlike report echoed across the field. The airplane faltered.

"Has blown cylinder!" Stavoras shouted. "Engine might still run, but need to emergency land!"

They watched in horror as Buford rolled the aircraft into a 180-degree to turn back toward the landing field.

"No, no, no!" Ben screamed, waving his arms. "Land straight ahead! Go for one of those fields out beyond the trees!"

Buford continued his turn, pulling the nose up to clear the trees. The engine seized with a shriek, and the propeller stopped abruptly, snapping the fighter into a vicious roll. Buford recovered; but the additional drag robbed the trainer of flying speed, and it stalled, dipping the left wing. Buford wrenched the airplane level as it dived and smashed with sickening crunches into the uplifted arms of the tallest trees. The wings sheared off, and the fuselage torpedoed between the trunks, hurtling nose first into the ground. The engine plowed a long furrow, and the tail flipped forward. The wreckage smashed upside down in a cloud of dust and dirt.

The Americans ran toward the crash as the fire engine and field ambulance clanged past. They reached the wreckage as the rescue crew released Buford's safety harness and lowered him to the ground. His face was bloodied, his head twisted at an odd angle. He had been killed instantly. The pilots stood in shocked silence.

"He always was afraid of those goddamned trees," Randy Schuller sobbed.

They buried Buford with full military honors. Silverman said it was best to bury the dead quickly and get on with flight operations. Dwelling on the accident would erode morale.

He spoke to the remaining eleven pilots. "All right, gentlemen. We're going to miss Buford. He was special. But we still have a big challenge ahead of us. Let's focus on what we have to do."

Ben and the others listened in silence. Easier said than done.

Their second loss came when influenza swept the camp. Many succumbed to violent vomiting, dysentery, and high fever. Al Saunders, the biggest man among them, went down the hardest. Silverman ordered him transported to a Barcelona hospital. He died there three days later. Silverman drove into Barcelona to arrange the funeral.

Randy Schuller, his Florida constitution not fit for the cold wet winter of Catalonia, struggled to fight off an influenza attack. He survived, but emerged from the Barcelona hospital pale and weakened, not fit for flying in the open cockpit Russian airplanes. Silverman negotiated his release from the Republican Air Force and got him aboard a tramp freighter returning to New York.

Ed Pearson and Al Brewster qualified next in the I-16, following Ben and Ted, and joined them on the replacement pilot list. Silverman took the Iowa farmers, Art Rawlings and Brad Collins, into his I-15 attack squadron, along with Fred Jones, Rudy Groenke, and Clarence Schenk. They would remain at Igualada Aerodrome, flying the large biplanes on ground-attack missions supporting Republican army units fighting along the Ebro River. Ben was assigned to Zaragoza Aerodrome as a replacement pilot for Russian Pursuit Squadron 27.

Silverman gathered the Americans. "This is where we go our separate ways," he began soberly. "We knew this day was coming, so let's not mope about it. Let's concentrate on doing what we came here to do."

He broke out a case of rough red Spanish wine, and they toasted Ben on his way.

Chapter 30

ZARAGOZA

Silverman walked Ben along the Barcelona train platform. "When the train arrives at Zaragoza, stand next to the sign that says Estacion Una, or Station Number One," he said. "Someone will ask if you are Señor Blanco, or Mr. White. You respond, '*Si, yo* Señor Blanco de Barcelona.' Yes, I'm Mr. White from Barcelona. Got that?"

Ben nodded, trying to swallow a lump in his throat.

"Good. Relax. The man will drive you to the aerodrome. An English-speaking pilot should be there to meet you." An ancient steam engine huffed into the station pulling five battered passenger cars and screeched to a stop. "Good luck!" Silverman shouted as Ben clambered up the wooden steps. "Ted should be joining you shortly!"

The train chuffed slowly out into the rolling foothills that ringed the city. As they headed southwest, the terrain blended into a high dry plateau. Ben squirmed on the hard wooden seat. His eyes watered in the acrid tobacco smoke that enveloped the compartment.

Several passengers, noting his sergeant's uniform and the wings insignia over his right breast pocket, greeted him.

Ben stammered, "*Yo* Americano."

This caused a stir. Word passed about the *piloto* Americano traveling with them. Ben heard several "*salutos*" and grinned back at the friendly waves.

"You from where in America?" a young woman asked.

"Ah, you speak English," Ben said. "Wonderful!"

"I teach English in the school," she responded. "Unhappily, my school was badly damaged in the bombings, so I am without a position. I am returning home." She asked again, "You are from where?"

"I'm from Michigan. I lived on a farm there."

"Michigan, yes, where the Great Lakes are!" she said proudly. "I have read much about the Estados Unidos. I know about Michigan. It is beautiful there, I think."

Ben felt his throat clutch as an image of his farm swarmed into his mind.

"You have come a long way to participate in our war," she said. "And you did not come alone. Were you not with the group of American pilots who arrived recently in Barcelona?"

How'd she know that? Doesn't look like a spy, but better be careful.

The young woman became involved in a heated conversation with other passengers. Some were frowning at her.

"They tell me it is not proper for an unaccompanied woman to speak with a stranger," she explained. "We have strict social rules in Spain. But they said to tell you they are grateful you are here, and they thank you for helping us."

Ben nodded and looked out the window. The train was running along a large river, the Ebro. Zaragoza must be close.

The train lurched to a stop in Zaragoza's station. The tracks and sidings around the station showed bomb damage. He smiled broadly at the young woman.

"*Muchas gracias,*" he said. Clutching his barracks bag, he descended the steps to a chorus of best wishes.

A young Spaniard stood under the Estacion Una sign. Ben said, "*Buenos dias. Yo* Señor Blanco *de* Barcelona."

The man snapped to attention, saluted, and gestured for Ben to follow him. An Hispano Suiza saloon sat at the curb. Ben climbed into the back seat. When they arrived at the front gate of the Zaragoza Aerodrome, a guard examined his papers and waved the car through.

At base operations, his escort said, "You go here, Señor." He motioned to the door. "Commander Castiliano, he . . . he awaits you there."

"*Muchas gracias,*" Ben said. He clumped up the steps on rubbery legs and was greeted by a young, grim-faced Spaniard seated at a battered table.

"Sgt. Pilot Benjamin Findlay, reporting," Ben croaked. "I am to see Commander Castiliano."

"*Sus documentos, por favor,*" the young man said, extending his hand without acknowledging Ben's salute. The young man studied his orders and passport carefully and handed them back.

"*Si*, Señor Find-alloy," he said, struggling with Ben's last name. "You come by me."

Ben followed the young man down a dimly lit hall to a door marked with Castiliano's name. A young Spanish officer there introduced himself as Captain Ramon. He announced Ben and beckoned him to enter. Castiliano sat erect behind a polished desk. His thin, dark face was masklike. His lips formed a tight line beneath a neatly trimmed black mustache.

Again, the eyes, Ben thought. They were deep brown, almost black. Castiliano stared at him unblinking. Ben braced at attention, saluted, and stumbled into the Spanish phrase Silverman had taught him.

"I have good English," Castiliano said evenly. "You may speak English."

"Thank you, sir!" Ben said. "Sir, I am Sgt. Pilot Benjamin Findlay, reporting for duty." He thrust his papers across the desk

Castiliano returned his salute and slowly read the papers. Ben noted his long slender hands and fingers. Castiliano's jet-black hair was slicked down and brushed back. His neatly pressed uniform was starched.

Must use Brylcreem. Can't tell how tall he is sittin' down. Could be about six feet.

"All seems to be in order, Sergeant Pilot Findlay," Castiliano said, interrupting Ben's inspection. "Stand at ease, Sergeant Pilot Findlay. Be seated."

Ben sat down, remembering to square his shoulders.

"So you have come to help us fight the Fascists," Castiliano said. "What has prompted you to come all this distance from, from your Michigan state, to do this?"

"Sir, I love to fly, and I want to help Spain fight for freedom," Ben stammered, trying unsuccessfully to lock eyes with Castiliano. "And I think we have to make a stand against the Fascists here before they attack the rest of Europe." Ben cringed inwardly. *That sounded dumb. Really dumb.*

"I see," Castiliano said evenly. "You have a broad view of the world, Sergeant Pilot Findlay. Do you also have a good understanding of what is happening in Spain? Do you know why we so fiercely fight our brothers and sisters?"

"I don't know all the details, sir," Ben said quietly. "But I understand how long political unrest led to civil war." He breathed another thanks to Brice for his basic history lesson on what led up to the Spanish civil war. "We had a civil war in America too, in the 1860s," Ben added. "Had to fight each other to settle differences between the North and the South."

"I'm well aware of your civil war," Castiliano said. "Our civil war has causes that are both simpler and yet more complex, if I may say so."

Ben was puzzled.

"Beyond our political differences, which are clearly defined, are regional, ethnic, cultural, and religious issues we have been disputing for centuries. Unfortunately, when the monster of war was unleashed, the beast that lies within even the most civilized people also was unleashed. We Spaniards have done, and are doing, terrible things to each other.

"Now we have no choice but to continue the senseless slaughter to the end. And you, Sergeant Pilot Findlay, have come all the way to Barcelona from your Michigan to help us in that endeavor."

Ben sat stunned. He had no idea how to respond. *What'd I expect? To be welcomed as a hero like ole Brice helpin' the French and British fight Germany? Is this a glorious adventure or what?*

"Yessir," he said. "I want to do what I can to help."

"Good. Your record shows you have excellent piloting skills. You will be assigned to Squadron 27, commanded by Comrade Maj. Yuri Grigorevich Golenkinov, a famous Russian pilot who brought several squadrons of Polikarpov I-16 fighters to Spain. Do you have any questions?"

"No, sir! Uh, perhaps one, sir. Will I be assigned as wingman to a particular pilot, or will I stand in reserve?"

"I believe you will be assigned as wingman to an Englishman. But Comrade Golenkinov will give you those details. Captain Ramon will escort you to Comrade Golenkinov's office."

Ben snapped to attention, saluted, and followed Captain Ramon out the door.

The Hispano rattled over an unpaved road to Squadron 27's operations area. Ramon handed Ben off to a stone-faced Russian, who wore the usual peasant blouse uniform belted at the waist. He also wore no rank. With a brusque "follow me" gesture, the Russian headed for a ramshackle wooden structure, squadron headquarters.

At Golenkinov's door, his escort knocked, entered, and waved Ben inside. Ben had heard of short stout men described as fireplugs, but had never met one. The squat major standing next to a crude wooden desk fit the description perfectly. His large round head was topped with a ragged crew cut. His ears jutted out like twin jug handles. He had no neck, at least one that was visible!

Ben saluted. "Ah, sir, Sergeant Pilot Findlay, Benjamin Findlay, reporting for duty, sir!" he stammered.

Major Golenkinov stared at him, his round face impassive. Deep pockmarks on his cheeks showed through the rust-colored fringe of a three-day beard. His bright red shoulder boards extended like small wings from just below his ear lobes.

"*Umph!*" Golenkinov snorted, returning Ben's salute. "Stand to ease, Pilot Finn-el-ee," he growled. "Sit! Sit! Sit!" he added, gesturing to a scruffy wooden chair.

The Russian maneuvered his square bulk into a swivel chair that squawked in protest, slammed two hamlike fists onto the desk, and peered intently at Ben. His thick lips pouched out, and his small black eyes were hooded by bushy brows.

He has little pig eyes.

"So, Sergeant Pilot Finn-el-ee!" Golenkinov rumbled. "You are Americanski, no?"

"Yessir! Ah, from Michigan, sir!"

"You look like boy! Are dere no man pilots in America to come help us? Must dey only send us childrens?"

"I'm eighteen," Ben said defensively. "Been flying for two years. I know how to handle an airplane."

Golenkinov snorted and thumped a huge fist on an open file in front of him. "Da, da, records say you know how to fly. But you know also how to fight? Have you stomach for vat we do? Have you, what is Americanski saying? Ah, have you flames in gut?"

"That's fire in the belly, sir," Ben offered timidly.

"So!" Golenkinov roared. "Have you dis? Can you shoot down Fascist bastards vidout mercy? Can you shoot enemy soldiers in trenches? Can you do so day following day?"

Ben rocked back in his chair as if he'd been punched in the nose. "Yessir," he stammered. "I think I can do this."

"*Tink!*" Golenkinov shouted. "Pilots who *tink* dey can do dis are not needed! Vat needed is pilots who *know* dey can do dis. You unnerstan' me?"

"I understand you, sir!" Ben said hotly. This Russian bear was beginning to piss him off. "Just give me a chance, and I'll prove to you that I can! I haven't shot anybody down yet, but I think . . . I *know* how to, and I *know* I can!"

"*Umph*," Golenkinov snorted. "Dat ve see." He demanded, "How you called at home? Sergeant Pilot Finn-el-lee is too difficult for Russian tongue. How you called?"

"Ah, I don't understand, sir!"

"Diminutive! Vat is diminutive you are called by your mother?" Golenkinov shouted.

Not having a clue what "diminutive" meant, Ben said, "My mother calls me Benjamin, but only when she's mad at me."

"Hah! Crazy Americanski way. Dis no diminutive! Dis full name! In God's name, wery strange, but so it is! You are Benjamin! Here we use no rank, except mine!" Golenkinov roared. "From now forward, you are Comrade Benjamin! You unnerstan' me?"

"Yessir, Major Golenkinov."

"*Comrade* Major Golenkinov, Americanski idiot!" Golenkinov snarled. "You Comrade Benjamin and me, Comrade Major Golenkinov! You unnerstan' me?"

"Yessir, Comrade Major Golenkinov!"

"Good! Ve accomplish someting anyways. Now you fly vid me and show you know how stay on ving of *real* pilot." Golenkinov clumped out of his office.

"He sure moves fast for a guy with such short legs!" Ben muttered.

They grabbed helmets and parachutes and headed for the flight line. Ground crews leaped into action when they saw Golenkinov lumbering toward them. They stared bemused at Ben, trotting along behind him.

Golenkinov slapped Ben's shoulder and propelled him toward one of two Polikarpov I-16s parked on the line. "You fly dat one, Comrade Benjamin, and I dis one."

Shouting commands in Russian, Golenkinov clambered into the cockpit. Ben scrambled into his aircraft. The ground crewmen barely had time to help them strap in before Golenkinov started his engine and waved away the wheel chocks.

"What's he doin'!" Ben exclaimed. "He's taking off without engine checks or anything!"

Ben frantically started his engine, waved away the wheel chocks, and tried to complete his cockpit checks as they taxied out. Ben started his pretakeoff control checks. Golenkinov gave an impatient wave and pointed forward. He opened the throttle, and his airplane trundled down the field. Frantically shoving the throttle lever forward, Ben hunched down and concentrated on keeping pace with Golenkinov's rapidly accelerating airplane. He glanced at the other airplane out of the corner of his eye. He worked to keep his position off Golenkinov's left wing.

"Watch the angle of his fuselage," he coached himself. "Tail comin' up. He's about to lift off. Let him go first. Then follow. Now!"

The airplanes rose into the air seconds apart.

"Stay close but loose," Ben muttered, recalling Brice's instructions. "Behind and below his wing. There! He's turning right!"

Ben swept into a climbing right turn, hanging on to Golenkinov's wingtip like a bull terrier clamping a rat in his teeth. Golenkinov rolled level. Ben followed.

Golenkinov banked into a climbing left turn, a sure way to cause a midair collision with an unwary wingman. Ben dived below his airplane and turned left with him.

"Sonofabitch!" he hissed through clenched teeth.

He regained his position on the Russian's left wing. Ben saw his elevator droop. *Pitching into a dive! Stay with him!*

The two I-16s nosed down into a steep dive. Ben dared not glance at the airspeed indicator or altimeter. He had to rely on his leader not to fly them into the ground. The Russian's elevator slapped up, and Ben was ready. He pulled hard on the stick, and the g-forces pulled his guts downward. His eyes sagged; his goggles slipped and pinched his nose.

"I'm hangin' on, you Russian bastard!" he shouted. "Look out! Here he goes to the right!"

Golenkinov led Ben through abrupt maneuvers, including a low-level ground-strafing run. Finally, he pulled up into a steep climb and leveled out. Flying straight and level again, Ben inched his wingtip closer to Golenkinov's.

"I'm still here, Comrade Major Golenkinov!" he shouted into the airstream swirling past the cockpit. "What're we gonna do now?"

Golenkinov looked at him for the first time since takeoff. He flashed a wolfish grin and nodded. Pointing over his shoulder, he swept into a descending right turn, causing Ben to accelerate quickly to stay with him while flying a wider arc. They approached the field, and Golenkinov signaled they'd be making an overhead approach to the left. Ben jockeyed his throttle and slipped into trail position behind Golenkinov's airplane.

As they approached the runway, the Russian rolled his airplane into a tight left turn. Ben rolled in after him. The landing gear came down on Golenkinov's airplane halfway through the circling turn, and Ben spun the gear crank on his airplane. Both pilots turned onto final, and Ben slid to the left of Golenkinov's airplane as they dropped toward the field. Ben let his airplane settle, then flared and touched down first, with a three-point landing. Golenkinov extended his final flare and made a wheel landing ahead of him.

As they taxied back to the flight line, Ben leaned his head out into the propeller blast and sucked a deep breath. Sweat dripped from his helmet and ran down around his goggles. His sodden uniform shirt and blouse clung to his chest and armpits. Water trickled down his spine. *Flying with this mad Russian's gotta be more dangerous than dogfighting with the enemy!*

They wheeled their airplanes into the tie-down spots as ground crewmen clung to each inner wingtip to tighten the turn. Ben pulled the fuel mixture control and shut off the fuel and master switch. He raised his goggles and pulled off his sweat-drenched helmet. His hair was a matted mess.

Golenkinov hopped out of his cockpit. "Come to office after return gear to supply room," he rumbled as he stumped past Ben's cockpit.

Ben wriggled out of his safety harness and hoisted himself out of the cockpit. His knees buckled as he hopped off the wing. Slinging the parachute harness over one shoulder, he walked unsteadily to the supply room. He ducked into the latrine for a quick pee. Washing his hands, he looked at his red sweaty face and matted hair in the mirror.

"You look a mess, Comrade Benjamin. Better freshen up before you go see Comrade Major Golenkinov!"

At Golenkinov's office, the stone-faced Russian doorkeeper intercepted Ben and gestured for him to wait. The Russian knocked twice, stepped inside, and closed the door. Ben could hear a muffled conversation in Russian. The door opened, and Ben stepped inside.

Golenkinov sat at his desk, looking surprisingly fresh. As Ben braced to attention, he cut him short with a wave of his pudgy hand and gestured to a chair.

"Sit, Comrade Benjamin. Ve don't vaste time on military ceremony bullshit!"

He sat hunched and studied Ben through furrowed brows, like a man peeking from behind twin bushes.

"You comfortable vid I-16, Comrade Benjamin? You still believe you can stay on wing of combat pilot?"

"Yessir!" Ben nearly shouted. "I know I can."

"Da, I believe so also," Golenkinov said. "I send you to Englishman pilot. But first . . ."

He pulled a bottle of vodka and two grimy glasses from the bottom desk drawer. Ben watched with alarm as the major poured the two tumblers nearly full. "To health!" Golenkinov roared. "And death to all Fascist bastards ve get in gunsights!" He swallowed the vodka in one slurping gulp.

Ben took a mouthful and choked as the fiery liquid attacked his tongue and throat. Gagging, he struggled to keep his glass upright. The vodka burned down his throat and splashed into his stomach like a firebomb.

"Hah!" Golenkinov shouted. "Dis happens vhen sip vodka! You must to swallow whole. Don't let stomach know iss coming. Finish, finish." he commanded, pointing at Ben's glass with the bottle. "Next one go smoother."

Ben shook his head, holding the glass away from his face and wiping tears from his eyes. "Nnnn-no thanks," he sputtered. "This'll be enough, Comrade Major Golenkinov." He wondered how he was going to get the rest of the fiery liquid down. Maybe he could drop the glass, spill the rest. *Naw, the mad Russian would only fill it again.* "I'll just finish this one, Comrade Major."

Golenkinov snorted as he refilled his own glass. "Send me goddamned childrens, eh," he muttered.

Ben watched in awe as Golenkinov swallowed two more glasses of the clear liquid. The major wiped the back of his hand across his mouth. He gestured for Ben's glass and returned the bottle and glasses to the bottom drawer.

"So, Comrade Benjamin!" he bellowed, smacking a meaty fist on his desk. "Now ve send you to fly on wing of Comrade Percy!"

"What?" Ben exclaimed, interrupting Golenkinov. "Um, sorry, sir, uh, Comrade Major Golenkinov. What did you say the English pilot's name is?"

"Percy, Reginald M. Percy. You know him?"

"Comrade Major, he must be an old man by now. He flew—"

"*Old man*?" Golenkinov roared. "Damn fool kid! To you everyone look like old man. Bah! What in hell you know about anyting?"

"Sorry, sir, Comrade Major!" Ben blurted. "I've never met Reginald M. Percy. But I know someone who flew with him in the war in 1917 and 1918, an American. My instructor, Brice, Mr. Curtis Brice, was his wingman. He was an exchange pilot assigned to Leftenant Percy's Royal Flying Corps squadron."

"Impossible!" Golenkinov shouted. "Comrade Percy is young man. Not damn fool kid like you. But young man. Maybe has twenty-five years. Dat means he born in, what, 1912 maybe? English let five-year-olds fly in Great War? Hah! I tink not!"

"What's his full name?" Ben asked.

"Reginald M. Percy," Golenkinov snapped. "Like fancy Englishman."

"Wow! Ben exclaimed. "He's gotta be the son of the man Brice, my instructor, flew with in the war. How about that!"

"How 'bout, indeed!" Golenkinov snorted. "You have grand reunion vid Comrade Percy later."

I'd like to take a nap before meeting Comrade Percy.

Chapter 31

THE ENGLISHMAN

Comrade Reginald M. Percy wasn't what Ben imagined a British pursuit pilot would look like. He sprawled on a cot in the ready room as Ben entered. He turned slowly and fixed Ben with hooded gray eyes. A large straight nose supported by a thick rust-red mustache dominated his angular face. His bushy eyebrows were black, his thick hair red, combed straight back.

Snapping to attention, Ben raised his right hand to salute. Percy cut it short with a languid wave of his hand.

"I say, old boy," he drawled, "we don't stand on ceremony on the flight line." He kicked a campstool toward Ben with a foot encased in a scruffy knee-high boot. "Assume you're the lad from the colonies who's going to fly on my wing?"

"Yessir, Comrade Percy!" Ben exclaimed, perching on the stool. "I just passed my formation flight test with Comrade Major Golenkinov."

"Gooood shooow," Percy drawled. "And lived to tell about it. Our fearless Russian leader is quite mad, but I suppose you've tumbled to that." Rolling to a sitting position, Percy extended his right hand. "How'dja do? Findlay. Umm, Benjamin D. Findlay, right? Pleased to meet'cha. And you can forget the comrade bullshit. Ah, except when the comrade major is around."

Percy straightened his soiled khaki blouse, reknotted his silk scarf, and made a pass at rearranging his jodhpurs, which had pulled loose from his boots.

"We also don't spend much time grooming our uniforms," he said, noting Ben's stare. "Focus our attention on shooting down 'Fascist zons of beeches,' as the comrade major would say."

He stood and stretched his long, lean frame. Over six feet tall, even with a slight stoop, Ben noted. His mind flashed back to the farm and his old man railing at him to "square your shoulders—stand up straight!"

Percy yawned. "I say, interested in a dram?"

"Pardon?" Ben asked. "Dram?"

Percy pulled a bottle of scotch whiskey from a locker.

"A drink, snort, belt, you know." Percy tipped his right thumb to his lips. "What do you call it in the colonies?"

"Ah, no, sir," Ben responded. "Major Golenkinov gave me a drink after our flight. That's all I need right now, thanks."

"Right-ho," Percy responded with a guffaw. "The mad major's infamous postflight vodka toast. No doubt in a tumbler that hasn't been washed in years. He had two, I suppose?"

"Three, actually," Ben said, crossing his arms over his stomach where the fire continued unquenched.

"Well, avoid any future toasts. That stuff will erode your brain, destroy your liver, and shrivel your willie."

Ben was about to ask who Willie was when he realized what Percy meant.

"Bob's your uncle," Percy said, and drained the glass in one long draft.

Nobody around here drinks. They just swallow.

"The proper response to that is, 'And Tillie's your aunt,'" Percy said. "But how were you to know that, where you come from? By the way, where the hell do you come from?"

"I was raised on a farm near Flint, Michigan," Ben said.

"Michigan, eh. That's somewhere in the midland, isn't it?"

"Midwest," Ben corrected.

"Umm," Percy responded, a smile playing across his thin lips. "Where dja learn to fly?"

"Baker Airport, close to our farm." Brice's grizzled face swarmed into his mind. "That's an interesting story, by the way," Ben said eagerly. "And, and I think you're gonna be surprised."

Percy arched an eyebrow. "Really? Do tell."

"Yeah, well, talk about a small world! Does the name Curtis Brice mean anything to you?"

Percy shook his head. "Not right offhand, old bean. Who might he be?"

"Well, your father flew for the Royal Flying Corps in the war, right?" Ben asked eagerly. Percy nodded, and Ben pressed on. "Did he ever mention an American exchange pilot who flew with him near the end of the war?"

Percy squinted, this time really pondering what Ben was trying to tell him. "Dunno," he muttered. "Indeed, Pater flew with the RFC in France. But look, old boy, let's dispense with the quiz. Just tell me."

"My instructor at Baker Airport was Curtis Brice. We all called him Brice. He was posted to your dad's squadron as an exchange pilot. He flew as your dad's wingman!" Ben exclaimed. He saw Percy's interest build. "Brice told me your dad taught him how to fly in combat, and that's how he survived! Ended up scoring five victories, an ace!" Ben rocked back on the stool, his flushed face beaming.

140

"Well, I'm dammed!" Percy puffed. "Now that you mention it, I do remember Pater talking about this crazy American who'd been posted to his squadron. Natural flyer, he said. Mad as the March Hare, but one hell of a pursuit pilot. He was quite pissed off when they assigned this wild man from the colonies to him, but found him the best wingman he'd ever had."

Ben shouted and clapped his hands, and tumbled off the campstool.

"Steady on!" Percy exclaimed. "I trust you fly better than you can manage that stool. Now get up off the floor and tell me more about this, whatshisname, Brice?"

Ben grinned sheepishly as he righted the stool and sat down. For the next half hour, he regaled Percy with stories about flying with Brice, and how Silverman had recruited him.

"And here I am, assigned to you!" Ben shouted, waving his arms and barely staying on the stool.

Percy stared at him. "Well, I'm blowed. What're the odds?" He twisted the ends of his mustache. "What'll Pater say when I tell him I'm flying with the spawn of his old wingman?"

"Ah, sir," Ben ventured. "How do I refer to you? You said you didn't want any of that comrade bullshit when the comrade major isn't around, so . . ."

"Right you are!" Percy exclaimed. "Need to sort this out."

"By the way, what does 'dimuni-' something mean?" Ben asked.

"Diminutive!" Percy chuckled. "Ah yes, the mad Russian again. Russians are obsessed with, umm, nicknames, you'd call it. Did he shout, 'vat does yur mudder call you?'"

Ben nodded.

"What'd you tell him?"

"Benjamin, but only when she's really mad at me," Ben said sheepishly.

"Hah! I'll bet that went down smoothly with our Russkie friend. What'd he say then?"

"He said he'd call me Comrade Benjamin."

"Then it's settled. Comrade Benjamin it is, except when the mad major isn't around. Then it's just plain Benjamin."

"And how do I address you, sir?"

"Not as sir, that's for damn sure," Percy said. "My diminutive is Reggie, at least that's what they called me at Oxford. So there you are. From now on, I'm Reggie. Except that is, when our benighted commander is within earshot. Then it's Comrade Percy."

"Can I really call you just plain Reggie?" Ben asked.

"Why not? If you can call your beloved flying instructor Brice, why in hell can't you call me Reggie?"

"Well, this is a military organization. And, and I thought I'd have to use rank and call you sir, like that," Ben stammered.

"Benjamin, me boy, you'll soon discover that this ain't a military organization, not by half. Everybody here is in this for his own private reasons. The Spaniards are too busy knocking the shit out of each other to be concerned about the niceties of military protocol. The Russians are here because they hate the Germans."

Reggie paced the room. He turned to face Ben. "I'm here because I got bored at Oxford and needed a little excitement," he continued. "I guess I was inspired by Pater's stories from the war and wanted to savor some of that for myself. Was fed a lot of left-wing bullshit at Oxford, but I'm no Communist. I do think, however, the Nazis and Fascists pose a real threat to Europe."

Pater? Who the hell is this fella Pater he keeps talkin' about?

"And you, Benjamin," Reggie said, jabbing a finger at him. "Why are you here? America shouldn't feel threatened by what's happening in Spain."

"Well, I, ah—" Ben started.

Reggie cut him off. "Looking for a little excitement? See yourself as some noble knight on a sacred crusade?" Reggie plowed on. "I know a lot of your countrymen are wild-eyed romantics, joined the Lincoln Brigade and the like. They see this as some kind of holy war against Fascism. That what drives you, Benjamin?"

Ben sat silently, then said, "I thought we were talking about military protocol. How'd we get into all this?"

"Too true, Benjamin," Reggie said quietly. "Didn't mean to mount my soapbox. This ain't Speaker's Corner, don't you know. But you see, since we're all here for our own reasons, there's no cohesiveness. Everyone just wants to get on with the business of fighting the Fascists. We've all come from different backgrounds, different traditions. Whose military protocol would we use?"

Dropping onto the cot again, Reggie fixed Ben with a hard look. "So here we are, each doing whatever to help win this filthy war. Overlay that with the Spanish sense of melancholy and despair, and you have what you see—organized anarchy." Ben didn't know how to respond. "Point is, old man, we have neither the time nor the inclination to bother with a lot of military protocol bullshit. So you can call me Reggie and not worry about it."

Why the hell didn't you just say that in the first place?

"Okay," Ben said. "Reggie it is."

Chapter 32

FIRST BLOOD

Ben and Reggie flew several training missions together, and Ben admired Reggie's smooth flying skills. He telegraphed his maneuvers, making it easy for Ben to stay in position. Reggie seemed pleased he had a dependable flyer on his wing. He pressed Ben into increasingly complex situations. Ben struggled and felt discouraged, but finally mastered the technique of close formation flying.

"Benjamin, I think we're ready to get into the fray," Reggie said. "I've put our names on the active duty list."

Combat at last!

They were assigned a week later to their first two-ship combat patrol. Reggie exuded confidence in the premission briefing. It was given in a mixture of Spanish, Russian, and English, which didn't help clarify what was being said.

"Reggie, I don't understand what going on here," Ben whispered. "Where're we supposed to go, and what're we supposed to do?"

"Steady on, Benjamin," Reggie said. "Hush, so I can concentrate."

Reggie had enough of Spanish and Russian to get by. Ben understood only that Reggie would fly lead, and he would fly off his left wing. Ben would serve as a second pair of eyes searching for enemy aircraft. If they got into combat, he was to protect his leader and cover his six o'clock, or tail, position.

Ben studied Reggie. *Can't keep my knees from shaking or my gut from churning,* he thought. *And there he is carrying on like we're goin' for a Sunday drive.* This was Ben's first experience with the British stiff upper lip. Memories of Brice's "piece of cake" lecture swarmed into Ben's mind.

Reggie explained the mission as they walked to their airplanes. Ben trudged along in silence, hoping his stomach would settle down and that he wouldn't make any serious mistakes. The preflight checks, engine starts, and taxi to the runway passed in a blur. Advancing the throttle for takeoff, Ben felt an adrenalin surge.

"Hot damn!" he yelled. "Goin' to war!"

Ben's formation takeoff was a little ragged. But with the landing gear cranked up and climbing to altitude, he shifted back in the seat and relaxed. He focused on staying close to Reggie. Not so close that he had to work at flying tight formation, but close enough so they functioned as a coordinated team. Glancing across at Reggie, Ben saw him raise his left hand in a cheery salute. His spirits soared, and his knees stopped shaking.

Their mission was to fly northwest for a quick look at Nationalist troop movements and, more importantly, look for Condor Legion fighters and bombers. The exhaust from the I-16's mighty M-62 radial engine roared in Ben's ears as the slipstream swirled through the open cockpit. He hunched forward behind the windshield, his eyes sweeping the sky for enemy aircraft.

The two Messerschmitt Bf 109 fighters sliced across overhead and swooped into a diving attack behind them, and Ben was in his first dogfight. He nearly lost control of his airplane but scored his first enemy airplane kill, more by luck than by skill.

That night the exhausted American fell into a deep sleep, dreaming of his Michigan farm home.

Ben awoke just before dawn. His body ached, but he felt refreshed and alert. The morning air was clear and crisp. He felt famished and hurried to the mess tent. Reggie appeared about half an hour later and managed to down only black coffee before they headed to the operations tent for the morning briefing. They were to fly as part of a six-ship routine patrol.

"As if any patrol in this bloody war could be routine," Reggie growled.

But the patrol was routine, and they returned to the field frustrated at having seen no action. They continued flying patrols for over a week without contacting enemy airplanes. Something was happening. Was the Condor Legion preparing for a massive attack?

Comrade Major Golenkinov was waiting for Ben in the briefing room. "Comrade Benjamin!" he rumbled. "You know Americanski pilot name Anderson?"

Ben nodded apprehensively.

"Also goddamn child pilot?" Golenkinov demanded.

"*No*! He's older than me, couple of years at least. Has something happened to him?"

"Not yet," Golenkinov growled. "He comes fly vid Squadron 26. Tomorrow, I tink."

"Yeow!" Ben yelled, pumping a fist in the air. "That's great! Ted, umm, ah, Comrade Anderson is my best friend. This'll be really swell!"

"Ve see," Golenkinov said and stumped away.

The next afternoon, Ben greeted Ted with a shout and a bear hug. "Am I ever glad to see you!" he yelled, punching Ted on the shoulder. "Haven't had much action here lately, but we think something big is about to happen."

Ben had asked Reggie to arrange for the two of them to sleep in the same tiny cubicle, even though they were assigned to different squadrons. They sat on their bunks jabbering like boarding-school roommates catching up after summer vacation. Ted sat openmouthed as Ben regaled him with details of his first dogfight and his first kill.

"It happened so fast!" Ben said. "It musta been over in less than a minute. If I hadn't lost control and flopped around the sky, that German mighta nailed me instead. Afterward I got sick to my stomach and nearly barfed!"

They talked into the night, finally drifting off to sleep around 0100 hours.

At 0630 they were at the morning briefing. Ted, assigned as wingman to a tall, dour Russian in Squadron 26, sat with a look of total bewilderment as the multilingual conversation swirled around him.

Ben nudged him. "Stick close to your lead for the first couple of missions," he said. "You'll get a feel for it."

Chapter 33

THE LOSS

The enemy air offensive burst over them the following week. Waves of Condor Legion bombers attacked Republican positions south of the Ebro River. More bombers hit Barcelona. Ben and Ted met only as they trudged exhaustedly back to their bunks after flying multiple sorties. Ted teamed with his lead pilot to shoot down a Heinkel He 111, drawing first blood. When stalking the formations of bombers, the Russian fighters swooped in at low level and popped up to attack from below. Their intelligence sources said shaken German bomber pilots nicknamed their stubby Russian fighters "Rats" because they seemed to pop up from holes in the ground.

Two days later, Reggie was grounded with a severe head cold. Ben flew as wingman for Major Golenkinov. Ted went out with Squadron 26, flying wing on his taciturn Russian. Golenkinov led Squadron 27 over Nationalist territory and into a head-on confrontation with a large patrol of Bf 109s. The encounter degenerated into swirling individual dogfights. Airplanes slashed past each other, barely avoiding collisions. Several I-16s spun out of control and dived smoking into the ground. A Bf 109 broke away and fled southwest, streaming oily smoke.

A Bf 109 cut across in front of Ben. He mashed the firing trigger, and his guns shredded the German airplane from nose to tail. It tumbled away trailing fire. Ben pulled into a gut-wrenching climbing turn to avoid the streaming debris. He spotted a Bf 109 closing on Golenkinov's I-16. The German was concentrating on Golenkinov's airplane and didn't see Ben coming. Another long burst ripped through the Condor Legion airplane. It rolled inverted, broke apart, and tumbled to the ground.

Golenkinov pulled his fighter into a tight turn and pumped a fist at Ben. Suddenly the sky was clear of enemy aircraft. Ben marveled at how massive dogfights could end so abruptly. As they pulled up, Ben saw that three I-16s were missing. He hadn't seen them go down. The Condor Legion lost five airplanes, the smoke columns on the ground attesting to their fate; and one, badly damaged, had limped back toward base.

The Squadron 27 re-formed on Golenkinov, who signaled the return to Zaragoza. They swept over the field. The Russian major, who had shot down one Bf 109 and shared in the destruction of a second, pulled up in a vertical victory roll over the field as the others sailed in and landed.

Back at the flight line, Ben hopped off the wing and slipped his parachute harness to his left shoulder. Golenkinov, his helmet pushed back above his sweating face, strode up to him and gave him a breath-stopping bear hug. He then crushed Ben's right hand in his meaty paw.

"Good shooting, Comrade Benjamin," Golenkinov growled, a grin creasing his melonlike face. "You shoot one sonofbitch Kraut right offa my tail and blow other into smoking pieces! Dat give you two more kills!" he shouted, holding up two sausagelike fingers. "By God, make ace from you yet!"

Ben grinned, hiding the pain in his right hand. "Thanks!" he said, heading for the briefing room. "It helps when they fly right in front of you." *What are the chances of that ever happening again? Gotta find Ted. I got three kills, and he's only scored one half.*

Reggie intercepted him outside the door. "I say, Benjamin, have a moment?" He had an odd look on his face.

"Sure," Ben said, glancing around. "Is Ted back yet?"

"Sorry, old boy, but there's no easy way to put this," Reggie said. "Ted isn't coming back."

Ben doubled over as though he had been punched in the stomach. "Wha . . . what happened?" he gasped.

"Long story, my friend," Reggie said. "Ted was in the six-ship flight from Squadron 26 this morning. His squadron commander said they were bounced by Bf 109s and got into one hell of a fray. Two pilots from 26 were shot down immediately. Ted got on the tail of one of the 109s and shot him down."

Ben's head spun. Reggie's voice sounded like it was coming from miles away.

"As he was pulling out, another 109 got on Ted's tail and hit him pretty hard. His airplane burst into flames. One of the 26 pilots saw his airplane roll inverted, and Ted fell out. His chute opened fine, and he looked okay."

"Was it over enemy territory?" Ben cut in. "He's been taken prisoner?"

"No, Ben," Reggie said. He hesitated, and then shrugged. "Ben, umm, another 109 pilot circled in and strafed Ted hanging in the chute. The others didn't see him hit the ground, but they're certain he was killed in his chute."

"*What!*" Ben screamed.

He shoved a knuckle into his mouth and bit hard trying to hold back a guttural howl. Blood spurted from his knuckle.

"I say, I say!" Reggie said. "Steady on there, Ben! You'll bite your bloody finger off!"

Ben pulled his hand from his mouth. He stared dumbly at the blood running down his finger and dripping off his palm.

"Why would the dirty bastard do that?" he yelled. "*Aren't there rules about that*? I mean, I know we're in a war, but we don't kill in cold blood, do we?"

"Right you are, Ben. But this has been a dirty war from the beginning. Nobody is playing by the rules, whatever the bloody hell they are. Face it, Ben, we're fighting for the Republicans, Socialists, Communists, leftists, whatever. The Germans think we're all Bolshies and they'd better kill us now because they're going to have to fight us later."

"But we're not Communists!" Ben yelled. "I sure as hell am not, and you aren't!"

"They don't know that, Ben," Reggie said gently. "We're flying Russian kites, some with big red stars on the fuselage and wings. Furthermore, the Republicans have done some beastly things to the Nationalists. We're all fair game as far as the Huns are concerned."

"Reggie, Ted is . . . was an American. You're a Brit! We haven't done any of that dirty stuff!"

"Hang on, Benjamin!" Reggie said. "The enemy pilots don't know who the bloody hell we are! What do you suggest, old boy, that you wave the Stars and Stripes and I the Union Jack while we dogfight the bastards? Might make them hate us even more."

"Can we find out what pilot did this?" Ben asked coldly. "Because I want to go after the son of a bitch myself!"

"The other pilots said the German was flying a 109 with a red spinner. He also has a black eagle painted on each side of the fuselage. They've seen him before. He's damn good. Has a string of kills painted on his tail. He appears to aim for the cockpit. Apparently doesn't want any pilot surviving."

Reggie added, "We'll all be gunning for him. Don't go blundering after him in a fit of rage. He'll nail your arse for sure, if you do."

Golenkinov strode up and pounded Ben on the back. "You telling English here how you shoot down two Kraut bastards this mornin', Comrade Ben?" he roared. "Damn good fight, English. How you say, 'bloody good show,' da?"

"No, I didn't tell him," Ben muttered. He turned and trudged off to the barracks.

"What's wrong wid young Americanski, English?" Golenkinov demanded. "I say wrong ting?"

"No, Yuri Grigorevich, it wasn't anything you said. I just told Ben that Ted had been killed."

"Vat happened?" Golenkinov asked.

Reggie repeated the story of Ted being strafed in his parachute. The squat Russian's face blossomed red and then turned purple. Veins on his neck bulged like thick ropes.

"Filthy Kraut bastard!" Golenkinov roared. "Ve make dem all pay for dis!"

Golenkinov exploded with a stream of Russian obscenities. Reggie, who had picked up a basic knowledge of Russian, as usual mostly the swearing vocabulary, stood speechless at the breadth of Golenkinov's cursing.

"The Hun with the red spinner is a marked man," Reggie muttered.

Ben kicked open the door to the room he had shared with Ted. He stared at the neatly made cot his friend wouldn't be sleeping in tonight. Hot tears of rage welled in his eyes. He kicked the nightstand, and Ted's tinny alarm clock clattered to the floor. Ben scooped it up and opened the nightstand drawer to put it away. He found a sealed envelope addressed to Ted's parents in Minnesota.

"Oh god!" Ben sobbed. "I gotta mail this."

PART 4

FORGING THE WARRIOR, SPRING 1938

Chapter 34

DEALING WITH DEATH

Ben's sorrow over Ted's death congealed into cold fury. He was obsessed with finding the pilot with the red spinner and—and what?

"Reggie's right," he muttered. "Gotta keep my wits. Not do anything dumb. But I'll find him no matter how long it takes. He's gonna end up in a smokin' hole!"

Ben lost his appetite and couldn't sleep. When not flying, he moped around the aerodrome looking pale and spent. Many recent missions had been unproductive. They missed on several intercepts of Nationalist bombers, and two times, Bf 109s drove them off. Shunning breakfast again, he gulped a cup of black coffee and went to check the mission board.

He and Reggie weren't on the schedule. He wanted to get out there and get revenge. Shoot some enemy bastard out of the sky! Instead he clumped back to the barracks and flopped irritably onto his bunk.

"Guess I better get Ted's things packed up for shippin' home."

He'd put off that awful task for over a week. Now he had to get it done. He stepped to Ted's narrow closet, hesitating at the door. He didn't want to touch Ted's things, but he had to pack them for shipment home. Ted's folks deserved at least that. Steeling himself, he opened the door and found a letter addressed to him.

"God help me. I don't want to do this," he sobbed.

The letter was short. Ted wanted Ben to know how much he enjoyed his friendship. They had some great experiences—their big dinner in New York, their flying, and the voyage to Spain. Their idea about opening a flying service somewhere in the Midwest was a swell one. What a life that would have been!

"But since you're reading my letter, Ben, none of that's going to happen," Ted wrote. "Thanks for being such a great pal. Your friend forever, Ted."

Ben groaned. Tears streamed down his cheeks. He crumpled the letter in his fist. Shocked when he saw the ball of paper in his hand, he quickly smoothed it flat.

"Gotta keep this and read it often," he sniffed. "What I do from now on is for both of us."

Chapter 35

A BREACH OF DISCIPLINE

Ben and Reggie flew in a large patrol searching for Condor bombers reported heading for Barcelona. Scudding along at low level, they spotted a formation of Heinkel He 111s above them, a flight of Bf 109 escorts flying top cover. The Russian flight leader signaled a climbing attack. The I-16s slashed up through the bombers and blasted two out of the sky. Two more were sent smoking to the south. The 109s dived to meet the attack.

Ben, screaming wildly, broke away from Reggie and flew directly into the oncoming fighters, all guns blazing. The German pilots, unnerved by the frontal attack, broke off and tried to reform. Ben plunged into their ragged formation, shooting down one airplane and nearly colliding with another. The German formation disintegrated. Individual pilots wheeled and fled.

Back at Zaragoza, Reggie vaulted out of his airplane and strode over to Ben's as he shut down the engine.

"Just what the hell do you think you're up to, my good man?" Reggie shouted, his face twisted with rage. "If you do another goddamn dumb thing like that, I'll have you grounded and kicked out of my squadron! Who do you think you are, your Superman comic-book hero?"

Ben slumped in his cockpit, too exhausted to reply. He knew he'd lost his head; he was still dealing with his rage over Ted's death. Big mistake. Not only did he abandon Reggie, he had taken dumb risks.

"Sorry, Reggie," he mumbled.

"Sorry my arse, old boy! That kind of stupid behavior is just not on! Time for you to grow up. Understand?"

Ben nodded dumbly.

"All right. There's the end to it," Reggie snapped. "Now get inside to the debriefing."

Reggie stayed aloof from Ben for two weeks as they flew routine and unproductive patrols. Conversation was limited to mission details.

Ben finally exploded. "Look, Reggie, I'm real sorry for messing up in that big fight. I've got myself under control now. Can we get things back to normal?"

"Good point, old boy," Reggie replied lightly. "Let's do just that. I hear we have a big show coming up."

They indeed had a big show coming up, flying cover for a massed raid of I-15 bombers against key Nationalist aerodromes. Reggie pulled Ben aside after the briefing.

"Old bean," he began. "Umm, I have a bad feeling about this one. I want you to stick close to me, understand? No more haring off on your own. We'll need to pull as a team."

"Sure, Reggie. Why the bad feeling?"

"No idea. Just a feeling."

Reggie's concerns proved legitimate. The raid degenerated into a disaster for the attackers. The Nationalist bases were on high alert and had several squadrons of Bf 109s aloft and waiting. The attack was broken up with the loss of four I-15s and three escorting I-16s. Ben worried that Silverman, now commander of the combined I-15 group, was leading the first wave of bombers. But Ben was busy helping Reggie battle the 109s and had no idea how Silverman was faring.

The I-15 bombers broke off their attack and headed north. Golenkinov signaled the I-16s to cover their retreat. A swarm of 109s pursued them. Ben singled out a German fighter and attacked. The enemy pilot racked his airplane into twisting tight turns, but Ben matched his maneuvers and circled into firing position. Instead of turning into Ben's arcing attack, the German pilot rolled the opposite way to escape. Ben cut him off and fired three long bursts.

"Big mistake, fella!" he yelled.

The 109 bucked under the hammer blows of Ben's guns. Bits of wing and fuselage blew away in the slipstream. The canopy shattered, and the German plane spun downward. Ben saw no parachute before the crippled airplane exploded on the ground.

Ben rejoined Reggie and accelerated to catch up with the I-15 bombers. A lone 109 sliced out of the sun and raked Reggie's airplane with a well-directed burst. His aircraft shuddered and smoke streamed from the engine, but Reggie kept the airplane flying. Ben wheeled on the 109 and fired a long burst that shredded the German's wingtip. The 109 wheeled away.

Ben closed on Reggie's crippled I-16, was relieved when Reggie waved, indicating he wasn't wounded. But he patted the instrument panel and drew his hand across his throat. His mount was mortally wounded, and he was going to have to bail out over Nationalist territory. Ben spotted an open level field ahead and signaled Reggie.

Reggie studied the field and nodded. Cranking down the landing gear, he slipped his smoking fighter in for a landing. He jumped out of the cockpit as the airplane bumped to a stop and burst into flames.

Ben slowed to just above stalling speed and swept overhead. *There's a lot of room behind my seat, why the hell not?*

He pounded his chest and pointed down to the field. Reggie understood his intentions. He ran up and down the field, stomping on the grass as Ben circled. The rest of the field was solid. He waved Ben in for a landing.

As Ben circled, he spotted an armored car leading a truck full of troops toward the field where Reggie's burning fighter had shot a column of smoke into the sky. Ben dived toward the two vehicles and ripped them with a long burst of fire. The shells from his guns slammed into the vehicles and blew soldiers out of the truck bed.

Wheeling into a climbing turn, he swooped back for a second strafing run. A guttural howl filled his eardrums. He was startled when he realized it was coming from him. His lips curled as he saw both vehicles burst into flames, crumpled bodies strewn around them.

Gasping for breath, Ben turned back for Reggie. He cranked down the landing gear and slipped over the fence for a rough touchdown. Reggie raced to grab a wingtip to help turn the airplane for the trip back up the field.

"Reggie . . . just strafed an armored car and truck comin' down that road!" Ben yelled. "More are comin'. No time to taxi back! Get your ass in here! Let's go!"

He cranked his seat far forward. Reggie squeezed in behind him.

"Nice of you to drop by, old boy," Reggie joked. "Now kindly get us the hell out of here!"

Ben groped back for the throttle. "Push back! Gimme room!" he yelled at Reggie.

The I-16 hurtled down the field. Ben held it on the ground to gain airspeed, then pulled the stick back under his chin at the last moment.

"Come on, you Russian tub, *fly!*" he snarled. They cleared the fence by inches and climbed out just as two more armored cars roared into view.

Back at Zaragoza, ground crews stared at the I-16 taxiing up with two heads sticking out of the cockpit.

"Thanks for the lift," Reggie said, cuffing Ben on the side of his head. "Do the same for you sometime."

Ben grinned. "Next time I hope I pick up somebody prettier."

The next months were frustrating. By August, more than midway through the "critical year of 1938," the weather turned sour, preventing even routine patrols. News from the frontlines continued to be depressing. The Battle of the Ebro River valley raged as Republican forces fought to block a major Nationalist thrust against Barcelona. Others dug in to defend Valencia, south on the Mediterranean coast, against the Nationalist army's attempt to drive a wedge between Barcelona and Madrid.

And worse, Germany shipped large numbers of late-model Bf 109s to the Condor Legion, giving it the tools to achieve clear air superiority. Still mourning Ted's death, Ben's morale sagged. He moped around the base and slowly sank into a black mood. Reggie tried to boost him out of his funk, but with minimal action in the air, his efforts prove futile.

Chapter 36

A Break for Benjamin

Concerned about Ben's deteriorating condition, Reggie went to Golenkinov. "Yuri Grigorevich, I need to get Benjamin away for a bit. He's obsessing over Ted's death, and it's ruining his health. At this point he's not much use to me as a wingman, not that we've been able to fly much in this filthy weather."

"Da!" Golenkinov spat out. "I see dis too. Ve don' vant push him to break point. Some new I-16s arrived Barcelona Harbor. Two assembled ready for test flight. Take Comrade Benjamin, and bring airplanes back to squadron, eh?"

"Excellent!" Reggie said. "We'll leave in the morning. There's a small hotel near the base where we can spend the night. Maybe I can find Ben some diversion to get his mind off Ted."

Golenkinov flashed a leering smile. "Da, diwersion. Maybe find some yourself, eh?"

Ben slumped in the rear seat and stared out the window. Lopez, their Spanish driver, muttered about watching for enemy aircraft, but seemed eager to make the trip.

"Relax, Benjamin. The war'll still be here when we return. Chance to clear the cobwebs from our brains. And we'll fly two brand-new I-16s!"

Ben grudgingly agreed, stretched, and yawned. Later he jolted awake as Reggie shook his shoulder.

"Stopped for a bit of lunch. Shake it off, old boy. I'm famished."

They parked in front of an adobe-walled cantina. A thick oak door stood open, held by an iron hook. A heavy burlap curtain fringed with leather hung in the doorway. Reggie smacked it aside and gestured Ben and Lopez inside. Smoke-darkened wooden beams crisscrossed the low ceiling, supported by large, equally darkened wooden posts. A thin haze of smoke wafted along the ceiling like an early morning mist rising from an airfield. The rhythm of a flamenco guitar pulsed through the murmur of conversations from the crowded tables.

"*Cerveza, por favor,*" Reggie said to a waiter. "Nothing like a cold beer to wash away the dust of the highway. I say, Lopez, what looks good?"

"No much on the menu, Señor Leftenant Percy. But I think roast wild boar will be, how do you say, tasty?"

"Capital! Roast wild boar it is. With roasted potatoes and whatever vegetables."

The beer arrived, and Lopez gave the waiter their order.

"Cheers!" Reggie said.

Their meals arrived on plates heaped with steaming shredded pork, roasted potatoes, and French-style green beans.

"Now we need a large *frasco de vino tinto*, Lopez," Reggie said. "Ask the waiter to bring good Spanish red wine, not that rough Algerian stuff."

The three men finally eased back in their chairs, satiated by the big meal, their senses dulled by the wine.

"Siesta!" Reggie said. "Wonderful Spanish custom! What say we indulge in it?"

They paid their bill and walked to the car. Reggie and Ben stretched out in the backseat and Lopez curled up in front. It was late afternoon when they awoke.

"Señor Leftenant Percy," Lopez said urgently. "We must go along. I do not want to drive in the darkness."

They arrived at the temporary Russian base near Barcelona Harbor at dusk. Reggie splashed through the rain and checked in with Comrade Major Petrov, commander of the base. He returned shortly.

"They sleep in tents here," he said. "Told the good major we had reservations in the Hotel Granada, and that we'd report in at 0730 hours tomorrow. He didn't seem too pleased."

"How do we rate hotel rooms?" Ben asked.

"My treat, Benjamin."

The Granada was a modest hotel. Lopez said he would stay the night with his cousin and would meet them in the morning. After he left, Ben asked if Lopez really had a cousin here.

"Not ours to ask," Reggie smirked.

Ben noted how warmly the desk clerk greeted Reggie.

"Stayed here before?" Ben asked.

"On occasion. Let's meet in the lobby at 2000 hours."

"Have a special treat in store," Reggie said. "Going next door to El Catalan. We'll eat a little, drink a lot, and enjoy the best flamenco dancing you've ever seen. There are a couple of beautiful señoritas who'll dance their way into your heart."

El Catalan's tables formed a semicircle facing a low stage with a highly polished wood floor. Again, everyone warmly welcomed Reggie.

"Been here before, Reggie?"

"Time or two. Now sit back and prepare to be royally entertained. Reckon you'll find the floor show exciting!"

159

The wine waiter arrived with a small leather bodega bag hanging from his shoulder. He raised the wineskin and pointed a small nozzle at his mouth. A thin stream of red wine hissed into the back of his throat. Maintaining careful aim, he extended his arms until the wine stream was about two feet long. Swallowing steadily, he moved the wineskin in closer and aimed a reduced stream at his upper lip. The wine snaked around his lip and into his mouth. Holding his head back, he slowly moved the stream of wine up along his nose and onto his forehead. The wine, following the wetted path on his face, continued to flow into his mouth.

"Wow!" Ben exclaimed.

The waiter snapped the wineskin upright, cutting off the stream with a flourish. "Now you, Señor," he said, offering the wineskin to Ben.

Ben shook his head.

"This way, then," the waiter said. "Open mouth, and swallow steadily."

The waiter sent a stream of wine into the back of his throat. Ben gulped and then raised his hands, signaling for a stop. The waiter cut off the stream with a flick of his wrist.

Dinner arrived, delicious seafood paella. Ben waved agreement as Reggie called for "*mas vino, por favor!*"

Ben felt fuzzy-headed. *Hope I don't have to pee. Not sure I can walk to the head.*

"Now for the flamenco!" Reggie exclaimed.

Three guitarists in colorful costumes eased into small chairs and launched into a flashy flamenco routine. They steadily increased the tempo and ended the piece with a flourish that brought the restaurant patrons shouting to their feet.

"Here come the dancers!" Reggie yelled.

Ben tried to focus on the lithe young women and slender man who glided onto the stage. The women flashed bright smiles and tossed their heads. Each wore her shiny black hair swept into a tight bun. The male dancer stood erect as a bullfighter. His broad shoulders tapered to an incredibly small waist. The guitarists took up a frenetic flamenco rhythm, and the dancers stamped their heels and clapped in staccato unison.

"Sounds like gunfire" Ben yelled. "Fantastic!"

The dancers swirled past Ben's wine-befogged eyes. Heels pounded, upheld arms waved, hands clapped like pistol shots, castanets snapped. Two female dancers seemed particularly interested in the two pilots. They flashed dazzling smiles and winked as they swirled past.

One blossomed her skirt and brushed it across Ben's face. Ben blushed when he realized he'd become aroused. He squirmed in his seat, hoping the bulge in his pants wouldn't show. Reggie grinned devilishly and saluted.

"A pair of these fair maidens have their eyes on us, Benjamin. The one on the right is Manuela, and the other is Angelica. What do you think we should do about it?"

"I dunno, Reggie, but I'm beginnin' ta see what you have in mind."

"Capital!" Reggie shouted. "When the show's over, we'll invite the ladies to our table!"

The show's final number overpowered Ben, who slumped in his chair. The dancers glided across the stage, bowing to cheers and whistles. Reggie gestured to Manuela and Angelica.

Reggie said casually, "Ben, I'd like to introduce two friends of mine, Manuela and Angelica. Ladies, my wingman, Benjamin Findlay."

"I'm really pleased to meet you, ladies," Ben said. "Won't you join us?"

Reggie gave him an amused look.

The evening became a blur, but Ben stayed focused on Angelica. Her swept-back jet-black hair accentuated her rounded forehead and high cheekbones. Her flashing almond-shaped eyes bored into him. He noted her smooth tawny skin and thought it must be soft. Her long, straight nose accentuated a full-lipped mouth outlined with bright red lipstick. *She's the most beautiful woman I've ever seen.*

Ben struggled to hold up his end of the conversation and heard himself spinning a long-winded yarn about something. He was being very funny, he thought, ignoring Reggie's smirks.

"Señor Percy say you are from America," Angelica said softly. "From where, may I ask?"

Ben leaned back in his chair and nearly tipped backward. "Uh, raised on a farm in Michigan. In the Upper Midwest, Great Lakes and all that."

Images of the farm swirled into his mind, bringing a wave of homesickness. Without warning, he bellowed a song.

> *That's why I wish again, that I was in Michigan,*
> *down on the farm; with a milk pail on my arm,*
> *Far away from any harm.*

Angelica and Manuela shrieked with delight and clapped their hands.

"*Mas, mas*, sing more," they shouted in unison.

Encouraged, Ben started over. "It goes like this."

> *I was born in Michigan and I wish and wish again*
> *that I was back in the town where I was born!*
> *There's a farm in Michigan and I'd like to fish again,*
> *in the river that flows beside the field of waving corn.*
> *A lonesome soul am I, here's the reason why.*
> *I want to go back, I want to go back, I want to go back to the farm.*
> *Far away from any harm, with a milk pail on my arm!*

Tears coursed down his cheeks. "Sorry," he slurred. "There's a couple of more verses, can't . . . can't sing'em right now."

Angelica flung her arms around his neck. "Sing them, Benjamin! This song is from your heart! It is about your home place!"

Reggie rolled his eyes to the ceiling. This was a Ben he'd never seen.

"*Sing!*" Angelica commanded.

"Okay," Ben relented. "After you sing, 'with a milk pail on my arm,' comes the refrain."

He cleared his throat and ignored Reggie's alarmed look. Embolden by what he took to be an adoring look from Angelica, Ben took a deep breath and continued.

> *I miss the rooster, the one that used ter wake me up at 4:00 a.m.*
> *I think your great big cities very pretty . . . nevertheless I want to be there,*
> *I want to see there a certain someone full of charm.*
> *That's why I wish again that I was in Michigan, down on the farm.*
> *I want to go back, I want to go back, I want to go back to that old farm.*
> *Far away from any harm, with a milk pail on my arm!*

He ended with a flourish. The restaurant erupted in applause. Few understood the words the Americano was singing, but Angelica told them he was singing of his homeland. Ben looked startled.

"You've struck a resonant chord, old bean," Reggie said dryly.

"Benjamin, you must to teach us the song of your home place!" Angelica pleaded.

Ben repeated the lyrics until they had learned most of them. Later the foursome reeled out of El Catalan arm in arm, singing lustily.

Ben didn't remember navigating back to the hotel. Reggie led him into his room and shoved him onto the bed. He helped Ben shuck his shoes and strip to his underwear, then headed for his own room. Ben flopped back, smirking at the ceiling.

A short while later, a knock on his door roused him. He wobbled to door, expecting to find Reggie. Instead he stared into the dark eyes of Angelica, wrapped in a fluffy dressing gown.

"You invite Angelica inside, or must she stand in drafty hall?" she asked sweetly.

Ben stumbled back, embarrassed that he was in his underdrawers and more conscious than ever of the bulge in the front.

"Ah, I notice you are pleased to see me," Angelica said with a sly smile as she pushed him back to the bed. "Maybe you like Angelica make you comfortable? To relieve tension?"

Ben's wine-besotted mind whirled as they rolled onto the bed. He sobered quickly. He had fantasized about this moment for years, but now? *Dunno. Can't tell her never done it before. Is this how it's s'posed to be?*

Angelica quietly took control. She slipped out of her nightgown, and Ben gasped at the beauty of her naked body. She slipped off his underwear, and they relieved the tension twice; that he remembered. Suddenly it all seemed so natural.

Chapter 37

THE AFTERGLOW

A loud pounding roused Ben.

"Uhhhh," he clutched his head as he sat up. The pounding seemed centered between his throbbing temples.

"Come alive! Benjamin! Rise and shine, old bean!" Reggie shouted through the door.

Ben moaned. "Oh god, we're supposed to fly this morning. I can't do it. I can't!"

He opened the door. Reggie, hands on hips, surveyed him.

"Sorry to say, old bean, but you look like hell!"

Ben snarled and stumbled back. "Can't fly. Feel sick."

"Steady on, steady on, Benjamin! Look out the window. It's raining the proverbial cats and dogs, friend. We ain't going to be flying today!"

"Thank God!" Ben breathed. "What time is it?"

Reggie grinned, "0600 hours. Won't be flying, but have to report in to Comrade Major Petrov at the aerodrome by 0730."

Comrade Major Petrov was not pleased as he studied the two pilots standing before his desk. He stood and squared his shoulders. Ben squinted at him. *Doesn't look Russian.*

Petrov was tall, close to six feet, and trim. His uniform looked tailor-made. He had blond hair and blue eyes. He had a square jaw and full lips topped with a neatly trimmed mustache. He lacked the high cheekbones of most Russians Ben had encountered.

"You sleep las' night or jus' drink and fiddle vid vomen?" Petrov asked sourly.

"Comrade Major," Reggie said stiffly, "we had an arduous journey here yesterday, taking back roads to avoid Nationalist airplanes. We knew the weather would be bad this morning, so we felt we could relax a bit last night."

"*Umph*! Relax!" Petrov snorted. "You relax in soft varm hotel bed! Here ve relax in cots under leaking tents! Next time, Comrade, you take Petrov vid you, unnerstan'?"

Reggie nodded vigorously. "We understand, Comrade Major!"

"Good! Now go out to aerodrome and oversee work of mechanics," Petrov said with a tight smile.

The two pilots slopped around the drenched camp for the rest of the morning. They watched the Russian mechanics assemble another pair of I-16s under a makeshift tent hangar. The aircraft they were to deliver to their squadron sat on the flight line with tarps covering the open cockpits. When they reported back to Petrov, he told them the weather forecast for tomorrow morning was for clear skies.

"Report here at 0730 hours and do test-flying," he said. They saluted and turned to leave. "You stay in hotel again tonight?" Petrov demanded.

Reggie raised an eyebrow to Ben, and turned to the major. "Why, yes, Comrade Major. Would you care to join us?"

Petrov squinted at him. "Cannot stay for night," he said evenly. "Must be back at aerodrome. But can join for dinner and maybe some relaxation."

"Of course, Comrade Major," Reggie said. "Why don't you join us at the Hotel Granada at 2000 hours. We'll have a drink, then slip next door for dinner and a show at El Catalan. I'll make the arrangements."

Petrov nodded vigorously. "Da, make *all* arrangements, eh?"

In the car, Ben turned on Reggie. "Why the hell invite ole Petrov along tonight," he demanded. "He's gonna ruin everything!"

Reggie fixed him with a hard look. "Ease up, my boy. It was clear what the good major had in mind. Couldn't very well deny him that, now could I?"

Ben grudgingly agreed.

"Besides, we're going to be back at the hotel in time for a quick spot of lunch. And then it's siesta time! Perhaps we can persuade Manuela and Angelica to join us for a little relaxation."

Ben grinned at the thought. Lunch with the two young dancers was delightful. The shared siestas were even better.

Major Petrov appeared promptly at 2000 hours, resplendent in full dress uniform, his blouse bedecked with medals and ribbons. Ben gaped. *Wow! Pretty impressive, a soldier's soldier.*

The bartender stared wide-eyed at Petrov. Obviously he didn't see many Russians at his bar. Petrov ordered vodka, followed quickly by a second and then a third. Ben carefully sipped a beer. *Another swallower. How can they do that and still stand up?*

The dinner and flamenco show matched those of the night before. Angelica directed smoldering glances at Ben as she swept past him. At one point she aimed a pelvic thrust at him that nearly knocked him off his chair. He grinned delightedly, remembering their passionate tussles under the covers. Reggie made an arrangement with another dancer, Carmen, who focused her attention on Major Petrov. He responded with upraised glass and shouts of "*Salud!*"

The women joined them after the show. Ben nursed a glass of beer. He really had to be in shape to fly tomorrow. He noticed Reggie pacing himself as well. Petrov drank with abandon and nuzzled Carmen, who seemed flattered by the attention of an important Russian officer. Ben signaled Reggie that he and Angelica were going to slip out. Reggie nodded toward Petrov and heaved a resigned shrug.

Ben grinned. "Work out your own arrangement," he whispered.

He reached for Angelica's hand. Later that night, he snuggled against her in bed, content just to hold her soft, warm body next to his.

"You are to leave tomorrow?" she whispered. "You go back to war?"

He clutched her tightly. "Yes, Angelica, I have to leave tomorrow. Reggie and I need to continue the fight."

She shuddered and sighed. Ben felt warm tears dropping on his arms.

"Hey there," he said softly. "Don't cry, Angelica. Somehow I'll get back here to see you."

"When?" she asked.

He had no answer, so he hugged her closer.

After a silence, she murmured, "You no come back. Men go to war and no come back."

Their lovemaking had a special intensity that night. Ben felt he was becoming quite accomplished at this. He slipped into a deep and dreamless sleep, unaware that Angelica lay awake weeping. Near dawn, she then eased out of bed, dressed, and left.

Ben awoke and reached for her. He was alone. *Didn't even give me a chance to say good-bye!*

Reggie knocked on the door at 0600. "Right-ho!" he exclaimed. He glanced around the room and looked at Ben, who stared back with a blank face.

"Okay!" Reggie said heartily. "Let's get a bite of breakfast and be on our way."

In the car, Ben turned from the window and looked steadily at Reggie. "Angelica and Manuela are they, umm, er, are they . . . ?"

Reggie smiled. "Are they what, old man? Are they, umm, prostitutes?"

Ben turned away quickly. "No! Ah, I mean. Well, you know," he said. "It went so easy with us, an', an' it kinda makes ya wonder."

"Ben, let me tell you a bit about these ladies," Reggie said solemnly. "I've known them for nearly two years, ever since I arrived in this wretched corner of Spain. They've had very tough lives. Great hurts. They're looking desperately for, oh hell! I don't know. Looking for what, comfort, companionship? Manuela is a widow. Was married six weeks when her husband was killed in '37. Angelica had a boyfriend. He was called up and marched off to war. She never heard from him again. The army never said whether he was killed, captured, or missing in action. Nothing! This bloody war has caused a lot of casualties on the home front as well, Ben."

Ben stared out the window. "Bloody war indeed!" he snarled. "Reggie, I didn't even get a chance to say good-bye. What's going to happen to them? If the Nationalists capture Barcelona, I mean, what do they face?"

Reggie sat silently for a while. He turned to Ben. "I've given this a lot of thought myself, Ben," he said. "And by the way, don't feel hurt that Angelica slipped out without saying good-bye. I'm sure that's what she wanted. She's been through one too many heartbreaking good-byes. Besides," he grinned, "I think the two of you said your fond good-byes last night . . ."

As Ben started to protest, he said, "All right, all right! It's none of my business! Anyway, old bean, I'm afraid they don't have much of a future. The siege on Barcelona is inevitable. And even if they survive that, they won't have much to look forward to."

Ben whirled. "Then it's up to us!" he shouted. "We've gotta get them out to safety somewhere!"

"Get them out, Benjamin?" Reggie said. "Be serious! What are we supposed to do, tuck the ladies behind the seats of our Russian tubs and fly them away to sanctuary? Look, even if we could, where the hell would we take them?"

Reggie added, "If we tried to fly across the border into France, we'd probably be shot down. Even if we were able to land safely, we'd all be arrested, and Manuela and Angelica would be hustled right back across the border into Spain. That'd make them fair game for anyone, especially the Fascists!"

"Well," Ben said. "I'm not gonna give up that easily. I still think there's something we can do."

At the aerodrome, Major Petrov looked a bit ragged. He eyed them closely. "You two much better than yesterday morning," he grumbled. "You behave las' night after vent separate ways?"

Reggie beamed at him. "Right-ho, Comrade Major! Benjamin and I paced ourselves with the drinking and then went right to bed."

Ben stifled a snicker.

"And you, Comrade Major," Reggie inquired solicitously. "Was the evening to your satisfaction?"

Petrov glared at Reggie. Slowly a smile softened his stone face. "Da!" he said heartily. "Carmen is nice lady. Tank you for introduction. Now get to test-flying, no?"

Ben tried to slide Angelica to the back of his mind and keep focused on the test flight. He brightened as they strode out to the flight line. Reggie was right, he did have a lot of cobwebs that needed clearing away. The last two nights were a good start. They had briefed on flying the dual test flight, a formation takeoff, aerial formation, then break off for mock dogfighting.

"Remember, we need to keep an eye out for enemy airplanes," Reggie cautioned. "Wouldn't do to get jumped and shot down while we're horsing around. I'll signal when it's time to return to the aerodrome."

The takeoff went smoothly, as did the maneuvers for the routine flight-test checks. As they lined up for their mock dogfight, Ben tightened his safety harness, adjusted his goggles, and tensed for the encounter. Reggie beat him badly on the first go, but Ben quickly refined his attack profile and ended up in firing position of Reggie's tail two times in a row.

"Not bad, not bad," Reggie said as they walked back from the flight line. "I'm glad you're flying on my wing and not in some German Bf 109."

Praise of the highest order!

"Flight back to Zaragoza will take less than half an hour," Reggie said. "When we get there, let's beat up the field a bit, giv'em a low-level formation flypast. I mean grass-cutting height. Okay?"

Ben could feel his juices flowing.

"And we'd best call them first so they'll expect us and not try to shoot us down. After our flypast, we'll do a couple of vertical zooms and roll in for a formation landing."

"That sounds swell!" Ben said.

Their flypast was closer to grass-cutting level than Ben could have imagined. His heart thumped as he clung to his position off Reggie's left wing while zooming the length of the field.

"*Wow*! Never flown this low with the wheels up!" Ben shouted. "Feels like I should be taxiing!"

They landed without incident. Major Golenkinov sat scowling behind his desk. "Damn fools!" he roared. "I send you for new airplanes, and you try crash dem in front everybody?"

Reggie tried to look contrite, but failed. "Comrade Major, we were just trying to give the ground troops a little boost. You know, something to celebrate."

Golenkinov held his scowl. "Something celebrate!" he yelled. "Bah! Vat dey celebrates picking up pieces of new airplanes vid pieces you two mixed in? How low you damn fools fly?" he asked with the beginnings of a smile. "I tink we find propeller chops in field, no?"

Reggie relaxed. "Not quite, Comrade Major. But I think we clipped a few of the taller weeds."

"Hokay, hokay. Jus' no more, unnerstan'?" Golenkinov said gruffly. "Don' wan' lose you two. Also don' wan' start, vat's word? Da, competition! Don' start low-flying competition, unnerstan'?"

The two pilots stood like misbehaving students in front of the principal's desk.

Reggie said, "By the way, the new I-16s are beautiful machines."

"Da!" Golenkinov said. "Dat's good. You get fly one, an' I get udder. Now dismissed!"

Outside Reggie clapped Ben on the back. "Sorry about the new airplanes, old bean. I get to fly one, and the mad major gets de udder. I say, take you back to your bloody cows in Michigan?"

Ben waved off the wisecrack as not funny. He slept soundly that night. Angelica played a leading role in his dreams.

Chapter 38

THE END NEARS

Ben, unable to get leave to visit Angelica, slipped back into depression. He wrote her several notes, and she responded with a short note in Spanish, which Lopez translated. It was stilted, conveying none of the feelings Ben had included in his notes to her. This did not brighten his outlook.

The squadron's operations yielded occasional successes, one notably against a squadron of Junkers Ju 87 Stuka dive-bombers. The Condor Legion had brought the single-seat, gull-winged aircraft back into Squadron 27's region, thinking they had achieved air supremacy along the entire front. Reggie and Ben were part of a six-ship flight sent to intercept the Stukas reported heading for Republican positions along the Ebro. They arrived just as the German pilots pushed over into their near-vertical bombing dives. The I-16 pilots followed, and as the Stuka pilots pulled up, they presented full planform targets to the pursuers.

A German aircraft filled Ben's gunsight. "So long, bastard!" He depressed the firing button. The Stuka shuddered, its canopy exploded in bloody splinters, and it dived into the ground.

"Yahaaaa!" Ben screamed as he pulled up into a steep climbing turn. He snapped his head around, looking for other enemy aircraft. Three other Stukas tumbled to the ground, trailing smoke and flames. The Bf 109 pilots, not wanting to engage the I-16s in a low-altitude fight, marshaled the remaining Stukas and headed for home base.

Ben landed and taxied to the flight line feeling light-headed and exuberant. "By God, we showed 'em we're still in this fight!" he yelled.

They trooped into the debriefing room, slapping each other on the back. Their delight was short-lived.

Reggie and Ben flew several more missions to escort I-15 airplanes attacking Nationalist positions. Each time they were repulsed by superior numbers of Condor

Legion fighters. Once they tried to intercept Heinkel He 111s attacking Barcelona, but again were unable to penetrate the Bf 109 fighter cover.

Reggie signaled Ben after dinner. "Let's take a stroll," he said. They walked along the flight line, found two ammunition boxes, and sat down. Both stared into the sunset as the blood-red disc slipped toward the horizon.

"Things ain't goin' so dandy, as they say in the East End," Reggie muttered, mimicking London's Cockney street performers. "Afraid we're going down like that sun."

"Whadda you mean?" Ben asked anxiously. "We givin' up?"

"Look around you, Ben. We're not getting replacement pilots. We're short of airplanes. Ground crews are cannibalizing otherwise serviceable crates for parts. Comrade Major is in a deep funk and drinking heavily. Our political commissar friend left the base a couple of days ago. Bad signs, old bean. Bad signs."

Reggie kicked the dirt with his toe. "Methinks Uncle Joe Stalin is about to cut his losses here and pull out. He can read the signs. Spain's a lost cause. 'sides, he must be worrying about what Herr Hitler might be planning for Russia. He needs all his troops and airplanes back home."

"Where does that leave us, Reggie?"

"With our knickers badly twisted if we don't come up with an escape plan of our own, Benjamin."

"But what about that son of a bitch with the red spinner?" Ben yelled.

"Okay, okay, calm down," Reggie said. "Hopefully we'll get a chance to deal with him. But Ben, we have to look out for ourselves. Need a way out before all this goes to hell in a handbasket!"

"But Reggie!" Ben snarled. "There's unfinished business here!"

"Calm down, goddamnit!" Reggie snapped. "Get your emotions under control! This calls for some clearheaded planning, not childish lashing about."

Ben mumbled an apology, and they discussed their options. Both knew how badly the Nationalists were treating prisoners of war, torturing and killing most. Civilians in areas overrun by the rebel forces were treated even more brutally. Clearly they needed an escape plan.

"A bolt-hole, Ben. We need a back door and need to figure how to get to it. Know where we can get some personal transportation? Even an 'orse or two would do. Get us into the mountains and hopefully over to France."

"Will the French let us in?"

"Dunno. Cross that bridge when we get to it."

"Okay," Ben said. "But what about Manuela and Angelica?"

Reggie shook his head impatiently. "What the hell do you expect us to do, set up an air evacuation service?"

Ben stifled an urge to tell Reggie how much he had fantasized about tucking Angelica behind the seat of his I-16 and flying her off to safety. But where to?

The two Spanish armies continued to surge back and forth across the Ebro River, but the Republicans' strategic situation deteriorated as 1938 slipped into autumn. Reggie, Ben, and their fellow pilots were hard-pressed to do more than defend their own small bit of airspace, occasionally breaking through the superior Condor Legion units to give their ground troops minimal support. They continued to lose I-16s, and the I-15 units suffered horrendous losses. Ben wondered about Silverman and his five other American friends who had joined the attack group. Ed Pearson and Al Brewster were assigned to I-16 squadrons nearby. But Ben had no word on any of them. He felt very alone.

By mid-November, Nationalist forces stormed across the Ebro to stay, and prepared a final drive toward Barcelona. Valencia fell, and the siege on Madrid began. The I-16s were pulled back to Igualada Aerodrome in a last-ditch effort to defend Barcelona. There, Ben found Silverman and learned that the two Iowans, Art Rawlings and Brad Collins, had been shot down and listed as missing in action. Rudy Groenke, Fred Jones, and Clarence Schenk still flew with Silverman. Ben grimaced. *So much for our grand adventure.*

One bright spot was Pilot Ivanovich, a.k.a. the naked warrior. He had reemerged newly uniformed, none the worse for his legendary drinking voyage, and continued to cut a swath through Nationalist bomber and fighter units. In one mission, his guns jammed as he closed on a Heinkel He 111 making a bombing run. He rammed the bomber, slicing off most of its vertical fin with his right wing. The bomber spun and crashed, his nineteenth kill. Ivanovich guided his wing-and-a-half fighter back to base for a successful belly landing. He strode away from the wrecked airplane without a backward glance.

Ben caught brief glimpses of Sergeants Stavoras and Golenko. They flew with Squadrons 24 and 25, respectively, from the satellite aerodrome where Pearson and Brewster were based. Their I-16 squadrons joined Ben's occasionally on large missions. Now that they were all grouped at the overcrowded Igualada Aerodrome, Ben found Stavoras and learned that Golenko had been shot down in flames and presumed dead.

"Comrade Sergeant Pearson also shooted down," Stavoras said sadly. "Escape by parachute, but probably prisoner of Fascists."

"And Sergeant Brewster?" Ben asked.

"Do not know, Comrade Finneley. No one saw him shooted down. He just not comes back."

Ben felt he might vomit. He shook Stavoras's hand and stumbled back to his barracks.

Six of the original twelve young American pilots gone! Buford, in the early training accident; Al Saunders, dying from influenza and Randy Schuller, invalided out by the same sickness; and then Ted, Ed Pearson, and probably Al Brewster, killed in aerial combat. How had the grand adventure gone so wrong?

"Damn, damn, damn!" He slammed the door.

Weeks passed with no word on Brewster. By December, Nationalist forces had Barcelona under full siege. It was only a matter of time before they broke through. That would be the end.

Ben's thoughts turned to home. He was going to miss another Christmas, and wondered how his mother was doing. He wrote her a long letter, hoping it would make it aboard one of the freighters still operating out of Barcelona. He told her the flying jobs were keeping him on the move. But he skirted the truth of where he was and what he was doing. *Am I really fooling her?*

He closed by telling her how much he loved her and missed her, slipped a ragged ten-dollar bill into the envelope, and sealed it. He wrote to Brice, detailing his combat experiences and thanking him again for the training that kept him alive. *Wonder if I'll ever see ole Brice again?*

Reggie pounded on his door and strode in. "I say, me boy, believe I've found us an 'orse, our way out of here."

"What?"

"An 'orse, an 'orse, my good man. Transportation! Motorcycle, actually. Found it tucked away in the equipment shed. Belonged to that young fellow Salazar. Didn't return from that big I-15 sortie fortnight ago. Listen, Ben, it's an old crock. But it has a sidecar. It'll serve our purposes perfectly!"

"Reggie, that's stealing!"

"Borrowing, Benjamin, borrowing. Besides, Salazar won't be needing it. If he wasn't killed when he was shot down, the Nationalists have done for him by now. We'll collect a bit of extra petrol, and when this place goes down the chute, we'll head for the frontier."

"Deserting?"

"Could call it that, I suppose, but the alternative is to hang around here and get captured. As prisoners, our best option, and I do mean our best, would be a quick session with the firing squad. Sort it out, Benjamin. In the end, it's going to be everyone for himself. I'm for a run to the French border."

Ben nodded dumbly. "Never thought it'd come to this."

Christmas 1938 at Igualada was miserable. The Spaniards gathered for a somber year-end secular service in keeping with the Republic's antichurch policy. Even the Russians didn't go on their usual drinking voyages. Vodka, like everything else, was in short supply. And the Russians were quietly packing up and moving equipment to the port of Barcelona. Soviet freighters waited offshore. Uncle Joe Stalin indeed was ordering them home.

With operations suspended during the holiday season, Ben and Reggie wheedled a three-day pass from Golenkinov. Lopez agreed to drive them into Barcelona. It would allow another visit with his "cousin." They were saddened to find the Hotel Granada damaged by bombs, even more shocked to find El Catalan closed.

"What happened next door?" Reggie demanded of the hotel desk clerk.

"Eet has been closed since three weeks, Señor Percy," he said. "No one has money for dining out. Besides, there are so little food supplies. There was no choice, I think."

"I see," Reggie said. "What happened to the flamenco dancing troupe? Still in this area?"

The clerk shook his head. "Some still remain, but several lady dancers go with Señora Manuela to her home place in the mountains near Seo de Urgel in the north. It is very near border with Andorra. Perhaps they cross into Andorra and maybe to France from there."

"Who went with her?" Ben burst in. "What other dancers?"

The clerk sighed. "I believe Angelica and Carmen and maybe one other dancer. I do not know for certain."

"Did they leave any address?" Ben asked anxiously.

The clerk shook his head.

Ben stumbled outside. He felt sick. Reggie followed.

"Look, old man, there's an end to it. If they get into Andorra, and it's quite likely they can, they'll be okay. And they probably stand a good chance of getting into France from there."

Ben shook his head and shuffled down the street.

That night, he and Reggie sat sullenly in the hotel bar. Reggie knocked back several scotch whiskies. He was incredulous when the bartender produced the bottle.

"We have so few guests, Señor," the man said. "No one requests the whiskey anymore."

Ben drank wine. He felt as depressed as he ever remembered. He surfaced shakily the next morning. He groaned and held his head as he shuffled to the bathroom and peered into the mirror.

"Didn't get drunk on purpose," he muttered. "But I guess I did it anyway." Even Reggie looked worse for the wear.

"No sense in staying around here, Benjamin," Reggie mumbled. "Let's call Lopez and tell him we've been recalled."

"We gonna give up on Manuela and Angelica?" Ben asked.

Reggie sighed and looked at him wearily. "Certainly can't chase them up north. Just have to assume they're okay. Bloody hell! Not the way either of us wanted it to end."

"Yeah," Ben snapped. "Let's get back to Igualada."

Chapter 39

COLLAPSE, SPRING 1939

The new year began darkly. In mid-January, France allowed arms shipments to reach the beleaguered Republicans. But it was too late. Depression hung over the aerodrome like a burial shroud. The I-15 squadrons flew occasional missions, but the I-16s were grounded by lack of spare parts, fuel, and ammunition.

"Benjamin," Reggie said one evening. "It's time. We make our move soon."

"Okay," Ben shrugged.

Two days later, Ben saw Silverman in the briefing room with I-15 pilots clustered around him.

"Sir!" Ben called out. "What's going on?"

"Briefing for an attack on Nationalist positions along the lower Ebro salient. They're about to break through, which'll giv'em a clear shot at Barcelona. Been ordered to delay them."

"Sir, you can't! We don't have enough I-16s to give you any fighter cover!"

"I know." Silverman turned back to his solemn-faced bomber pilots.

Ben ran back to the barracks. Reggie was sprawled on his cot.

"What's up, Benjamin?"

"They've ordered Silverman to attack Nationalist positions along the Ebro salient! We weren't even told!"

"Damn!" Reggie spat. "We can't do anything about it. Don't have more than a handful of operational I-16s. Let's find Golenkinov."

The major slumped behind his desk. "Whaddaya wan', English," he slurred. "Ah, de Americanski too!" He was drunk.

"Yuri Grigorevich!" Reggie shouted. "What the hell is going on? Silverman's group is being ordered out with no fighter cover!"

"Da! Vat you vant me do? I don't got squadron no more. Go look at flight line! I been told fly last airplanes to field near Barcelona Harbor. Mechanics take dem apart and put on ships. Destroy rest. We go home, Comrade Reginald."

Ben had never heard Golenkinov use Reggie's first name.

Engines roared along the flight line. Reggie and Ben ran outside and found Silverman organizing the mass sortie.

"Frank!" Reggie yelled.

"Later, Reg." Silverman strode to his airplane.

The I-15s took off, Silverman in the lead.

"Noooo! They can't do this!" Ben yelled. But they did.

That afternoon, a pitifully small number of I-15s straggled back to the base. Fred Jones stood dumbly among survivors milling around the debriefing room.

"Fred!" Ben called in relief. "You're back! How about Silverman and . . . ?"

"Dunno. We got shredded. Didn't even get close to our targets. Fellas got shot down all around me. Saw Silverman's plane hit. Think he bailed out, not sure. Dunno about Schenk or Rudy."

"Gawdalmighty!" Ben shouted. "Fred, we're the only ones left from our group."

Fred's shoulders heaved. His eyes filled with tears. "Yeah, I know."

"Listen, Fred," Ben said. "Reggie has found a motorcycle. We've got extra gas. We're gonna make a run for the French border very soon. Come with us!"

"You guys deserting? They shoot deserters."

"Fred, if we stay here and are captured, the Nationalists will shoot us anyway. The Russians are bailing out. We need to get out."

They found Reggie packing a kit bag in his room.

"Fred's comin' with us, Reggie!"

"Right-ho! Don't stand there with your thumbs up your bums. Pack up the old kit bags, and let's be on our way. Don't forget your passports and logbooks."

They marched into Golenkinov's office. He snapped upright in his chair. "Wha . . . ?" he muttered. "You go someplace?"

"We've come to say good-bye, Yuri Grigorevich," Reggie said quietly. "It's over here. You know that. You've shifted most of your equipment to the port. And as you said, the rest will be destroyed before you leave. That leaves us in the soup."

"Soup, soup?" Golenkinov snarled. "Why tink of eating at time like dis?"

"No, no, not real soup. I mean we . . . we'll be stuck here and likely taken prisoner. And you know what that means!"

"Da! Fascist bastards first cut off balls, den shoot you!" Golenkinov roared. "So come vid us."

"Thanks, but can't do that, Yuri. There is one thing we'd like, however," Reggie said. "We'd like to take our personnel files. May need them in the next lifetime."

"Take vat you vant," Golenkinov said, waving his arm clumsily toward file cabinets along the far wall. "I got no need for dem now."

Reggie shoved Ben toward the cabinets. "Pull both of our file folders, Ben. And if Fred's is there, pull that one as well."

Ben soon had three folders under his arm.

"Okay, Yuri," Reggie said. "I guess we'll be off. We're heading for France."

"You valk to border, Reginald?"

"We have a motorcycle," Reggie said. "When the French open the border, we'll make a run for it. Wanted you to know. Couldn't leave without saying good-bye."

"Hah! English always do manners," Golenkinov snarled. He rubbed his bloodshot eyes with bulging knuckles. "Hokay! Go! Be careful, English, an' take care of Comrade Benjamin. You both damn good pilots. Maybe we meet somewheres again."

Chapter 40

ESCAPE TO FRANCE

France opened the border six days later. Most of the Russians left Aerodromo Igualada for Barcelona. They loaded their serviceable airplanes on ships for home. Republican Spanish squadrons across the aerodrome also disbanded, and pilots flew their aircraft to fields along the French border. Ground crews joined infantry units for a last stand on the outskirts of Barcelona.

Reggie and Ben clambered onto the motorcycle, and Fred squeezed into the sidecar. They headed north, hoping to reach Port-Vendres on France's Mediterranean coast. From there, they'd try to find a boat.

"And go where?" Ben asked.

"Hopefully, Gibraltar," Reggie said. "From there, I can get some help from Pater, and we'll beat our way home to sunny England!"

They were arrested at the frontier, held overnight in a French border jail, then transferred to a prison in Marseilles. The French were preparing to ship them back to Spain to face desertion charges when the Nationalists overran Barcelona. Catalonia had fallen under Nationalist control. The Republican army no longer existed. French authorities shrugged their collective shoulders. Who would they send the pilots back to?

France and England recognized Generalissimo Francisco Franco's regime in late February, and within a week, the remnants of the Republican government escaped into exile in France. Nationalist forces overran Madrid in late March with a massive infantry assault supported by Condor Legion fighters and bombers that swooped overhead unopposed. Republican defenders suffered terrible casualties until white flags of surrender appeared. The Spanish civil war sputtered to a violent end. Generalissimo Franco entered Madrid in triumph, and a tense peace settled over Spain. But the bloody reprisals were only beginning.

PART 5

FRANCE TO ENGLAND, SPRING 1939

Chapter 41

RELEASED

Police Inspector Henri Louiseau of the Marseilles Sûreté twitched his ragged mustache and scowled at the three men standing before his desk.

"You 'ave now been delivered to me, but I 'ave no reason to keep you," he said sourly. "I cannot send you back to La Espagne, because zer iss no one in official capacity to take charge of you. And ef I jus' push you across ze border, you probably vill be shot. Zat vould not be nice."

He smiled thinly. "You 'ad not so pleasant a time in Espagne, I believe. Ve 'ave watch with much concern ze 'appenings across ze border, and are much disquieted for Generalissimo Franco to come into power. Ze Germans and ze Legion Condor also are cause for concern. I 'ope dis does not forecast a future for France!"

The three pilots shifted uneasily.

"Hitler and Mussolini are pressing Franco to enter ze Axis Pact," Louiseau continued. "Ef zey succeed, France will 'ave potential enemies all along 'er eastern and southern frontiers. Zis vould be very bad. But . . . perhaps it vill not come to zat."

Louiseau shrugged and rubbed his face with both hands. "And now Les Boche 'ave occupied Bohemia and Moravia," he muttered. "I 'ave wery bad feelings . . ."

"I'd like to be able to reassure you, Inspector," Reggie said quietly. "But we were in the thick of it in Spain for years. We saw how Germany and Italy used Spain as a proving ground for their military, especially their air forces. I'm afraid the pessimists are correct. This is only the beginning. There's going to be hell to pay in Europe!"

Louiseau shrugged and pouched out his lips. "*Poff!*" he spat out. "You may be correct."

He reached into his desk drawer. "Your records and passports," he said. "You shall see zey 'ave been properly stamped, indicating you enter France legally." He shrugged again. "One little ting ve can do, I suppose."

"Thank you," Reggie said. "We appreciate your kindness and understanding."

"So! You are free to go. I suggest you return to Angleterre as soon as possible," he said to Reggie. "And you two," he said, looking at Ben and Fred. "Go home to America. Zis is not your problem—not yet anyway."

He gave them a long doleful look. "Au revoir."

They stepped out onto the streets of Marseilles. Tension coursed through the city.

"Out of the cauldron of Spain and into the smoldering fire of Europe," Reggie muttered. "Right! First, we find the nearest post office. We'll cable Pater and ask for help in getting a ship out of Gibraltar."

"Reggie," Ben said. "This fella Pater you been talkin' about. Who's he?"

Reggie stared. "Pater? Pater! Umm, you know, . . . Father."

"Pater is your father?"

"Well, ducky, if he ain't," Reggie said, striking a pose, "that would make me a bastard and me mum a woman of questionable virtue!"

Ben looked more confused than ever.

"*Pater* is Latin for 'father,'" Fred interjected.

"How'd you know that?" Ben demanded.

"My Latin class at college."

There I go again. They must think I'm the world's biggest dummy!

"I say, Benjamin, you never came across the word in a Latin class?" Reggie asked.

Ben whirled on him. "I'm the farm boy from the colonies, remember?" he snapped. "I went to a one-room school for the first eight grades, okay? Went to a small high school in a nearby town, an', an' . . . I didn't even finish that! Left before graduating to join Captain Silverman's group. I guess that's what makes me so dumb!"

"Sorry, Benjamin. Didn't mean to poke fun or embarrass you. You're far from dumb, my friend. And I can't think of anyone I'd rather have flying on my wing! As the Spanish say, *sempre a du lado, amigo mio*! Always by your side, my friend!"

Ben squared his shoulders and smiled.

"Now then, we need some civilian clothes," Reggie announced. "I'm sick of this Spanish uniform! How much money do you lads have?"

Ben had $50 left from the advance Silverman had given them, Fred $65.

"I've a small bundle of sterling," Reggie said. "I should think that's enough to get ourselves rekitted, into a hotel for a night or two, and book passage at least to the big Rock."

A patrolling gendarme saluted as they approached, touching the bill of his cap with his white baton. He eyed their Spanish air force uniforms suspiciously.

"*Papiers*," the gendarme said. "*Votre documentation, si'l vous plait.*"

Reggie handed over their documents, and the gendarme's eyes widened when he saw one British and two American passports.

"*Qu'est-ce que se passé, ici*? (What's going on here?)" he inquired icily.

In heavily accented French, Reggie told the gendarme what they had been doing in Spain. They had just left Inspector Louiseau at the Sûreté, he said, and that their passports were stamped officially for legal entry into France. The gendarme chewed his mustache, grunted, and gave them directions to the post office.

"That's it, gents!" Reggie snapped. "We find a tailor and get some civilian duds!"

An hour and a half later, they emerged from a clothing shop looking like Hollywood movie mobsters in ill-fitting blue serge suits, striped shirts, black neckties, and cheap leather shoes. They stuffed their uniforms into their kit bags.

Reggie dispatched a cable to his pater in England. Ben and Fred bought stationery, envelopes, and stamps. Just before leaving Spain, Ben had received two long-delayed letters via the New York post office box. One was from his mother, the other a scrawled note from Brice.

Gotta answer them tonight. Boy, I'll have a lot more to tell Brice! Better finally explain all this to Mom, but how the hell do I do that without givin' her a heart attack?

They booked two garret rooms at the Hotel de la Gare. Ben and Fred bunked together.

"I'm famished," Reggie said. "Think a large bowl of bouillabaisse will be just the ticket." Seeing Ben didn't know what he was talking about, he hurried on, "You gents like fish chowder, don't you? Marseilles is famous for its bouillabaisse."

Settled in a corner booth of a smoky bistro, the three men sipped raw Algerian red wine. An accordion wailed in the background. Fred stared gloomily into his glass.

"You're rather quiet, Fred," Reggie said. "What's on your mind?"

Fred looked up slowly. "Lot's of things, I guess. I mean, I'm thinkin' about our friends back in Spain . . . about Captain Silverman . . . Art and Brad, Ed and ole Schenk. Wonder if I'll ever see any of those fellas again? Ya know, when I left Chicago an' met Ben and the others, I thought we were off on a big adventure. Gonna do something I could really brag about when I got back home."

He sighed deeply. "Didn't turn out to be all that great . . . I mean, we didn't accomplish a damn thing 'cept gettin' a lot of friends killed!"

"Umm," Reggie mused. "Can't say I entirely disagree with you, Fred. But look, we took a stand, fought for something we believed in . . ."

"I didn't," Fred said quietly. "I didn't know what the hell I was doin' in Spain! I still don't. What was solved by half the damn Spaniards tryin' to kill the other half? Is Spain any better off now than before?"

"Actually, no," Reggie said, "and getting worse as we speak, I should think. But maybe Spain has been a wake-up call. Maybe the rest of the world will draw a lesson from all that went on with the civil war."

"You really believe that?" Fred asked. "I sure as hell don't!"

"You're probably right," Reggie said. "An ugly monster is growling below the surface in Europe. Any lessons learned from Spain soon will be forgotten." He added, "There *is* going to be hell to pay."

"Well, I don't see that anything good came out of the civil war," Fred said stubbornly. "All I saw was a lot of unnecessary destruction an' killin'. An' . . . an' we left a lot of friends behind. Who's gonna tell their families what happened to 'em? Captain Silverman kept all the records. He wrote Buford's family an', I guess, Al Saunders' family too. Who's gonna do it now? Is he even alive? Who's gonna inform *his* family he's missin'?"

"I sent Ted's things and a letter back home to his folks," Ben said quietly. "At least they know. But you're right, Fred, the others won't. I gave a letter to Captain Silverman . . . I, I guess you did too. But I don't know where he kept them."

"Well, I'm sick of the whole goddamn mess!" Fred snarled. "I'm goin' home and try to forget about it!"

"I say, steady on, Fred," Reggie said. "Let's not be rash about this. I'm for getting back to England and joining the Royal Air Force. I have an uneasy feeling they're going to need a lot of pilots."

"I'm with you, Reggie," Ben said evenly. "Got some unfinished business with the Luftwaffe."

"I know, laddie. But remember what I said: keep your wits about you, or our man with the red spinner will have your arse!"

"Ah, this is all bullshit!" Fred snapped. "I'm hearin' the same crap I heard in Spain! I'm goin' home!"

"At least travel to England with us, Fred," Reggie said. "Me old man is a chief maven in the Air Ministry. He'll help Ben and me get into the RAF. And he can help get you on a ship back to America."

Fred muttered, "Okay. I appreciate that."

"What's a mav—?" Ben began to ask, then bit his tongue. Reggie cut him off.

"Pater is deputy for procurement in the British Air Ministry. He handles the purchase of all equipment and airplanes for the RAF."

Ben looked at Fred. "Reggie's father was a pursuit pilot with the Royal Air Corps in the World War. Brice, my—you remember me tellin' you—Brice, my instructor back in Michigan was in the U.S. Army Air Corps, an exchange pilot with Reggie's dad's squadron. He flew as his dad's wingman. An' now here I am Reggie's wingman! Isn't that something?"

"Okay for you, I guess," Fred said gloomily. "An' I suppose you gonna continue flyin' on his wing with the RAF?"

Ben nodded.

"Well, no more of that bullshit for me. I'm goin' home!"

The waiter served the bouillabaisse. They ate in silence.

That night, Ben reread letters from his mother and Brice. Brice described how the old man stormed into Baker's Flying Service about two weeks after Ben left for New York. He was belligerent. He had been drinking.

"Threatened to call the police, sue us all," Brice wrote. "Simpson let him ramble on and then told him to get out. Haven't heard from him since."

Ben wrote several pages to Brice, recounting his last weeks in Spain and his escape to France. He detailed his association with Reggie, the son of Brice's flight leader in the Great War. "What're the chances of that?" he asked. "That'll make the old boy sit up and take notice," he chuckled.

The letter to his mother was a challenge. Did she still have no idea where he was or what he was doing? His letters had been vague.

"Everything's fine," he wrote. "I'm doing a lot of flying, and have met a lot of nice fellas. Also, I'm eating my vegetables," he had added, trying to lighten the tone. He knew it wouldn't work.

Now he told her that the New York job "led to a flying job in Spain." Not an outright lie, but not the full truth either. He'd been doing a lot of flying in Spain, he wrote, but left the impression he was hauling cargo and medical supplies.

"We're through in Spain, Mom, and now headed for England. I expect to get a flying job of some sort there as well." No need to burden her with the added worry of his joining the RAF.

Before sealing the envelope, he slipped a wrinkled ten-dollar bill into the letter. "Here you go, Mom," he said softly. "Hope this helps."

At breakfast the next morning, he asked Reggie what return address he could use in England in case his mother wanted to write him.

"Use my home address, me lad," Reggie said brightly. "Calvert Hall, Romsey Forest, Hants—that's short for Hampshire—England. Ben scribbled it down, asking for spellings along the way.

That morning they prowled the docks along Marseilles Harbor, looking for a ship that would call in at Gibraltar. They found the *Phoenix*, a small freighter of Greek registry, and booked two small cabins on the aft deck. She sailed at 2000 hours.

Chapter 42

GIBRALTAR

The three pilots watched from the railing as tugboats nudged the *Phoenix* into the main Channel. The lights of Marseilles harbor receded into the gloom. Next, Gibraltar; then, England!

At daybreak, the *Phoenix* steamed southeast along Spain's Mediterranean coast. Ben's throat tightened as he thought of Angelica and his lost pilot friends. He shivered as the morning air swirled around him. Fred seemed to be shivering as well. But Ben realized his friend was sobbing.

"Come on, Fred, let's go inside."

"No!" Fred muttered. "I wanna watch this damn country go past. Just make sure it's gone. Won't ever come back here again!"

Ben sighed deeply. "Yeah. It didn't turn out like we had hoped."

He recalled his conversations with Ted on the way to Barcelona more than a year ago. They would get the job done in Spain, visit North Africa on their way home, then look for an airfield to buy. *God, how dumb we were!*

"No sense dwelling on it, lads," Reggie said softly. "We all did a lot of growing up there. Now it's up to us to carry on."

"To hell with your British stiff upper lip!" Fred snapped and strode away.

On their trip to Barcelona from Brooklyn, the *Escobar* had slipped through the Strait of Gibraltar at night and hugged the North African coastline until the ship was well into the Mediterranean. The pilots had seen Gibraltar's lights, including those high atop the Rock.

Now in daylight, the Rock loomed high over the narrow peninsula, this sharp end of Spain that thrust southward like a dagger toward Morocco. As *Phoenix* maneuvered into the harbor, the pilots had a good view of Gibraltar's unique airport. Its single runway cut across the isthmus connecting the northern part of the peninsula to Spain's southern border.

"That runway is built partly on the peninsula and juts out into the bay on that causeway," Reggie said. "The main road into Gibraltar from the Spanish border crosses the runway. There's a traffic signal to stop road traffic when airplanes are using the runway."

The pilots lined up for immigration control, passports in hand. Reggie stepped to the counter first.

"Good morning, sir. Where are you arriving from?" the passport control officer asked, eyeing Reggie and his companions in their ill-fitting Mafia-like costumes.

"Morning," Reggie said. "Arriving from France—Marseilles, actually, stopping over en route to England."

"What was your business in France?" the control officer asked. "And how long were you in that country?"

"Actually we were in France less than a month," Reggie responded, not mentioning that most of the time was spent in a French jail. "You see, I . . . ," then indicating Ben and Fred, "we've been in Spain for the past year or so, flying for the Republican Air Force. We crossed into France when the Republic collapsed. You can see the entry stamp in my passport there."

The control officer riffled through Reggie's passport. "Umm, ah, are these other two gentlemen with you?"

"Yes, we served together as volunteers in the Republican Air Force. These two are Americans."

"Americans?" the control officer asked quickly. He gestured for Ben and Fred to step forward. "Where are you gentlemen from?"

"We, we came from Marseilles with Reggie . . . uh, Left . . . uh, Mr. Percy," Ben stammered.

"I assumed that," the control officer said, giving Ben a skeptical look. "I meant, where are you from in America?"

"Oh, sorry. I lived on a farm in central Michigan, near Flint. Fred here is from Chicago . . . that's in Illinois."

"I'm familiar with Chicago," the control officer said blandly. "You say you flew in the Republican Air Force, as well as, umm, Mr. Percy?"

"Yes, they did," Reggie interjected. "All quite legal. They were sworn in as volunteers, as was I. All quite aboveboard. Their . . . our passports are quite valid, and—"

"I'm certain they are," the control officer interrupted. "I see nothing amiss here. But I am interested in the fact that you two are Americans. Were there just two of you, or did you volunteer with a group?"

"With a group," Fred said. "There were twelve of us—actually, thirteen, with our leader."

"And you, sir?" he asked Reggie. "You served with these gentlemen?"

"I was not part of the group of American pilots who arrived together. Mr. Findlay was a replacement pilot assigned to fly with me. He was my wingman in a Russian pursuit squadron—"

"Russian?"

"Yes, does that present a problem?" Reggie asked archly. "I might point out that Russia was the only country to officially aid the Loyalists. The rest of the world's nations, including ours, I might add, sat back on their collective arses and let the Fascists take control of Spain. I repeat, do you have a problem with our volunteering to help the Russians in their efforts in Spain?"

"No, not at all. But I have to ask you to step out of line . . . over here, please. I must call my supervisor."

"Now see here!" Reggie protested. "Our passports are in perfect order. We crossed legally into France." Not exactly true, but Reggie wasn't about to dwell on that. "We're en route to England. I don't see that there should be any problem!"

"Please, sir, bear with me a moment. There is no problem, but I want you to talk to my supervisor, Captain Sampson."

"Right!" Reggie snapped. "Bring on Sampson!"

Sampson was a tall, spare man with a long face dominated by a bushy red mustache and an aquiline nose that bore a strong resemblance to an eagle's beak. His sandy hair was slicked back, and his impeccably tailored uniform closely fit his thin frame.

"Mr. Percy?" he inquired, raising his right hand in a diffident salute. "Right, would you and your colleagues follow me, please?"

They trooped into a small office in the rear of the terminal.

"Please be seated," Sampson said.

"I say," Reggie began. "I don't see why we're being singled out for special scrutiny. Our papers, our passports, are in—"

Sampson cut him off with a raised hand.

"Kindly allow me to explain," he said evenly. "Your passports indeed appear to be in order. I called you in here because you gentlemen may be able to assist us in another matter. Can you provide us with names of other Americans who served with you in this . . . this Russian squadron in Spain?"

"I suppose we could," Reggie said warily. "Why would you ask?"

"Well, we're currently holding a man who was arrested at a remote location on our coast. He was dressed in ragged civilian clothes and had no papers or passport. He claims to be an American."

"What's his name?" Ben and Fred shouted in unison.

"I'd rather not disclose that until you share with me the names of other Americans you served with in Spain," Sampson said evenly. "If you can give me the names, I'll know whether our, umm, guest has been telling us the truth. So names, please?"

Ben looked at Reggie, who nodded.

"Well, sir, I'm Benjamin Findlay. And this is Fred Jones. But I guess you know that from our passports. Anyway, we were part of a group of twelve American pilots recruited by Captain Silverman, Capt. Frank Silverman. He led us through our training and took us to Spain."

At the mention of Silverman's name, Sampson arched an eyebrow and began writing.

"I see," Sampson said. "And the other names?"

Ben's heart thudded as he recited the names of the ten others. Fred coughed with a strange choking sound.

"I say, very good," Sampson said. "Now I'd like you to accompany me to our holding facility."

He made a brief hushed phone call and signaled them to follow.

Chapter 43

REUNION

Sampson ushered them into a darkened room with a small window giving a view of an adjoining room. Five men stood on a raised platform.

"Silverman! Third man from the left looks like Silverman," Ben gasped.

The thin, bedraggled man's face was marked with barely healed wounds. He held his left arm at a strange angle.

"That's him! Silverman . . . Captain Silverman," Ben shouted. "Third from the left . . . He's alive!"

"Well, I'm damned," Reggie puffed. "Said you saw him go down, Fred. But he survived. Fantastic!"

"You've obviously made an identification," Sampson said quietly. "Third man from the left, you say. He's been insisting he was Frank Silverman. But of course, we had no way of confirming that. The U.S. consul here couldn't confirm, either. Has cabled Washington, but it'll take a week or so to verify his identity."

"Can we see him?" Ben asked.

Sampson ordered a guard to take Silverman to his office.

Silverman stood staring at the three, with no recognition.

"Hullo, Frank," Reggie said heartily. "Fancy meeting you here."

Silverman looked confused. "Who . . . uh, Reg? My god, is that you? And who's this with . . . ?"

Fred jumped forward and grabbed Silverman in a bear hug. "Oh god, am I glad to see you, sir!" he gushed.

"Fred? Is that really you?"

Embarrassed, Fred stepped back, face flushed.

"Hello, Capitan Silverman," Ben said.

"Ben!" Silverman exclaimed. "Gawdalmighty! Wouldn't have recognized you in those outfits. Where'd you get those awful suits?"

"Steady on, Frank," Reggie said. "You're not exactly dressed in the best tradition of Savile Row yourself. Did what we could, don't ya see, with the limited means at our disposal."

"Yeah, well, my means were even more limited," Silverman said, adjusting his rough fisherman's shirt, corduroy pants, and scuffed boots. He grabbed Reggie's hand and gave it a hearty shake.

"Well, now," Sampson said. "It appears we've verified your identity, Captain Silverman. Tell me again how was it that you arrived on our shore without a passport or any identity papers?"

"I was leading a ground attack squadron during the last Ebro River campaign. We were told not to carry any identification on missions . . . in case we were shot down and captured. The Nationalists didn't treat prisoners of war very kindly. Most were tortured and shot."

Sampson recoiled. "Tortured and shot?"

Ben recalled Major Golenkinov's parting words, "Da! First cut off balls and den shoot you!"

"Yes. Fortunately when I bailed out, Loyalist sympathizers picked me up. They smuggled me south to Valencia. There another group took charge. They figured my best chances were to get to Gibraltar, so they put me on a small fishing boat. Slipped down the coast to Gibraltar. They landed me on the beach where your people picked me up."

"And your injuries?" Sampson asked.

"Shrapnel in the face. My airplane took several hits. I bailed out. Wrenched my shoulder when I landed. Not too handy with a parachute. Hit pretty hard and tumbled."

Reggie exhaled. "I say, damned good show, Frank!"

"Yeah," Silverman mumbled. His head drooped, and he swayed.

"Have a seat," Sampson said quickly. "And a glass of water."

"Now then," Reggie said. "What do we have to do to get Captain Silverman released? We're arranging transportation to England. Like to take him with us."

"Let's not be too hasty here," Sampson sniffed. "We'll have to get the American authorities involved if we're to get Captain Silverman a passport. And how are you going to arrange transport to England?"

Reggie hesitated. He didn't relish pulling rank on anyone. "Well, you see, my father happens to be Lord Reginald Montgomery Percy, deputy minister for procurement in the British Air Ministry. I cabled him from Marseilles. I'm certain he has arranged some means of getting us home."

Sampson coughed softly into his hand. "Ah, Lord Percy. I see. Well, that puts a different perspective on things, doesn't it? But Captain Silverman still must have a passport, and that's up to the Americans."

"Yes, yes, of course," Reggie said testily. "I realize that! But he's exhausted and hurting. Need to get him to a doctor. And then get him some solid food and rest. Can't you draw up a release document that'll make him my responsibility?"

"How do we ensure he won't try to leave, Gibraltar?" Sampson said.

"Leave!" Reggie exploded. "How in hell could he leave? He can't slip back across the border into Spain, that's for certain! Neither can we. And how could he get aboard any ship without a passport?"

"Yes, yes, of course," Sampson muttered. "Of course."

"Good! Then give us a letter saying he's in our custody until his new passport comes through. We'll check with the Americans. Meantime, let's get him some decent clothes and a good meal. We'll book him into a hotel with us and find a doctor to check him over."

"Agreed," Sampson said. "My adjutant will do the letter. At what hotel will you be staying?"

"We don't have a booking," Reggie said. "What hotel do you recommend?"

Sampson said the Cannon Hotel.

The Cannon Hotel was a short taxi ride away. It was an old-style hotel near the center of Gibraltar. When the foursome approached the front desk, the manager stared at them suspiciously.

"We must be a strange-lookin' bunch," Ben muttered. "Is he gonna give us rooms?"

"Not a problem, old bean," Reggie said airily.

Ben was right; the manager fixed them with a cold stare. "Can I help you, uh, gentlemen?" he said, arching an eyebrow.

"Quite right," Reggie said. "I'm Reginald Percy. These are my colleagues. You've had a call from Captain Sampson's office booking three rooms in my name."

The manager spent a long moment perusing the reservation list. "Umm, yes, sir," he said, slowly raising his gaze to Reggie. "And these other three gentlemen?"

"Mr. Frank Silverman, Benjamin Findlay, and Fred Jones. They're Americans," Reggie said.

"I see," the manager said slowly. "May I see some identification?"

The manager consulted his list. "And the other gentleman . . . ? Um, Mr. Silverman, is it?"

"Indeed," Reggie said with authority. "Here is a letter concerning Mr. Silverman, ah, from Captain Sampson."

The manager read the letter slowly, eyebrows arching as he glanced up at the men before him. "Is the gentleman, umm, Mr. Silverman, ill?"

"Not exactly," Reggie said, leaning toward the man. "You see, he's just escaped from Spain. He was, actually, all four of us were, combat pilots . . . volunteers in the Republican Air Force. Mr. Silverman was wounded in an aerial combat, parachuted, was rescued by Republican Loyalists, and spirited out of Spain. Had a very difficult trip here to Gibraltar. When the Republic collapsed, the three of us crossed into France and came here by ship."

The manager took a step back.

"Which explains his condition and our appearance," Reggie said, leaning over the desk. "You see, we've all had a bad time of it. Mr. Silverman the worst. So kindly get us into our rooms as quickly as possible. All right?"

Ben puffed a long breath and flopped on his bed. Fred stretched out on his.

"I'm sure glad Reggie took charge down there," Ben said, staring at the ceiling. "I wasn't sure we'd get by that fella at the desk."

"Yeah, Reggie is a take-charge kinda fella," Fred said. "You enjoy flyin' on his wing?"

"He's a swell flight leader!" Ben said quickly. "Kept me alive in the early goings. I learned a lot from him, an' I want to continue flyin' with him in the RAF. I really hope we can stay together."

"So you're gonna go on with this stuff, eh?" Fred said, rolling on his side and looking at Ben. "You didn't get a bellyful in Spain? There isn't even a war goin' on anymore. Spain's over. Why do ya want to stay over here? I've had enough. I'm goin' home."

"Reggie says it isn't over," Ben said hotly. "Spain was only the preliminary. He thinks Germany and Italy are gonna make a lot of trouble in Europe. Look at what they've done already. Italy in Sardinia, and Germany pushing everybody around, reoccupying the Saar, and tellin' the French to take it or leave it.

"They took part of Czechoslovakia and are threatening Poland. England has pledged to support Poland, so Reggie thinks it only a matter of time before there's serious war in Europe. Amazing how this is happening just like Brice said."

"Okay, okay," Fred said impatiently. "Why the hell are you concerned? What business is it of yours? America got involved in the Great War, and what'd we get for it? Not a goddamned thing 'cept a lotta dead and wounded! And what'd it settle? Reggie says they're ready to go at it again? Okay! Then the Great War didn't solve a damn thing! That's why I say it's all bullshit!"

"I don't agree, okay?" Ben said. "Besides, I got a personal reason for stayin' over here."

"You mean, what happened to Ted?" Fred asked quietly.

"Yeah," Ben said through clenched teeth. "I got a score to settle."

"I'd be real careful about that," Fred said.

"Yeah, yeah, that's what Reggie says all the time. I'll be careful. But that's why I'm joinin' the RAF."

The room became quiet, and soon heavy breathing sounded from both beds.

Chapter 44

TAILOR-MADE

Ben bolted upright, startled awake by pounding on the door. He stumbled to the door and flipped the lock.

Reggie strode in, waving his arms. "How can you sleep when we've got business to attend to?" he shouted. "Doctor's seen Frank. Still a bit dehydrated, but otherwise in fairly good condition. Wounds healing nicely. Should be right as rain in a couple of days. Now then, let's get to the general post office and see if there's a cable from Pater. Should have news on a ship home and, thank you very much, a bit of the King's lolly."

"Lolly?" Ben asked.

"Money, me young friend. Cash, scratch, dough, pounds sterling. We'll need it to get us some decent clothes, pay our hotel bill, and book passage home!"

Cables from Pater confirmed passage for three on the freighter *Halifax*. It would arrive in two days from Portsmouth.

"Have to increase that to four. Frank'll be coming with us," Reggie said. He let out a whoop after reading a second cable. "I say! The old boy has been most generous. What you see here, gentlemen, is a sizeable draft on the Bank of Gibraltar! This will get us all outfitted in respectable rags, while we wait for the Halifax to see us home."

Turning to Fred, he said soberly, "Once there, Fred, we'll book passage for you and Frank to America . . . unless you decide to stick with us."

"Thanks, but I'm not gonna stay," Fred muttered. "Don't want to sound ungrateful. You're doin' a lot, helpin' me get outta Spain an' all. I really appreciate it, Reggie. But, but, I hafta go home."

"Right-ho! Your decision. No quarrel with you on that score. We'll work out passage home for you and Frank soon as we get to England. Now let's get to the Bank of Gibraltar and then find us a tailor shop fit for gentlemen of our station!"

They found Winston's of Savile Row near the center of Gibraltar.

"What does Say-Vile Row mean?" Ben asked.

"Special street in London," Reggie said. "In Mayfair. Has a storied history as the tailoring center of London . . . of the world, according to some English clothes snobs. All the best tailors have shops there, where gentlemen such as we will find the best in bespoke tailoring, don'tcha know?"

Ben's mind swirled. At the risk of again sounding like a country bumpkin, he asked what "bespoke tailoring" meant.

Reggie pursed his lips. "When purchasing a Savile Row suit, one begins by selecting the material, you know, from a bolt of cloth. That means the material has been spoken for. Hence the term 'bespoke.'"

"What do ya do with the bespoke material?" Ben asked.

"Well, the tailor measures one, adds whatever special features one wants, and makes final adjustments before sending a pattern to the cutting room. One returns for the first fitting a day or so later and then comes back for whatever additional fittings are needed to get everything just right. We'll be a bit pressed for time, so we'll tell the tailor to get it right after two fittings."

"You mean they're gonna make special suits just for us?" Ben asked. "Why can't we just go in, find a suit we like on the rack, and buy it?"

"Not on, Benjamin old boy," Reggie chortled, waving the cable. "Pater said to get properly outfitted. And tomorrow we'll get Frank up and about and escort him down for a fitting."

Reggie led the charge into Winston's, hailing the manager. "Good day to you, sir!"

The manager, a slightly built man of indeterminate age, eyed their mobster suits with alarm. He took two steps backward. "Umm, can I help you, umm . . . you gentlemen?" He narrowed his eyes, obviously hoping they had just stepped in to ask for directions.

"You can, indeed, my good sir!" Reggie said, striding forward.

The manager slipped behind the counter, eyes widening.

"We've come in for some of your best tailoring," Reggie said affably. "Our temporary garb leaves much to be desired. Don't be put off by these," he added, flapping the wide-notched lapels on his suit jacket. "Bought these in Marseilles under pressing circumstances. Had just slipped out of Spain, don'tcha know."

The manager swallowed twice and looked around nervously. Reggie leaned forward across the counter. The manager fingered his precisely knotted tie. His eyebrows seemed to merge with his carefully coiffed brown hair.

"Now then," Reggie continued, ignoring the man's discomfort. "Shall we start by you showing us some of your best worsted? Something in a charcoal gray, perhaps with a red thread running through it?"

"Umm, the gentleman seems to know precisely what he wants," the manager said, visibly relieved. He began pulling several bolts of fine woolen cloth from the shelves. "Would any of these do?"

Ben sniggered and poked Fred in the ribs.

"I like this one," Reggie said, after inspecting several bolts of cloth. "What looks good to you gents?"

Ben pretended to inspect the cloth bolts and finally pointed to one. Fred spent even less time looking them over and pointed to another one.

"Don't think you're giving this process the serious attention it deserves, gents. But if those are your choices, so be it," Reggie said. Then to the manager, "Seems we've made our selections. Shall we proceed with the measuring?"

The manager called for his chief cutter. A small balding man, peering over half-glasses, approached them brandishing measuring tape and chalk. Reggie shucked his suit coat and stood with legs slightly apart. Ben and Fred did the same. Reggie seemed quite relaxed during the process, but Ben fidgeted as the tailor measured him. Fred flinched and stepped back when the tailor began measuring his inseams and got alarmingly close to his privates.

"If the gentleman would stand still, this would go much more smoothly," the cutter muttered.

The rest of the process required a bewildering series of decisions from Ben and Fred. How the hell did they know what waistband height they wanted, much less pleats or no pleats, shoulder contours, watch pockets, linings, cuffs, and myriad details they'd never considered before?

Finally, the patterns emerged and were sent with the material to the cutting room. The manager reached for his order book and said, "Umm, today is Thursday. Would Tuesday next do for the first fitting?"

"'fraid not," Reggie said. "Bit pressed for time. Have to be getting on home to England. How about late tomorrow afternoon for the first fitting? And tomorrow morning, we'll be bringing another colleague who'll need to be outfitted as well."

"Umm, I'll have to work my cutters and tailors overtime to make that schedule," he said. "I'm afraid that will add to the cost—"

"Kindly do what needs to be done," Reggie interrupted. "Now then, we'll need a few other items, blazers, trousers, shirts, socks, and informal jackets. How about something with a bush-coat cut? Shoes we'll get somewhere else, I expect."

"Why, yessir! Indeed! I think we can see to all your needs," the manager said, rubbing his hands. "Except the shoes, of course. I can direct you to Baxter's just up the street."

The remaining purchases took far less time. Ben noted they were now buying things right off the rack.

They soon had a hefty pile of clothing on the counter. Reggie had added shirts, trousers, socks, and a jacket for Silverman. "He's about my size. These should fit," he said.

As the clothing was being bundled up, Reggie sealed the order with a sizeable down payment. He swept out the door with Ben and Fred in his trail, looking like Sherpa porters clutching large bundles.

"That's how gentlemen shop!" Reggie said.

Purchasing shoes at Baxter's was less of a production, but nevertheless took more time than either Ben or Fred had ever spent buying a pair of shoes.

"Shopping makes me peckish!" Reggie announced. "Let's get back to the hotel and see if Frank can have a spot of lunch with us."

"Not gonna ask him what 'peckish' is," Ben whispered to Fred.

"Think it means hungry."

They knocked on Silverman's door. He was lying on the bed, dressed in pajamas and a dressing gown. A young man rose from a chair at Silverman's bedside.

"Hello, fellas!" Silverman said. "Meet Brian Wilson, deputy consul-general at the consulate here. Has good news. They've issued me a provisional passport. I can get to England with it. They'll issue a regular passport at the embassy in St. James's."

Looking at Ben and Fred, Wilson said, "I understand you two are Americans as well. Are your passports in order?"

They nodded.

"You'll be traveling back to the States with Mr. Silverman?"

"Fred is," Ben said quickly. "I'm gonna to stay in England and join the RAF!"

"The RAF, as in Royal Air Force?"

"Yeah, I got some unfinished business to see to after Spain."

Wilson paused. "I suggest you tread carefully there," he said gravely. "There was quite an uproar in Congress and at the State Department about volunteers fighting for the Republic in Spain. These same people are raising concerns over the deteriorating situation in Europe. There are strong voices demanding the U.S. stay neutral in any ensuing conflict. If war does break out, you can expect an executive order forbidding U.S. citizens from taking part in it."

Fred poked Ben. "I told ya we shouldn't get involved. If there's a war, it won't be ours. You could lose your citizenship!"

"Steady on," Reggie interrupted. "There isn't any European war at the moment, and there hasn't been any executive order about anything. Let's not get ahead of ourselves. If Ben wants to go to England with me and volunteer for the RAF, I don't see why he can't. It'll be the same as our participation in the Spanish civil war. We were volunteers, period! We didn't pledge allegiance to the Republic of Spain, and Ben won't have to pledge allegiance to His Majesty's government to join the RAF as a volunteer."

Wilson gave Reggie a long look. "That may be the case at the moment," he said. "But it could change very quickly if war breaks out."

"Ben can cross that bridge when he comes to it!" Reggie said hotly. "It's your decision, of course, Benjamin . . ."

"I'm goin' to England and volunteer with the RAF," Ben said stubbornly. "But thanks for the warning, Mr. Wilson."

Wilson pursed his lips and left.

Silverman, silent during the exchange, shook his head. "Ben, I'm sorry I ever got you fellows into this mess. I really thought we had a moral obligation to help the

Republic, especially with most of the world so indifferent. The only ones who made a commitment were our Russian friends . . . not that it made any difference in the end."

"This is getting far too heavy, gentlemen!" Reggie announced. "I say, Frank, how about joining us for a spot of lunch? We had a big morning shopping for some decent clothes," he added.

"Great! I need to get out." Silverman wobbled as he headed for the bathroom. "Let me get cleaned up. See you in the lobby in half an hour."

In the Red Fox Pub, they ate a typical English lunch washed down with pints of bitter. Ben noted that Silverman seemed stimulated by getting out.

Silverman gave him a long look. "Ben, are you certain you want to go to England and join the RAF? I know how you feel the burden of Ted's death, but—"

"It's no burden," Ben interrupted. "Ted and I got to be swell friends. It's the way he was killed. If I get the chance, I'm gonna find that German pilot with the red spinner and pay off my debt to Ted."

"Guess I'm the one carrying the burden," Silverman said softly. "Have a lot of letters to write when I get back to New York."

Fred covered his mouth with his napkin, stifling a choking sound. He sat back in the booth and closed his eyes. "All a bunch of bullshit!" he snarled.

The next morning, they headed for Winston's of Savile Row to start the fitting process.

"Mr. Percy, gentlemen, welcome," the manager gushed. "This must be Mr. Silverman. You gentlemen care for a cup of tea while we measure Mr. Silverman?"

As the chief cutter fussed around Silverman, Reggie turned up to the manager. "I say, should know your name."

"Whitford, sir."

"Right you are, Whitford. Good show and all that!"

Whitford of Winston's bowed them to the door, clasping and unclasping his hands, and assuring them that all four suits would be ready for the first fitting, "by late tomorrow afternoon . . . shall we say 4:00 p.m.?"

"Excellent!" Reggie said. Then turning to the others, he said, "What say to a pub lunch and then a quick tour of the Rock?"

Chapter 45

THE ROCK

After lunch, the four pilots piled into an old Austin taxi and set off for a tour of the Rock. As the Austin chugged up the narrow winding road leading to the summit, Reggie read from a tour book, "The Rock is primarily limestone, laced with networks of caves carved by water dissolving the calcite in the limestone. Must make a stop at St. Michael's Cave, just ahead."

The cave proved to be spectacular. The four men gaped at the huge formations of stalagmites, including one weighing many tons that had toppled on its side, and arrays of colorful mineral formations that created a natural cathedral.

"Book says we're to look for Lenora's cave, which archeologists think may lead to an undersea tunnel to Africa," Reggie said. "Ah, here it is! Fantastic! Scientists think that may be the way the Gibraltar apes got here."

As they left the cave and headed for the peak, Fred shouted, "Hey, look! The place is crawlin' with monkeys!"

"Those are the apes I was telling you about," Reggie corrected. "Known as Barbary macaques. Only wild monkey-type animals in Europe."

At the summit, the view was breathtaking. To the north lay the southernmost peninsula of Spain, with the deep blue Atlantic Ocean on the left and the light blue Bay of Gibraltar on the right. The town of Gibraltar nestled at the base of the mountain below.

"Wow! Feels like flying, except we aren't moving," Ben exclaimed, turning to take in the full panoramic view. "Look how close Africa is."

They stopped on the way down to inspect the ruins of a Moorish fortress and gallery tunnels that had been dug through the Rock's limestone to interconnect strategic gun batteries.

"What'll happen to an outpost like this if there's another European war?" Silverman asked. "It's a long way to England. Can it be defended?"

"Good question, Frank," Reggie said as the taxi wheezed back into Gibraltar. "War Ministry has plans, I'm sure. You saw the galleries. A small army group with the right kind of artillery could put up a strong defense."

They had their first fitting at Winston's the next afternoon. Ben asked why he was trying on his suit inside out.

"So they can fit and pin all the seams just right before the final sewing," Reggie said patiently. "They'll have it right side 'round tomorrow."

The suits were right side 'round the next day. Except for a few adjustments, they were ready. Ben felt like the suit was a part of him, an outer skin he had grown up with.

"Who says the clothes don't make the man!" Reggie said expansively; then to Whitford, "Well done, well done!" He slipped him a sizeable tip.

The *Halifax* had arrived in Gibraltar Harbor, and Reggie went to the quayside to verify their reservations.

"Good news!" he exclaimed, returning to the hotel. "The *Halifax* captain has been ordered to expedite unloading and head back to England as soon as possible. We're to be onboard by midnight."

Once under way, they gathered on the ship's fantail and watched Gibraltar's lights slip into the night.

"Watched a lot of interesting places fade into the mist," Ben said quietly.

Chapter 46

ENGLAND, SPRING 1939

Reggie showed Ben their destination on a wardroom wall map. "Portsmouth is here on the southern coast, in the county of Hampshire," he said. "It's one of England's largest ports. 'Ampshire also 'appens to be me 'ome as well," he joked. "Romsey Forest, the family estate, is located, ah, right here, on the way to Salisbury."

The *Halifax* arrived at Portsmouth shortly before midnight. Despite war jitters, the bustling port was ablaze with lights, presenting a contrast of deep shadows and brightly lighted roadways, warehouses, and cargo-handling cranes.

"I say, chaps," Reggie said. "Since it's so late, think we'd best sleep onboard tonight and clear immigration and customs in the morning. I'll give Pater a quick call. Tell him to work out travel arrangements for you, Frank and Fred. Try to get you on the way back to America as soon as possible. Then Ben and I'll get ourselves up to Calvert Hall."

Ben lay on his berth, feeling the slight rocking of the Halifax, and listening to the bustle as the dock crews unloaded her holds.

"Well, here I am in England, almost," he said to the ceiling. "What's next?" He drifted into a dreamless sleep.

At breakfast, Reggie said, "Frank, they've arranged passage for you and Fred on the *Normandie*. All goes well, you should be in New York by Friday next."

Silverman sighed deeply and sat back in his chair. "I'd like to see London again," he said quietly. "A wonderful old city . . . but I really must get back to New York."

"Can't leave soon enough, for me," Fred muttered. "Can't wait to get back to Chicago!"

After clearing immigration the next morning, the four booked into a small hotel near the harbor. They poked around the city of Portsmouth, ate in English pubs, and waited for the *Normandie* to sail. Silverman's passport arrived. He and Fred were cleared to return to America.

As departure approached, Silverman looked intently at Ben and Reggie. "This is good-bye," he said solemnly. "Maybe I should just say, 'so long.' I have a feeling we're going to meet again. We've been through quite a bit since I first met you at Baker Airport . . . Ben, if I'd had any idea, I don't think—"

Ben interrupted. "It won't do any good to dwell on that," he said firmly. "Nobody knew for sure what we'd get into."

Fred grabbed Ben in a bear hug. Ben felt him suppressing sobs.

"Have a good trip back home, Fred," he said, his voice also breaking. "An' stay in touch."

Ben and Reggie stood on the pier as the *Normandie* was nudged into the main Channel. Fred and Silverman stood solemnly at the rail. Both raised their hands in salute.

Ben felt his throat tighten. "This time, I'm on the shore that's disappearing into the mist," he whispered. What now?

Chapter 47

CALVERT HALL

The train to Romsey Forest chugged around Southampton, past Eastleigh and on to Salisbury. A local milk train, it stopped at nearly every station. Ben stared out of the window, noting the small fields, some barely an acre, bounded by stone walls and hedgerows. Back home, anything under twenty acres was a small field. Sadness swept over him at the thought of home. *Wonder how Mom's doin'? Hope she got my letters.*

The conductor announced, "Romsey Forest, next stop."

Ben and Reggie stood, straightened their Gibraltar suits, and checked their reflections in the large window.

"Reckon we'll pass for gentlemen," Reggie chuckled. He leaned out of the window and peered up the tracks. "Mother said she'd send Watkins to meet us," he called back over his shoulder. "Home is only a twenty-minute ride."

The train shuddered to a stop with a screech of brakes and hissing steam. Reggie glanced along the platform. "I say, Watkins!" he called out, raising his hand. "There's a good fellow."

A trim, elderly man in a dark uniform and cap trotted up, raised a gloved hand in a crisp salute, and reached for the duffel bags.

"So good to see you again, sir!" he smiled. "So good . . . Umm, 'ave a pleasant trip, did you, sir?"

"Did indeed, Watkins," Reggie said affably. "Had a spot of trouble getting out of Spain, don'tcha know, but the French were most accommodating. And here we are."

"Watkins, this is Mr. Findlay, Benjamin Findlay," Reggie said. "He was my wingman in Spain. I 'spect you've heard about him."

Watkins dropped the duffel bags, snapped to attention, and gave Ben another crisp salute.

"Oh, indeed, sir!" he said. "We 'eard a great deal about Mr. Findlay, 'im protecting you an' all. Landin' in the field where you'd crashed an' snatching you outta the grasp of the enemy. Fair excitin' it were!"

Ben eyed Reggie. "How'd he know all that?"

"Oh, I write a pretty good letter when I put me hand to it."

"Right this way, sirs," Watkins said. "I've parked the motorcar just there."

When they stepped out of the station, Ben stared. The "motorcar" as Watkins called it was a gleaming black Rolls-Royce Phaeton with an open driver's seat. Ben blinked at what looked like a gold crest on the door. Inside, he sank into the plush upholstery of the rear seat. Freshly cut flowers sprouted from small vases on the sidewalls.

"Ah, Reggie, what's that insignia painted on the driver's door?"

"Insignia . . . ? Oh, you mean the family crest. Lions rampant on a field . . . all sorts of symbolism. Ha! Pater had that added when he was elevated to the peerage. I did tell you he's now formally known as Lord Percy, didn't I?"

Ben blinked. "Lord Percy?" He had heard Reggie say that in Gibraltar. Was his father related to the King? He wasn't sure, but decided not to ask.

"Home, Watkins," Reggie said cheerily. "And damn glad to be able to say that."

"Right you are, sir!" The Rolls-Royce purred away from the station.

Ben pressed his nose to the window. Reggie gave him an amused glance. "The old village of Romsey is quite lovely, isn't it, especially the thatched cottages? We also have some of the finest pubs in all England."

The little houses and the stately old buildings with black cross timbers flooded Ben's senses. The people, he noted, whether on foot or pedaling bicycles, appeared more relaxed than those in Spain. He had a strong urge to raise his hand in a palm-waggling wave as he had seen the King of England do in a newsreel.

"Reggie," he said quietly, "this is one of the most beautiful places in the world!"

"Not that you've seen that much of the world, me lad, but you're right. It is a beautiful place. It'll always be home to me."

Watkins eased the Rolls between imposing gate pillars. A large brass plate on one pillar read "Calvert Hall—Romsey Forest."

"Is this where you live?"

Reggie chuckled. "Aye, 'umble though it be, it's me 'ome."

The Rolls swept up a circular gravel driveway and eased to a stop in front of an imposing granite building that looked like a hotel. Tall stone columns flanked the front entry. A man dressed in a long black coat with tails stood at attention between the columns.

"Umm, who's that?" Ben asked.

"That's Bates, the butler," Reggie replied. "A bit stiff and old-fashioned. He's been the family butler for more than thirty years. Place wouldn't run without him."

Watkins opened the passenger door and stood aside as Bates stepped forward. "Ah, Mr. Reginald. Welcome home, sir. So good to see you again," he said. "M'lady is waiting anxiously inside, sir."

"Hello, Bates. Good to be home. Thanks. How *is* Mum?"

"Not getting around too well because of her hip, sir. But in good spirits, especially now you're home."

"Bates, this is Benjamin Findlay . . . my wingman in Spain," Reggie said. "Bates is like a member of the family, Ben. He's really the one in charge here. Anything you want, just ask Bates."

Ben mumbled, "Hullo, pleased to meet you, sir."

Bates smiled broadly. "'tis an honor to meet you, Mr. Findlay. We've heard a great deal about you."

What did Reggie write about me?

Ben tried not to gawk at the size of the entry hall with its marble floor, dark oak paneling, heavy-timbered ceiling, and huge framed portraits of important-looking people. A straight-backed lady in a full-length blue gown trimmed with lace stood before them. Her beaming face was crowned with silvery-white hair.

She let out a cry of joy, dropped her cane, and wrapped her arms around Reggie's neck, holding him in a fierce hug, tears spilling down her cheeks. "Reggie, Reggie, Reggie," she whispered. "I'm so happy and relieved you're home at last. We were so worried . . ."

"Hullo, Mum," Reggie said, patting her softly on the back. He kissed her cheek. "You needn't have worried. I was very careful, as I promised I'd be."

She held him at arm's length, studying his face. "You look . . . You look older," she said. "You weren't wounded, were you, dear?"

"No, Mum, I'm just tired. We've had a fairly long journey." Reggie turned. "Umm, sorry. Mother, this is Benjamin. Ben, this is my mum . . . Lady Percy. Mum, Ben was my wingman from Spain."

She limped forward and wrapped Ben in a hug. "You're the brave young man who saved Reggie after he crashed," she said. "We can't thank you enough!"

Ben blushed. *Sure enjoyed that hug. She smells like some kinda sweet flowers.*

"That's okay, ma'am," he said. "I was just doin' what a wingman is s'posed to do, covering his lead's a . . . ah, you know, looking after his lead. Reggie would've done the same for me."

"Of course, of course! But that does *not* diminish what you did for Reggie . . . and for us," she said. "Now then, let us not stand here in the draught. Come into the drawing room. We have a nice fire going."

A loud shriek pierced the air from an upper floor. Ben gave Reggie a startled look. Reggie shrugged and raised his hands. "Elizabeth," he said with a wry smile. "My little sister. Just realized I'm home, I 'spect."

A young woman dressed in white hurtled down the stairs, her long auburn hair flowing out like a horse's mane. *"Reggie, Reggie!"* she screamed. *"You're home, you're home! Why didn't someone tell me?"*

She leaped into Reggie's arms, smothering him with kisses.

"Hullo, Peanut," Reggie chuckled, as she leaned back to beam into his face. "How've you been?"

"Don't call me Peanut anymore," she pouted. "I'm nearly thirteen—that makes me almost a grown lady!"

"Almost grown, I'll agree," Reggie said, laughing. "But a lady? Not quite yet, m'love."

She pinched his cheek and then flung her arms around his neck, kissing him again and again.

"Okay, okay," Reggie gasped. "I'm pleased to see you again, Miss Elizabeth."

This taunt earned him another pinch on the cheek. Reggie eased her to her feet.

"Elizabeth," he said. "I'd like to introduce Benjamin Findlay. Ben was my wingman in Spain—"

"Oooh!" Elizabeth squealed and grabbed Ben in a fierce hug. "You're the one who saved Reggie! I'm so pleased to meet you." She gave him a wet kiss on the cheek.

"Pleased to meet you, ma'am, uh, er, miss," Ben stammered. He gave Reggie a bewildered look over Elizabeth's shoulder.

"Not to worry, old bean," Reggie grinned. "'tis the way we reserved English greet all our guests."

Elizabeth slipped out of Ben's arms. "I've never met an American before. What do we call them, Mum, Yankees?"

"Some call them Yanks, dear," Lady Percy said quietly. "But with his permission, we shall call him Ben."

Ben, flustered at being the center of attention, nodded dumbly. Elizabeth stared at him with adoring eyes, making him feel even more uncomfortable.

"Now then, into the drawing room," Lady Percy ordered. "Bates, tea, please."

Bates bowed and backed out of the hallway. "Of course, ma'am. Right away, ma'am."

After tea, Reggie took Ben for a stroll around the grounds to see the gardens and stables.

"Reggie, this is like a palace!" Ben exclaimed. "You said your father is Lord Percy. Does that mean he's royalty? You know, related to the King?"

Reggie chuckled. "No, Ben, his title comes from the peerage system. The King awards titles to individuals who make major contributions to society, industry, and the country. Pater's been a big help in getting the RAF modernized."

They entered the stable yard, and Ben stared at the sleek horses peering over the half doors of their stalls.

"How many horses do you have?" he asked.

Reggie pursed his lips. "'bout a dozen, I should think. We also stable several horses for Pater's friends. I say, Benjamin, do you ride?"

"I rode a lot of workhorses on the farm, and our neighbor owned a real riding horse. But I've never ridden horses like these. Are they all thoroughbreds?"

Reggie nodded, "What say we take a ride tomorrow morning? Grand way to see a good bit of the Calvert Hall estate."

They strolled the grounds for another hour, reminiscing about Spain.

"You know, Ben," Reggie said quietly. "By my count, you had six victories and one probable in Spain. That makes you an ace, and a damn young one at that, but I doubt there's any record of it."

"Yeah, an', uh, well, I guess I'm proud of that. But I feel real bad about all the friends we lost," Ben said. "Sometimes I think maybe Fred is right. What'd we really accomplish except shootin' down some other fellas?"

Ben asked, "But what about your victories? You scored nine kills. Were they ever recorded?"

"Doubt it," Reggie shrugged. "But we know what we did. That's enough for me."

They speculated on getting into the Royal Air Force.

"I 'spect it'll be straightforward, especially for me," Reggie said. "With the war fears spreading as they are, the RAF will need all the pilots they can find. I shouldn't think you'll have any problems, either."

The sun dipped toward the horizon, casting long shadows from the ancient oak trees lining Calvert Hall's grounds. A breeze full of the promise of spring rippled the grass and early blooming flowers.

"Let's head back," Reggie said. "I intend to put me feet up and then bathe before dinner. Normally we'd dress for dinner, but I think it'll be acceptable if we stay in our Gibraltar Savile Row suits."

Ben frowned. *Of course we'll dress for dinner. Sure wouldn't come down in our underdrawers, would we?*

He nearly blurted that out, but caught himself. At dinnertime, Reggie escorted Ben down the curved stairway to Calvert Hall's drawing room. Reggie introduced him to the other guests. When Ben saw the ladies in fancy dresses and the men in tuxedos, he understood "dressing for dinner."

Men gathered around Reggie and Ben, asking about Spain. They muttered noncommittal "indeed!" and "I say!" as Reggie recounted the most memorable missions with Ben flying on his wing. When Reggie gave an embellished account of how Ben "swooped out of the sky and saved my arse after I crashed," one man smiled patronizingly at Ben.

"I saaay, gooood show," he said smoothly. "Didja learn that trick flying out on the American prairie? You know, battlin' Indians and all?" Other men snorted. "Understand large parts of the colonies are still untamed," he added.

"There're still Indians in Michigan, in the northern part," Ben mumbled. "But I dunno about them bein' untamed. There weren't any livin' near our farm."

"Farm, eh?" another chimed in. "How'dja ever get from a Michigan farm to flying in the Spanish civil war? I mean, how didja even know where Spain was?"

Ben wasn't prepared for this type of teasing. "I was recruited by a man named Frank Silverman and—"

"Silverman?" one of Reggie's cousins interrupted. He sucked in his cheeks and gave Ben a condescending look. "I say, have you many Hebrew friends? What was he doing fighting in Spain, and with the Russians yet? The Russians haven't been any kinder to the Jews than the Fascists, have they now?"

"Okay, okay," Reggie interrupted. "Put a sock in it. Find your sport somewhere else. Benjamin is our special guest. See that you treat him as such!"

This elicited several *umphs* as the dinner gong sounded.

Reggie gave Ben an "I'm sorry" look. Ben shrugged and marched into the dining room. He stared at the wooden-beam ceiling, the huge paintings lining the walls, and the enormous table set with gleaming china, crystal, and silverware, and lighted with four large candelabras. He saw multiple knives, forks, and spoons at each place and wondered how he was going to figure out when to use the right ones. Reggie poked him in the ribs.

"Steady on, me lad," he whispered. "Just keep an eye on me. I'll signal which tool to use."

Lady Percy directed Ben to a place across from Reggie and took her seat at the head of the long table. "I cannot tell you how happy I am to welcome Reginald back to our table," she said to the assembled guests. "And also to welcome Mr. Benjamin Findlay, Reginald's friend from America who, by the way, rescued Reginald when his aeroplane crashed."

All raised their glasses and toasted Reggie and Ben. "Hear, hear," several murmured.

Ben squirmed. To his left sat a distant, elderly female relative—distant, because her near-total deafness isolated her from the world around her. Lady Bayswater, one of Reggie's more formidable aunts, sat on his right. Elizabeth sat farther down the table on Reggie's side.

Ben watched apprehensively as servants offered food on large silver platters. He was as uncomfortable as a mouse in a cage surrounded by cats. *Keep your eye on Reggie. Don't do anything dumb!*

Several around the table watched with undisguised amusement as Ben took his cues from Reggie on which utensil to use. Lady Bayswater cast haughty looks down her long sharp nose. Her nostrils flared as though she was testing the air for an unpleasant odor. Ben tried to start a conversation, but with little success. Finally, she turned to him.

"Reginald tells me you live on a, umm, ranch in Middle America," she said.

"No, ma'am," Ben replied. "I'm from Michigan, which some call the Midwest. But we don't have a ranch. Ranches are bigger, an' they're mostly out West, states like Montana, Wyoming, places like that. Also in Texas. They have really big ranches in Texas."

"So I'm given to understand," she sniffed. "Everything, it seems, is large in Texas. Is yours a large farm holding?"

Ben said it was a small family farm.

"Oh, I see . . . Is it remote as they are in Australia . . . far from civilization?"

This woman is beginnin' to piss me off. I've had it with Reggie's stuck-up friends and relatives.

"Oh yes, ma'am," he replied. "We're so far out in the country that by the time ya get to our place, you're on the way back."

Lady Bayswater stiffened and shuddered.

Ben picked up his knife and fork, cut a large chunk of roast beef, put his knife down, and shifted his fork to his right hand. He speared the beef chunk and popped it into his mouth and chewed contentedly. Lady Bayswater's eyes widened as he reached for a slice of bread, folded it neatly in half, and took a huge bite. He then used the folded bread in his left hand to push vegetables onto his fork. Lady Bayswater snatched her napkin to her mouth and made a croaking sound. She didn't speak to Ben for the remainder of dinner.

Reggie also covered his mouth with his napkin and barked a cough to cover the guffaw clawing up his throat. His face reddened as he struggled to suppress the laugh. He gave Ben an enormous wink.

Glancing down the table, Ben saw Elizabeth watching him, wide-eyed. Other guests stared, openmouthed. Ben continued his performance through the rest of the dinner, not daring to look at Reggie. He was greatly relieved when dessert and coffee were finished, and Lady Percy announced that the gentlemen could adjourn to the drawing room for brandy and cigars.

The remainder of the evening passed quickly. The men pressed Reggie for more details of his exploits in Spain, studiously ignoring Ben. One by one, they excused themselves and left Reggie and Ben nursing final brandy nightcaps. A fire snapped in the large fireplace. Ben felt snug in the dark-paneled room.

Reggie, who had been struggling to suppress a smile, finally erupted in laughter. He mopped tears from his eyes, struggling for control.

"I say, Benjamin," he gasped. "One helluva show you put on tonight! Didn't half-give the Lady Bayswater a shock. Wouldn't have missed that for anything!"

"Whadd'ya mean?"

"'So far out in the country that when you get to our place, you're on the way back' . . . ! Hooha! I say, old bean, permission to use that sometime . . . proper credit, of course?"

Ben grinned and nodded.

"And the knife-and-fork bit!" Reggie choked. "Come on, you know how to eat with the back of the fork, as we say. And, and . . ." He chortled again. "The gambit with the folded bread! Brilliant!"

"Yeah, Reggie," Ben grumbled. "Lady Bayswater really pissed me off. Treated me like some kinda, whaddaya call it, barbarian. So I decided to act like one."

He sat up quickly. "Say, Reggie, I hope I haven't caused any trouble. Is she important, being a 'Lady' an' all?"

Reggie gave a dismissive wave. "Not at all, Ben! She's a lady by title only. Put her in her place, you did, and good on you for it. The old girl's filthy rich. Not her money, of course, her late husband's. No children, so when she goes, somebody in the family inherits a packet. That's why everyone tolerates Her Royal Imperiousness and pretends not to notice what a pain in the arse she is."

Reggie snorted, wiped the tears from his eyes, and stood. He raised his glass. "I say, I must apologize for some of the cousins. They're so impressed with themselves they don't half-take pleasure in trying to make others uncomfortable. Bloody pricks!"

Ben shrugged. "Aw, I didn't mind, really. I just wasn't ready for all that kidding. I hope I didn't embarrass you."

"Not in the least, Benjamin. Damn good show. Really!" he said heartily. Now it's off to beddi-bye. Tomorrow we ride. You know the way to your bedroom."

Ben squirmed in his chair. "Ah, Reggie, your cousin, the tall, blond one."

"Brewster. What about him?"

"Well, um, ah, what he said about Captain Silverman. You know, him being one of my Hebrew friends? Why'd he say that?"

"Oh, that's Brewster, narrow-minded, bigoted prick of the first order. Whadd'ya mean?"

"Well, I know Captain Silverman is Jewish, but your cousin called him a Hebrew, like it was some kinda insult."

"Why, yes, Benjamin, that's exactly what he meant it to sound like. Does Silverman being a Jew present a problem?"

"Captain Silverman is someone I respect. Hell, I followed him to Spain, didn't I? He trained me. Probably saved my life. What difference does it make if he's Jewish?"

"Exactly, Ben. That just the point. What difference *does* it make that he's Jewish?"

"None," Ben said quietly.

"Quite, old man. So write off cousin Brewster for the complete ass he is. Sod him! Good night, sweet prince!"

The next morning, Reggie provided him with proper riding clothes. Ben felt ill at ease in his jodhpurs, calf-length riding boots, silk shirt, and black riding coat. He fidgeted with the black riding helmet and crop as he clumped down to the dining room. Reggie was waiting, and they had a quick breakfast. Ben avoided the fried fish Reggie called kipper. After breakfast, they headed for the stables.

They walked the horses along a narrow trail under cathedral-like archways of ancient oak trees. A cool breeze wafted a bouquet of spring scents from the surrounding fields and woodlands. Ben settled back in the saddle and allowed his body to slip into the rhythm of his mount.

"Shall we step up to a canter?" Reggie asked.

Ben nodded, took a tighter grip on the reins, and set his feet firmly in the stirrups. He concentrated on moving with the horse. Their mounts stepped up the pace, and soon they were galloping along the path. Ben relaxed, settled back, and savored the scented breeze. They slowed the horses to a walk and rode in silence for about twenty minutes, enjoying the English countryside.

As they entered the stable yard, a sirenlike scream rent the air. Both horses snorted and jumped.

"Elizabeth," Reggie said, shaking his head. "Apparently has some news to share."

"*Reggie, Reggie!*" Elizabeth shouted as she flew into the stable yard. "Papa's coming home! Papa's coming home! He'll be here tonight and will stay for the weekend!" She bounced up and down on the cobblestones. A delighted grin creased her flushed face. "We haven't seen Papa in such a long time!" she shouted.

That evening, Ben looked every inch a gentleman in one of Reggie's tuxedos. It fit him fairly well. But as he descended the broad staircase, the stiff shirtfront bulged up under his chin. He resembled a penguin imprisoned in a straight jacket.

Lord Percy was waiting for them in the library. He was a formidable figure, tall like Reggie, with broad shoulders, but much stouter. Ben noted the ample belly bulging under his boiled shirtfront.

Lord Percy's thick white hair was combed straight back. But errant tufts sprouted throughout the mane. Bushy white brows bristled over clear blue-gray eyes. An equally bushy white mustache seemed to support his bulbous red nose, flanked by ample cheeks. He stood hunched, head slightly lowered and chin jutting forward. He clasped his hands behind his back. His critics accused him of emulating Winston Churchill's famous stance.

"Hello, father!" Reggie said, stepping forward to shake his hand. "It's good to see you, sir."

"Harrumph!" Lord Percy rumbled. "Good to see you, Reginald!" The elder Percy peered intently into Reggie's eyes. "Survived your Spanish adventure in one piece, I see."

"Yessir, with the help of my friend here," Reggie said. "Father, I'd like you to meet Benjamin Findlay, my wingman in Spain. Ben, my father, Lord Percy."

"Aha!" Lord Percy said. "The lad who snatched Reginald from the jaws of the enemy, eh? Pleased to meet you, young man." He clenched Ben's right hand in a crushing grip. "Very pleased to meet you," he repeated, pumping Ben's arm.

"Ah, I'm, ah, honored to meet you, Lord Percy," Ben stammered. "And, and thank you for helping us get out of France and here to England."

"Not at all! Least I could have done," Lord Percy boomed.

"Umm, Father," Reggie said. "You recall me writing you about the American flyer named Brice? He was an exchange pilot. Flew on your wing."

Lord Percy raised his brows. "Umm . . . Yes, yes. Of course! Brice. Mad as a hatter, but a damn fine flyer. Excellent wingman. Saved the old arse a couple of times."

"Well, as I told you, Brice was Ben's instructor," Reggie said. "Trained him so well, a recruiter for the Republican Air Force swept him off to Spain to do battle with the Fascists. He ended up flying on my wing. Saved my old arse a couple of times, as well."

"By God! Didn't he half!" Lord Percy barked. "Didn't make that connection at first, lad," he said to Ben, crushing his hand in another mighty grip. "Brice, Brice! Bloody hell! Is he still flying? Hasn't come a cropper in a tree or flown into some other immovable object, eh?"

"No, sir," Ben said, grinning. "I last flew with him in '37, just before leaving for Spain. But I've had a couple of letters from him since then. I guess he's okay. He's still instructing."

"Damn fine flyer! Fearless! Had a wild way about him," Lord Percy said. "Hasn't been caught out by some irate husband, I expect. Hah! I could tell you some tales about your friend Brice." He chuckled. "*Umph*! Indeed, indeed. Talk about Brice later. Now then, let's have a whiskey before dinner."

They eased into overstuffed leather chairs.

Lord Percy raised his glass, toasted their health, and sipped his whiskey. "Wonderful to have you back in one piece, Reginald," he said. "Your mother is quite relieved. But before we go in, I'd like to hear some details of your adventure in Spain, especially your evaluation of the Luftwaffe's Me 109 fighter. And, of course, the proficiency of their pilots." He took a healthy swallow of whiskey.

"The Me 109?" Reggie asked. "We were up against the Bf 109. Same airplane?"

"Yes, yes, same airplane," Lord Percy said. "They changed the designation from Bf 109 to Me 109 when Willy Messerschmitt bought the Bayerische Flugzeugwerke Company last summer. Messerschmitt designed the Bf 109. Renamed the company Messerschmitt AG and redesignated the airplane as the Me 109. Bit confusing—bloody Germans still use both designations. Same airplane. Newer version, of course. Bigger engine, increased armament."

Lord Percy sat forward. "Afraid we're going to face Les Boche again soon," he said dourly. "How'd they perform in Spain?"

"Too damned well, I'm afraid," Reggie said. "Tipped the balance and helped Franco win the war." Reggie described how the Condor Legion cycled pilots and airplanes through Spain on a rotating basis. "As you know, we flew the Russian Polikarpov I-16, an open-cockpit fighter, if you believe. Quite a rugged old tub, though. Had its strong points, didn't it, Ben?"

"Yeah! In the right conditions, mainly at low altitude, we could beat the 109," Ben said. "We tried mixing it up with them at altitude when they were escorting bombers, but they beat us more than we beat them. So we used to sneak under the bombers at low altitude and attack by zooming up through the formations. Worked great. Most of the time the bomber pilots didn't see us until we started firing at 'em."

Lord Percy shifted in his chair and reached for the whiskey. "What other machines did you face?"

"The main Condor bomber we saw was the Heinkel He 111," Reggie said. "And as Ben said, they were particularly vulnerable to attacks from below. We also came up against the Junkers Ju 52 bomber and the Ju 87 Stuka dive-bomber. The Stukas were bloody effective if they had good fighter cover. Without it, they were sitting ducks. We'd follow them through their dives and hit them as they pulled up. Gave us a full planform target, and we chopped 'em up."

Ben gave Reggie a broad smile, remembering how he shredded one Stuka into bloody splinters.

"The Germans pulled them from our sector, then brought them back after they thought they'd regained air superiority. We still had a couple of good goes at them, didn't we, Ben?"

"Yeah," Ben responded. "After that one fight, when we downed, what, four or five in one swoop, they withdrew 'em again."

"The Condor Legion fielded advanced variants of the Heinkel He 112 fighter, especially late in the war," Reggie continued. "But we didn't encounter any around Barcelona. They also had several squadrons of Heinkel He 51C biplane attack aircraft in Spain. We were told they were particularly effective, especially with good fighter cover, but we didn't encounter them either."

"What about the Bf 110, or Me 110, whatever the hell the Luftwaffe is calling it now?" Lord Percy asked.

"Bf 110?" Reggie responded. "The twin-engine fighter, right?"

"Yes," his father responded. "Could call it either a heavy fighter or fighter-bomber. The Luftwaffe uses them as bomber escorts."

"We didn't see any in the Barcelona sector," Reggie said. "But they were pretty effective around Madrid. We also didn't encounter the Italian Fiat Cr 32, which was a pretty formidable bi-plane fighter, but it carried only two wing mounted 7.7 mm machine guns. A bit outdated now, but they were damned effective in the early years of the war."

Lady Percy entered the room. "Dinner is served, gentlemen. Shall we go in?"

She offered her arm to Ben, who gave Reggie a startled look. Reggie raised an eyebrow and inclined his head toward the dining room. Ben caught the signal and escorted Lady Percy to her seat. Ben made a point of minding his manners. Under Elizabeth's watchful eye, he got through the meal without incident. Reggie smiled approvingly and winked.

In the drawing room after dinner, Lord Percy plopped into a chair by the fireplace. Reggie poured a round of brandy.

"Quite interested in what you have to say about the Luftwaffe's machines and their pilots," Lord Percy said quietly. "Want you to share your experiences with our intelligence boffins. Can we arrange that?"

"Of course!" Reggie said quickly. "Can give them chapter and verse on what we encountered. I must say, their pilots seemed to be well trained, disciplined, and well equipped. Amazing, since the Versailles Treaty forbade them to develop an air force after the war."

Lord Percy responded with a hearty *"harrumph!"*

"Overall, they were formidable opponents. Fought fairly—" he stopped and looked at Ben, who was staring at the floor. "With one exception that we know of," Reggie added quietly.

"Oh?" Lord Percy rumbled. "And what was that?"

"One German pilot violated the rulebook, if there is such a thing," Reggie said.

"I say, what're you talking about?" Lord Percy demanded.

"This bastard machine-gunned one of our pilots in his parachute!" Ben said hotly. "His 109 has a red spinner and special tail markings. The son of a bitch killed my best friend as he was hanging helpless in his parachute. And I hope to find him some day!"

"Hmm. Bad show, bad show," Lord Percy mused. "Sounds like you're bent on a personal vendetta. Is that wise in combat?"

"No, it isn't!" Reggie interjected. "I've told Ben that many times! Seems the message hasn't sunk in yet."

Ben glanced gloomily into the fire. "Sorry, Reggie," he mumbled. "I got the message. That just slipped out."

"You damn well better have received the message," Reggie snapped. "If we get into the RAF and if, as it bloody well seems inevitable, we go to war with the Germans, you won't last long if you're always thinking about that damn Kraut with the red spinner!"

"Didn't mean to stir things up," Lord Percy said. "Let's get on with your assessment of the Luftwaffe."

Reggie and Ben spent the next hour sharing impressions of the Condor Legion, detailing the Luftwaffe aircraft they faced, pilot proficiency, and tactics.

"Werner Molders was their leading ace in Spain," Reggie said. "What little information the Republican intelligence people could garner pointed to him as the originator of the Rotte-and-Schwarm formation their pursuit squadrons used."

"Rotte and Schwarm?" Lord Percy cut in. "You mean using two airplane units, lead and wingman, as the basic formation, or Rotte, and then joining two Rottes into a Schwarm, or a four-machine attacking unit?"

"Exactly," Reggie said. "You're familiar with these?"

"Should be," Lord Percy huffed. "The Huns used the same pursuit formations in 1914-18. We picked up on it late in the war and used it effectively. Then some fools in the reorganized Royal Air Force, who didn't know the first damn thing about aerial combat, dreamed up the so-called fighting-area attack formation. Strung everybody out line abreast. Expected the pilots to peel off one at a time and dive in for the attack!"

Lord Percy snorted into his brandy. "You know, 'tallyho and in we go!' Bloody nonsense! Won't work in actual combat, of course. S'pose we'll have to learn that the hard way if we go up against the Hun again, as seems likely."

"We also switched to the Rotte and Schwarm in Spain when we saw how well it worked for the Condor Legion," Reggie said. "That's how Ben came to be assigned as my wingman. Worked fine. Gave us the flexibility of launching two-ship patrols or

212

joining the formations into a finger four. Also let us form bigger gaggles for large-scale attacks."

The three men fell silent, swirled their brandies, and watched the fire.

"Good show," Lord Percy said finally. "Our operations chaps will find all this quite interesting. S'pose now you'd like to hear what's happening on the political and diplomatic fronts."

"Quite!" Reggie said. "Ah, and we'd also like to hear how quickly Ben and I can get into the RAF."

"Not a problem for you, Reginald. I'll pave the way. Might be a bit more involved for Ben, but the RAF are badly in need of pilots, so it shouldn't be all that difficult for him either."

Reggie paced around the room. "Without sounding too impatient," he said, "I'd like to get started on that process as quickly as possible. I mean, from what I'm hearing, we may be at war again with Germany by summer."

Lord Percy waved a hand and snorted. He gestured for Reggie to refill his brandy glass. "Herr Hitler seems bent on making that happen," he grumbled. "This business in Czechoslovakia, for example! Goddamnit all! If that didn't signal his ultimate purpose, I don't know what would! And the PM pussyfooting 'round with his futile hopes for peace!"

Reggie noted Ben's confused look. "Question, Ben?" he asked.

I'm gonna sound stupid again, but what the hell. "I'm confused," he said. "I mean, what's a 'pm pussyfooting round'?"

Lord Percy regarded him with arched eyebrows.

"Father was speaking of Prime Minister Neville Chamberlain," Reggie said quickly. "He's referred to as the PM."

"And he's a pussyfooter!" Lord Percy interjected. "Not to mention a fool. Haring off to Germany to *reason* with Herr Hitler! Bloody damn nonsense! Then coming home and waving a copy of the Munich agreement as if it meant anything! Tell the wretched Czechs that. And now, it looks like it'll be the Poles next."

Lord Percy angrily mopped his mustache. "And what's the piece of paper he signed with Herr Hitler say?" he nearly shouted. "Our two people pledge never to go to war again. Hah!"

"Won't a move into Poland be the breaking point?" Reggie asked. "I mean, we're committed to go to their aid if the Germans invade, aren't we?"

"Right you are, my boy! We've finally drawn a line in the sand. But it'll mean war. If we'd stood up to the Little Corporal a year or so ago, we might have contained him. Bloody small chance of that now!"

They talked into the night, with Lord Percy reminiscing about his experiences in the Great War and how much he valued Brice as his wingman. As fascinating as it was, Ben felt his eyelids drooping. The late hour and the whiskey, and now the brandy, on top of the wine with dinner, hit him hard.

"Ramblin' on too much," Lord Percy muttered. "'fraid I've worn out our American friend," he added, nodding toward Ben, whose chin had sunk to his chest.

"Sorry," Ben said sheepishly.

"We've had a long day," Reggie said.

Lord Percy drained his glass and handed it to Reggie. He levered himself out of his chair, and grunted and puffed as he stretched and shrugged his shoulders. "Had a bit of a day myself," he said. "I'm off to bed. G'night."

He turned and gazed at Reggie and Ben. "You two make a fine-looking pair," he said. "The RAF will be fortunate to have you. I'll start that process soon as I'm back in London on Monday."

Lord Percy left for London early. Watkins chauffeured him in the Rolls-Royce. A somber mood pervaded Calvert Hall. War loomed.

Chapter 48

JOINING THE ROYAL AIR FORCE

"We're off to Londontown on the early train tomorrow morning," Reggie announced before dinner. "Pater has paved our way into the RAF. We see Wing Commander Watkins-Jones at 1100 hours."

At RAF headquarters, officials reviewed their logbooks and flight experience in Spain and inducted the two pilots immediately. Reggie, enlisting as a British citizen for the duration, was commissioned a flying officer. Ben, a noncitizen volunteer, was assigned the rank of pilot officer. They were rushed through a physical examination and given a thirty-minute mental acuity test.

"Reggie, I can't wait to get back into a cockpit," Ben said.

Instead, they were told it would take at least a week to process their orders, and to return home.

"Now to get our uniforms," Reggie said gamely, trying to boost Ben's spirits. "Moss Bros. in King Street is the place."

"Reggie, are we gonna go through all that bespoke-tailoring bullshit again?" Ben asked plaintively. "I mean, the fitting and inside-out stuff like in Gibraltar?"

"No, me lad," Reggie said. "Moss Bros. have specifications for all uniforms in the King's military. We'll be getting ready-made togs. They'll have us kitted out in no time—rank, insignia, all the trappings."

Ben spent the next several days pacing Calvert Hall like a caged lion, growing increasingly restive under the placid routine of life. Elizabeth, who said Ben looked "so handsome" in his uniform, pursued him doggedly, testing his patience.

Finally, the morning post brought large envelopes addressed to Flying Officer Reginald Percy and Pilot Officer Benjamin Findlay. Bates found Reggie and Ben lingering over a late breakfast on the patio. "Official-looking correspondence for you, sir," he said.

"Here it is, Benjamin," Reggie said quietly. "Our call to active duty and our posting. We're going to RAF Grantham training base, assigned to the Number 12 Service Flying Training School. 'spect we'll get indoctrination there and our pilot evaluation flights. Could be in the Miles Master or the Harvard. Shouldn't think either'll be much of a challenge."

Ben knew nothing about either the Miles Master or the Harvard, but decided not to ask. "Where's RAF Grantham, Reggie?

"North, not far from Nottingham."

"Nottingham!" Ben said. "Isn't that where the sheriff in Robin Hood is from?"

"Right you are, Ben," he chuckled. "Sherwood Forest, where the evil sheriff chased the dashing Robin Hood. It's a bit north of Nottingham."

"How're we gonna get there?"

"Have a '35 MG," Reggie said. "Should do us nicely. Up to London, see a few points of interest along the way, and then onto the A1 and north."

Ben grimaced. Another travel-and-sightseeing adventure loomed. "How about what's important? When do we get back to flying?"

"I say," Reggie said, looking at Ben closely. "What's the matter?"

"Ahh, I dunno. But how much time are we gonna spend with this pilot evaluation stuff? We're experienced combat pilots. All we need is to check out in the Spitfire, and we're ready to do some serious flyin'!"

"In due time, Benjamin," Reggie said. "Let's not go haring off until we go through all the procedures. I mean, what's the hurry?"

"I'll tell you what the hurry is!" Ben snapped. "You heard what your father said about Germany! Reggie, we gotta to be ready!"

"We aren't at war yet," Reggie said.

Ben gave an impatient wave.

"Look," Reggie said quietly, "I hear what you're saying. But we can't rush these things. The system is going to move at its own pace, especially with some of our leaders clinging to the hope there's a last-minute chance of avoiding war!"

Ben was certain this was a vain hope.

"Okay, I'm eager to get going as well," Reggie said. "We'll motor up to London, get on the A1, and hie off directly to RAF Grantham. Umm, speaking of London," Reggie mused, scanning their orders, "we have a week before we report to Grantham. Let's launch for Old Londontown day after tomorrow, spend a few days doing the sights, and then motor on north to Grantham?"

Ben nodded, but didn't look forward to another sightseeing tour.

As Ben and Reggie were preparing to leave, Elizabeth found Ben on the patio outside the library, writing a letter.

"There you are, Benjamin!" she said eagerly. "Am I interrupting anything?"

"No, no," Ben said. "I just finished a letter to my mom. What's on your mind?"

"Well, you see," Elizabeth said, "you've spent a lot of time with Reginald—do you really call him Reggie? But I haven't had a chance to really talk with you about America. I've never met a Yankee. Umm, what do we call you again? Oh yes, a Yank! All right if I call you a Yank? Mum said only *some* people call you Yanks. But whatever, I want to hear all about America, where you lived, what your farm is like, what you eat, and, and just *everything*! Because you see, I've never been—"

Ben raised his hands in surrender. "Hey! Catch your breath. I'll tell you what I can about America. But I haven't seen much of it myself. I know about Michigan, and I've been to Detroit and New York City and New Jersey. But I haven't seen much else."

"You've been to New York City? You visited Manhattan and, and the Empire State Building?" she gushed.

"Well, yeah," Ben said nonchalantly. "I've been all over Manhattan." His sightseeing bus trip with Ted swarmed into his memory.

"New York must be a fantastic place!" Elizabeth said. "Is it bigger than London?"

"Never been to London," Ben said quietly. "But Reggie and I are going there tomorrow for a couple of days, on our way up to RAF Grantham."

Elizabeth's shoulders slumped. She stared at her hands in her lap. "I do wish you didn't have to go away so soon," she mumbled. "I've hardly got to know you. And you're Reggie's best friend!"

"We'll be back for visits," he said.

"Really? Can you come back after your training at . . . where is it again?"

"RAF Grantham," Ben said. "Up north, near Nottingham."

"Do you think there's going to be war again?" Elizabeth asked, catching Ben off guard.

"I dunno. Lots of people, including your father, think so. He says Hitler probably will attack Poland, and England has pledged to protect the Poles . . . But hey, you wanted to talk about America."

"Oh, yes, yes, of course," Elizabeth said. "Tell me about America."

"Haven't seen all that much of it," Ben said. "A huge country. I haven't been out west or to the South, either. Haven't even seen Washington, DC."

"Are there really cowboys and Indians out west, like in the cinema?"

"Well, yeah, but not like in the movies," Ben said. "There're huge ranches in the West and especially in Texas. And there are Indians, but they mainly live on reservations. They don't roam around in tribes like they used to."

"I want to see *all* of America one day!" Elizabeth said.

"Yeah, me too," Ben said. "If, ah . . ." He caught himself. "*When* I get home." He added, "Anyway, I wanna travel all across America, learning what my country is all about."

"Oooh! That's so exciting!" Elizabeth said. "Maybe you could show me all those fascinating places."

Time to change the subject. "But let me tell you about the part of America I do know," he said.

They spent the next hour chatting about Michigan, farming, and the Great Lakes. Elizabeth, totally absorbed, plied Ben with questions.

Just as he was winding down, Reggie strode onto the patio. "Ah, here you are, Benjamin and Elizabeth," he said. "Deep into some fascinating subject?"

"Ben is telling me all about America!" Elizabeth said brightly. "All about his farm and Michigan and the Great Lakes and New York City. Fascinating!"

"Sure," Reggie said patiently. "Look here, Elizabeth, Ben and I have to go over some details about our departure tomorrow. Do you mind?"

Elizabeth looked crestfallen, then smiled. "All right!" she said brightly. "But Ben has promised to visit again soon, right after you finish training at RAF Grantham. You did promise, didn't you, Ben?"

Ben nodded.

"And someday, Ben and I are going to tour all over America and see lots of wonderful sights!"

Reggie raised his eyebrows. Ben shrugged.

"Okay, Elizabeth. That sounds wonderful," Reggie said. "Now I really have to talk to Ben."

Elizabeth planted a big kiss on Ben's cheek. "Okay!" And she skipped away.

"You've made a bit of an impression, old bean," Reggie said.

Ben grimaced and rubbed his cheek. "Yeah, okay. What's up?"

"A change in plans. Pater just telephoned. Wants us to share some of what we learned from fighting the Condor Legion in Spain. Seems the intelligence boffins want to see us in London."

"Intelligence boffins?"

"Quite! Want to pick our brains. Hear what we may be going up against in the near future."

"'Intelligence,' I understand," Ben said. "But what're boffins?"

"Boffins, boffins! You know, ah, oh hell, what would you call them in America? Experts, I suppose, or specialists. I say, dammit all! Pity we don't speak the same bloody language."

"Couldn't agree more," Ben muttered.

"Anyway," Reggie continued, "we're to report to the Air Ministry by 1700 hours."

Dinner at Calvert Hall was a small somber affair that evening. Lady Percy tried to keep the conversation flowing, but it was difficult, with only four of them seated at one end of the big table. The meal passed with long silences. Elizabeth ate sparingly; her sad eyes lingered on Ben.

Reggie and Ben agreed to forgo brandy in the library. They bid his dispirited family good-bye, saying they'd be leaving in the morning following an early breakfast.

"Shall I be driving you up to London?" Watkins asked as Reggie and Ben came down the stairway the next morning.

"Ah, thanks, Watkins," Reggie said. "We'll take the MG. After a couple of days in London, we'll motor on up to RAF Grantham. Just collect our bags and pull the MG around front. We'll launch right after breakfast."

"Yes, sir!' Watkins said, cap in hand and touching his forelock.

Chapter 49

LONDON, LATE SPRING 1939

The drive north through Hampshire was exhilarating, the English countryside lush and green in brilliant sunshine. Towering cotton-ball clouds floated overhead. The breeze wafted scents of blossoming trees and wildflowers through the open car. Ben felt strange sitting on the left side, especially during turns when he thought Reggie was heading for the wrong lane.

"Almost like flying the old pot-bellied Polikarpov, eh?" Reggie said over the steady hum of the MG's engine.

They pressed on to Farnham and stopped at the Rope and Anchor Pub.

"Recommend a gourmet pub lunch," Reggie announced. "Scotch egg and top it off with a steak-and-kidney pud."

"Umm, what's a Scotch egg?" Ben asked warily.

"Hard-boiled egg wrapped in a layer of minced meat and breadcrumbs, and then deep fried," Reggie said. "You eat them cold."

"And steak-and-kidney pud, what's that?"

"Steak-and-kidney pudding, me lad. One of the most delicious things ever to emerge from an English kitchen."

Ben savored the Scotch egg. When the steak-and-kidney pudding arrived, he sniffed his plate with growing alarm. "Never had anything like this before," he said, swallowing a small bite. *And hope I never do again. Tastes terrible!*

The drive into London went quickly, and they arrived at the Air Ministry with time to spare.

"Remember how we briefed this," Reggie whispered to Ben as an immaculately uniformed sergeant led them upstairs and quickstepped along a long marble-floored hallway. "When we're ushered inside, high-step smartly up to the presiding officer. We'll report to Air Vice-Marshal Sir Anthony Whitney-Jones. Come to attention and salute. Hold the salute while I report in and the air marshal acknowledges us. Remain at attention 'til he puts us at ease."

"What'll I say to an air vice-marshal?" Ben hissed. "Hope I don't piss my pants!"

At the command of "Come!" they entered the room and found themselves facing seven senior RAF officers seated at a long table. At one end sat Lord Percy. Like a pair of toy soldiers, they quickstepped forward and snapped to attention. They held their salutes as Reggie reported, "As directed," to the officer in the center, Air Vice-Marshal Sir Anthony Whitney-Jones.

"Right," Sir Anthony said. He brought his hand to his brow in a diffident return salute. "Stand at ease, gentlemen."

The two young officers slapped their hands behind their backs but continued to stand rigidly. Ben felt his knees shaking as he chanced his first look at the air vice-marshal. He stared at his long, impassive face topped with silver-flecked hair that was brushed back. Dark eyebrows accentuated unblinking gray eyes. The only softening touch was a thin dark mustache at the base of his long aquiline nose.

"So you're our Spanish civil war veterans." A statement, not a question. "Come to tell us about your experience with the Luftwaffe, have you?"

"Yessir!" Ben and Reggie responded in unison.

"Neither of you looks old enough! But that's the way war works, I suppose," Sir Anthony said. His jaw barely moved when he spoke. "And you, you've come all the way from America to join this show," he said to Ben. "I expect there's a story there."

"Umm, yessir, I've come to . . . umm, I mean, yessir," Ben mumbled.

"We met in Spain, sir," Reggie said quickly. "Ben—ah, Pilot Officer Findlay—was my wingman. We flew the Polikarpov I-16 with a Russian squadron and—"

"Know all about your record, thank you, Flying Officer Percy. We'd like now to hear your impressions of the Luftwaffe pilots you met in the Condor Legion, their machines, and their tactics."

Sir Anthony introduced the six other officers. When he came to Lord Percy, he said with a thin smile, "And I think you know this gentleman. Now be seated, gentlemen. Let's make this a relaxed and informal exchange of information."

Ben fumbled for his chair. *Relaxed? How do I relax facing a bunch of generals? God, don't let me fall offa my chair!*

"Flying Officer Percy," Sir Anthony said. "Start with some general impressions."

Ben sat amazed as Reggie calmly recounted their experiences in Spain, emphasizing their respect for the skill of the Condor Legion pilots and especially the capabilities of the Bf 109 fighter.

"We matched the early models of the 109 with our Polikarpov I-16s, "Reggie said. "But in the latter stages of the war, the Luftwaffe brought in newer variants of their fighter. Put us at a distinct disadvantage. And I should think they've since developed even more advanced models."

Sir Anthony grunted. Reggie pressed on, describing tactics and formations and other aircraft they faced, such as the Heinkel He 111 and Junkers Ju 52 bombers and the Ju 87 Stuka dive-bomber. He told how effectively they attacked the He 111s by swooping in at low altitude and slicing up through the formations, and how vulnerable the Ju 87 Stukas were without strong fighter escorts.

An hour into the session, Sir Anthony turned to Ben. "Pilot Officer Findlay," he said, "what are your general impressions of combat with the Condor Legion?"

Ben stiffened. "Well, . . . umm, well, sir, ah, I started flying at an airport near our farm in Michigan. And, umm, I got to be a pretty good pilot. And, umm, then I was recruited and ended up in Spain flying with the Republicans, and—"

"Yes, yes," Sir Anthony said impatiently. "But you had minimal training before you went against experienced German pilots flying the Bf 109. I understand most of your fellow pilots were shot down, killed, or captured. Tell us how it is you survived."

Ben shot a look at Reggie. "Sir, umm, good training, great instructors, and then I was lucky to be assigned to fly on the wing of Flying Officer Percy," Ben said. "He kept me alive until I learned how air combat works."

Reggie stirred uneasily.

"I see," Sir Anthony said. "So you think the secret to your success, if not your survival, was being assigned to fly with a highly experienced leader?"

"Oh, yessir! No question!" Ben responded.

"Hmm, and the German pilots you faced?"

"Most were good flyers, pretty tough fighters," Ben said. "And most of them, except for one that I know of, fought fairly."

"Except for one?" Sir Anthony asked.

"Yessir, this one bast—umm, this one German pilot shot down my best friend and then, ah, and then strafed him in his parachute. He has a red spinner on his—"

All seven officers stiffened. Sir Anthony's eyebrows shot up. "He shot your friend in his parachute?"

"Yessir! But we're gonna find—"

Reggie laid a restraining hand on Ben's arm. "Sir, this is a highly emotional issue with Pilot Officer Findlay," Reggie said quietly. "I must say, however, that this was the only instance of this kind of behavior I heard of in the nearly three years I flew against the Condor Legion. I feel certain this is not acceptable practice in the Luftwaffe."

"I should hope not!" Sir Anthony said. "Killing the enemy is what we're forced to do in war, but killing a man who is helpless is a criminal act!"

"Sir, I think this was aberrant behavior by a rogue pilot." Reggie gave Ben a hard look. "I'd like to move on to the question of armament, if we may."

Sir Anthony nodded. Reggie then described the placement of the four 7.62 mm machine guns, two in the I-16's wing leading edge and two nose mounted guns firing through the propeller. "The gunsight was rudimentary, so we had to compensate by maneuvering to close range before firing," he added.

"The Bf 109s we faced were B and C variants," Reggie said. "They had a 20 mm cannon that fired through the propeller hub, and two 7.9 mm machine guns mounted in the engine cowling. It made for a formidable concentration of fire."

"Ah yes," Sir Anthony interjected. "We've had considerable discussion about aircraft armament. On both the Hurricane and Spitfire, one of which you gentlemen no doubt will fly, we decided on eight wing-mounted .303-inch Browning machine guns. No cannons yet."

"The 20 mm is a very effective aerial weapon," Reggie said. "It has a slower rate of fire, but has a much longer effective range than a machine gun. And a hit anywhere on one's aircraft from one of its high-explosive rounds causes quite a bit of damage."

"Well, now," Sir Anthony said, nearly two hours into the briefing, "this has been most productive, and I thank you both. Is there anything else you'd like to say—any questions for us?"

"Umm, yessir," Reggie said hesitantly. "Pilot Officer Findlay and I are anxious to get into an operational squadron."

"I shouldn't think getting the two of you prepared for squadron service would take much time," Sir Anthony said. Turning to an officer on his left, he asked, "Wing Commander Nicholson, where do these two officers go from here?"

"They've been assigned to No. 12 Service Flying Training School at RAF Grantham, Air Vice-Marshal, for indoctrination and advanced training on the Harvard."

No. 12 was one of the first RAF units to get the Harvard, which the U.S. aircraft company North American originally built as the AT-6 trainer. The AT-6 evolved from North American's earlier BT-9 trainer.

"Advanced training!" Sir Anthony snorted. "Good God, man, these two should be able to handle the Harvard straightaway. Can probably fly circles around most of the instructors at Grantham! Can't we get them on a quick pace to squadron service? It's not as though we're awash in experienced pilots."

"They will be, Air Vice-Marshal," the officer said. "I should judge a fortnight or even less at Grantham will do nicely. Give them an opportunity to brush up on their piloting skills, provide a bit of indoctrination into life in the RAF, tactics . . . that sort of thing."

"*Umph!*" Sir Anthony responded. "Perhaps so. At any rate, I want that process accelerated as much as possible." He frowned at Reggie and Ben. "How does that sound to you, gentlemen?"

"That sounds fine, Air Vice-Marshal," Reggie said.

Ben nodded vigorously.

"Right then! You're dismissed."

In the outer hallway, Reggie blew a puff of relief and arched his back. Ben flicked perspiration from his brow.

"Benjamin, old bean, I think that went rather well," Reggie said, smiling. "Made it worth their while, we did. Now we'll hie ourselves up to Grantham and get on to the Spitfire. But first, we have two days to do a bit of London."

Ben frowned, then smiled resignedly.

Lord Percy caught up with them in the hallway. "Nicely done, my boy," he said, shaking Reggie's hand. He turned to Ben. "And for a farm boy from Michigan, you acquitted yourself quite admirably. Now then, what're your plans?"

"We have a couple of days, Father, and I thought I'd show Ben about Londontown, maybe take in a show," Reggie said. "Don't expect there'll be much diversion at Grantham. I've heard it's a rather sparse place."

"Capital!" Lord Percy said. "Where'll you bunk? There're extra bedrooms in my Ministry flat. You're welcome to stay with me, that is, if it won't cramp your style."

"Won't cramp my style, but I can't speak for Benjamin," Reggie joked. "Bit of a hell-raiser, don'tcha know."

Lord Percy left for his office at the Air Ministry. Ben and Reggie headed for his father's flat in London's Mayfair district.

"Not bad digs." Reggie looked around the drawing room. "Could get accustomed to this style quite easily. Think we can be comfy here for a couple of days, Ben?"

Ben surveyed the large paneled room with its high-timbered ceiling, crystal chandelier, and floor-to-ceiling French windows. He noted the thick Oriental rugs on the parquet flooring and the overstuffed wing chairs by the fireplace. Lord Percy's butler already had poured them a whiskey.

"Yeah, comfy."

"Good, I'm glad it meets your high standards," Reggie joked. "Now then, we'll dine tonight in style at Simpson's in the Strand."

"I dunno what Simpson's is, but it sounds fine," Ben said. "Umm, something other than that steak-and-kidney thing, I hope?"

"Wait 'til you see, Benjamin," Reggie said with a laugh. "We'll find you something edible, I shouldn't wonder."

That evening, Reggie said he'd do the ordering, and the dishes began appearing. Ben worked his way through lobster bisque, a baked oyster plate, and Beef Wellington, a succulent cut of beef encased in pastry and garnished with roasted vegetables and potatoes. They started the meal with a chilled white burgundy and washed down the beef with a robust pinot noir.

Relaxed over coffee and brandy, Ben regarded Reggie. "A thought keeps runnin' through my mind," he said.

"What's that, old bean?"

"Like, how the hell did I get from the farm in Michigan to London and with all those strange places and experiences in between? I can't believe I'm here!"

"Right you are, laddie," Reggie replied. "And you've grown up a bit in the process. Now I'm going to spend the next two days showing you even more some of the major points of interest in Olde Londontown. You know, Ben, it occurs to me you soon may find yourself into a life-or-death struggle for this beloved land of mine. I'd like to give you a taste of the history, culture, and heritage—you know, what you'll be fighting for."

The next morning, Ben joined Reggie and Lord Percy at breakfast. Lord Percy waved a crumpled copy of *The Times of London*. "Bloody Austrian corporal!" he sputtered. "Who the hell does he think he is, demanding the reunification of Danzig with the goddamned fatherland? Is there no end to this madman's audacity? Mark my words, he'll make a move on Poland next, and then the fat's in the fire!"

"Couldn't agree with you more, Father," Reggie said. "That's why Ben and I are anxious to get up to Grantham and get on with our indoctrination and flight evaluations. I've a feeling we're going to be needed in an operational squadron before long."

Lord Percy harrumphed and tossed the paper aside.

"S'pose your right. Best get to it," he grumbled. "Help yourself to breakfast. I need to be on the way. Another busy day at the ministry. Reginald, tell my driver I'll be down in five minutes. What are the two of you up for today?"

"Giving Benjamin a quick historical tour of London," Reggie said. "Show him what he might soon be fighting for."

Lord Percy gave them a thoughtful look, nodded approval, and strode out of the room.

Reggie spread out a map of London. "Don't mean to belabor the point, Ben, but I want to show you what puts the 'Great' in Great Britain. Let's start with Parliament. We can trace its history back to 1066, when William of Normandy brought the feudal system to these shores. Under Edward II, parliament was organized with two houses, the House of Lords and the House of Commons."

Ben squirmed.

"Point is, in the Year of Our Lord 1939, in the reign of George VI, we face yet another threat to our basic democratic institution. We've the second-oldest parliament in the world. Only Iceland's is older, dating from 930. Ours has served its people nobly for 873 years. We're not about to give that up. Right-ho! Only have time for a quick whip-round, so we'll take the MG."

They wound through the narrow streets of Mayfair, swung past Marble Arch, Hyde Park, and Speaker's Corner, and on to Buckingham Palace. "That's where the King and family hang their hats," Reggie shouted. Ben remembered seeing newsreel films of the royal family waving from the balcony. "We'll see the changing of the guard here and at the horse guards tomorrow." Reggie said.

He reversed course and headed up the Mall to St. James's Palace. "There's the American Embassy," he said. "Let's whip down Horse Guards Road to Westminster Abbey and Parliament."

Ben felt small and humbled as he gaped openmouthed at Westminster's high vaulted ceiling and its long sanctuary. They walked across the street to the House of Commons and sat in the visitor's gallery.

"It's the PM's question time," Reggie whispered. "Think you'll be interested in how the debate works."

Ben recognized Prime Minister Neville Chamberlain, a tall, thin figure who stood slightly stoop-shouldered in a long, black morning coat. His starched wing collar and thin tie reminded Ben of the wedding picture of his grandfather standing stiffly next to Ben's grandmother. Chamberlain's thinning hair was combed straight back. He looked haggard. His mustache drooped under his prominent beaklike nose. He rose from his front row seat, stepped to a table in front of him, and rested his hands on a battered black box. He spoke in a thin, reedy voice.

"That's Winston Churchill seated in the front row to the PM's right," Reggie whispered. "He's been taking Chamberlain to task over his attempts to pacify Hitler."

Ben jumped when Churchill and others loudly interrupted Chamberlain with cries of "Shame!" and stamped their feet in unison.

"Democracy in action," Reggie chuckled. "Debate in Commons is open and freewheeling. All quite healthy."

As the debate droned on, they slipped out, had a quick look at the ornate, gilded House of Lords Chamber, and stepped outside. Big Ben in the Parliament tower toned eleven times.

"I'll show you No. 10 Downing Street, the PM's office and residence," Reggie said.

Ben stared. "There's no fence or barrier. Is there only one policeman guarding this place?"

"We're a civilized nation, lad," Reggie said. "Now then into the MG. Westminster Bridge over the Thames and cut across Southwark to Tower Bridge and the Tower of London."

As they approached Tower Bridge, Ben said, "This is London Bridge, right?"

"Nay, lad, many make that mistake." Reggie pointed left up the Thames to the next bridge. "That air be London Bridge, matey. This 'ere be Tower Bridge."

"This is more like a walled-in town than a tower," Ben said, gazing at the Tower of London.

"Its formal name is His Majesty's Royal Palace and Fortress," Reggie said. "Built around 1078-80 as a fortress, his royal palace, and a prison. Lots of heads lopped off here."

"Your ancestors were a bloodthirsty bunch," Ben observed.

"Right," Reggie said. "They didn't shrink from dealing severely with their enemies, and neither do we today." Ben began to understand what Reggie was doing with this whirlwind tour of London.

In addition to a large armory and treasury, the Tower housed the Royal Mint and observatory, Reggie said. "Crown Jewels been kept here for centuries."

Ben surveyed glass cases filled with dazzling arrays of jewels, pins, broaches, gold chains, and crowns. "What's all this stuff worth?" he exclaimed.

"An incalculable amount of money, Ben, even if one could replace it. This is England's heritage."

Outside, two Yeoman Warders strolled past in their dark-blue-and-red uniforms and crownlike hats.

"Who're they?" Ben asked.

"Yeomen Warders," Reggie said. "Better known as Beefeaters. Retired military, been patrolling the Tower since the 1400s." He added, "We'll lunch at the Hangman's Noose a few blocks away."

"I'm famished," Ben said. "But no more of that steak-and-liver stuff."

"Steak and kidney, Ben, steak and kidney. Can't call yourself a true Hinglishman 'til you've developed a taste for steak-and-kidney pud." Then Reggie announced, "Last stop of the day will be St. Paul's Cathedral. Want you to see it because of what it represents."

Inside the cathedral's main doors, Ben shook his head in weary surrender as Reggie recited a bewildering list of ancient dates.

"I'm making a point here, Ben, so pay attention," Reggie snapped. "St. Paul's has endured fire, sacking by vandals, and the disfavor of kings. But she's still here, an important part of London's persistent history of surviving disasters. That's why the line in our favorite national song 'Rule Britannia' says, 'Britons never, never, never shall be slaves.'"

They returned wearily to Lord Percy's flat. His valet said His Lordship would be attending a working dinner at the ministry. Cook had left a cold supper.

Lord Percy looked haggard and drawn at breakfast the next morning. His drooping eyes and gray complexion gave him the look of a doleful bloodhound. He cleared his throat with a loud *haruump* as Reggie and Ben joined him.

"Don't want to sound like your guardian," Reggie said. "But what time did you get home?"

"In the wee hours. Working dinner turned into a lengthy affair. Too bloody much going on. Japs and Russians bashing each other. Russians also mucking about with Finland. Don't like the looks of that one bit. And Herr Hitler is stepping up the pressure on Danzig. The bloody fool seems determined to push us to the wall!"

Lord Percy slumped, exhausted by his outburst.

"I say, Father, aren't you pushing yourself a bit much?" Reggie asked. "I mean, shouldn't you pace yourself, you know, back off some, take a little time to recharge?"

"Recharge! Recharge!" his father roared. "How the bloody hell can any of us sit back and recharge when that Austrian madman is bent on plunging the world into another war?"

Reggie bowed his head and raised his hands in an apologetic gesture.

"Sorry, Reginald, I shouldn't take it out on you," Lord Percy said. "Old fuse is more than a little short these days. Just don't see how we can avoid going to war again with the Hun. The prospect sickens me!"

Then Lord Percy said, "Tell my driver to have the car ready in ten minutes." He rose slowly from his chair and shuffled out of the room.

Reggie straightened and gestured toward Ben's plate. "Finish your breakfast, laddie. Have a few more stops on the grand tour today. Then up to Grantham tomorrow and back in the cockpit!"

The day passed in a blur. Later, Ben remembered Reggie grimly marching him through the British Museum, the Science Museum in South Kensington, and the National Gallery. They made it to both Changing of the Guard ceremonies, and Ben was impressed by the precision of the exercises. They lunched in a quaint pub on Fleet Street, and Reggie pointed out the offices of London's leading newspapers and Broadcast House, home of the British Broadcasting Corporation.

"We have a free and open press, Ben," Reggie said. "England has some of the best and some of the worst newspapers in the world. Point is, they're free of government censorship. We cherish that, as you do in America."

That afternoon, they toured the Old Bailey, England's Central Criminal Court, located in a sprawling complex of buildings known as the Temple.

"Sorry, Reggie. Not sure I can stuff any more history into my aching brain."

"Of course, of course," Reggie said hastily. "Last stop. Promise."

They spent an hour in the spectators' gallery observing several trials. Reggie noted Ben drooping and guided him to the exit.

As he drove Ben back to Mayfair, Reggie glanced at Ben slumped against the car door.

"Okay, I've given you the fire hose treatment," Reggie said. "Later on, I hope you'll think about what I've shown you. Think we're in for one hell of a time. If you ever sit back and wonder why you got involved, maybe you'll think back to what you've seen these two days and understand."

Despite his last-stop promise, Reggie zoomed past Lord Percy's flat and drove onto Baker Street.

"You a Sherlock Holmes fan?" Reggie stopped in front of a plaque indicating the address 221B Baker Street. "This is where Sir Arthur Conan Doyle said his famous detective lived with Dr. Watson. A lot of people think he was a real person and actually lived here."

Ben nodded wearily, unable to respond further.

That evening, refreshed by a nap, they dined in a small restaurant near the Leicester Square theater district and sat spellbound through a flashy musical review. Ben slept soundly that night. When he awoke in the predawn darkness, images of their whirlwind tour of London paraded through his mind.

Chapter 50

FLYING WITH THE RAF, SUMMER 1939

A thick fog oozing rain hung over London like a sodden burial shroud. It was still dark when Reggie and Ben entered the breakfast room.

"Need to get an early start for Grantham," Reggie said. "It'll be slow going on the A1 north."

Lord Percy joined them as they finished their coffee. "On your way this morning?" he asked. "None too soon, I shouldn't wonder. Can't help but feel we're careening toward war. Need a good many lads like you, I'm bound."

Their good-byes were perfunctory. Reggie clasped his father's hand in a long, firm handshake. Ben shook Lord Percy's hand, and the older man nodded grimly.

It was slow going on the A1. Wind-driven rain lashed the little car, cutting visibility to a minimum. Water leaked around the windshield and side curtains. The MG had no heater to take the chill off the wind whistling around them.

At Grantham Aerodrome, the sergeant on guard duty saluted smartly and asked to see their orders. "Right you are, sirs," he said. "You'll want to report to the adjutant's office. Second turning on the left and third building on the right." He raised the gate and waved them through with a crisp salute.

Ben saw trainer aircraft parked on the flight line. "Hey!" he shouted to Reggie, "They've got BT-9s here. Great! I flew one of these with Brice before leaving for Spain! Checking out in this is gonna be a piece of cake!"

Reggie smiled at his "piece of cake" reference. "Actually, they're Harvards," he said. "Variants of the BT-9's successor, the AT-6. These have retractable undercarriages and bigger engines. Probably handle much like the BT-9."

The sergeant in the adjutant's office snapped to attention. The adjutant was away on special duty, he said, as he escorted them to the No. 12 SFTS commander's office.

They stepped up to Wing Commander Cecil Finchly-Morris's desk, saluted, and reported. The wing commander regarded them with the pinched-face look of a man who had encountered a bad odor or suffered from constipation. He was a small man, standing barely five feet, four or five inches. His round, flat face bore a dour expression, accentuated by a brow wrinkled into a permanent frown. A pencil-thin mustache did nothing to improve his looks. Reggie and Ben waited for him to speak.

"So you are the two aces from the Spanish civil war I've been told to expect," he said in a nasal twang. "The combat-hardened veterans we're supposed to expedite through this bothersome training business as quickly as possible."

Ben stiffened. *Uh-oh. Don't like this fella. Better watch our step.*

"You're correct about our combat experience in Spain, Wing Commander," Reggie said. "I flew fighters with a Russian unit there for nearly three years. Pilot Officer Findlay was my wingman for about half that time. We were based in the Barcelona sector and escaped to France when the Russians withdrew just before the Republic collapsed. We're here to—"

Finchly-Morris interrupted him with a dismissive wave and looked at Ben. "You're the American, I presume?" he said sharply. "How is it you're here?"

"Sir, I started flying at age sixteen at an airport near my farm . . . in Michigan," Ben said hesitantly. "I was recruited to fly for the—"

"Yes, yes!" Finchly-Morris snapped. "That much is in your records. I asked how is it you're here? In the event you didn't understand the question, I meant, why are you here?"

"Why, ah, to fly with the RAF and fight the Germans if there's a war, sir," Ben stammered. "I want to help."

"I see," Finchly-Morris said. "Consider yourself Roger Rudder, out to help steer the free world in its time of need?"

"Ah, umm, no, sir. I mean, I think more people ought to be concerned about what Germany might do in—"

"Indeed!" Finchly-Morris sniffed.

"Wing Commander, if I might put in a word," Reggie said evenly. "We answered what we considered a legitimate call to help the Republican government in Spain and—"

"Help?" Finchly-Morris snapped. "Flying with the Bolshies? Think you could have chosen better colleagues, or should I say, comrades."

"All due respect, Wing Commander," Reggie said. "If by Bolshies you mean the Russians, they were the only ones who came to the aid of the Spanish Republic. Continued their support, at no small sacrifice, until the bitter end."

"Their sacrifice was self-serving," Finchly-Morris snapped. "They were there because Comrade Stalin wanted a Communist regime in Spain. He wasn't driven by any high ideals about Spain's future except under a Russian-style dictatorship. And he wanted to deal a blow to the Fascist regimes in Germany and Italy. When everything began going badly, he had no hesitation about withdrawing his forces and quietly slipping away!"

"Sir, I think there was much more to it than that." Reggie struggled to control his anger. "Granted, we were quite close to the situation and that might have affected our understanding of what was going on. However, the Russian pilots we fought with were highly skilled and dedicated to the task at hand."

Finchly-Morris snorted. "Not a matter for further discussion," he said. "The task I've been given is to get you, and many other pilots, qualified for operational squadrons. We'll set about that tomorrow at 0700 hours. See Sergeant Benchly for details. Dismissed!"

The two pilots saluted, turned, and stepped out of his office. Ben confronted Reggie. "What was that all about? As Brice would say, that fella's got a big angry bug up his ass!"

"Ben, Finchly-Morris is his own bug up his ass!" Reggie snapped. "He's obviously barely qualified to command even a training unit, much less to be trusted with any operational assignment. He's frustrated, watching combat pilot candidates pass through this dreary place and on to frontline fighter units, while he rots here. Sod him! Our challenge is to get into Harvards, qualify, and get the hell out of here!"

Reggie and Ben were nonplussed when they were assigned to an indoctrination class taught by a nonpilot flight lieutenant. He began with a recitation on the history of the Royal Air Force, its customs, and courtesies. This was followed on subsequent days by a basic course in aeronautics and an introduction to the Harvard trainer and its flight characteristics. By the end of the first week, Ben was frothing.

"Goddamnit, Reggie!" he exploded. "They're treating us like dummies who've never seen an airplane. I'm about to bust a gut! We're combat veterans! Don't they care?"

"Right you are, Benjamin! Finchly-Morris is a complete ass! Hate to use Pater's rank, but we have to get this moron out of our way!"

The next morning they stood at attention in front of Finchly-Morris's desk.

"Seems you two have some high-level connections," the wing commander said with a sour expression. "I've just received a telephone call telling me to get you into Harvards without delay. I'm to get you qualified, moved up to the Spitfire and on to an operational squadron. You'll have your first flights tomorrow. Report to the operations center at 0630 hours."

"Sir!" Reggie responded. They saluted, wheeled, and marched out.

Ben's instructor was Sergeant Pilot Wheeler. He deferred to Ben's rank but made it plain he was in charge and that they'd fly by the numbers. As they approached their airplane, Ben felt his pulse quicken. At last, back in the cockpit!

Wheeler led the walk-around inspection. Ben smiled as he moved the aircraft's control surfaces and examined the cowling containing the 600-hp Pratt & Whitney R-1340-AN-1 Wasp radial engine. *Boy, 200 more horsepower than the BT-9. Can't wait to fire you up.*

Ben was struck by how much bigger the Harvard was than the tubby Polikarpov I-16. Its thirty-foot length was slightly longer than the BT-9 he had flown in New Jersey. Its wingspan was forty-two feet, and its empty weight 4,158 pounds.

Ben strapped into the front cockpit. The combined smells of leather and gas fumes revived a flood of memories. *Wonder what ole Brice is doin'? Wouldn't he like to see me now!*

Wheeler strapped into the rear seat. With his BT-9 experience, Ben had all the critical airspeeds memorized and was ready to go. "Don't forget the retractable undercarriage," he reminded himself.

The Harvard's radial engine snorted into action. Wheeler keyed the intercom radio and told Ben to taxi into takeoff position.

"I'll let you do the flying, but I'll follow on the controls," he said.

Ben soon had them airborne and over the practice area.

"How do you feel?" his instructor asked.

"Okay," Ben responded.

"Good. Show me some basic maneuvers."

All right! Ben grinned. *Hang on, fella! Hope your seatbelt is tightened.*

Ben racked the airplane into a maximum bank 360-degree turn to the left, crossed an imaginary point in the sky, and rolled into a maximum bank 360-degree turn to the right.

"Christ!" crackled in his headset.

"There's your horizontal figure eight!" Ben grunted. "Now here's the Cuban eight."

Ramming the throttle open, he pushed the Harvard into a dive and then pulled up into a loop. Once over the top, he rolled upright on the downside. He heard "bloody hell!" in his headset and felt the instructor pulling on the control stick. Ben snatched it away from him and bore on. Letting the aircraft accelerate, he pulled into a second loop and again rolled upright on the downside, completing the Cuban eight. He then launched into the full aerobatic routine Brice had drilled into him and completed the routine with three aileron rolls. He leveled the airplane and sat back in the seat, grinning like a half-wit.

"What the bloody hell d'you think you're up to?" his instructor screamed into the intercom.

"You said to show you some basic maneuvers," Ben replied calmly. "Those were pretty basic aerobatics. I can show ya some advanced ones."

"Give me the bloody aeroplane!" the instructor yelled and wrested the control stick away from Ben. "I could wash you out and send you packing!"

"Based on what?" Ben asked innocently. "You wanted me to show you I can handle this airplane, so I did."

Ben heard a chuckle, followed by a loud laugh. "Too bloody true, Yank, you cheeky bugger!" the instructor said. "Truth be told, you caught me unawares. Thought you'd gone totally bonkers. Hah! Nothing I can show you about flying this wee beastie. Take us back to the aerodrome. Think I can certify you as capable of moving up to the Spitfire."

For good measure, Ben threw in an overhead circling approach to the landing.

When Ben entered the barracks, he found Reggie stretched out on his bunk.

"What're you lookin' so smug about?" Ben asked.

"Reckon I passed," Reggie said nonchalantly. "How about you?"

"Reckon I passed too." Ben tried to mimic Reggie's accent.

Ben shared details of his check ride. Reggie barked a loud laugh and admitted he had given his instructor a similarly wild time. Fortunately his instructor also had accepted it in good humor and signed him off as ready for the Spitfire.

Several hours later, they again stood at attention in front of Finchly-Morris's desk. The wing commander's white face twitched with anger. "I've just read your instructors' reports," he snapped. "Seems you both put on quite a show. Not the brightest thing to do. But you've made your point, however crudely."

Finchly-Morris cleared his throat. It sounded like a snarl. "Report to No. 12 Operational Training Unit and start upon the Spitfire."

Chapter 51

THE SPITFIRE

Ben and Reggie met with ten other pilots as they filed into the operations briefing room. A large cutaway drawing of a Supermarine Spitfire hung on the front wall.

"*Attention!*" The pilots jumped from their seats and stood rigidly.

A squadron leader, trailed by two other officers, mounted the stage. "At ease, gentlemen!

I'm Squadron Leader Clarke. I'll be leading you through your transition onto the Spitfire. This will be fast-paced. We haven't time to run you through the full course. So open your pilot's manuals, sit up, and take notice!"

The squadron leader tapped the cutaway drawing of the aircraft with a wooden pointer. "The Spitfire is a straightforward design," he said. "Has no major vices, although it has some idiosyncrasies you need to be aware of."

Clarke pointed out the light alloy monocoque fuselage design, the single-spar wing, the stressed aluminum skin covering, and the fabric-covered control surfaces.

"The Spit was designed by Reginald Mitchell and draws heavily on the earlier Supermarine S-series seaplanes built for the Schneider Trophy competition," Clarke said. "One of those set the world speed record of 407 mph in 1931. But the Spit is a more direct descendant of the Supermarine Type 224. It was spawned by the Type 300-upgraded design on which Mitchell used the elliptical wing that distinguishes the current machine."

A sergeant projected images of the evolving designs on the screen.

"The Spitfire Mark I you'll be flying is powered by the Rolls-Royce Merlin engine. This is a Vee twelve-cylinder, a design that produces 1,030 horsepower," Clarke continued. "The Merlin is what gives the Spit its distinctive sound and its excellent rate of climb and top speed. The Merlin also generates a bloody great torque on takeoff. You'll need full right rudder, and sometimes right aileron, to keep your runway alignment."

Ben scribbled notes in his manual. *Over a thousand horsepower. God almighty, can't imagine that much power!*

"Mitchell wanted to keep the Spit's nose cowl as streamlined as possible, so he located the radiator for the glycol cooling system under the starboard wing," Clarke said. "Two smaller radiators for the oil cooling system are located beneath the port wing, as shown here. The carburetor air intake is under the center fuselage here."

He tapped the cutaway drawing. "This radiator arrangement results in one of those idiosyncrasies I mentioned earlier. When the undercarriage is down, the right leg obstructs the intake on the underwing glycol radiator. The engine's temperature limit of 115 degrees Centigrade can be reached easily during lengthy ground run-ups, or if one stooges about while taxiing. The temperature also can rise early in the takeoff run, until sufficient cooling air reaches the radiator. Keep an eye on the temperature gauge until you get a sense of how to time your ground operations. Minimum engine temperature for takeoff is 60 degrees Centigrade."

Ben underlined the temperature limits in his manual.

"The Mark I Spitfire has a wooden two-blade, fixed-pitch propeller," Clarke continued. "Isn't the best, but still gives the machine good performance. De Havilland are developing a new three-blade, constant-speed propeller that'll be easier to manage and will give us an increase in top speed. And Rolls-Royce also are promising higher-powered versions of the Merlin."

Clarke said the Mark I Spitfire weighed 5,280 pounds, had a low wing loading that gave it good maneuverability. It carried 85 imperial gallons of fuel in two tanks—48 and 37 gallons, respectively—stacked just ahead of the windscreen. Maximum speed was 362 mph in level flight, and maximum diving speed, 450 mph. He listed maximum speeds with undercarriage down and flaps extended, and told the pilots to mark in their manuals the critical takeoff, approach, and landing speeds.

"The Spit's top speed provides a slight edge over the Luftwaffe's frontline Messerschmitt Bf or Me 109 fighter," Clarke said. "The Spit's initial climb rate is 2,500 feet per minute, which translates to about eight minutes from takeoff to 20,000 feet. Combat range is 395 miles, depending on power settings."

Clarke added, "Of particular interest is its high roll rate. This is critically important in combat maneuvering, either while pursuing an enemy fighter or trying to evade one attacking from the rear.

"A bulletproof laminated glass plate is laid over the windscreen, here, and a rearview mirror is mounted at the top of the windscreen frame, here," Clarke tapped the drawing. "But the only way to be certain you're not coming under attack is to keep your head on a swivel. Keep looking around, especially above and behind you!"

He added another cautionary note. "The ailerons are fabric-covered and tend to balloon as speed increases. This makes aileron control heavy during high-speed maneuvering."

Turning back to the Spitfire drawing, Clarke continued.

"Standard armament is eight .303-inch Browning machine guns, four in each wing leading edge, and fed with three hundred rounds of belted ammunition. The debate over how to arm the Spitfire continues. One school maintains 20 mm cannons have superior destructive power with their longer range and explosive projectiles. But initial tests with the cannons have not gone well, so we must make do with the Brownings for the present."

He added, "The eight Brownings were harmonized for maximum shell concentration at four hundred fifty yards, although there is talk about reducing this to two hundred fifty yards. This means you'll have to maneuver considerably closer to your target before you fire. Each gun has only three hundred rounds, so limit your fire to short bursts. The last twenty-five are tracers to warn that you're running low on ammunition."

Tapping his pointer on the Spitfire cockpit, Clarke said, "The reflector gunsight is mounted here. Rule of thumb is, fill your reflector sight with the enemy aircraft, then fire."

Clarke also indicated the main controls and placement of the instruments and switches. The spade grip on the control stick facilitated switching hands while raising and lowering the undercarriage, he added.

"Most of you have flown aeroplanes with brakes controlled by the rudder pedals. The pneumatic braking system on the Spitfire is a bit different," Clarke said. "The lever is mounted behind the space grip. Pull it back for full braking. Pushing either pedal while pulling the brake lever provides differential braking, to facilitate turns during taxi."

Clarke said the Spitfire had limited forward visibility on the ground, with its tail wheel undercarriage and long nose needed to accommodate the Merlin engine. Taxiing required S-turns to give at least a partial forward view. On takeoff, the tail came up quickly, so forward visibility on takeoff and in flight was greatly improved, he added.

"The Spitfire has two flap positions, fully retracted and fully deployed," Clarke continued. "Partial flaps are not available for takeoff. Flaps are used only on landing. After takeoff, the undercarriage is retracted with this lever."

Clarke pointed to the gear lever on the projected view of the right-hand side of the cockpit.

"Activating the lever requires switching hands on the control grip, so watch for pitch changes after takeoff."

Ben nudged Reggie. "After hand cranking the gear on the Polikarpov, this should be a piece of cake," he whispered.

Clarke reviewed the starting procedures and the sequence for engine and systems checks prior to taxi. "Add a propeller check to your cockpit routine, even though the Mark I has a fixed airscrew," he said. "On operational service, you'll be flying a Mark IA variant with a two-position propeller that must be set in fine pitch for takeoff and landing, and coarse for cruise."

He ran quickly through procedures that pilots were to use in preparation for landing, after landing, and prior to engine shutdown.

"Stalling speed is 64 mph in landing configuration and 73 mph with undercarriage and flaps retracted," Clarke added. "On initial approach you should be at 100 mph, and speed over the fence should be around 90 mph with power, and closer to 100 in a power-off glide."

"Doubt we'll have time during scramble takeoffs on intercept missions to refer to checklists," Reggie whispered to Ben. "Better memorize the lot."

Clarke cautioned the pilots to get the feel of the airplane on initial flights before trying advanced maneuvers. "If you want to practice spins, do not start the maneuver below ten thousand feet," he said. "And start your recovery above five thousand feet."

He stepped to the front of the platform and stared at the pilots. "You all have experience in various advanced trainers and lead-in aeroplanes. The Spit is a beautiful flying machine," he said. "Relax and enjoy it. Any questions before we go fly?"

The pilots stirred in their seats. No one raised a hand. All were anxious to get into the cockpit.

"Reggie!" Ben hissed. "I gotta pee! My question is, where's the head?"

Reggie raised his hand.

"Yes, Pilot Officer," Clarke said.

"Squadron Leader, thank you for an excellent briefing. I think we're ready to go fly. But several of us need to spend a penny. Can we work in a visit to the Gents on the way to the flight line?"

This drew a raucous laugh from the pilots and a chuckle from Clarke. "Right you are, you'll have a loo call just before drawing your flight gear. Now if no one has any more pressing needs, you're dismissed!"

As they trooped to the flight line, Ben tugged at the straps on his Mae West flotation vest and fumbled with his leather helmet and goggles, gloves, and oxygen mask. His guts churned—with excitement, not fear, he told himself.

A sergeant pilot led him to his Spitfire, introduced him to his aircraft ground crew, and walked him through the preflight inspection. The Spit was beautiful. Its sleek fuselage and graceful elliptical wings made it appear eager to fly. Ben's eyes widened. *Wow, that engine looks huge! This'll be one helluva big step up from our Polikarpov tubs.*

His escort showed him how to unlatch the small hinged door on the left side of the cockpit to ease entry and exit. Ben settled into the seat, savoring the aromas and snug feeling of the tight cockpit.

"This door has two latched positions, partially open and closed," his escort said. "Lock it partially open on takeoffs and landings. That prevents the hood from sliding shut in the event you prang and need to get out quickly. To bail out whilst airborne, run your elevator trim to full nose down and hold the stick back, jettison the hood with this overhead lever, roll inverted, and let go of the stick after you hit the release on your

Saunders safety harness. The aeroplane will pitch up inverted, and you'll pop free. If you're right-side up, jettison the hood, drop the door, and dive out behind the wing."

"I'll master flyin' this beast first, and then I'll worry about how to bail outta it," Ben said through clenched teeth.

All cockpit checks completed, the sergeant pilot reviewed the engine start and pretakeoff sequence. "Remember, after you've taxied out, to do TMP, fuel, flaps, and radiator," he said. "TMP means trimming tabs set for elevator one notch nose down and rudder to full starboard, mixture full rich, and practice adding prop lever fully forward in fine pitch. For fuel, verify that both fuel cocks are open, and check the contents of the bottom tank. Flaps are to be set at zero, and the radiator shutters fully open."

The sergeant pilot clung to the side of the fuselage as the mighty Merlin engine fired. When the twelve cylinders roared into action, a surge of energy vibrated through the airframe and up Ben's spine. His spirits soared. He completed the final cockpit checks and signaled he was ready to taxi. His escort hopped off the wing with a thumbs-up gesture and shouted "Cheerio!"

"Concentrate, concentrate. Don't mess up," Ben coached himself as he S-turned out onto the grass field, his knees twitching. "Gawdalmighty, that nose is huge!"

"Okay, TMP, fuel, flaps and radiator," he mumbled. "All set. Ready to go."

Getting a green-light clearance from the tower, Ben eased the throttle lever forward to the gate stop at the rated-boost power setting. The Merlin bellowed. Ben pushed on the right rudder pedal to maintain runway alignment as the airplane accelerated, and the tail rose into the flying position. The Spitfire lifted smoothly into the air. Ben switched hands on the stick's spade grip and raised the undercarriage. The airplane accelerated quickly through 140 mph. Ben simulated adjusting the propeller and pulled back on the stick.

"Wow!" he yelled, trembling with excitement. "This is smooth!"

Ben eased the stick back until the airspeed indicator settled at 185 mph, the optimum climb speed, and watched the altimeter rapidly wind up. He leveled off and throttled back to cruise at ten thousand feet, feeling the airplane through his butt as Brice had taught him. "Brice, hey, Brice," he yelled. "What a fantastic flyin' machine! Wish you could see me now!"

Ben banked the airplane through several gentle turns. The Spit responded immediately, eager to please. Emboldened, he racked the airplane into steeper turns, finally winding it through a horizontal figure eight. *Fantastic! Okay, Spit, let's try a loop. Up and over we go!*

After forty-five minutes of increasingly aggressive maneuvering, Ben radioed Grantham tower for clearance to land. He lowered the undercarriage, slid the canopy hood open, and configured the airplane for landing. He rolled into a descending left turn onto final approach, lowered the flaps, and held a steady 100 mph as the airplane slowed and dropped toward the field.

Over the fence, he chopped the throttle and eased back on the stick. The Spitfire flared smoothly, bounced slightly on touchdown, and then rolled across the grass.

Ben S-turned to the flight line and shut down the Merlin engine. He sat, momentarily stunned by the silence, then yawned to clear his ears. "This is gonna be swell!" he exulted.

They flew three, and sometimes four, training sorties a day. Ben often joined Reggie as his wingman as they practiced navigation and formation flying. Gunnery training followed until they were comfortable with firing the eight wing-mounted Browning machine guns.

Ten days after starting their training, Squadron Leader Clarke informed them they all were certified in the Spitfire. "Good luck," he said. "Remember what you've learned here. Your job will be to go out there and kill the enemy, not yourselves."

Again they were summoned to Finchly-Morris's office. "I've had yet another telephone communication concerning you," Finchly-Morris snapped. "Been encouraged to expedite your transfer to Operational Squadron 104, a Spitfire unit based at Duxford Aerodrome. Your instructors tell me you've qualified in the Spitfire, so I'm releasing you."

Ben shivered with excitement.

"Your orders have been prepared," Finchly-Morris added, pushing several sheets of papers across his desk. "You're to report to Duxford forthwith. Dismissed!"

The wing commander neither acknowledged their salutes nor watched as they quickstepped out of his office. Outside, Ben whooped for joy and grabbed Reggie in a bear hug.

"All right, old bean!" Ben mimicked one of Reggie's favorite forms of address. "Let's get our arses south! Uh, is that where Duxford is, south?"

Reggie laughed and punched him on the shoulder. "Right you are! South and east actually, to Cambridge. Duxford's on the outskirts. Can't wait!"

Chapter 52

OPERATIONAL, AUGUST 1939

They quickly packed their gear and sped through Grantham's front gate before Finchly-Morris or anyone else could change their minds. Reggie drove to Cambridge in record time.

Ben scrunched low in his seat and hung on. His emotions swung from exhilaration to abject terror as Reggie whipped the MG over hills and around sharp curves, all the while regaling Ben with details of Cambridge's historical significance. They gulped a quick pub lunch along the way and arrived in Cambridge in late afternoon. Ben girded himself for yet another historical tour of the old city and the university grounds.

But Reggie sped through the city, gesturing and making quick references to points of interest as they flashed past. They entered the village of Duxford and into the Duxford Aerodrome gate at dusk. A ramrod-stiff sergeant checked their papers and gave them directions to the aerodrome commander's office. He waved them through with a crisp salute.

"Should be a lot livelier here than at darkest Grantham," Reggie observed. "We're about to go operational, Ben. You can feel it in the air!"

Ben nodded eagerly. *Flying combat ops in the Spit*! "A beautiful base!" Ben shouted, admiring the ivy-covered brick buildings they passed.

"Dates only to 1918, I believe," Reggie said. "Practically brand-new."

Wing Commander Douglas Archer, station commander at Duxford, read their orders and skimmed their record files. "Umm. Interesting," Archer said. He fixed them in a steady stare. "Stand at ease, gentlemen. So you're the two Spanish civil war veterans I've been hearing about. I think we'll be able to put you to work straight away. Now tell me a bit about yourselves and your experiences in Spain."

Ben studied the wing commander. He appeared to be in his early forties, although his black wavy hair was flecked with gray. A formidable appearance, with chiseled features and a strong chin. His eyes belied a softer inner man. *Reminds me of Brice. Tough but fair. Gonna like flying for him.*

Archer gave Ben a quizzical look. Ben gulped and shifted his gaze above Archer's head. *Hope I wasn't starin' with my mouth open.*

Reggie gave an abbreviated account of their assignment with the Russians in Spain and their assessment of the Luftwaffe pilots they fought.

"And you, Pilot Officer Findlay. You've come a long ways from America to join us. Anything to add?"

Ben hadn't been listening to Reggie's briefing.

"Ah, umm, I mean . . . No, sir," he said. "As Reggie, ah, Flying Officer Percy said, we came up against some pretty tough Luftwaffe pilots. Ah, the Bf 109 is a good fighter. But, but, ah, I think we can match it with the Spitfire."

Archer smiled tightly and turned to Reggie. "Right, Flying Officer Percy," he said. "Sergeant Gardener will escort you to your quarters. I'll see you later in the officers' mess."

Their quarters were spartan but clean, the beds firm but comfortable. Airman Orderly Winthrop greeted them and said he was their batman.

Ben whispered, "What the hell is a batman?"

"Winthrop is a combination butler, personal servant, and errand boy," Reggie said. "You know, a general dogsbody."

"Dogsbody? Don't think I'll ever understand English the way you English speak it," Ben muttered. "Never had a personal servant! Wait'll I tell ole Brice!"

As they entered the officers' mess, a tall, red-haired pilot gestured wildly and called Reggie's name. He charged Reggie and wrestled him in a rough bear hug. "I say, Reggie, you old bastard! What the hell brings you here?" he shouted. "Are you joining this motley bunch?"

"Stitch!" Reggie shouted. "If I'd known they let the likes of you in this outfit, I'd have run the other way!"

Turning to Ben, Reggie said, "Meet Stitch, umm, Flight Leftenant Thomas E. Threadwell, a fellow sufferer from Oxford days. Stitch, meet Benjamin Findlay, my wingman from our Spanish adventure."

"Pleased to meet you, Benjamin," Stitch said, pumping Ben's hand. "Can't imagine you surviving that bunfight flying on this character's wing, much less trailing along with him for another go at it."

Ben mumbled that Reggie had kept him alive in the early days and had taught him everything he knew about combat flying.

Reggie interrupted. "Ben literally saved my arse when I crash-landed my Polikarpov tub in a field behind enemy lines. Landed his crate in the same field, crammed me behind the seat, and flew me 'ome fittin' an' proper."

Stitch pulled on his bright red mustache and regarded Ben closely. "I say, good show, Benjamin," he said. "Sounds as though you two had a bit of excitement along the way. What say we arm ourselves with a pint, and you can tell me some real war stories?"

Stitch listened intently as Reggie told about flying I-16s with the Russians and his assessment of the Condor Legion pilots and the Bf 109.

"If the balloon goes up in the near future, as seems likely, you lads may end up facing some of the same Jerry pilots," Stitch said.

Reggie said that although the endeavor in Spain turned out to be futile, it had been a worthy cause.

"Futile undertaking in Spain!" Stitch said. "Brings to mind the story of the errant knight Don Quixote and his loyal companion Sancho, gallantly tilting at windmills."

He promptly dubbed Reggie as Don Quixote and Ben, Sancho. The nicknames stuck. Ben remembered *Don Quixote* portrayed the Knight of La Mancha and his faithful servant Sancho as misguided but heroic figures.

Stitch and Ben became close friends. Stitch said he read medieval history at Oxford, whatever that meant. Ben admired the lanky, loose-framed man, whose flaming red hair and mustache made him stand out in any crowd. He had a laconic air and appeared relaxed almost to the point of indifference. But after flying a few sorties as his wingman, Ben realized Stitch was a consummate flyer.

Reggie and Ben settled smoothly into the 104 Squadron routine. Their commander, Squadron Leader Hamish P. (Mac) Macintosh, was a no-nonsense Scotsman with a droll sense of humor. Ben never was sure when he was kidding, primarily because he had trouble understanding his accent.

"Everything is wee this and wee that," Ben complained to Reggie. "Half the time I think he's clearing his throat when he's actually sayin' something! I hafta keep asking him to repeat stuff. He must think I'm really dumb."

Macintosh stood five feet, seven inches tall. His thick wavy hair was as black as Stitch's was red. He stood ramrod stiff and walked with a purposeful stride, as if attacking the ground with his feet. His uniform, always immaculate, was in stark contrast to most of the squadron's pilots whose uniforms included turtleneck sweaters, sheepskin vests, and, it seemed, any item of clothing that happened to be lying about.

Other 104 Squadron pilots treated Don Quixote and Sancho as new boys, but respected the fact that they had scored aerial victories, albeit in that "little sideshow" in Spain. Reggie and Ben were quickly drawn into the Mess rugby matches. These usually erupted after dinner, when a few drinks prompted the pilots to relax by knocking each other about in rough-and-tumble gang-wrestling matches.

"Reggie, I don't feel good about this scrimmage business," Ben said one evening. "Tonight I head-butted a guy and knocked him on his ass. It was Wing Commander Archer. He thought it was great fun! I nearly pissed my pants!"

"Relax and enjoy it," Reggie hooted. "I saw you knock the old man's ass over the teakettle. Don't worry about it. Good way to blow off steam. Wing Commander Archer is still the boss, but in the officers' mess, he's one of the chaps. It's good for morale."

Ben and his squadron mates flew multiple training sorties daily, as the pace of operations intensified in response to the deteriorating situation on the Continent.

Each day they heard of aggressive German maneuvering along the Polish border and elsewhere.

"Germany's probing her borders like some bloody wild beast trying to escape from a cage," Stitch said. "Won't be long before we're in for it."

Governments throughout Europe, Scandinavia, and as far away as South Africa, Latin America, and South America hurriedly declared their neutrality, hoping to dodge the war that seemed inevitable. England mobilized her armed forces.

Chapter 53

War! 1939

On September 1, German forces rolled into Poland. Two days later, a distraught British Prime Minister Chamberlain announced on the BBC that as of 1100 hours, England was at war with Germany. That evening, French Premier Edouard Daladier told the French by radio that a state of war existed with Germany.

The next day, RAF Bomber Command launched fifteen Blenheim bombers to attack the German navy's pocket battleship *Admiral von Scheer* near Wilhelmshaven. It was Britain's first attack in the day-old war.

"The BBC reported five bombers were lost in the attack, and the *von Scheer* wasn't damaged," Reggie grumbled. "Not exactly an auspicious beginning."

Duxford and RAF bases throughout England went on highest alert. Airfield defenses were bolstered and squadron aircraft dispersed.

"Okay, Reggie, looks like we're in it," Ben said soberly. "What happens now?"

"Dunno, Sancho." Reggie had adopted Ben's new nickname. "Seems to me there's a lot of mindless scurrying about while we sit with our thumbs up our bums, waiting for someone to tell us what to do."

That afternoon, Squadron Leader Macintosh gathered squadron personnel in the base operations' briefing theatre. "First order of business will be a code name for our squadron," he said. "We'll not be using our official squadron designation over the RT, so let's consider what we'd like to be called. Myself, I favor Loch Ness, but I'll leave it open for suggestions."

"We have Don Quixote and Sancho in our squadron, Squadron Leader," one pilot called out. "Why not call us La Mancha Squadron?"

There was a murmur of approval, and Macintosh put it to a quick vote. The pilots voted unanimously for La Mancha.

Macintosh pondered this. "Aye, all right, La Mancha will be our code call sign on all missions. We'll use color codes for our flight. Avoid using names in any RT broadcasts. A Flight's six aeroplanes will be red and B Flight's blue. Your flight leaders'll give you your designations."

"Since I'll be Red Leader, Ben, that makes you Red 1," Reggie whispered.

"Now ye'll be wantin' ta know what's happenin'—the big picture, so to say—and how we're to proceed from here," Macintosh continued. "We have Wing Commander Wilkinson from 12 Group here today to give us a wee briefing on operating procedures. Wing Commander . . ."

Wing Commander Christopher R. Wilkinson, deputy head of operations for RAF 12 Group, directed a sergeant to unfurl a large map of Britain. "Good morning, gentlemen," he said. "I'm here representing 12 Group Commander, Air Vice-Marshal Trafford Leigh-Mallory."

He tapped the map with a long wooden pointer to indicate Duxford. "Your squadrons here are part of 12 Group, whose southernmost boundary extends west along this line to the North Sea coast near Lowestoft. To the east, the line extends to the Bristol Channel just north of Cardiff.

"The northern boundary extends from slightly north of Flamborough Head, here, west to the Irish Sea south of Lancaster, here. This gives 12 Group an area encompassing the Midlands, Norfolk, Lincolnshire, and North Wales. And of course, Duxford is headquarters for 12 Group's southernmost sector.

"Duxford is on the northern border of 11 Group, commanded by Air Vice-Marshal Keith Park, so we hope to be working closely with them. The area covered by 11 Group encompasses southeastern England, including metropolitan London and the major dock areas in the Thames Estuary. Its western boundary runs here, just past Southampton.

"A chain of radio direction-finding stations is being completed along the eastern coastline and eventually will stretch from north of Aberdeen to the tip of Cornwall," Wilkinson said. "This will give early warning of enemy airplanes approaching from the Continent and provide altitude, bearing, and numbers of aeroplanes, which is relayed to the operations centers at each group headquarters. Ours is at RAF Watnall Station and Fighter Command headquarters in Stanmore.

"Enemy formations are plotted on the central display table at Fighter Command, and sent to whichever group will make the intercept. Group relays the information to the appropriate sector. When the scramble alert is sounded, ground controllers will give you pilots the bearing and altitude of the approaching formations, the number of aeroplanes involved, and direct you to the intercept."

Reggie nudged Ben. "Sounds good in principle," he whispered. "Let's hope it works in actual practice."

Wilkinson continued, "When you're assigned your attack altitude, it will be given as 'Angels ten, that is an altitude of ten thousand feet' or whatever. And when the controller says 'Buster, Buster,' that means throttles to the stops, gentlemen. Get there as quickly as possible."

The system proved less than smooth. False alerts were common. Pilots scrambled on one fruitless intercept after another. Several times, RAF pilots were shot down by friendly aircraft.

"Terrible cock-ups," Reggie fumed one evening in the officers' mess. "Hope the new identification friend or foe system, or IFF, makes it easier to sort out the good guys from the bad guys."

After a series of training missions, they spent many boring hours flying patrols along England's east coast.

"No wonder the newspapers are calling this the Phoney War," Reggie groused. "Damn! I wish we could show them something different."

Excitement coursed through the unit at news that several squadrons would be sent to France to support the British Expeditionary Force, the first positive news since Poland's depressingly quick defeat.

"I hope that includes us!" Ben said. "I'm itchin' to get back into action!"

Weeks later, after the deployed squadrons encountered disasters in France, Ben was glad their squadron had not been involved. They watched from across the English Channel as the war stagnated on the Continent.

The year 1939 drew toward a dreary and inconclusive close.

Chapter 54

CHRISTMAS AT CALVERT HALL, 1939

104 Squadron was ordered to stand down over the year-end holidays. Squadron Leader Macintosh issued the pilots fortnight leaves, subject to immediate recall. Reggie and Ben piled into the MG and headed for Calvert Hall. Bates, impeccably dressed despite their late arrival, met them at the front door.

"Welcome home and a happy Christmas to you both," he said with a slight bow. "M'lady is waiting up for you in the upstairs study. I'll take the bags, sir."

"Reginald, Reginald," she whispered. "I'm so happy to see you, my son." Then, "Hello, Benjamin."

Ben stood quietly, savoring the warmth of her embrace.

"I must say you two look a bit bedraggled. Difficult journey?"

"Sort of, ma'am," Ben said. "But this sure makes it worth it."

They sat chatting by a roaring fire when Bates entered, bearing a tray with tea, sandwiches, and scones.

"I say, Bates, wouldn't have a drop of Scotland's best about, would you?" Reggie asked. Bates produced a crystal decanter of whiskey. "A plentiful splash of this'll cap our day nicely," Reggie added.

A piercing "Elizabeth scream" roused Ben from a dreamless sleep.

"God, I feel like I've slept only an hour or two!" he groaned.

He heard Elizabeth pound on Reggie's bedroom door and then attack him with an exuberant welcome.

"*Reggie, Reggie, Reggie*, you're home, you're home!" echoed down the hall. "Is Ben here too? Can I see him? How long is your leave? Do you think Papa can get home for Christmas too? Which room is Ben in?"

This was followed by rapid knocks on Ben's door. Without waiting for a reply, Elizabeth burst into the room. She bounded onto his bed and gave him a fierce hug and a wet kiss on the cheek. Recovering her composure, she hopped off the bed and stood grinning through a scarlet blush.

Ben sat blinking like an owl awakened in bright sunlight. "Um, hello, Elizabeth," he stammered. "It's good to see you."

This loosed a breathless torrent of comments, questions, and declarations from Elizabeth. Ben stared impassively at her. She finally took the hint and slipped out so he could get dressed.

The next two days swirled by in a flurry of Christmas preparations. Lady Percy handed Ben two recently arrived letters, one from his mother and the other a scrawled note from Brice. Ben eagerly read them twice and that evening wrote long replies to both. He regaled Brice with details of the Spitfire's performance. He again was circumspect with his mother, although he did tell her he was flying with the Royal Air Force and could get involved in the war with Germany. He slipped his last ten-dollar bill into the envelope. *Too late for Christmas, but I'll bet she can use it.*

With Bates's assistance, they decorated two trees and hung bunting and garlands throughout Calvert Hall. Elizabeth danced with excitement among all the preparations.

Lord Percy arrived on Christmas Eve, looking pale and drawn. He barely had his hat and coat off when the telephone rang. "Damn and blast! Can't get away for a moment," Lord Percy grumped.

He rejoined the family in the study, shaking his head and muttering. "Just got confirmation from Uruguay. Captain Langsdorff, commander of the German battleship *Admiral Graf Spee*, is dead," he said wearily. "Committed suicide after he scuttled his ship outside Montevideo, where our navy had him bottled up in the Rio de la Plata. Nasty business, nasty business."

The family staged a proper, albeit forced, Christmas dinner of a huge beef roast, a roasted goose with all the trimmings, and a selection of fine wines. It was topped with an Elizabethan Pantry pudding, which Ben considered a big improvement over the traditional American fruitcake. He was amused when everyone linked arms at the table and pulled in unison on twisted paper crackers. He felt foolish wearing the paper crown that popped out of his.

"Old English custom," Reggie noted dryly, canting his paper crown over one eye. "No one knows for sure exactly where it came from. Guess we all want to be kings or queens for the day."

Lord Percy pushed back with a sigh of satisfaction as the port wine was passed. "Wonderful feast, m'dear," he said, smiling at Lady Percy. "May be one of our last for a while, what with meat rationing about to be imposed. 'fraid we're in for some dreary times until we get this thing sorted out with Herr Hitler."

They adjourned to the study to hear the King's Christmas address on the wireless. It did little to lift their holiday spirits as the King spoke gravely of challenges that lay ahead.

The remainder of the holiday passed in a desultory manner. The New Year's celebration was muted, even with a large contingent of Reggie's family in attendance. All conversation revolved around the war. Even Elizabeth was quiet and subdued, nowhere near her usual effervescent self. Lord Percy, who had spent much of the holiday conferring on the telephone, left for London on New Year's Day.

The next morning, Reggie and Ben packed their gear in the MG. As they roared down the long driveway, Ben looked back at Elizabeth and Lady Percy standing dejectedly in Calvert Hall's entrance.

"Wonder if I'll ever see this place or those wonderful folks again?" he whispered.

Chapter 55

AWAITING THE LUFTWAFFE

Duxford buzzed with activity as they wheeled through the front gate.

"New airplanes!" Ben shouted. "Look at the flight line, Reggie. Those are the Mark IA Spits we've been hearing about. They have the new three-bladed variable speed props. Probably the bigger Merlin engines too."

"Hot damn!" Reggie exclaimed. "We'll show Jerry what for with these new mounts!"

That evening in the officers' mess, Ben noticed a squadron leader stumping in with a strange, stiff-legged gait. His round grinning face was topped with a thatch of dark curly hair. He boomed a cheery hello to all and headed for the bar.

"Reggie, who's that?" Ben asked.

"Squadron Leader Douglas Bader, commander of 242 Squadron," Reggie whispered. "Lost both legs in the early 1930s when he pranged doing low-level aerobatics. He was invalided out of the service, but he's wrangled his way back on active duty even with two peg legs. One hell of a pilot. He'll get things stirred up around here."

Reggie was right. Bader launched 242 Squadron on a furious pace of operations. All squadrons flew increasingly aggressive patrols over the English Channel and shot down several Luftwaffe fighters and bombers attacking coastal shipping.

Ben flew steadily on Reggie's wing, all the while looking intently for the Me 109 with the red spinner and distinctive tail markings. He became increasingly frustrated at not finding any enemy airplanes to engage. In April, a combined British-French expeditionary force launched the Norwegian Campaign to counter Germany's thrusts into Denmark and Norway. Several RAF fighter squadrons were dispatched to Norway to provide air support.

104 Squadron was left behind again, and Ben ranted about another missed chance at combat. His anger cooled when word filtered back that the squadrons had encountered operational disasters in Norway and were being withdrawn with large

losses of airplanes and pilots. Within the month, the total expeditionary force was withdrawn.

The disaster in Norway was shoved to the background when the German army, closely supported by the Luftwaffe, launched its blitzkrieg against western Europe. The Wehrmacht slashed into Belgium, Luxembourg, the Netherlands, and France. British Prime Minister Chamberlain resigned in disgrace, and Winston Churchill formed a coalition government to lead Britain's participation in the Battle of France. But time had run out. Ben and his fellow pilots listened to the wireless reports with dismay. Germany's offensive, which overran the lowland countries in a matter of days, pushed deeply into France, trapping over three hundred and forty thousand British and French troops at Dunkirk.

Ben and Reggie flew numerous sorties over the beaches at Dunkirk and inland to intercept Luftwaffe bombers headed for Dunkirk. They attacked the Luftwaffe bomber and fighter fleets at high altitude, which masked their activities from the troops trapped on the beaches below. And bad weather often frustrated their attempts to continue effective air cover for Operation Dynamo, the improvised evacuation of Allied troops across the Channel to England. Ben clashed with several Me 109s with no results, but sent a Ju 87 Stuka dive-bomber smoking east across France. Defying the odds, the Royal Navy and a hastily assembled flotilla of private yachts, fishing boats, and almost anything else that would float, churned across the Channel to rescue most of the combined Allied armies trapped on the Dunkirk beachhead. Their weapons, equipment, and supplies were left behind.

The dark mood in the Duxford Officers' Mess was barely lightened by accounts of aerial victories scored by Bader and several other squadron pilots. Within days, France capitulated, joining the four lowland countries as German-occupied territory.

Squadron Leader Macintosh gathered the 104 Squadron pilots. "Aye chaps, we're seeing some dark times ahead," he said heavily. "Britain stands alone in this fight wi' the Nazi hordes. An' the Luftwaffe is soon to be attacking us from just across the Channel. Those of ye who've been itchin' for action are about to get yer fill."

Shortly after occupying airfields along the French coast, the Luftwaffe launched major attacks against ship convoys in the English Channel and sent bombers on northern arcs to strike Scotland and Wales. German bombers also struck RAF bases all along Britain's East Coast, primarily in 11 Group's sector. Their mission was to destroy the RAF, gain air superiority over the Channel, and pave the way for a German amphibious invasion.

Ben alternated flying with Reggie and Stitch. Ground controllers guided La Mancha Squadron to intercept waves of Luftwaffe bombers covered by fighter escorts. The RAF pilots exacted a heavy toll on the enemy fleets. They had a distinct advantage, fighting along the inner perimeter of the battle, aided by early warning from RDF stations. But each aerial victory was hard-won. Ben and Stitch shared in shooting down a Heinkel He 111. Both returned to Duxford with damaged airplanes, the result of being jumped by several Me 109s escorting the bombers.

Chapter 56

THE BATTLE OF BRITAIN, JULY, 1940

The pace of scramble-and-intercept operations increased, pushing pilots and ground crews to the limits of endurance. Ben rubbed his itching eyes and yawned as he stumbled into the operations shack following his third mission of the day.

"Can't even remember what day it is," he mumbled. "How many ops today?"

"Grab a cuppa, Ben," Reggie said. "This bloody war is being run on tea and biscuits."

On the flight line, ground crews, fitters, and armorers scrambled to service and rearm their Spitfires. The pilots had barely completed their postmission debriefing when the alert phone rang. Scramble again!

"Bloody hell," someone yelled as they ran for their airplanes. "Bastards are beginning to play on my nerves!"

"Case you haven't heard," Stitch called out. "Winston says this is the Battle of Britain. Makes it seem a bit grander, don't it?"

Ground control gave La Mancha Squadron a southerly heading and told them to climb to Angels 12, or 12,000 feet. "Buster, Buster!" They were directed to help 11 Group squadrons of Spitfires and Hawker Hurricanes intercept a large number of bombers headed for the docks in London's East End. 104 Squadron arrived too late.

"Damn!" Ben yelled as he saw the enemy airplanes wheeling away from the flaming docks and heading back to France.

Squadron Leader Macintosh and his wingman managed to shoot down a lagging Heinkel He 111, but the rest of 104 Squadron returned to Duxford without firing their guns.

"Goddamnit," Ben snarled as he stepped off the wing of his Spitfire on the flight line. "That was a waste of time. Goin' all that way and not even getting a shot."

Reggie grabbed his elbow. "Come on, Sancho, we're done for the day. Let's get cleaned up and head for the mess. Maybe you can work out your frustrations by knocking Wing Commander Archer on his ass again."

The after-dinner rugby scrum was especially intense, and almost everyone ended up drinking too much and getting knocked on his ass. The pilots soon succumbed to fatigue and stumbled off to their bunks.

Chapter 57

SHOT DOWN

Ben and Reggie were promoted to flying officer and flight lieutenant, respectively. Within days, they launched in a mass gaggle scrambled to intercept a huge formation of Do 10 and He 111 bombers. Enemy aircraft blackened the sky.

"La Mancha Leader calling," Macintosh radioed. "Tallyho chaps! Bandits eleven o'clock. This time we have the buggers below us!"

"Christ!" someone yelled over the radio. "Where'd all these blighters come from?"

"Who's left 'ome mindin' the sausage factory?" another pilot quipped.

"La Mancha Leader calling," Macintosh responded, "Knock off the chatter. Keep this channel open."

Ben's squadron slashed into the Me 109s escorting the bombers, providing cover for RAF Hurricanes that attacked the bombers. Multiple smoke trails stitched the sky as burning fighters and bombers spun out of control. The smoke wove through vapor trails from aircraft engines. The sky blossomed into a massive lacework.

Ben attacked an Me 109. His Spitfire shuddered, and cordite fumes swirled into the cockpit as he fired two long bursts ripping it from nose to tail. It exploded in a fireball.

"Yahoo!" Ben screamed as the smoldering wreckage tumbled to the earth, its smoke column joining others marching across the English countryside.

A second Me 109 flashed past Ben on the right. He rolled sharply and fired, and shells from his eight guns hammered the fuselage. The German fighter rolled inverted and dived, trailing smoke. Twisting in his seat, Ben looked over his left shoulder into the ugly snout of another Me 109.

"*Oh shit!*" He snapped his airplane to the left.

The Me 109 rolled after him. Maneuvering desperately, Ben flicked his Spitfire right and quickly rolled back to the left. Snapping to the right again, he glanced in the rearview mirror.

"Dammit! Can't shake him!"

Flashes spouted from the German aircraft's twin machine guns and 20 mm nose cannon. Ben pulled harder on the stick and climbed as shells slammed into his Spitfire. A giant blacksmith seemed to be hammering on his airplane. Something hit his left thigh. Smoke curled in the cockpit. The engine sputtered, caught, and sputtered again. He smelled more smoke mixed with glycol. His engine seized with a shriek. The propeller froze, and his Spitfire rolled violently.

Get out! Get out!

Ben yanked the overhead handle to jettison the canopy, dialed in nose-down trim, and rolled inverted. The airplane spun out of control, smashing him against both sides of the cockpit. It rolled upright and pitched nose down.

Wind whipped his helmet as he dropped the small side door on the cockpit. He unplugged his headset, slapped the quick release on his Saunders safety harness, and dived out behind the wing. The left horizontal stabilizer slashed past, missing him by inches.

Tumbling, Ben clawed at the parachute release ring and pulled. He heard the drogue chute pop, followed by a cannonlike boom as the main chute blossomed. Ben jerked upright and dangled awkwardly, reaching frantically for the riser cords to control the swaying parachute canopy. An Me 109 bore down on him.

"Omigod! He's gonna strafe me!" he yelled.

The 109 broke off at last minute, and the pilot circled Ben, tossing him a derisive salute. Ben raised his right arm, middle finger extended in the internationally recognized insult. The Me 109 flashed past and headed east across the Channel.

"Hope you saw my return salute!" Ben yelled.

Ben tried to position his body for landing. A gust of wind hit his parachute, and he slammed into the muddy ground, landing hard on his left shoulder. Ben rolled several times. His helmet was torn off as he was dragged across a mucky, rain-drenched pasture. His harness tangled in a gorse bush, and he jerked to a stop.

Struggling to undo the harness, he peered through mud-caked eyes. Figures loomed toward him. Three farmers clumped up and surrounded him. One pointed an ancient shotgun, and the two others brandished pitchforks.

"Stay where ye be!" roared the farmer with the shotgun. "I'll use me blunderbuss if I 'ave ta!"

"I'm an RAF pilot!" Ben sputtered, wiping mud from his face and uniform, hoping they'd recognize the RAF blue. "I was just shot down by an Me 109. That's my Spitfire, or what's left of it over there," he shouted, pointing to a black smoke column about half a mile away.

"I told ye to stay where ye be!" snarled the farmer, pushing the barrels of the shotgun toward Ben's face. "Ye don't talk like no Hinglishman! I 'ears a fooney accent. I think ye're a Jerry, an' I've mind to blow yer goddamn head off!"

"No, no!" Ben yelled. "I'm an American! I'm flying with the RAF! Look at my uniform, for God's sake!"

"Yer covered in muck!" the farmer yelled. "'sides, America ain't in this war. We's holdin' off the bloody Jerries all by ourselves, an' I think yer one of 'em."

"No!" Ben yelled. "I'm an American volunteer flying with the RAF! I swear!"

"Whadda ye think, gents?" the shotgun-toting farmer asked his companions. "Do ye believe 'im?"

"Blowed if I know," one muttered. "Got a fooney accent, 'e do fer sure. Ain't no Hinglishman, not by 'alf. But I dunno know what 'e be."

Ben's head swam. He felt faint. Pain stabbed through his left shoulder. *Dammit! My shoulder's broken!* He shifted, and pain seared down his left leg.

"Ay tol' ye to stay where ye be! Er so 'elp me, yer a dead bloody German!"

"Yah! Soddin' Kraut, is what 'e is!" the third farmer snarled. "Comin' over 'ere, droppin' bombs on us and all. Killin' our wemmen and kids. Look at 'im, blond 'air, blue eyes. 'E's one of them bloody Aryans, that's fer sure!"

"Goddamnit!" Ben finally snarled. "I'm an American. I'm from Michigan!" *Now why the hell did I say that?*

"Mitchigan?" one farmer roared. "Where in 'ell is Mitchigan? Somewheres in Germany?" he asked his companions.

"Dunno."

"Hallo there!" a voice called. "Be he all right or is 'e wounded?"

A heavyset farmer puffed up, his face beet red from running across the field in mud-caked Wellington boots.

"Hallo, Simpson," the shotgun-toting farmer said. "Seems ta be hurtin', I reckon. But ah don't see no blood on this 'ere muck-coated bastard. We got us a Jerry fer sure, an' we'd soon as not kill 'im right now! Says he's from Mitchigan, wherever the 'ell that be!"

"Nay, nay!" Simpson shouted. "I saw the whole thing. This 'ere fella come outta that Spitfire what's smashed yonder. T'were a wonder ta see! I think 'e shot down a couppla Jerries before one got 'im!"

He asked Ben, "Are ye hurt, lad? Ye shot or somethin'?"

"I hurt my shoulder when I landed," Ben croaked. "I think it might be broken. And, and there's something wrong with my left leg."

Simpson reared back with a startled look. "By gor, yer a Yank!" he said. "What in 'ell are ye doin' 'ere?"

"He's a bloody Kraut!" snarled the first farmer, brandishing his shotgun. "Lissen ta 'is fooney accent!"

"Don't be a bloody fool!" Simpson shouted. "This 'ere's a Yank! Only I'm blowed if I know 'ow 'e got 'ere! America ain't in this war, is it?"

"I volunteered to fly with RAF," Ben stammered. "I . . . I, umm . . ." His head swam. He was going to faint.

"Steady on, lad," Simpson said. "Ye jus' lay back. We'll get ye ta 'ospital."

Ben's flopped back into the mud and darkness. He was vaguely aware of being moved, of jouncing along in some kind of rough cart. He passed out again.

Ben awoke with a snort, surrounded by whiteness—whiteness and light. White figures swarmed into view as he struggled to focus his eyes. *Have I died? Am, am I in heaven?*

"Well, hello there!" a soft female voice said. "Ever so nice to see you awake. You were a bit of a mess when they brought you in."

Ben stared into the most beautiful light gray eyes he'd ever seen. They were set in a smooth face with a straight nose, high cheekbones, and a luscious mouth.

"Am, am I in heaven?"

Her laugh was like a pealing bell. "Gracious, no!" she giggled. Her broad smile was dazzling. "You're in hospital. Here in Cambridge. I'm your nurse. Nurse Brewster."

"Oh god!" Ben groaned. "I must have sounded pretty dumb."

"Not at all!" she said. "You've had a nasty shock. You were quite out of your head when the farmers brought you here."

"Farmers?" Ben mumbled. Then he remembered. "That's swell! They thought I was a German pilot. The big one with a shotgun was ready to blow my head off. Said I had a funny accent. Made 'em suspicious. My uniform was covered in mud."

"Well, you *do* have a funny accent," she said mockingly. "And you were covered in muck. The farmers said you were from Mitchigan. Where's that?"

Ben groaned. "Michigan, Michigan! I was raised on a farm in Michigan! That's in America."

She smiled brightly and placed a hand on his forehead. Ben flinched, then relaxed. "Seems your fever is about gone," she said soothingly.

Angelica has soft hands like hers. Oh god, I miss her! Wonder if she got out of Spain okay?

He gazed at Nurse Brewster. Her blond hair framed her angelic face. *She's beautiful! Different from Angelica, but beautiful.*

"Well, anyway, we checked with the aerodrome. And they confirmed who you are. Fancy that, you coming all the way from Mitchigan in America to help us fight the Germans."

"Michigan, Michigan," Ben said "Oh hell, whatever . . ."

"Still a long ways from home," she said.

"Yeah," he blushed. "At the time, volunteering seemed like a good idea. I flew with the Republicans in Spain. We escaped at the last minute and got to England where two of us joined the RAF."

"We?" she asked.

"Yeah. Four of us. Captain Silverman, my friend Fred—ah, they went home—and an Englishman. I flew as his wingman."

"Ah yes, that would be Flight Leftenant Percy. He's been here twice to see you, but doctor had you asleep with morphia. I'm to ring him up as soon as you're awake."

"Reggie was here!" Ben exclaimed. "Is he okay? We were in one helluva fight. Ah, 'scuse me!"

257

"Not a problem," she said, flashing another dazzling smile. "Leftenant Percy is fine. But he's not half-worried about you. He also said it was one helluva fight, and that you shot down two Germans before you got hit."

"Ah ha," another voice joined in. "I see our Yank is back with us. I'm Dr. Cooper. I see you've met Nurse Brewster. How are you feeling? You took a bit of a bashing, I must say. Nothing broken, I'm happy to report. But you do have a nasty sprain of the left shoulder. And I extracted a piece of shrapnel from your left thigh. All healing nicely, however. You'll be right as rain in a fortnight or less. We should have you out of here in a few days. Then we'll send you off for a short recuperation leave."

He watched amused as Ben turned a doleful gaze back to Nurse Brewster.

"Ah, umm, where will I go to recuperate?" Ben asked.

"To Bournemouth, on the Dorset coast," Dr. Cooper said. "The War Ministry have requisitioned several hotels along the seaside. You'll find a full staff there to help you back to full health."

"Can I rejoin my squadron?"

Dr. Cooper smiled, knowing there were two reasons for Ben wanting to return. "I should think so. We're just taking every precaution before we clear you for operational service. Meanwhile, Nurse Brewster is at your beck and call."

Gotta find out her first name. Maybe I can get a fever so I'll have to stay longer.

He quickly pushed that thought from his mind. Feeling ashamed, he knew how short his squadron was of experienced pilots. He'd have to get back as soon as possible. He drifted into a deep sleep. A burst of noise startled him awake. Reggie, followed by Stitch and several other pilots, hove into view.

"I say!" Reggie hooted. "Look at 'im, lying there like some Egyptian potentate, being fussed over by a beautiful woman."

"Do they have potentates in Egypt?" one of the other pilots asked.

"Damned if I know. But if they do, then like as not, this is how they're treated." Reggie peered into Ben's face. His exuberance faded when he saw the pain his friend was in, but he pressed on. "Now then, Sancho, old bean, tell Reggie where it hurts. Did that nasty Jerry poke a hole in you anywhere? Or did he just shoot up your aeroplane?"

"Naw, no bullet holes," Ben said. "I did catch a piece of shrapnel here in my left thigh though."

"Bloody fortunate it wasn't a bit higher, eh?" one of the pilots chimed in.

"Right you are!" Reggie said. "It was one helluva fight, Benjamin. Didja know you blasted one of the Huns and sent another off trailing smoke?"

Ben nodded. "Guess I didn't see the third one comin'."

"Not a wonder with the number of aeroplanes involved," Reggie said. "Never seen such a circus."

They launched into a raucous replay of their biggest air battle. Hands flew, accompanied by mouthed engine and machine-gun noises as the group recounted the battle. Ben broke into a sweat and slumped back on the pillow.

"All right!" Nurse Brewster said firmly. "You've overtaxed my patient. It's time you lot were out of here!"

Flying hands stopped in midair, and the pilots stepped back like reprimanded schoolboys.

"Only trying to cheer him up a bit," Reggie said defensively.

"You've cheered him up quite enough for one day," Nurse Brewer snapped. "Now out of here!"

"Promise to behave, Mum." Reggie hung his head and stifled a guffaw. "Cheerio, Ben."

One pilot cracked, "She's a beaut, eh? A real tough one, but damn easy to look at."

Nurse Brewster's scowl softened into a smile as she bent to straighten Ben's bedcovers. Ben gulped as he gazed at the swell of her breasts against her starched white uniform.

Another nurse peeked into the ward. "Everything all right in here, Gwen?"

Her name is Gwen! Great, thank you.

Nurse Brewster nodded and turned back to Ben. "By the way, who's Angelica?" she asked with a twinkle in her eye. "You've been calling her name. She your sister?"

"Ah, no. She's not my sister. She's, she's, ah, a lady I met in Spain."

The week flashed by. Ben desperately wanted to stay in hospital, close to Nurse Gwen. But he knew he had to free a bed and then get back to his squadron. Ben was released and, despite his protests, Gwen rolled him to the front door in a wheelchair.

"Doctor's orders and hospital regulations," she said firmly. "Can't have you falling on your face or some other part of your anatomy now, can we?"

Ben clutched orders assigning him to a fortnight rehabilitation leave in a converted seaside hotel in Bournemouth. A RAF car pulled up to take him to the railway station. As Gwen helped him out of the wheelchair and steadied him, Ben turned and stared into her beautiful gray eyes.

"Thanks so much, Gwen. Ah, umm," he stammered, "after I get back on ops with the squadron, ah, could I come by and see you?"

"I'd like that ever so much," she said softly, guiding him into the backseat of the car. She smiled brightly and waved as the car pulled away.

Ben slumped back in the seat with a grin. "You can bet I'm sure gonna stop by and see you again, Gwen!" he muttered.

Chapter 58

RECUPERATION

Bournemouth's Norfolk Royale Hotel had been the Duke of Norfolk's summer residence in the 1800s. It still was elegant despite extensive modifications that transformed it into a hospital and rest center. It was in the heart of Bournemouth, a few blocks from the city's golden sand beaches. A clerk registered Ben and signaled an orderly, who wheeled Ben to a large third-floor suite converted into a six-bed ward. He cringed when he saw his wounded ward mates, one of whom had suffered horrific burns on his face and hands. *I don't belong here. I'm in pretty good shape compared to these fellas.*

Ben greeted his ward mates and said he was a Spitfire pilot in the RAF. Had been shot down but not seriously wounded. This prompted a snort from an army captain in a bed by the window. "Lost my bloody leg when the Jerries bombed us on the beach at Dunkirk," he snarled. "Where the hell was the Royal Air Force when we needed you?"

"I was part of 12 Group's air cover," Ben protested. "We made regular sweeps over the beach, a lot of it at high altitude. You probably couldn't see us. But we couldn't maintain continuous coverage. Also attacked the Luftwaffe bombers inland before they got to the beach. Besides, bad weather made it damn difficult to cover the whole evacuation."

"Do say," the soldier snapped. "Soddin' Luftwaffe seemed able to find Dunkirk, even with the overcast and rain." He rolled on his side and stared out the window.

Ben resolved to demand as little as possible from the overworked staff. Dr. Harold Watson cleared him to get out of bed and prescribed walking therapy. Ben noted that the doctor's bloodshot eyes blinked rapidly as he peered through thick glasses. His narrow face etched with deep fatigue lines and his stoop-shouldered shuffle testified to long hours on duty.

The head nurse, Margaret Opie, presented a stark contrast. A stout Cornish woman, her round body was topped by an equally round face with rosy cheeks and sparkling blue eyes. She beamed a broad, snaggly-toothed smile. She loved chatting with her "Yank." Ben smiled through most of their conversations, understanding little of her thick Cornish accent.

He left the depressing ward at every opportunity and hobbled along Bournemouth's beaches, their beauty marred by coils of barbed wire and tangles of obstacles to ward off enemy landing craft. He wrote his mother that he was on a rest leave at an English seaside hotel. He also wrote to Gwen, closing each letter with a line about how anxious he was to see her again. She responded with a sweet-smelling note, apologizing because her heavy schedule allowed little time to write. His spirits soared when he read her closing line; she was anxious to see him too.

Ben bore down on his walking therapy and pestered the doctors to certify him early for operational service. They relented, and Ben caught a morning train for London. He sent a telegram to his squadron's adjutant with his arrival time. A RAF car was waiting for him at the Cambridge station.

At Duxford, Ben signed in, posted a quick note to Gwen, and headed for the officers' mess. Reggie and Stitch pounced on him and quickly bought him a pint.

"Damn glad to see you, lad," Reggie said, grabbing him by the shoulders. Ben grimaced, but Reggie didn't notice. "Looks like the sea air and sunshine did you a world of good. Umm, how were the nurses, eh?"

The image of round Nurse Opie flashed through Ben's mind as he told Reggie and Stitch about the curvaceous and willing beauties who had tended him in Bournemouth. Glancing around the room, Ben noted several new pilots and the absence of familiar faces. "Uh, Reggie, where are Stevens and, uh, Wilson and Shepard? And who are these new fellas?"

Reggie and Stitch exchanged a long look. Stitch shrugged. "Stevens and Wilson bought it in a big fight last week," he said. "Shepard was shot down two days ago. He bailed out. He's in hospital with serious wounds. The new chaps are replacements. Introduce you later, if they survive the next day or so."

"We taking heavy losses?" Ben asked.

"Our share, but we're also making Jerry pay for them," Stitch said. "Problem is the new replacement chaps. Some have less than twenty hours total time, only a couple in Spits, and no combat experience. We tell 'em to stay close to their leads, but most don't make it past the first week."

Chapter 59

SETTLING A SCORE

Ben commandeered a bicycle after breakfast and pedaled to the hospital to see Gwen.

"Hello, Mitchigan," she said, smiling broadly. "You look ever so much better than when I last saw you."

Wanna grab her and kiss that beautiful mouth. But I better go easy. "Hello, Gwen. Great to see you," Ben said. "Umm, I only have an hour or so. Thought I'd drop by and say hello and ask, uh, ask if maybe you'd like to go out with me. We could see a movie, or maybe take a picnic somewhere."

"Ben, I'd love to do that," she said.

They bicycled out of Cambridge Sunday afternoon, along the River Cam. They sat watching punters on the river and flocks of geese and ducks scrambling for crumbs tossed from the boats.

"Uh, Gwen, I, uh, I really like being with you," Ben stammered. "And I get the feeling you like being with me. Um, are there any other fellas in your life?'

Gwen didn't respond.

"Sorry, sorry, I, uh, I shouldn't have asked," Ben said.

"That's all right, Ben," Gwen said quietly. "I was . . . I mean, I am married. My husband, Tony, and I were together less than a year when his destroyer was sent out on convoy duty. He wasn't gone but a short time when his ship was sunk. He's listed as missing in action and presumed dead. But . . . but I haven't heard anything more."

Ben gripped her hands. "I'm so sorry," was all he could say.

Ben managed brief meetings with Gwen. Their relationship progressed to passionate embraces and kisses during long walks on the hospital grounds. Ben learned that Gwen was living with her mother in a small village on the outskirts of Cambridge.

One Sunday afternoon, when he had a four-hour pass, Gwen invited him to tea with her and Mum. He spent the time gazing fondly at Gwen and trying not to ignore her mother, a plump, rosy-cheeked woman who beamed at him. Her laugh had the same bell-like quality as Gwen's.

"Me 'usband, Gwen's Da', went off to war in 1917," she said softly. "Umm, 'e come home with terrible wounds. 'ad been gassed, and 'e, umm, 'e died when Gwen were just three. And now Gwen faces the same. Jus' don't know what the world's comin' to," she added, dabbing tears.

The frequency of bomber attacks on Duxford lessened as the Luftwaffe shifted its focus from RAF airfields to London. Several days earlier, an errant Luftwaffe bomber unit had struck a London suburb. Prime Minister Churchill, thinking this was a reversal of Hitler's policy not to attack civilians, ordered RAF Bomber Command to bomb Berlin. The Germans reciprocated in kind, and soon their aerial blitzkrieg transformed London into a living hell.

104 Squadron was scrambled repeatedly and directed south to help repel attacks on London. On one mission, Ben circled over London chasing Luftwaffe bombers that had pounded the East End and were working toward Central London. Despite the heat of battle, Ben spotted significant landmarks Reggie had shown him on their whirlwind tour of the city.

"My god!'" he shouted into the radio. "The bastards are attacking St. Paul's!"

The great cathedral's dome stood defiantly amid a swirling sea of smoke and flame that consumed huge portions of the city around it.

"Easy, Red 1," Reggie radioed in response. "Stay focused, else you'll have Jerry up your arse."

Ben wrenched his Spitfire toward the mass of bombers and fighters. An Me 109, with a red spinner and eagles and multiple kill insignias on its tail, flashed into view.

"You bastard! You killed Ted!" Ben screamed and dived after him.

They dueled, twisting, turning, and diving to a low altitude. Ben howled like a madman as he pursued the German and ignored the danger as they swooped to near-rooftop level. The German pilot snapped his airplane left and right, pitched up, and dived, trying to throw Ben off his tail. Ben grunted as the g-forces pulled at his body, but he clung to the German like a mad rat terrier.

"You're dead, you sonofabitch!" he screamed.

Ben fired burst after burst at the writhing Me 109, driving the German pilot even lower. He fired again. The German airplane rolled onto one wingtip, dived toward a large park, and slashed into the trees. It cut an ugly gash across the forest canopy and disintegrated in a ball of flame.

Ben pulled up abruptly, skimming the uppermost tree braches. "Ted! I got him!"

Ben rolled his Spitfire into a climbing turn and circled, fascinated by oily black smoke coiling up from the wreckage. He didn't see another Me 109 slicing in behind him until he heard cannon fire. He twisted in his harness to scan the sky as 20 mm explosive shells hammered his airplane. The impact knocked the stick out of his hand. The rudder pedals slapped his feet.

"What the hell?" he yelled as he rolled into a violent turn and searched wildly in his rearview mirror. "Oh god! Brice. Brice! I didn't see him! He came outta the sun—"

A voice crackled in his earphones. "Break hard right, Red 1, I'm on him." It was Stitch.

Ben nearly blacked out as he slammed his Spitfire into a gut-wrenching climbing turn. When he could get his chin off his chest, he glanced back and saw Stitch firing bursts into the Me 109. The German fighter rolled inverted and dived into the Thames.

Smoke swirled into Ben's cockpit. The engine coughed and backfired. Oil splattered his windscreen. More smoke! "Oh god, oh god!" Ben croaked.

"Stitch, am I on fire?" Ben radioed, forgetting to use the color code.

"You're smoking, lad, but don't see flames," Stitch responded calmly. "Head north. Let's see if you can make Duxford. I'll cover you."

The run north seemed interminable. Ben watched in alarm as the oil pressure dropped. The engine surged, producing just enough power to keep him airborne. He exhaled a puff of relief when he spotted Duxford on the horizon. Ben called Duxford tower for an emergency landing and slipped his battered Spitfire over the fence. The airplane bounced roughly onto the grass. The mighty Merlin engine backfired, belched black smoke, and quit.

Ben slumped sideways and sat shaking in the cockpit. The fire rescue crew roared up. Hands reached into the cockpit and undid his Saunders harness. They dragged him over the wing and onto the turf. A medical orderly started to cut open his tunic.

"Okay. I'm okay," Ben croaked. "Not shot. Just beat up. Need water."

"Better than that, old chap," the orderly said. "We've a tea thermos. How about a nice hot cuppa?"

Ben grinned wearily. "Bloody Brits. A cuppa tea is your answer for everything."

Reggie and Stitch were waiting when Ben shuffled into operations. Ben smiled weakly at Stitch and gripped his right hand. "Thanks, Stitch. As Reggie would say, you saved me arse right and proper."

"So you got your red spinner?" Reggie said evenly.

"Yeah, I got him. Sent the sonofabitch smashing into the trees," Ben said. "Paid my debt to Ted like I promised in Spain."

"Good," Reggie said. "Now you've exorcised your demon, maybe you can settle down and put your mind to the greater task at hand, which is to kill the enemy but stay alive. I keep telling you to stay alert, stay focused! You won't always have someone hanging around to save your arse when you let your guard down."

"I don't think I deserved that," Ben retorted.

"I think you did," Reggie snapped, and walked away.

That evening in the officers' mess, Macintosh announced it had been a banner day for La Mancha Squadron: five verified kills, two probables, and three enemy airplanes damaged—two bombers and a fighter. He said it was "his shout"—he'd pay for drinks for everyone. The pilots stood openmouthed as he bought a full round of pints, an unusual gesture for their frugal squadron commander.

Reggie raised his glass to Ben and nodded. "Now we get serious, Benjamin. I want you on my wing full-time. Let's show these Jerry bastards what for."

Ben grinned and quaffed half of the pint.

Chapter 60

LOVE

Ben's squadron flew a staggering number of missions, rising to meet Luftwaffe bomber attacks seven days a week, often racking up five sorties a day. The Battle of Britain raged. The pace took its toll on pilots, ground crews, and airplanes. Fighter Command ordered Macintosh to stand down 104 Squadron for a twenty-four-hour rest.

Ben telephoned Gwen to say he had a day pass. "Could we maybe have a picnic somewhere today?" he asked. "Do you know a nice place?"

"That'd be delightful, Ben! There's an ever so nice spot along the River Cam. I'm off duty until this evening. I'll pack a hamper and bicycle to our meeting spot. See you in, what, an hour and a half?"

"Swell! I'll bring a pint or two. See you!" Ben rang off and searched for a bicycle.

"Off on a mission?" Reggie asked as Ben rushed past.

"Got a picnic date with Gwen!" he called over his shoulder, and bolted out the door.

They bicycled along the riverbank, basking in the summer sunshine. They found a secluded spot under an ancient oak and spread their blanket and picnic. As they ate, Ben stared at Gwen with puppylike eyes. *Can't believe how beautiful she is!*

She fixed him with a long look. "What are you thinking, Mitchigan?" she said softly. She had adopted Mitchigan as her pet name for him.

Ben blushed. "I'm thinkin' how beautiful you are, an'—" She leaned forward and planted a luscious kiss on his mouth. He felt a jolt through his body, and was aroused. "Gwen, I, um—"

She clamped her index finger on his mouth. "Let's shift the blanket around behind the tree into those bushes," she said softly. "Gives us a little more privacy."

Ben scrambled to comply. Stretching out on his back, he pulled Gwen toward him. "Gwen, I'm happier than I've ever been," he said. "Nothing else matters when I'm with you. Not this dirty war, nothing!"

He pulled her on top of him.

"Oh!" she gasped. "You are happy!" She quivered and pressed herself against him.

"And gettin' happier by the minute!" he said.

Scooting deeper into the bushes, they fumbled with each other's clothes and spent the next hour making each other very happy.

Ben muttered and smacked dry lips as he awoke. He lay on his back and emerged from a dream like a deep-sea diver floating to the sunlit surface through a halo of bubbles. *Man, what a dream!*

Gwen lay across his chest. She stirred and mumbled. It wasn't a dream! She raised her head and stroked his face. "Morning, Mitchigan," she giggled. "Have a nice nap?"

"Gwen!" he gasped. He pulled her down and crushed her mouth with his. "Gwen, I . . . Ah, I don't know what to say."

"Don't say anything, silly. Just bask in the afterglow."

He began caressing her.

"Not again, Mitchigan." She pushed his hands away. "Look at the time. Must be getting back. I'm on duty in less than two hours. And you, Mitchigan, are due back at the aerodrome, in case you forgot."

Chapter 61

CASUALTIES OF WAR

Controversy swirled through RAF Fighter Command as the commanders of 11 Group and 12 Group argued over how to combat the large Luftwaffe bomber formations swarming across the Channel. Air Vice-Marshal Keith Rodney Park, commander of 11 Group, the closest to London, favored launching individual squadrons on slashing hit-and-run attacks. He wanted to get his fighters airborne as quickly as possible and have them attack the German formations in waves before they reached London.

Air Vice-Marshal Trafford Leigh-Mallory, commander of 12 Group, proposed mass attacks under the Big Wing concept, also known as the Balbo formation. It was named after the Italian aviator Italo Balbo, who led large formations of aircraft on long international flights in the 1920s and 1930s.

Critics of Park's approach argued that 11 Group squadrons were suffering heavy losses because their fighters were strung out during the attacks and more vulnerable to interception by Me 109 escort fighters. By contrast, Leigh-Mallory's Big Wing tactic allowed 12 Group squadrons to press concentrated attacks that broke up the enemy bomber formations. They also kept the RAF fighters more closely grouped for mutual protection.

Park contended that 11 Group's squadrons were much closer to where the Luftwaffe bombers penetrated England's airspace and therefore didn't have time to form massed attacks. Commanders in 12 Group, led by Bader, pressed Leigh-Mallory to continue the Big Wing tactic; and the dispute over the best defensive strategy continued unresolved.

"Reggie, what's all this fuss about?" Ben asked. "Why can't they settle on one approach, and then we'll all know what the hell we're supposed to do?"

Reggie gave him a long look and shook his head. "As Tennyson wrote:

> Theirs not to make reply
> Theirs not to reason why
> Theirs but to do and die.

Let's keep our heads down, Sancho. Concentrate on flying our sorties and staying alive."

A week later, Fighter Command Headquarters ordered 104 Squadron shifted south to RAF Biggin Hill Aerodrome, one of the primary fighter bases protecting London.

"I've flown over Biggin Hill but haven't landed there," Ben said to Reggie. "That field's been pounded. Why are we bein' sent there?"

"Pounded is right," Reggie said. "Biggin Hill's on the southeastern edge of London, along one of the Luftwaffe's favorite attack routes to the city. Jerry has tried repeatedly to wipe them off the map to clear that approach. They've had the hell of a time trying to operate while dodging bombing and strafing attacks. We're going in as temporary replacements. Give the chaps there a respite."

"Not sure I like the sound of this," Ben muttered.

"Nor do I, Sancho, but there it is."

Biggin Hill looked bedraggled and war-torn. As the 104 Squadron pilots landed, they had to dodge bomb craters. A smoky haze wafted over the field. All hangars were damaged. Some were blackened hulks barely standing.

Ben and his fellow pilots soon were ordered into action amid the wailing of air raid sirens. Every scramble was a "Buster, Buster" call for maximum speed as the pilots clawed for altitude to meet the waves of Luftwaffe bombers streaming across the Channel. The next three weeks passed in a blur. The exhausted pilots flew multiple sorties every day, straggling back to Biggin Hill in twos and threes after each engagement. There, ground crews swarmed over their airplanes, refueling and rearming them.

Following one fierce battle with a large bomber force, Ben, Reggie, and Stitch barely had time to relax when the Klaxon sounded again.

"La Mancha, scramble, La Mancha, scramble!" the squadron controller yelled. "Heading 090, Angels 12. Buster, Buster!" The pilots grabbed their helmets, flotation vests, and other gear.

"Not even time for a proper pee or a relaxing cuppa," Stitch puffed as they ran to their airplanes. "Helluva way to make a living."

The ground crews had the fighters' engines running and helped strap the pilots in before the green flare signaled a formation takeoff.

Ben's crew chief shouted, "Good hunting, sir!" and jumped off the wing.

Ben waved his thanks and reached for the throttle lever. "God," he muttered. "I'm beat. Dunno if I can keep this up."

The takeoff was ragged, but the squadron formed up and raced east as they climbed toward twelve thousand feet.

"Not gonna make it," Ben snarled. "Not enough time to get above the bastards. Dammit! See what these Biggin Hill fellas have been up against."

La Mancha Squadron was too low to intercept the lead bombers, which penetrated to London and rained bombs on the East End. Several squadrons of Hawker Hurricane fighters joined 104 Squadron in the pursuit.

"La Mancha Leader calling," Macintosh radioed. "We'll take the second wave. Watch for the high fighter escort. Buggers are lurkin' up there in the sun."

"Bastards!" Ben snarled into his oxygen mask as he and Reggie dived into a formation of Heinkel He 111s. They both targeted the same bomber and fired simultaneously. The German's top gunner turret shattered, and the .303 shells from the sixteen guns of the two Spitfires raked across the wings. The left engine exploded, and the bomber spiraled out of control, dragging a plume of smoke into the mist.

"One o'clock, 109s, high! Break left, Red 1!" Reggie yelled into the radio. He then rolled to the right.

Ben snapped his Spitfire into a climbing left turn to meet the enemy fighters. Ben heard Stitch ordering other pilots to break and engage the attackers; then he plunged into a swirling mass of fighters. *Gawdalmighty, who's who?*

He spotted an Me 109 slicing toward a Hurricane, whose pilot appeared intent on hammering a bomber.

"Hurricane attacking the Heinkel! Break right!" Ben shouted into the radio. "Jerry on your tail!"

As the Hurricane snapped to the right, Ben rolled in behind the German fighter. He closed until its image filled his reflector sight and fired three quick bursts. Pieces flew off and flashed past Ben's cockpit. The German pilot rolled left, a fatal mistake that put him inside Ben's turning arc.

"So long," Ben snarled. He depressed the firing button and watched a long burst shatter the cockpit of the German fighter. Ben didn't see where it crashed.

"La Mancha Leader. Where are you?" Ben radioed as he climbed back to altitude. The sky had suddenly cleared as the air battle swept past.

"La Mancha Leader here," Macintosh radioed. "Low on petrol and ammo. Headin' home."

Ben was one of the last pilots to straggle back to Biggin Hill. He taxied to the flight line, shut down his airplane, and trudged to the operations shack. As he stepped inside, several pilots grabbed him and pinned his arms. Reggie poured beer over his head.

"I christen thee La Mancha's latest ace!" Reggie shouted as Ben coughed and shook beer from his face. "That Me 109 you smoked was your fifth kill. Bloody double ace you are, if we count your kills in Spain."

The frenetic pace of scramble missions continued for two weeks. The pilots stumbled about like zombies, flying by instinct. But they continued to extract a heavy toll on the attacking bombers. Ben scored his sixth kill. That evening Macintosh called them to a meeting in the operations room.

"Bit of good news, laddies," he said. "We're goin' home to Duxford tomorrow mornin'. Two refreshed squadrons are comin' in ta relieve us. Pack yer kits, chaps! Takeoff is at 0700 hours, assumin' we're not scrambled aforehand."

Duxford had been badly damaged. Bomb craters pocked the landing field, and several buildings were reduced to burned-out shells. Ben was frantic when he heard the Cambridge hospital had been hit. After several phone calls, he was relieved to learn Gwen had not been on duty during the raid. But he heard her neighborhood may have been hit.

Ben coaxed a four-hour pass from Squadron Leader Macintosh, commandeered a bicycle, and pedaled furiously to Gwen's home.

"What happened?" he gasped as he skidded to a stop before several women gathered on the sidewalk.

"You lookin' fer someone, lad?" one inquired.

"Ah, Gwen, um, Gwen Brewster and her mom," Ben stammered, looking at the charred ruins of their house.

"Oh, poor Gwen and her mum," the lady said sadly. "Aye, that were their 'ome there. 'er mum was killed, God rest 'er soul. Gwen was injured, burns and all. Believe she's in 'ospital in Cambridge."

Ben found Gwen in a hospital ward like the one in which she had tended him. She was swathed in bandages. He stood fingering his cap at the foot of her bed.

"Hullo, Ben," she whispered. "Ever so nice to see you."

"Are you okay? I mean, are you feelin' better?"

"I'm much better, Ben. Thanks ever so much for coming by. Lovely of you . . ."

"Sorry, umm, ah, sorry to hear about your mom," Ben said.

"Thank you, sweet Ben. It was over quickly for Mum. Don't think she felt any pain. The house, it . . . it just collapsed. Beams and everything. Some neighbors pulled us out of the wreckage. I don't think Mum suffered."

Tears welled in Ben's eyes, and he reached out to Gwen. "I'm so sorry," was all he could say. "Ah, can I touch you? Will it hurt if I touch you?"

"No, Ben, it won't hurt. Give us a bit of a hug then."

He held her in a soft embrace, sobbing into her shoulder. "Thank God you're okay," he whispered. *I'll get even for this! I'll make those Kraut sons of bitches pay! I'm gonna take this war to their backyards!*

He kissed Gwen good-bye, stumbled out of the hospital, and vomited in the bushes.

Ben's squadron flew multiple missions every day, and it was another week before he could visit Gwen again.

"Gwen! Hey, Gwen, you look great!" Ben said, handing her flowers. "Say, isn't this quite a switch? I mean, me carin' for you in the hospital?" He stopped short when he saw her worried look.

"Sweet Ben," she said softly, grasping his arm. "Have something I need to tell you. But I, umm, I don't know how." Tears welled in her eyes.

"What is it, Gwen? Just tell me."

"Umm, Ben, I've had news of Tony," she whispered. "They've told me now he's alive."

Oh god, this can't be happening! Just when I get her back, I'm gonna lose her?

"I've just heard from the Red Cross, Ben. They said Tony's alive. Oh, Ben, I don't know what I feel. He . . . umm, was presumed dead when his destroyer was sunk . . . ," she choked back a sob. "I've had no word for months and months. But, but now . . . now, they tell me he was rescued by a German submarine. And he's alive. He, umm, he was badly wounded. But he's alive in a prisoner of war camp."

Ben felt numb, unable to respond or offer Gwen comfort.

Gwen was released from the hospital at the end of the week. The doctor said she needed several months of convalescence. She told Ben she was going to Bristol to live with her aunt. Ben arranged for a staff car to take her to the train station. He helped her aboard the train and stood holding her hand through the open window. They managed brave smiles through their tears.

"So long, Gwen," Ben choked. "I'll never forget you."

"G'bye, Mitchigan." She leaned out and kissed him. "I'll write, I promise. Maybe we'll meet again."

Ben stared dumbly as the train chuffed out of the station.

The air battle over London reached a crescendo as the Luftwaffe launched one massive attack after another. RAF Fighter Command threw squadrons of fighters at them. The German losses mounted. Ben had no time to dwell on losing Gwen. He flew and fought with a cold calculating fury and scored three more kills—a Do 17 bomber, an He 111 bomber, and another Me 109.

"Sancho, I can't tell you how great it is to have you on my wing," Reggie said one evening as they trudged back to the operations shack. "You've become one of the best pilots in the squadron."

Ben grunted his thanks.

"Which is why I've put you in for promotion," Reggie continued. "You're to take my place, Flight Leftenant Findlay. I'm moving up to Squadron Leader and will take command of 104 Squadron. Our friend Macintosh is moving on to Group Headquarters."

Ben stared at Reggie. "Flight leader?" he said.

"Right you are. Leader of A Flight. Stitch will continue to command B Flight."

Chapter 62

THE BATTLE WON:
THE WAR CONTINUES

On his first mission as flight leader, Ben drew newly arrived Pilot Officer Bainbridge as his wingman.

"Stay close," Ben instructed. "I'm Red Leader, and you're Red 1. Your job is to ride my wing and cover my tail. If I tell you to break right or left, do it without delay. There'll be no harin' off by yourself, understand? Stick with me, and I'll get you through the early days. They're the most dangerous."

Bainbridge stuck to Ben like a flea on a foxhound's tail. He returned from each sortie pale and shaken, relieved to be alive.

Reggie led 104 Squadron with authority. Their losses, like those for all of Fighter Command, dwindled as the Luftwaffe's rose. Scramble missions blended into one another as the Battle of Britain raged on into September.

On September 15, 1940, as Ben would remember, the pilots of 104 Squadron rolled out of their bunks before dawn, gulped a breakfast of tea, toast, and bacon, and headed for the dispersal shack. Some smoked, some paced. Ben and Stitch stretched out on lawn chairs and drifted into troubled sleep. Both snorted awake when Reggie called "La Mancha Squadron!" They hadn't heard the alert phone ring.

"Good news, chaps! We're to stand down. No bogies on the big board! Herr Goering apparently isn't sending any visitors this morning."

The pilots exchanged baffled looks. Was this the squadron leader's idea of a joke?

Stitch looked at his watch. "Bloody hell! It's gone past 0900 hours. Should be airborne by now."

"Right-ho," Reggie shouted, striding out of the shack and kicking Stitch's chair out from under him. "I think the Luftwaffe have had enough. Can't be certain yet, but I believe we've given Jerry what for!"

The Battle of Britain, the biggest air conflict ever fought, dwindled to a halt; although sporadic day air battles continued through the end of October. By early November, the German high command apparently realized its Luftwaffe could not gain air supremacy over Britain and suspended all-day bomber attacks. Hitler postponed the amphibious invasion across the English Channel.

RAF Fighter Command's exhausted air and ground crews, stunned by how suddenly the battle ended, reveled in the respite. But for civilians, particularly in London, the Blitz had only begun. The Luftwaffe shifted to massive night-bombing attacks on the capital and other major cities across the country. The RAF, with no credible night fighter force, could not defend them.

The most infamous Luftwaffe bomber attack occurred on November 14, a night raid against Coventry, an industrial city in the West Midlands. Waves of He 111s and Do 10s leveled the city's medieval center and destroyed Saint Michael's Cathedral, which dated from the late fourteenth century. It had been the largest cathedral in England. Coventry became the rallying point for British resistance to Hitler's Third Reich and created anti-Nazi sentiment throughout the Western world.

Reggie, leading La Mancha Squadron in the West Midlands soon after the attack, flew them over Coventry, giving them a panoramic view of the destruction.

"Take a close look, chaps," he radioed. "This is what we're fighting for. Given his head, the Hun would reduce all England to rubble like this. The cheeky bastards passed nearly overhead of Duxford in the night, to make these raids."

Ben keyed his radio to shout angry agreement. An inner voice urged caution, and he switched off the radio. "Learning not to shoot off my mouth," he mumbled. "But by God, some day I'm gonna take this war directly to the Krauts!"

As 1940 drew to a close, major responsibility for pressing the air war against Germany shifted to RAF Bomber Command's night raids. At sea, the Royal Navy struggled to secure Britain's critical supply lines in the Mediterranean and across the North Atlantic. In North Africa, the British Western Defense Force scored early victories against the Italian army.

There was a resurgence of daylight operations by the Luftwaffe in late November. Mixed fleets of German and Italian bombers and Ju 87 dive-bombers attacked shipping in Channel waters along Britain's east coast. RAF's 11 Group met the threat effectively, scoring multiple kills against the vulnerable Ju 87. Meanwhile, 12 Group's contribution dwindled to routine patrol flights.

Morale in La Mancha Squadron sank to a low ebb. They had drawn the short straw and were ordered to stand in ready reserve during the holidays. Other squadrons received a fortnight's leave.

"Sorry, Ben, but no Christmas at Calvert Hall this year," Reggie said. "'fraid it's going to be a pretty somber affair."

Ben, still mourning the loss of Gwen, muttered that he wouldn't be very good company anyway. He wrote long letters to his mother, Brice, Simpson, and his brother, Joe. He spent the holiday nursing beers with his hard-drinking squadron mates in the officers' mess, and joined halfheartedly in their increasingly frenetic games of mess rugby.

Chapter 63

A New Beginning, 1941

Fighter Command's new commander in chief, Air Chief Marshal Sholto Douglas, faced a formidable task, defining a new mission for his fighter forces. Fighter Command had fifty-six squadrons—considerably more than before the Battle of Britain. But the command had lost many of its best pilots. Training command could not meet the demand for replacements, leaving at least half the squadrons undermanned.

The Battle of Britain officially ended on October 31. But ACM Douglas, certain the Luftwaffe would resume daylight bomber attacks the next spring, asked the Air Ministry for additional fighter squadrons. By April he had sixty-four; but again, not all were up to operational strength.

British intelligence reported Germany had shifted several Luftwaffe squadrons from Europe to the Mediterranean and Balkan theaters. Others were transferred to the Eastern Front as part of the buildup that led to Germany's invasion of the Soviet Union.

Against England, the Luftwaffe switched to new hit-and-run tactics, using Me 109E models fitted with centerline bomb racks and escorted by fighter versions of the airplane. Pilots of La Mancha and other squadrons eagerly joined in the chase, like hounds pursuing the fox. But the German raids were unpredictable and difficult to detect by radar, so the squadrons made few intercepts.

At Fighter Command Headquarters, ACM Douglas struggled to meet the demands of the Royal Navy and Coastal Command for better protection over shipping convoys in the Channel and along approaches to southern and western coast ports. Fighter units performed three levels of shipping support: escort, protection, and full cover. Ben thought the missions were boring because they resulted in few encounters with Luftwaffe attackers. And they were dangerous, starting with predawn takeoffs to get in position over the ship convoys at first light, then continuing in shifts until dusk. That meant the last fighters returned after dark—often in bad weather—and the aircraft were not equipped for instrument flight.

"Damn mindless waste of pilots and resources!" Reggie grumbled as they nursed pints during one of their increasingly frequent visits to the nearby Hangman's Dog pub. "We're burning up scarce petrol circling over ship convoys. Last two weeks, 12 Group lost five aircraft and pilots, mucking about in bad weather."

ACM Douglas called the year 1941 Fighter Command's difficult year. Morale ebbed. Germany invaded the Soviet Union on June 22, which caused a brief stir throughout Fighter Command, but no action. The Luftwaffe shifted more fighter and bomber squadrons to the Eastern Front, further reducing the possibility that Germany would launch massed daytime attacks on Britain. Ferocious fighting raged on the Eastern Front, and Ben thought of his erstwhile Russian comrades from Spain.

"Don't like sittin' out on the sidelines," Ben said. "Wonder where the Mad Major is? And Ivan, the naked warrior. S'pose he's still flying bare-assed?"

Behind them, their squadron mates were becoming increasingly boisterous. A typical officers' mess scrum seemed about to erupt.

"I doubt Ivan is still flying wearing only in his boots," Reggie chuckled. "It gets pretty cold in Mother Russia, even at this time of year. Poor bastards. They're really up against it. Hope they survive—"

Someone crashed onto a table. Glasses shattered on the floor.

Reggie wheeled on the miscreants. "I say, keep it down!" he roared. "Leave off the horseplay! That's for the officers' mess. We come here for somber, serious drinking. Landlord, shall we heave the blighters out?"

Turning back to Ben, he winked. "Lads really need to blow off a bit. We're all frustrated at not being able to nail the Huns on their night attacks. But we can't let 'em bust up the Hangman's Dog."

The Luftwaffe's nighttime Blitz against England continued unabated. Fighter Command fighters, unequipped for night fighting, could provide no credible defense. A few sorties were launched when the moon was bright enough to see the enemy bombers in the forlorn hope of bagging a lucky kill. However, these missions mainly succeeded in scaring the RAF pilots during the return to base for night landings with rudimentary runway lighting. The RAF tried several schemes to equip various fighters for night operations, but with limited success.

The RAF's mission was reduced to patrolling coastal shipping lanes, pursuing German reconnaissance aircraft that occasionally penetrated Britain's airspace, and joining daylight fighter and fighter-bomber sweeps over northern France. The main objective of the latter was to draw Luftwaffe fighter squadrons based in northern France into battles of attrition. A secondary objective was to force the Luftwaffe to shift Eastern Front squadrons back to France, thereby reducing pressure on Russian fighter squadrons. Both failed.

The fighter sweeps, often involving multiple squadrons, were code-named Rhubarb. Combined strikes, with a mix of fighters and bombers from Bomber Command, were dubbed Circus. If fighters on Rhubarb patrols lured no enemy fighters into battle, the

RAF pilots were authorized to attack any ground targets they could find. This enabled the pilots to vent some of their frustrations.

Combined Circus patrols achieved mixed results and soon bogged down in disagreements between Fighter and Bomber Commands over such important details as attack altitudes. Through mid-1941, neither Circus nor Rhubarb sweeps achieved their mission objectives. Deteriorating weather conditions further complicated mission planning and execution.

Reggie, Stitch, and Ben strolled the perimeter of their dispersal site.

"Need to chat with you about squadron discipline," Reggie said. "The chaps are getting sloppy, and—"

"And why the hell not!" Stitch snapped. "We've no bloody mission worthy of the name, and we're losing pilots and aeroplanes with no effect on the enemy!"

Ben butted in. "I agree! We all like the joyrides over France, but the Krauts hide in their bunkers, and we're left to roam around strafing old buildings and the occasional train. And I can't get anyone excited about training missions. They want real action!"

"If you gentlemen are through," Reggie said evenly, "I'd like to share something with you that might put a positive spin on the problem."

Stitch and Ben looked at Reggie.

"As you know, all hell is breaking loose in North Africa, and our forces on Malta are being pounded mercilessly," Reggie continued. "Fighter Command are looking at all its resources and considering which squadrons it can spare for those theaters. We're on alert with everyone else."

"That's great!" Stitch said. "It's bloody well past time we got tapped for some real operational assignments."

But 12 Group again was bypassed. Hawker Hurricane fighters were sent, and Spitfire squadrons remained on standby defensive assignment in Britain. Morale in 104 Squadron dropped another notch.

In early December, Ben was in Reggie's office working on holiday leave priorities. Stitch burst in, waving his arms and yelling, "The Yanks are now in it!"

"What the hell?" Reggie said. "Ever heard of knocking?"

"Sorry," Stitch said, trying to catch his breath. "Just came over the wireless. Japs have attacked Pearl Harbor! Launched waves of fighters and bombers from aircraft carriers. Caught the Yanks napping on Sunday morning. Blew hell out of the place. Sank most of the U.S. Navy's Pacific Fleet!"

Ben and Reggie sat, stunned.

"Where the hell is Pearl Harbor?" Reggie asked. Ben shrugged.

"Hawaii!" Stitch yelled. He didn't add that he had just learned that from the wireless report.

"And Guam and Wake Island also have been attacked. And the Japs are raising hell all over Southeast Asia—Malaya, Hong Kong, Singapore, the lot!"

"Ah, umm, what's that mean for us?" Ben stammered.

"Means America is officially in the war, Sancho!" Stitch exclaimed. "In the Pacific end of things, at least."

December 7, 1941, was a dramatic turning point. Japan quickly declared war on the United States and the United Kingdom, albeit after the fact. The U.S., Britain, New Zealand, and the Netherlands retaliated by declaring war on Japan. Australia and China quickly joined them.

In a bizarre flurry of diplomatic actions, Germany and Italy then declared war on the U.S., which reciprocated by declaring war on the two Axis nations. The conflicts in Europe and the Far East coalesced into a global struggle—World War II. Smaller nations joined the Allied or Axis camps, betting on who they thought would win. Spain, Portugal, Sweden, and tiny Switzerland declared their neutrality in desperate attempts to stay out of the fray.

The year 1941 ended with the world engulfed in a global conflict of unprecedented proportions.

Chapter 64

CHALLENGING TIMES, 1942

Following a desultory Christmas and New Year's break at Calvert Hall, Reggie and Ben returned to Duxford. Months of sporadic operations followed. Ben grew increasingly restive. America, now fully in the war, accelerated the buildup of U.S. forces in England. The U.S. Army Air Force organized a massive unit called the Eighth Air Force in England. Rumors abounded that it soon would gather thousands of airplanes in England: various fighter types such as P-47s, P-38s, and a few P-51s; B-17 and B-24 heavy bombardment wings; and B-25 and B-26 bomber attack squadrons.

Ben hoped the Americans were preparing massive daylight bombing attacks on the German homeland. Rumors also circulated that U.S. officers from something called the Inter-Allied Personnel Board had identified U.S. expatriate pilots flying with the RAF and would pressure them to transfer to the U S. Army Air Force.

The year dragged by as 104 Squadron saw little action beyond shipping patrols and occasional sorties over France. By autumn, Ben's depression deepened. Frequent weekend leaves in London did little to raise his spirits. The grand old city was cold, dark, short on food, beer, and liquor, and under bombardment nearly every night. It was an overall depressing place.

One afternoon in late November, Ben found Reggie in his office, shuffling papers.

"What's up, Ben? Reggie asked.

"Got a minute? Need to chat."

Reggie waved him to a chair.

"Reggie, I, ah, well, I dunno where to start. But, ah, I'm really frustrated with Fighter Command messin' around trying to find a mission for us. I mean, we hang around with nothin' to do, then we're sent off on these crazy cross-Channel sorties that don't seem to benefit anybody. I can't see how we're helpin' the war effort." Ben paced the office.

"Agree with you, Ben," Reggie said. "But dammit, our job is to follow orders and hope our fair leaders know what the bloody hell they're doing. They'll get it sorted out, me lad, and then we'll be back in the thick of it again. Meanwhile, we need to standby in case Jerry decides to launch day strikes against us."

Ben shook his head impatiently. "Not sure I agree, Reggie. And, ah, I've been thinking about these fellas from the, what's it called, umm, the Inter-Allied Personnel Board. I haven't been contacted, but I guess they'll sniff me out sooner or later."

"I expect they will. And when they do, what'll you say?" Reggie asked quietly.

"That's just it, Reggie. I dunno. I mean, I've been flyin' with the RAF for three years, been with you nearly five years, countin' Spain. I feel at home in the RAF, like I'm one of the blokes. I'm not sure I want to leave that."

Reggie smiled, "But . . . ?"

"But I feel drawn to the USAAF, you know? Like I should be fightin' with my own blokes. And now, ah, I know this is gonna sound crazy," Ben continued, "but I want to switch to bombers. I've been sayin' how I want to take the war to the Krauts' backyard. Give 'em a taste of what they did in Spain and what they're doin' here in England!"

"What the hell? A fighter pilot volunteering to switch to bombers?" Reggie asked incredulously. "It happens sometimes that fighter pilots in the RAF make the switch, but it usually ain't by choice, matey."

"Well, maybe it sounds nuts to you, but I've given it a lot of thought. It's what I want to do." Ben plopped into his chair. "Look at what those bastards did to Coventry and what they're doin' in the night raids on London and other cities! And what they did to Gwen and her mom. I don't wanna fight 'em one by one. I wanna fly over their damn country and bomb the shit out of a lot of 'em!"

"Steady on, old man!" Reggie exclaimed. "Steady on! Remember how you unnecessarily put your arse on the line going after the Hun with the red spinner. Don't make that mistake again."

Ben sat forward, started to protest, and then sat back.

"If you want to do this, Ben, make it a rational decision, and then go into it with a cool head. Think it through, laddie. I'd hate to lose you, but I'll support any decision you make, as long as you make it a rational decision. And I might point out that RAF Bomber Command is bombing the shit out of a lot of 'em on a nightly basis."

"I know, I know," Ben sputtered. "But I don't think Bomber Command has been very effective with night raids. I hear the American Army Air Force is planning huge daylight precision bombing raids on Germany with maybe a thousand bombers. Massed precision bombing! That's gonna make a difference! Besides, if some Inter-Allied fella catches up with me, staying in the RAF probably won't be an option."

An "Inter-Allied fella," Lt. Col. James Watson, caught up with Ben in late 1942, just before Christmas. Reggie called Ben into his office and introduced Watson.

"Excuse me, gentlemen," Reggie said, reaching for his cap, "I'll leave you to it. I've duties to attend to."

Watson, a heavily built man, looked steadily at Ben with hooded brown eyes. He clasped his hands across his slightly rounded belly and twiddled large sausagelike thumbs. His chin jutted out aggressively, but a smile played around his lips.

No wings. Not a flyer. What's Reggie call 'em? Oh yeah, paper-shuffling sods.

"Know why I'm here, Lieutenant?" Watson asked. Not waiting for an answer, he continued, "You know what the Inter-Allied Personnel Board is, what it does?"

"Not exactly, sir."

"Well, our job is to sort through issues that arise between the Allied forces, you know, misunderstandings due to differences in language, customs, military styles. That sort of thing."

"What's that have to do with me?" Ben asked.

"Very little directly, I suppose. But indirectly, you and other American expatriate pilots could find yourselves at the center of a dispute between the USAAF and the RAF."

Keep your mouth shut. Let him spell it out.

"Quite a few Americans like you are serving in foreign military services," Watson said. "Nothing dishonorable about that. You fellas came over here on your own, looking for excitement, acting on your principles, fighting for democracy, whatever. And you started earlier than most by going to Spain in '37."

Ben shifted in his chair.

"Hold on," Watson said, raising a hand. "Let me finish. Nobody's questioning your motives. Nobody's accusing you of being disloyal or anything like that."

"Then what's the problem?' Ben interjected.

"Let's call it a situation, not a problem," Watson countered. "The situation is, Uncle Sam would like to have all you fellas who've already shown your willingness and ability to do battle with the Axis enemy—he'd like to have all of you on our team. We can benefit from your combat experience."

"You're tellin' me I have to resign from the RAF and join the U.S. Army Air Force?" Ben asked quietly.

"Not saying you have to, not yet anyway. I'm here to encourage you to voluntarily switch to the USAAF," Watson said. "But I won't kid you. If not enough of you do so, it could become mandatory, in fact, probably will. But we want to go easy first."

"So I really have no choice," Ben muttered. "Question is, what's the advantage of doin' it now?"

"Ah, the advantage," Watson said with a smile. "Agree to make the switch now, and we'll do our best to get you the assignment you want. No guarantees, of course, but we'll try. And I might add, the USAAF is still getting organized over here, so there are a lot of choice assignments open."

"How much time do I have to think this over?" Ben asked.

"Not much. We haven't ironed out all the details of how this is going to work, so it'll be sometime in January before we meet again. Meantime, think this over. I'll be in touch. Okay?"

"Yes, sir," Ben said. Rising, he saluted and walked out.

Ben led La Mancha Squadron on several massed Rhubarb sweeps across the Channel. Usually the Luftwaffe did not launch fighters to challenge them. The RAF pilots attacked ground targets of opportunity before straggling back to their home bases. They were far from satisfied.

Returning from one mission in late December, Ben's mind was on his conversation with Watson and not on the task at hand. Flight discipline lagged, and La Mancha Squadron's mission degenerated into a ragged mess.

Ben shook his head angrily as he led the squadron back to Duxford. *Damn fool! Lost your focus! Made a mess of this mission, and the other fellas know it. Make your decision. Get this settled.*

That evening he told Reggie he had made his decision, but would have to wait until Watson contacted him again in January. Reggie nodded grimly and gave Ben his full support, as promised.

"Thanks, Reggie," Ben said. "I really appreciate that."

Ben stood to leave. "Ah, by the way, I'll take a pass on Christmas at Calvert Hall this year. I'll take standby duty. Let some of the other fellas get home."

As 1942 ebbed into the history pages, Ben felt very alone and increasingly frustrated.

Chapter 65

THE DECISION YEAR, 1943

Ben fidgeted through the first month of the new year. A wet cold front shrouded most of England, putting an even greater damper on the sporadic operational assignments La Mancha Squadron received.

In early February, Ben led the squadron on a coastal patrol when center control radioed that a flight of Ju 87 Stuka dive-bombers, covered by Me 109 fighters, was attacking an Allied ship convoy in the Channel.

"La Mancha Leader here," Ben radioed. "B Flight, go for the escort. We'll take the Stukas."

"Tallyho!" someone radioed. "Let's get the bastards!"

"Red 1!" Ben radioed to his wingman Bainbridge. "Stick to me. Follow the Stukas down, hit 'em when they pull out of their dives!"

Hurtling out of the sky, Ben spotted a pair of Stukas just as they dropped their bombs. "Red 1, take the one on the left! I've got the other one."

Both pilots opened fire. Bainbridge's target pitched up and dived into the Channel. Ben concentrated his aim on the second Stuka, which exploded and cartwheeled into the water.

"Red 1!" Ben grunted as they pulled into a high-g turn. "Two Stukas attacking that freighter to the right."

Again, two flaming Ju 87s spun into the water. Ben and Bainbridge broke off and circled.

"Red Leader, break right! Me 109 on your tail!" someone yelled over the radio.

Ben wrenched his Spitfire into a steep climbing turn and looked frantically in his rearview mirror. An enemy fighter sliced in behind him. The pilot pulled hard to bring his guns to bear on Ben's tail.

Suddenly the Me 109 bucked, broke off the attack, and began a twisting, turning escape. As Ben completed his turn, he saw a Spitfire pouring rapid bursts into the

German airplane. Ben could see the shells ripping into the fuselage. The Me 109 bucked again, burst into flames, and dived inverted into the water.

"You're clear, Red Leader," echoed in his earphones. It was Bainbridge.

"Remind me to stand you a pint or two in the mess," Ben radioed.

That night, the 104 Squadron pilots rattled the rafters in the Duxford Officers' Mess. They had broken up the attack on the convoy and shot down nine enemy aircraft. Their raucous celebration, which included pouring several pints of bitter over a grinning Bainbridge, allowed the men to vent months of frustration.

Chapter 66

Transition

Ben's spirits sagged further when Lieutenant Colonel Watson sent a message saying he wouldn't be able to meet until mid-March.

"Dammit!" Ben groused to Reggie. "Hate being left in no-man's land. I mean, Watson said they wanted me to transfer to the USAAF, and the sooner the better. What the hell's goin' on?"

"Steady on, me lad," Reggie said quietly. "I hear the new American Eighth Air Force is looking for a lot of pilots. You'll get a berth."

"Maybe!" Ben shouted. "But I've got myself all geared up to make the switch, and they leave me hanging!"

It was early April before Watson reappeared, apologizing that he had been busy with the turnover of British air bases to American forces and the construction of new bases.

Seated in Reggie's office the next afternoon, Ben glared at Watson.

"Look, I regret the delay," Watson said. "But I see from your records you haven't been sitting around doing nothing. Congratulations on breaking up the attack on that convoy."

Ben waved aside the compliment. "I've made my decision. I wanna switch to the USAAF *now!*"

"Capital!" Watson responded. "You won't regret it. You're joining the American air forces at an exciting time. Now to your choice of assignments—fighters, I'm sure. P-51, P-47, or P-38?"

"I want to fly heavy bombers, preferably the B-17."

Watson blinked. "Bombers! With your experience, you're a natural to join almost any fighter outfit now organizing in England. Transition from the Spitfire would be a snap. Change your uniform and airplane, learn some new tactics, and you're ready to go."

"I want heavy bombers."

Watson sat back and studied Ben. He chewed his lip. "Okay. But it's going to be one hell of a transition. You really want to switch to flying a big four-engine job?"

Ben nodded.

"You'll have to go back to the States for training."

"So I'll go back to the States," Ben said. "But I want assurance that I can get into B-17s, and that I can come back to England." *Not about to tell him how badly I want to bomb the Krauts.*

"I think I can do that," Watson said. "There's a big demand for bomber pilots. I'm just amazed you want to be one of them."

Ben didn't respond.

"I'll get your travel orders to USAAF Headquarters in High Wycombe, west of London," Watson said. "You'll be sworn in there and issued USAAF uniforms and identity papers. Transportation stateside will be on one of the airplanes making the transatlantic trip."

That night Ben wrote short notes to his mother and Brice, telling them he was heading home. *Wonder if I'll get there before these do?*

Much to Ben's disgust, it took four weeks for the transfer orders to come through.

"Finally got 'em!" Ben shouted, bursting into Reggie's office waving his orders. "Dammit, another month gone. At this rate, I won't get home until late summer."

Reggie gave him a long look. "Good for you, Sancho. On your way. Ain't happy about it, but there it is."

That night, Reggie told the La Mancha Squadron pilots to arrange a suitable send-off for Ben. Stitch was put in charge.

Chapter 67

HOMEWARD BOUND

Ben hunched forward in his seat as the train chugged toward London. He groaned. A fierce headache, stinging eyes, and a dry tongue reminded him his going-away party had been long, loud, and liquid.

Stitch, master of ceremonies, had outdone himself, rising to new heights with irreverent humor and bawdy jokes. Ben recalled getting angry over one insulting routine, gleefully staged at his expense. But he couldn't remember the details. What the hell, it had all been in good fun. Then there were tears and embraces before one by one, the intrepid warriors collapsed in scattered heaps.

I'm really gonna miss that bunch of silly bastards. Never had friends like that before. And Reggie.

Somewhere close to dawn, he and Reggie were the only partygoers still standing. Reggie grabbed Ben's shoulders and said, "Lesh go for stroll. Got somethin' I wanna . . . I wanna say."

The cool early morning breeze sobered them somewhat. They walked in silence; then Reggie turned to Ben. "Not going to get maudlin, Sancho. Hate to see you leave. Been through a hell of a lot—Spain and now here. Not sure I'd have made it without you."

"Know damn well I wouldn't a made it without you," Ben gushed.

"Now you're gonna go fly one of those lumberin' four-engine tubs, turd droppers," Reggie said. "Make yerself a bloody target for the Luftwaffe fighter boys. Sure you wanna do this?"

"Somethin' I gotta do."

They strolled for another hour, laughing raucously about Spain, their times with Angelica and Manuela, the escape to England, and their ferocious fights in the Battle of Britain. At their barracks, Reggie grabbed Ben in a fierce bear hug.

"Watch your arse, Sancho," he said, and headed to his room.

Ben stood surveying Duxford in the gray predawn, then stumbled off to bed. Later that morning, he slipped away before his worse-for-the-wear comrades were awake.

At High Wycombe, Ben stood before the adjutant's desk, bleary-eyed and still shaky from the previous evening's hilarity.

"You feeling all right, Lieutenant?" the adjutant asked.

"Yessir! My RAF squadron mates gave me a send-off last night. Bit of a bash, as they say. I'll be all right, sir."

"Okaaay," he said, eyeing Ben and smiling. "So let's get on with the business of getting you into the U.S. Army Air Force."

He was transferred as a senior-grade first lieutenant. The brief process ended with a perfunctory handshake and directions to the equipment supply room to collect uniforms and equipment. He was booked into the drab bachelor officers' quarters (BOQ).

"Welcome to Uncle Sam's air force," Ben mumbled. "Kind of a letdown. But what'd I expect, a brass band?"

Ben was stretched out on his cot when there was a knock on the door.

"Are you Lieutenant Findlay, Ben Findlay?" A slightly built first lieutenant peeked around the door.

"That's me. What's up?"

"I'm Lieutenant Cody. Ah, pleased to meet you. Mind if I sit down?"

Ben waved him to a chair.

"Ah, we—that's my crew and me—we've completed our twenty-five missions . . . Ah, we're in B-17s, see. And, ah, we were among the first crews to complete the big two-five and get our tickets home. We've been ordered to fly our airplane, ah, Buxom Baby, back to the States. We're supposed to take her on a war bond tour."

Ben stretched. "That was quick. How the hell did you get that many missions so soon?"

"Yeah. Well, we were in the first wave. We started operations last November. The weather was good, and we flew a lot. Mostly against targets on the French coast and in northern France. We were real lucky. Anyway, ah, I think you're gonna be offered a seat for the ride home on our airplane," Cody continued. "Well, not really a seat, but a space on our airplane. It'll speed up your trip back to the States."

"Really." Ben sat up, his interest piqued.

"Yeah, really. Ah, and we're scheduled to take off day after tomorrow at 0700 hours."

"Great!" Ben jumped up and shook hands with Cody. "Pleased to meet ya, and glad to get an early ride home."

"Ah, do I have it right that you have a lotta experience as a fighter pilot with the RAF and some, ah, outfits in Spain?" Cody asked. "And now you want to fly bombers?"

"Yeah, you got it right. But it's a long story."

"Well, ah, there's a rub, you see?" Cody examined his hands. "Ah, I was hopin' you might have some multiengine time."

"Nope. All my time's in single-engine trainers and fighters. Why, what difference does that make?"

"Ah, well, you see," Cody stammered. "Fred, he's my copilot . . . and is kinda sick. An' we're afraid if we send him to the flight surgeon, he'll be grounded, and we'll be stuck here 'til he gets better. I mean, we did our twenty-five missions, and we wanna get home. But with Fred sick, that might get all messed up. An' we don't wanna leave him behind."

"Where do I come in?" Ben asked.

"Ah, I was sorta hopin' that if Fred gets worse, maybe you could help me fly our ship back home. We'll get him on board okay and sittin' in the right seat at the start. I think we can handle the takeoff, but then Fred's probably gonna have to lie down, you know, back in the radio compartment. He goes in and out of fevers and gets the shakes, see, but he really wants to get home. And so do the rest of us."

Ben stared at Cody. Now that he had started the journey and switched to the USAAF, he wanted to get home too.

"Well, hell, how hard can it be?" Ben asked. "You get us all onboard, prop ole Fred up in the right seat, and I'll stand behind him. If you can get us airborne, I can slip into the seat, and you can tell me what to do."

Cody puffed a sigh of relief. "Hey, look, thanks a lot!" He pumped Ben's hand. "This'll be swell. We can make it work!"

On departure day, Ben reported to flight operations early. Cody and eight members of his crew entered.

"Where's Fred?" Ben whispered.

"We got him out to the airplane early. Tucked him in," Cody said. "I told the ops guys he was doin' a thorough walk-around inspection. 'fraid he's pretty sick. I'm really gonna need your help."

Cody gave Ben a quick summary of their flight plan. It could be a rough crossing, probably have to fight headwinds. They'd fly first to Prestwick, Scotland, then on to Reykjavik, Iceland. They'd overnight at Reykjavik and get a good night's sleep, Cody added, because the next stop—Bluie West One, a rough air base on Eriksfjord near Narsarssuak, Greenland—was a tough place to get into.

"Bluie West One, what kind of a name is that?" Ben asked.

"The U.S. military made up code colors for nearly every place in the world," Cody said. "For some reason, Greenland got blue, so Bluie West One it is."

Ben shrugged.

"They gave me and Art, our navigator, a special briefing about Bluie West," Cody said. "We gotta find a damn fjord called Eriksfjord, an' there're three of 'em close together that look alike. Then we have to fly about thirty miles up the fjord to find the base. They said we could expect to be in a narrow canyon under the clouds," Cody added. "No turnin' around, so we need to be sure we're in the right fjord!"

Ben grimaced. "This sounds dangerous."

"Bluie West has one five-thousand-foot runway, oriented sorta east-west, you know, 27 and 09. But the compass deviation up that close to the North Pole is 30 degrees, so I guess we'll actually be headin' southwest. Not sure, but Art'll know. And do ya know what the major landmark is?" Cody continued. "It's the rusted hulk of a ship that ran aground just south of the field! After passing the wreck, you don't see the runway until you make a final turn around a mountain, for Chrissake! The runway is pierced steel planking, on gravel. We'll refuel there and get the hell out and try to make Goose Bay, Labrador, for another overnighter."

Goose Bay was almost home, Cody continued. The final leg would be southwest to Floyd Bennett Airfield on the Brooklyn shore. Ben smiled thinly. *Full circle! Brooklyn, the jumping-off point for my grand adventure.*

They headed for Cody's B-17, Buxom Baby. Ben admired the well-endowed, scantily clad woman painted in vivid colors on the nose. Below her, two rows of painted outlines of bombs represented their twenty-five missions.

Ben gazed in wonder at the size of the bomber. This beast was a far cry from the trim Spitfire he was used to strapping into. "No wonder they call it a Flying Fortress," he muttered.

"Anything wrong?" Cody asked.

"Ah, nooo. It's just so damn big. Takes some gettin' used to."

"Aw, don't worry about that," Cody smiled. "She's a beauty to fly. Very forgiving."

Fred held up through the engine start and cockpit checkout procedures, but when Cody started to taxi, Fred slumped forward over the control yoke. Ben caught him, and he and the radio operator eased Fred out of the copilot's seat. By the time they got him settled on a bed of parachutes and flight bags in the radio compartment, Cody was calling from the cockpit.

"Ben, come on up here. I'm gonna need some help right away."

They completed the pretakeoff checklist and taxied into position on the runway.

"Lock the tail wheel with that handle," Cody said. "After takeoff, I'll tell you what to do with the landing gear and flaps."

They soon were airborne, flying north to Prestwick. From there, they'd fly a great circle route over the North Atlantic and then head south for Brooklyn. Ben settled into the copilot's seat, enjoying the expansive view of the horizon through the B-17's three-inch-thick windshield.

"On takeoff you didn't raise the tail to flying position before lifting her off," he yelled to Cody. Below ten thousand feet, they didn't need oxygen masks and could communicate without using the intercom.

"Right. The B-17's wing is set for maximum lift in the three-point taildragger position," Cody yelled. "We just accelerate down the runway until she flies herself off.

Important when you're carryin' a big bomb load. Then we get the gear and flaps up and ease her into a climb."

"I think I'm gonna enjoy flying this thing," Ben grinned.

Refueling in Prestwick and the overnight stay in Reykjavik went according to plan. Next morning, the weather briefing at Reykjavik was not promising. They'd face fierce headwinds as they flew westward, and Bluie West One was going to be at or below minimums when they arrived.

The forecasters were right. Out of Reykjavik, they bounced up and down in fierce turbulent headwinds. They approached Iceland and Bluie West One in rapidly deteriorating weather and with minimum fuel.

"Ben, no choice," Cody yelled. "Gotta slide under the cloud cover and hope to hell we find the right fjord. Have one shot at it. Keep your eyes peeled."

He called into the intercom, "Pilot to navigator . . . Art, are we there? We're down to eight hundred feet. When do I start lookin' for that damn fjord?"

"Skipper, we should see it soon. *There they are*! Aim for the middle one!"

"Here we go," Cody shouted, banking into the fjord.

"*Jesus!*" Harry yelled from his bombadier position in the glass nose. "You sure we're not flyin' up a box canyon?"

"Ben and Harry, watch for the wrecked ship!" Cody shouted over the intercom. "Ben, gimme first notch of flaps and the gear as soon as you see it! The runway should be somewhere around the next bend."

Ben saw the rusting hulk slide by, popped the flaps, and dropped the landing gear. "Got it, Cody!" he yelled. "Follow the fjord left to . . . *here*! Runway should be around that next hill there!"

"*God almighty!*" Cody yelled as he banked left and prepared for a steep right turn onto the final approach. "*Full flaps*! We're there!"

He swung the aircraft in a tight turn around the last mountain and slammed it onto the runway. They clanked along the steel-mat runway and rolled to a stop.

"*Damn!*" someone yelled over the intercom. "We still in one piece?"

The weather closed over them. For the next three days, they bugged the meteorological officer for word that the storm front was moving through. Fred's fever soared each night, and the crew took turns cooling him with wet towels.

The overcast finally lifted, and Cody fired up Buxom Baby. Their departure into low scudding clouds toward the 2,500-foot mountain off the end of the runway was as gut-wrenching as their wild-ass low-level approach along the fjord. But they were on the way to Goose Bay, Labrador.

Fierce headwinds again slowed their westward progress, and they arrived at Goose Bay late and exhausted. The flight engineer reported number four engine was running very rough and needed a thorough inspection.

"We're gonna have to spend the night here," Cody said. "Much as I want to get home, I'm not gonna risk taking off until we get number four looked at."

The final leg to Floyd Bennett Airfield in Brooklyn was uneventful. During the initial approach down the Hudson River, the crew was treated to a spectacular panorama of Manhattan. Ben's throat tightened as they turned over the Statue of Liberty.

"Last time I saw that lady in the harbor was in '37," Ben said. "When a bunch of us headed for Spain on the old *Escobar*—"

Cody's call for flaps and gear interrupted his reverie.

Floyd Bennett was jammed with airplanes assembling for transatlantic ferry flights. Cody taxied behind a Follow Me Jeep and parked Buxom Baby in a far corner of the ramp. The B-17's four engines coughed and shut down.

"Can't thank you enough, Ben," he said. "Couldn't have done it without you."

"My pleasure," Ben said, patting the control yoke. "I'm gonna enjoy flying these babies."

Cody said a quick good-bye and shook Ben's hand. He trundled Fred into a jeep and headed for the base hospital. Ben said good-bye to the crew, wished them well on their tour, and headed for the adjutant's office. He thought about the transatlantic trip. Would he ever see those fellas again? He was impressed with the B-17, convinced he had made the right decision to upgrade to the four-engine bomber. *I'm gonna give the Krauts a taste of what they've been doing to England.*

Chapter 68

OKLAHOMA!

The adjutant eyed Ben closely.

"Ah, Lieutenant, where the hell have you been?" he grumbled. "You were expected through here a month ago. Do a little dallying along the way?"

"Didn't do any dallying, sir," Ben said evenly. He started to explain, but let it drop. "Hitched a ride home on a B-17. Took us eight days to make the trip."

The adjutant grunted. He waved papers in Ben's face.

"According to these, you were due here in May. You were to get a ten-day home leave and then proceed to Altus Army Airfield for the next B-17 transition class. That class starts next Monday. You have three days to get your ass down there."

"Three days!" Ben exclaimed, recalling the weeks he spent cooling his heels in England. "Where's Altus Army Airfield?"

"Way-the-hell-and gone in the southwest corner of Oklahoma, nearly to Texas. Long haul from here." He was enjoying Ben's predicament.

"I don't get home leave?" Ben asked evenly.

"Maybe after transition training."

"I'm new to the USAAF. You have any suggestions how I get to way-the-hell-and-gone down to Altus from here?" Ben snapped.

"Thought you'd never ask, Lieutenant. Got a C-47 courier flight leaving here at 0630 hours tomorrow. Stops in Chicago and then runs on to Oak City. Check in at base ops there, and see if they got anything goin' south. If not, there's always the train, or you can get out on the highway and thumb a ride."

"But no home leave," Ben persisted.

"Not my fault, Lieutenant. Like I said, you were due through here a month ago."

Ben sent telegrams to his mother and Brice. "Back in U.S. Letter follows. Flying tomorrow Altus Army Airfield, Oklahoma. Write from there."

Ben slouched in his metal bucket seat as the C-47 transport droned toward Chicago. *Not sure I'm gonna like Uncle Sam's air force.*

By the time they reached Oklahoma City, Ben was butt sore. His ears ached from the throbbing engine noise that rattled the bare metal cabin. Base operations said they had no airplanes going to Altus that night. The duty sergeant suggested he check into the BOQ and come back in the morning.

"Gotta be there day after tomorrow," Ben said. "Appreciate it if you can find me a ride."

The next morning, Ben climbed into the right seat of a twin-engine Cessna UC-78 courier plane. The pilot said he had two stops at bases in southwest Oklahoma, but he'd get Ben to Altus by nightfall. The approach to Altus's long runway did nothing to improve Ben's spirits. It looked like a dreary place. He checked in with yet another adjutant, no friendlier than the others.

"Your name's on the list for the next transition class, but I don't have your Form 39-28 records file," he said, glancing up at Ben. "Where's your file?"

"I don't know what a Form 39-28 file is, much less where mine is," Ben said wearily. "I've just flown in from Floyd Bennett. Nobody there said anything about my records file. The adjutant said I was a month late or something, so I got here as quick as I could."

"What were you doing at Floyd Bennett?"

"I flew in from England."

"England! All our guys are going the other way. You better explain."

"I transferred to the USAAF from the RAF," Ben said. "I've been flying with the RAF since '39. Before that, I flew with the Republican Air Force in the Spanish civil war."

"Oh, one of those," the adjutant said, giving Ben a disapproving look. "That means you most likely don't even have a Form 39-28. And the Brits will take forever to send over whatever records they have on you. Probably never catch up with you."

"So what am I supposed to do?"

"I'll get you into the BOQ. You can eat in the officers' club or the mess hall. Report to Building Number 3265 tomorrow morning at 0700 hours and check in with the instructor."

Ben slipped into a front-row seat in the classroom, nodding greetings to the other officers. The instructor, Maj. Lawrence W. James, was a by-the-book officer who considered Ben's lack of records a major breach of army protocol. He made a point of standing ramrod straight and assuming a condescending tone to anyone he felt was inferior. That included nearly everyone.

"Highly irregular, highly irregular," he fussed, before finally allowing Ben to stay in his class. "But I suppose we have no choice, so let's begin."

He launched into the course introduction in a grating monotone. His black hair glistened as though he had slathered a full jar of hair cream on it. He smacked a wooden pointer into his left palm as he paced in front of the class. A neatly trimmed mustache twitched under his slightly upturned nose. Ben noted basic pilot's wings pinned on his uniform blouse. *Not even a command pilot. Not much flying time for a major.*

"The first thing I want to stress with all of you," James said, "is that you are being prepared to go into combat. I emphasize *combat*! As soon as you're qualified, you'll go off to war. Some of you won't come back."

He consulted his roster. "I see all of you will be going on to B-17 airplane commander school. You'll be in charge of a ten-man crew in the Flying Fortress, and likely as not, you'll be assigned to an Eighth Air Force unit in England. That means you'll be bombing occupied Europe and Germany."

"Your first taste of combat is going to be tough, very tough," James continued. "Our job is to prepare you for what you'll face."

Ben shifted in his chair. *This fella is pissing me off. Hasn't any idea what combat's like.*

"Yes, ah," James consulted his roster. "Ah, Findlay. You have a problem, a comment . . . ?"

Keep your mouth shut, Findlay. Not worth makin' waves.

"Findlay," James snapped, "I asked if you had a comment."

"Uh, no, sir. Umm, I mean, I was just thinking about what you said about combat. Ah, I, ah have combat experience. Actually quite a bit of it."

"Really?" James responded, clearly surprised and more than a little annoyed. "How so?"

"I flew with the Republican Air Force in Spain in '37 and '38 during the Spanish civil war." Ben said. "When the Republicans lost, I escaped to England and joined the Royal Air Force. Flew with the RAF four years, including the Battle of Britain."

James sniffed. "Really. What airplanes did you fly?"

"Russian Polikarpov I-16s in Spain and Spitfires with the RAF."

"Flew with the Russians, eh? All of your time is in fighters?" James asked. "Now you're switching to bombers? Had enough of facing the enemy by yourself?"

"Sir, I was an ace in Spain and with the RAF in England!" Ben retorted. "I'm not afraid to face the enemy. Besides, even in fighters you're not alone. You always have your wingman and your squadron mates."

"Interesting," James sniffed, although he made it clear he did not think it was. "It's a pity your records haven't caught up with you. We would have known that in advance."

He turned to the class as if dismissing Ben's claim. "So let's see how we all get along in this course."

Now that was dumb. Why'd I start off on the wrong foot with this fella by shootin' off my mouth?

Classroom training lasted three weeks. Ben found it interesting because, in addition to teaching him about flying multiengine airplanes, it gave him some insights into life in the USAAF. *Hell of a lot different than the RAF. These fellas sure are stuck on regulations.*

The pilots spent two more weeks flying the twin-engine, Cessna AT-17 Bobcat trainer. The airplane, dubbed the Bamboo Bomber because of its laminated-wood wing, was powered by two Jacobs R-775-9 engines rated at 245 horsepower, which gave it good performance. Ben soon mastered the intricacies of managing two engines and flying with one engine feathered. On completion of the course, Ben was assigned to B-17 airplane commander's school at Hendricks Field in Sebring, Florida.

This time the adjutant had good news. Ben was granted a two-week leave. He hitched rides on a variety of military airplanes that hopscotched him north, finally depositing him three days later at Baker Airport.

Chapter 69

FULL CIRCLE

Ben stood on the Baker Airport ramp. Passengers boarded two American Airlines DC-3s parked next to their military counterpart, the C-47 transport plane on which Ben had arrived. Four Stearman trainers stood in their wheel chocks in front of Simpson's Flying Service. Next to them were three BT-9 advanced trainers, one being fired up by its pilot. Ben saw a fourth BT-9 turn onto final approach, trailed by two more Stearmans.

"Wow!" he exclaimed. "This place has really changed in six years!"

He had telephoned his mother from Detroit City Airport, and she wept uncontrollably. Ben headed for the terminal, wondering if she'd remember his arrival time.

A frail, stoop-shouldered woman rushed toward him with outstretched arms.

"Hello, Mom," he said.

"Ben, Ben, Ben, oh Ben . . . ," she sobbed into his shoulder.

Tears streamed down her cheeks as she tried to speak; then she just gazed lovingly at him, patting him on the chest. Ben was shocked by her careworn appearance, her wispy gray hair. *She's gotten so old*!

"Ben, thank God you've arrived safely. How wonderful it is to have you back home. You look tired. Did you have a difficult trip? Have you had lunch? You look like you've lost weight. My Lord, how tall are you now? You look so grown up in that uniform. You aren't going to have to go back to that horrid war, are you? Oh, your father is here too. Now where is he? Oh yes, he's right over there. Ben, he's been so worried about you . . ."

Ben gave his father a steady look and extended his hand. "Hello, Dad."

"Hello, Ben. Ah, welcome home," his father said, gripping Ben's hand tightly. "Good, ah, good to have you back home."

"Thanks," Ben said. "Good to be here. I can't believe how this place has changed."

His mother held his hand during the drive home. Butch and Bertha growled and studied him warily through aged rheumy eyes. Then realizing who he was, they erupted into frenzied tail-wagging, yipping, and barking and threw themselves repeatedly against his legs.

"Hello, you two old bums," Ben said, fondling their fluffy ears and graying muzzles. "You remember me, eh?"

"I so wish you could have gotten home earlier, Ben," his mother said. "Joe was here for two days. He's a platoon leader in the Marines now. Said he was going to California to board a ship sailing to some place out in the Pacific Ocean. I worry about him going on such a long boat trip . . ."

"Damn, I'm sorry to have missed Joe," Ben said. *But the boat trip's the least of Joe's worries.*

That evening Ben insisted on doing the chores. His father, who had stiffly kept his distance, agreed. The smells in the barn triggered overwhelming memories. He slipped into the routine of feeding animals and milking cows as if he'd never been away. His two canine companions trailed him everywhere he went. He resisted the temptation to climb atop the windmill as he trudged to the house in the gathering dusk. *Maybe tomorrow. Wanna take another look at that far horizon.*

Ben felt uneasy as they sat around the kitchen table. He had so much to tell them, but didn't know where to start. His father tried several times to ask about the war, but his mother kept changing the subject. She didn't want to hear about all the killing and destruction.

"Look, I'm bushed," Ben said finally. "I need to hit the hay." *Ha! Easy to slip back into farm boy talk.*

"Like a cup of cocoa before going to bed?" his mother asked. "I made your favorite cookies."

"Thanks, Mom. I'll look forward to havin' them tomorrow."

He gave his mother a good night hug. His father cleared his throat.

"Ah, I don't know if you're aware of it, but we're building Tigercat tanks for the army. Haven't built a car since early '42. Anyway, tomorrow I have to drive down to the Willow Run Proving Grounds near Detroit to work on some transmission problems. Ah, I'll be gone at least a week. How long is your leave?"

"Took me nearly three days to get here," Ben said. "Probably take that long to get down to my next base, Hendricks Field near Sebring, Florida. So I guess I'll have a little over a week at home."

His mother stifled a sob.

"Oh," his father said. "Well, look, ah, I'll try to get back before you leave, okay?"

"Sure, Dad."

"Ah, the old pickup is still running. Guess you'll want to visit your friends at the airport."

Ben telephoned Al Simpson the next morning and said he'd drop by around noon. He could hear Brice bellowing hello in the background. Simpson said they'd have lunch at the Fly Inn.

A huge WELCOME HOME, BEN! sign hung from the ceiling. Red, white, and blue bunting was tacked to the walls. Simpson and Angie stood grinning like schoolkids. She ran to him and gave him a fierce hug and a kiss on the cheek.

"Wow, look at you in that spiffy uniform," she gushed.

Simpson clapped him on the back and gave him a crushing handshake. "Great to see you, Ben! By God, you've certainly grown up. And a first lieutenant yet!"

"Glad to be back," Ben grinned, looking around. "You've made some big changes. Simpson's Flying Service! Business must be good."

"Yah, sometimes too good. We got a big flight training contract from the army. That's why all the airplanes out there. I've hired four more instructors. Brice and I are working our butts off."

"Ah, where is the Ancient Pelican?" Ben asked.

Simpson pointed to the airport traffic pattern. "In that BT-9, where he is 'bout ten hours a day, six days a week."

Simpson and Angie peppered Ben with questions about his experiences in Spain and England. While they talked, the BT-9 landed, taxied up to the gas pumps, and shut down. Brice levered himself out of the rear seat, smacked the student pilot on the head, and stumped up to the office. He dropped his parachute on the floor and stood scowling.

Ben gaped at the shrunken form standing before him. *My god, he's aged fifty years.*

"Yah, whaddaya want, kid?" Brice rumbled, unsuccessfully suppressing a smile.

"Well, sir, umm, I wonder if I could get a job here—" Ben responded.

With a muffled sob, Brice lurched forward and grabbed Ben in a hug. Ben grimaced at the bony feel of Brice's sagging shoulders. "Let's have a look at ya, Ben," Brice said, stepping back.

Ben stood grinning foolishly.

"Nice-looking uniform, Lieutenant. And lookit, two sets of wings, RAF and USAAF. What're these ribbons for? Not good conduct fer sure."

"Actually, this one is," Ben said, pointing to one ribbon. "This one is the RAF's Distinguished Flying Cross, this one the Battle of Britain Clasp, and this one the Air Crew Europe Star. Don't have any from the USAAF yet."

Brice grabbed him again. "Let's get some chow at the Fly Inn! Al, I've canceled my schedule this afternoon. Let the young fellers take up the slack."

The lunch stretched into a three-hour raucous reunion. Simpson and Angie finally slipped away, but Brice held on to Ben's arm.

"Have another Vernors," he chuckled. "Don't s'pose they got any of that in Merry Olde England."

"Naw, but they've got ginger beer. Good, but it takes the skin off the roof of your mouth."

Brice roared and slapped the table. Ben noticed the waitress wink as she set down another draft beer in front of Brice. *Bet she's slippin' a little Irish in those.*

Brice plied him with questions about his combat encounters. Ben responded with elaborate hand-flying gestures. He retold the story of his first aerial victory while flying on Reggie's wing in Spain. Brice laughed uncontrollably as Ben described how he had inadvertently wrenched his I-16 into a high-speed stall, followed by a snap roll and another high-speed stall that caused his German pursuer to overshoot and become an easy target.

"By God, I'd have loved to see that!" Brice shouted, pounding the table with his fist. "Wish I'd been there."

"You were," Ben said quietly. "I could hear you in my mind, yellin' at me as if you were in the backseat coaching me through it. Brice, you trained me real good. Saved my life."

Brice blinked and swallowed hard. "You were easy to train, Ben. Natural flier. Hell, I wish they all were that easy. Bet that poor Kraut bastard was really surprised! Probably wondered where the hell you disappeared to. Damn! If you hadn't nailed him, he'd probably have gone back to his squadron and tried to teach the other pilots the great Russian escape maneuver!"

Ben held Brice spellbound with his Battle of Britain stories and the sheer joy of flying the Spitfire.

"With all your fighter experience—a double ace, for God's sake—why in hell are you switchin' to bombers?" Brice demanded. "I mean, the B-17 is one helluva airplane. But it ain't a fighter."

"Mind's made up, Brice. I wanna take the war to Germany. Bomb them for what they did in Spain and still are doing in England."

Brice grunted and signaled the waitress, who cheerfully replenished his augmented beer. Ben had switched to beer by now. Brice appeared not to notice. *Don't like to see him like this. He looks awful. Wonder if I should try to ease him outta here?*

"Whattaya thinkin', Ben?" Brice asked suddenly.

"My butt's sore. What say we move on."

"To where?"

"I dunno. The day's about gone. How about I drive you home? I'll pick ya up in the morning, and maybe we can find an hour or so for a flight in the Peril. You still have her, don't you?"

"You bet! Still got 'er. Bit ragged around the edges, but she still flies sweet as ever."

At home, Ben helped Brice partially undress and directed him to the bathroom. Brice returned and flopped onto the bed. His sonorous snoring filled the small house as Ben slipped out.

Next morning, Ben sat chatting with Simpson. Brice took a student pilot out for aerobatic training in a BT-9.

"I'm kinda worried about Brice," Ben said, watching Simpson for a reaction.

"Me too, Ben. It's his heart. That and his drinking. Stubborn old bastard refuses to see a doctor. Says he doesn't want to lose his medical certificate. I don't know . . . He's the best flight instructor I've ever seen, but I also can't take too many chances on his health."

"Yeah, of course," Ben said. "Is it bad enough that we have to worry about him having a heart attack in the air? When was his last physical?"

"Oh, 'bout six months ago. Can't prove it, but I think he quit drinking and shaped himself up before seein' the doc. Now he seems to be slipping again."

"Probably wouldn't do any good for me to talk with him about it," Ben said. "How about I go flying with him tomorrow? See if he still has the edge. Have any of his students complained?"

"You kidding?" Simpson laughed. "Most of them worship the man. A couple of the others are so scared of him, they wouldn't complain no matter what happened."

Ben did the chores again that night. He loved being in the barn, listening to the grunts and sighs as the animals settled in for the night. His aim with an upturned teat proved as good as ever, and he squirted warm milk smack into the open mouths of the gaggle of barn cats that lined up behind each cow. Before returning to the house, he climbed the windmill and sat surveying what once had looked like a far horizon.

"No matter where ya go or what ya do, that horizon's always out there in the distance," he mused.

Ben and his mother lingered over dinner. She filled him in on the latest news from their farm neighbors. Ben strained to show interest.

"Many of your friends from school have joined up," she said. "Donna, oh, I always thought you two would make a lovely couple . . . well, Donna joined the army. And her mother said she's driving a big truck! Can you imagine? And Barney, you and he were such good friends. Well, Barney joined the Marines. Say, do you suppose Barney and Joe might meet up out there in the Pacific? It'd be nice to have a friend from back home."

She sighed. "I don't know, Ben. I'm so worried about you and Joe and all the other boys and—and, I guess, girls—having to go off to this terrible war. 'Course, you went off before it was really necessary, didn't you?"

"Mom, it was necessary then, just like it is now," Ben replied.

"Oh, I guess so." She smiled. "You didn't think I knew you were actually fighting and not just flying supplies and the like. I could read between the lines, and I saw what they said in the newspapers. Guessed what you were really up to."

Ben looked at his plate. "I didn't really think I was fooling you."

"Oh Ben! I hate that all this awfulness is happening around the world!"

Ben rose early, got things going in the barn, and had a leisurely breakfast with his mother.

"Mom, I'm going to head to the airport. I want to fly with Brice, see how he's gettin' along."

"Is anything the matter? Is he all right?

"Don't know for sure, Mom."

Ben stepped back in time as he strapped into the back cockpit of the Yellow Peril. Brice pointed out one big improvement, a new two-way intercom. No more yelling down the Gosport Tube. Brice clambered into the front cockpit with the usual, "I'll get in the front hole up here an' try to keep you from killin' me."

They took off into the golden light of the autumn afternoon. Ben settled into the seat and absorbed the sights, sounds, and smells. He leaned his head to the side of the cockpit and let the Peril's prop wash buffet his face. *Close to perfect as it gets.*

"All right, Lieutenant!' Brice barked in his earphones. "We gonna just drone along on a straight line, or are we gonna do some *flyin'*?"

"What did you have in mind, sir?" Ben responded with a grin. "Could you show me some maneuvers I can try to learn?" *Smoke the old boy out. See if he's lost his touch.*

"Why hell, yes, kid. Lemme demonstrate sumthin' called aerobatics. Follow along on the controls, but lightly! Don't want ya stranglin' the stick!"

Brice racked the Peril into a high-g turn, starting a horizontal figure eight. Ben heard him grunting heavily. Two snap rolls followed, with a brief acceleration and pull up into a near-vertical climb that ended with a perfectly coordinated hammerhead stall. As they picked up speed in the descent, Brice pulled the Peril into a loop, rolled upright on the downslope, and pulled up into a second loop to complete the Cuban eight.

"Geee!" Ben yelled into the intercom. "This is exciting! Can you do some more?"

Brice responded with the full air-show aerobatic routine. He hit every crossover point exactly and transitioned smoothly from one maneuver to the next.

"Wow! Sure hasn't lost his edge," Ben chortled. "One helluva flyer."

"Okay, kid. Let's see what you can do."

Ben responded with a nearly identical routine, augmented with a few variations of his own. Brice roared with delight and waved both arms over his head.

"Damn! It's great to fly with a real flyer," echoed in Ben's earphones. "You musta been paying attention, after all."

Ben did two touch-and-go landings and then made a high-speed fighter break approach to the final landing. He smiled as the Peril slid onto the runway in a smooth three-point touchdown. The setting sun cast long shadows as Ben secured the Peril. Brice stared at him. Were those tears in his eyes?

"Brice, that was fantastic," Ben said, gripping the old man's beefy hand. "I really enjoyed it."

"Gawdalmighty! I missed you, Ben," Brice said, grabbing him in a bear hug. "Most of these new kids are ham-fisted. Not a natural flyer among 'em. But the army's clamoring for 'em. Can hardly keep up with the demand."

"You holding up okay?" Ben asked.

Brice squinted at him. "You been talking to Simpson?"

"No," Ben lied. "I'm just concerned you might be running yourself into the ground."

"Literally or figuratively?"

Ben smiled and shrugged.

"Well, the ole ticker has been actin' up a bit," Brice said. "If it gets any worse, I'll hafta quit flyin'. In the meantime . . ."

"Okay, Brice. I just hope you can take it a little easy."

"Sure, but ya do know there's a war on, don't ya?"

Ben's leave tumbled by. He flew with Brice two more times. He felt closer to Brice than ever before, which made it even harder to see how frail he had become. Ben spent as much time as he could with his mother, who became quiet and withdrawn as his departure time loomed. His father phoned from Willow Run.

"Ah, Ben, the job here is taking longer than I expected," he said. "Do you have to leave soon?"

"Day after tomorrow, Dad."

"Ah, okay. Well, I'll see you next time you get leave. Meantime, good luck."

"Sure, Dad. Thanks."

Brice picked up Ben at the farm on his departure day. Ben's mother clung to him weeping, unable to say more than, "I love you, Ben. Take care of yourself. Please be careful."

"I will, and I'll write often, Mom."

Following quick good-byes at Simpson's, Brice walked Ben to the terminal. A sergeant directed him to the C-47 courier plane on the ramp. Brice looked like a mournful hound dog. Tears streamed down his cheeks. "So long, Ben. I'm gonna miss you, kiddo."

Ben hugged him long and hard.

The flight to Chicago took all day, with multiple stops at air bases along the way. Ben caught a train that night, and after interminable hours in a coach chair, stumbled onto the platform in Atlanta. There a warrant officer checked his travel orders and issued him a ticket to Tampa, Florida. Ben arrived a near-zombie. A sergeant at the army travel counter said he could catch a courier flight at 0700 the next morning from nearby MacDill Field to Hendricks Field at Sebring, Florida.

Chapter 70

THE FLYING FORTRESS

The courier pilot plied Ben with questions about his combat experiences. Ben countered with questions about Sebring and Hendricks Field.

"What's the base like?" Ben asked.

"Big. Has to be, to handle so many Forts. It's got four runways, wide ones, three hundred feet, and one helluva lot of ramp area and taxiways. Hell, I can nearly land this crate crossways on the runways. They just started buildin' it in '40. Pretty much finished, but it's still a little rough."

Ben repaid him with several stories of his combat experience, especially in the Battle of Britain.

"Wow, that musta been some time!" the pilot said. "I sure hope I get a shot at combat. I'm sick of rattlin' around in this thing."

"Stick with it," Ben said. "You'll get your chance."

The Sebring base adjutant told Ben he had been assigned to B-17 Airplane Commander Class 10-43. Classes the first week would be devoted to ground school. The daily schedule then would switch to two hours of classroom work and four hours of flying instruction. Two student pilots would take turns on each training flight.

Ben's roommate was First Lt. George Sanderson from Tacoma, Washington. Sanderson had spent a tour in twin-engine Douglas B-25 attack bombers but had not deployed overseas. He and Ben hit it off from the beginning.

"What the hell are you doin' in B-17s?" Sanderson asked. "Didn't they offer you fighters when you transferred from the RAF?"

"Yeah, they did," Ben said. *Damn, I'm tired of explainin' this.* "I had a great time flying fighters. But I wanna fly B-17s, take some war to the Krauts' backyard. I saw Luftwaffe bomber squadrons do a lot of awful things in Spain, and they're still doin' it in England. I'm gonna try to pay 'em back."

"Jeeze, you sound like you're on some kinda crusade," Sanderson said.

"Might call it that."

Their classroom instructor introduced himself as Capt. Stanislas P. Jaworski from Minneapolis. "And no, I ain't Swedish."

Jaworski left no doubt they would be hard-pressed to keep up with the program.

"The B-17 is a big and complex airplane," he said. "You got a lot of systems to learn and not much time to do it. But you're also gonna have help from your copilot, navigator, bombardier, and flight engineer. They'll help you fly this bird by doin' a lot of the hands-on stuff. But that doesn't mean you don't hafta know the systems and how to manage 'em.

"Another big part of this course will be teaching you how to lead a crew of nine men. They're gonna look to you as their leader, not just their pilot. You'll be the boss. Having said that, big as the B-17 is, you're gonna be operating in cramped quarters under a lot of stress. You need to work as a team. Gotta treat your crew members like what they are, friends and buddies. The trick is hittin' the right balance."

Jaworski described the B-17G model they'd be flying: wingspan just short of 104 feet, length slightly over 74 feet, topped by a vertical tail that stood slightly over 19 feet. On the ground, the airplane sat in a three-point taildragger stance.

"She has an empty weight of over 36,000 pounds," Jaworski said. He tapped a large drawing of the B-17 hanging on the wall. "Gross weight is 65,500 pounds, and top speed is just shy of 290 miles per hour. Service ceiling is 35,000 feet and range is 2,000 miles, carrying a bomb load of 6,000 pounds. On short-range missions, this baby can carry over 17,000 pounds of bombs."

Jaworski added, "Learning to manage multiple engines will be the biggest challenge. But once airborne, the airplane is stable and has few bad flight characteristics."

He continued, "Your ground crew will keep your airplane in flying condition. Get acquainted real fast with your ground crew chief and his team. Your life depends on how good they do their jobs. But as airplane commander, you're responsible for seein' that your ship is flight ready."

Jaworski led them through the ground checks—not unlike those for other airplanes they've flown, but the walk-around inspection was more involved because of the B-17's complex systems.

"The B-17G is powered by four Wright Cyclone R-1820 engines," Jaworski continued. "They're nine-cylinder radial jobs rated at 1,200 horsepower each. That's with the General Electric turbosuperchargers stuffin' air big-time into each engine's carburetor. The superchargers are driven by turbine wheels located in each engine's exhaust stack. These are activated by cockpit controls that open or close waste gate valves in each stack. This means another system beyond throttles, prop controls, fuel mixture, and so on, that you hafta consider when operatin' the engines. See your manuals."

Wow! Nearly five thousand horsepower. Makes my Spit seem pretty puny.

Jaworski smacked the cutaway drawing and indicated the ten crew positions. "Pilot and copilot up here in the cockpit, with the flight engineer and top-turret gunner, behind them. Bombardier in the glass nose here, and navigator behind him here," he said. "Bombardier also has a nose gun. Radio operator's station is behind the wing, here. Ball turret is here in the belly. Tight quarters. You'll need a little guy to fit here. The two waist-gunner stations are here at open windows on the right and left sides of the aft fuselage behind the bomb bay, here, and the tail gunner is back here in the extended tail cone."

The first two days of ground school focused on the B-17G's systems. Ben's mind reeled as he struggled to absorb the details. Everything he was familiar with on the Spitfire was multiplied by four. On the third day, Jaworski talked about the airplane's flying characteristics; critical speeds for takeoff, cruise, and landing; flap settings; and techniques for achieving maximum performance. He also explained why the B-17 takes off from the three-wheel taildragger stance, eliminating the need to raise the tail to flying position.

"Today we're gonna talk about crew management and discipline," Jaworski said as the pilots gathered on the fourth day. "We got some experts here who'll give you some advice on how to interact with the nine other fellas on your team. Remember, you gotta be the boss. But you also have to win their support."

Jaworski introduced two captains, psychologists in civilian life and specialists in crew integration. He pronounced the last two words with a grimace.

Ben had trouble paying attention during these lectures, and he disliked the role-playing exercises the experts said would help emphasize their main points. The weeklong classroom portion of the program was completed. Jaworski said they all passed. The flight training schedule was posted that evening. Ben was delighted. He was teamed to fly with Sanderson.

Their instructor led them through the walk-around inspection and check of interior systems. As they completed the prestart checklist, the ground crew hand-turned the propellers on all four engines, to clear the cylinders. Ben was the first to fly; the instructor, in the copilot's seat, led him through the engine-start sequence. It was a two-man process that required the copilot to depress the start switch for fifteen seconds and the mesh switch to engage the starter to turn the engine. He pumped the hand primer to feed fuel to the engine.

Ben's first takeoff went smoothly. When his instructor expressed surprise at how quickly Ben developed a feel for the B-17, Ben explained he had logged some intense hours in the right seat of Buxom Baby. Ben moved to the top of the class and was the first pilot to qualify in the B-17.

"I really like the Fort," he told Sanderson as they relaxed on their bunks one night. "I thought handlin' four engines would be a big deal. But it really isn't, once you get comfortable with the controls, ah, and have a good copilot. The B-17 is just a big ole docile lady."

"Maybe for you," Sanderson groused. "I thought it'd be an easy step up from the B-25, but it's a totally different airplane, being a taildragger and all. I can't get comfortable with it."

"It'll come. Keep at it."

Two of the twenty-four pilots who started the course washed out and were sent off to fly C-47 cargo planes. After graduation, Ben was assigned to the 509th Heavy Bombardment Group being formed at MacDill Field. The 509th was scheduled to deploy to England as part of the Eighth Air Force. *Fantastic! Uncle Sam's army delivered, as promised.*

At MacDill, Ben was directed to the 509th headquarters to report to the commanding officer and meet his assigned crew. Maj. Harvey Patterson, the 509th's executive officer, intercepted Ben at the security desk and said he would escort him to the CO's office. *Not bad. A major taking me to see the boss.*

Patterson knocked on the door and gestured Ben inside. Ben stepped to the desk, raised his hand in salute, and stood openmouthed.

"What the—" was all he could say.

"Hello, Ben," said Col. Frank Silverman. "Welcome to the 509th." He stepped around the desk and pumped Ben's hand.

Ben stammered, "Frank! Uh, I mean, Colonel Silverman. Uh, this is quite a surprise! When we said good-bye in Portsmouth in '39, ah, I didn't think I'd ever see you again."

"Take a seat, Ben," Silverman said with a smile. "Sorry to spring it on you like this, but I couldn't resist. When I saw your name on the graduation roster at Hendricks Field, I grabbed you. You did very well there."

Ben sat grinning foolishly.

"I need every good flyer I can get," Silverman said. "The pressure's on to get the 509th formed and deployed to England. Now tell me what the hell you're doing in a bomber outfit. You went on to fly Spitfires with Reggie, didn't you?"

Ben shook his head. *Here we go again.* "Yessir. Reggie and I got into Spitfires just before the war," Ben said. "What a swell airplane. I flew all through the Battle of Britain—one helluva time, I'll tell ya—and then stayed with the squadron through early this year. Finally, an Inter-Allied Agency colonel said I had to switch to the USAAF."

"You still haven't told me how you ended up in bombers."

"Well, that's a long story, sir," Ben said. "I also wanna hear what happened to you after England."

"That's another long story, Ben, later," Silverman said. "Now let's find your airplane and get you teamed with your crew."

"Ben," Silverman said, stepping around his desk and extending his right hand again, "can't tell you how great it is to see you again. Major Patterson will introduce you to your crew."

"Yessir," Ben said, saluting. "I also want to meet with our ground chief, Sergeant Carter."

Ben studied the nine men lined up before him in the base operations center. He straightened his back and cleared his throat.

"Good morning," he said, reaching down for what he hoped was a mature bass voice. "I'm Lt. Benjamin A. Findlay, your airplane commander. I'm from Michigan, farm near Flint. Anyone here from Michigan?" *Damn, I almost said Mitchigan.*

"Close, sir. North Dakota. Master Sgt. Anderson, William A. I'm from Fargo. Flight engineer and top turret gunner."

Ben nodded.

"Almost as close, sir. Des Moines, Iowa. Technical Sgt. Stanley, Arthur J. Left waist gunner."

"Fellow midwesterners," Ben smiled. "Okay, let's start from the left."

"Second Lt. Baker, Gordon C., Denver, Colorado. Copilot. Friends call me Gordy."

"First Lt. Whitney, James A., suh. Bombardier. Ah'm from the wonderful city of Atlanta in the Peach state of Georgia. Friends call me Whit, suh."

"San Diego, sir. Second Lt. Jones, Bradford R. I'm your navigator. Tell you where to go, sir."

Wise ass. Hope he's as good as he thinks he is. "Next!"

"Still Anderson from Fargo, sir. Engineer and top turret." Ben nodded.

"Technical Sgt. Weisman, Leon H., sir. Radio operator and side nose gunner. I'm from New York." He pronounced it "New Yawk."

"Paddy, sir. Uh, Technical Sgt. Mahoney, Patrick K. Boston, Massachusetts, sir. You can tell by my size I'm your ball turret gunner."

"Right," Ben said. "Next?"

"As Andy said, sir, I'm still Sergeant Arthur. Left waist gunner."

"Umm, yeah," Ben said, and looked to the next man.

"Sir, Staff Sgt. Miller, John L., right waist gunner. I hail from Spokane, Washington, sir."

"Staff Sgt. Samuelson, Archibald R., suh. Otherwise known as Archie. Tail gunna, suh. Ah'm from Greenville, South Carolina." He pronounced it "Grenvull."

Motley mix of mutts, as Reggie would say. Hope I can make a crew outta them.

"Good. Stand at ease," Ben said. "We don't have a lot of time to get used to working as a team, so let's get a couple of things clear. I'm in charge of this crew. You all have jobs to do, and I don't expect to have to tell you how to do it. Teamwork's the key, but my decisions are the final ones."

He paced in front of the nine men, parroting some of the crew management lessons from his classroom work. He told them briefly about his combat experience in flying fighters with the Republican Air Force in Spain and the RAF in England.

"I've spent a lot of time working the other end of the stick, as the Brits say. My job was to shoot down enemy bombers, and I got fairly good at it," Ben said. "I think I can apply some of the combat lessons I learned to help us fend off Luftwaffe fighters. Now let's find our airplane. It's a new B-17G, tail number 43-268791."

They found their bomber on the flight line, dropped their gear under the nose, and stood looking at their mount.

"The nose looks pretty bare," Ben said. "We need a name, some nose art. Any suggestions?"

Several offered names he couldn't write home to his mother. They also suggested lurid pictures of scantily clad women in poses that emphasized their femininity.

"Okay, okay. I get the idea," Ben said, shaking his head. "But here's what I want. Let's name her Round Trip. With that comes the promise she'll bring us back from any mission we go out on. How's that sound?"

The men nodded their approval. They liked the thought of going out each time on a round-trip ticket.

"What about the nose art, sir?" Sergeant Weisman asked. "Couldn't we get a nice-lookin' babe painted up there?" The rest of the crew nodded eagerly.

"Ah, yeah, okay," Ben said. "But I see the drawing first."

He turned to the ground crew. "Okay, let's meet the most important fellas on this team. This is Master Sgt. Tommy Carter, chief of our ground crew. Sergeant Carter, introduce the rest of your crew."

Ben then faced the flight crew.

"Anderson, get to know Carter and his team. They're gonna make your job a lot easier by keepin' Round Trip in top flying condition at all times. Gunners, you get chummy with the armorers. When we're at thirty thousand feet and the outside temperature is minus forty degrees, you wanna know they've kept your guns and ammo in top operating condition."

Ben said to the other flight crew members, "The same goes for all of you. What these fellas do on the ground will keep us alive in the air. Make friends."

That night Ben and Gordy, his copilot, sat at the bar in the officers' club. Lieutenant Jones, their navigator, approached.

"Mind if I join you, sir? Uh, can I call you Ben?" he asked.

"Yes to both," Ben said. "What'll ya have?"

Ben ordered three more beers.

"Ah, Ben, I think you hit the right balance with the crew today," Jones said. "There's no question you're in command. You also made the crew feel comfortable, part of a team. We're gonna be okay."

"Thanks. But I won't stand for any bullshit. We've got a tough assignment ahead of us, so I'm gonna be tough when it necessary. It won't be all by the numbers, 'yes, sir, no, sir, right away, sir,' crap like that. We didn't follow a lot of military protocol in the RAF, but everyone knew who was the boss. We had a relaxed attitude, but we took our orders and got the job done."

Chapter 71

OPERATIONAL AGAIN

The 509th shifted into intense flight training. Ben took his crew out for solo flights in Round Trip to build their confidence in him and in each other. They proved highly spirited and motivated to work as a team. Colonel Silverman and Major Patterson flew several sorties in Round Trip as observers, evaluating their progress and Ben's effectiveness as a pilot and a leader.

Near the end of the training period, Weisman presented several nose art drawings to Ben. He rejected the most graphic ones before settling on a rosy-cheeked blonde posed provocatively, but not overly so, in a tight-fitting swimsuit. The crew gathered in front of Round Trip as the base artist put the finishing touches on Peaches, so named in deference to Whit, the bombardier from Atlanta.

"Okay, now we're official," Ben grinned. "You've all done a great job so far. Tomorrow we start the tough part—formation flying with the entire group. Everybody's gotta be on their toes. We'll be in the air with twenty-three other Forts, and Colonel Silverman will be on our butts to keep the formation tight. Eventually we need to be good enough to fly under a lot of stress wingtip to wingtip. Our survival under fire depends on it, so the sooner we get used to it, the better."

The 509th crews flew two training sorties a day for the next two weeks. The bombers formed into three-ship V formations, four of which were grouped into larger box formations. Ben's prediction proved correct. Silverman, riding in the top turret of the lead bomber, hammered them on the radio to "Close the formation! Get it tighter! Get into position, and stay there. Your lives depend on keeping the boxes tight!"

The crews were exhausted, but even through their fatigue, they saw they were making progress. They became increasingly confident that the 509th was becoming a formidable fighting unit. This was proved when the group completed its operational evaluation (OPEVAL) and was declared ready for combat.

Silverman and Patterson called the flight crews to the briefing room on a Friday afternoon. "Three announcements of interest," Silverman said when the men had settled in their seats. "First, we have our operational assignment! We deploy to England as part of VIII Bomber Command, Eighth Air Force. We'll be based at USAAF Station 153, also known as RAF Station Parham. It's in Suffolk, near the village of Framlingham northeast of London, due east of Cambridge. That'll put us in the front row for attacking Germany. We'll fly coordinated missions with the RAF's Bomber Command. They're bombing Germany by night, and we'll be attacking 'em by day. Keep the Krauts duckin' and bobbin' round the clock!"

The pilots cheered and stamped their feet.

Ben sat upright. *Cambridge! That puts us close to Duxford. Wonder if Reggie's still there? Hot damn! Images of Gwen swarmed into his mind. Gotta forget about Gwen, . . . but I can't.*

"Ground crews will ship out on Monday with their basic support equipment," Silverman continued. "We'll spend a week preparing for the ferry flight, using the North Atlantic routing. First stop will be Floyd Bennett Field in Brooklyn. From there we'll chart the ocean crossing according to the latest weather forecast. We're needed in England as soon as possible, so I'm sorry to say there won't be any leave before our departure."

This prompted a wave of muttered complaints.

"But we've arranged to have phone lines for those of you who want to call home. I don't know if there'll be enough for everyone, but it's the best we can do."

Ben stared at the briefing board. *Guess I'm not that disappointed about home leave. Saw them on the way down here. Don't know if I even want to call.*

"The second announcement has to do with a couple of promotions," Silverman said. "Lieutenants Findlay and Sanderson are hereby promoted to the rank of captain. Findlay will take command of A Squadron and Sanderson B Squadron. Congratulations!"

Ben sat stunned. Several pilots thumped him on the back. *Captain . . . Squadron Commander. Wow. Didn't see that coming.*

"And finally, this is a small gesture, since you won't get a transit home leave," Silverman said. "But you all have a weekend pass, starting immediately."

The pilots agreed it was a small gesture and shuffled quietly out of the briefing room.

Ben wrote several letters home that night. He gave his mother sketchy information, emphasizing that he was headed out on an operational assignment with a large group of fellow pilots. He couldn't tell her where he was going, but it would be a safe trip traveling in such a large group. Unfortunately they were needed urgently in their new assignment, so he wouldn't get a home leave before departure. He included more details in his letters to Brice and Al Simpson, but also couldn't tell them specifically where he was going. He penned a final letter to his brother, and wondered if it would ever catch up with him.

While the 509th flight crews made final preparations for the transatlantic trip, extra fuel tanks were fitted into bomb bays. These, with the help of westerly tailwinds, would enable them to make the ocean crossing in two hops.

"Glad we won't have to make that wild-ass approach up the fjord to Bluie West One!" Ben muttered.

Two days before departure, a telegram arrived for Ben. He ripped open the envelope with trembling hands. *Gotta be bad news.*

It was. Al Simpson told Ben that Brice had died of a heart attack, was found dead in bed. Details coming by letter. Ben sat stunned. Tears stung his eyes as he crumpled the telegram and tossed it into the wastebasket. He slumped into a chair. *Wonder if Silverman would consider a compassion leave?*

Ben lay awake that night. Memories of his golden moments with Brice swirled through his mind. Sobs welled up in his throat. He rose and paced the room. He peered into the mirror. "Brice was more of a father to me than the old man," he choked. "I'm here because of him. God, I'll miss not being able to share my experiences with him."

He told Silverman the next morning. Brice had made a deep impression on him too, but he took the news stoically. He needed to stay focused on the important mission ahead of him. Ben inquired about a compassionate leave to attend Brice's funeral. Silverman reluctantly denied it.

Two days later, the 509th gathered in loose formation over MacDill Field and turned north for Floyd Bennett Field. Ben smiled at Gordy, who grinned back. A Squadron moved smoothly into position on his airplane. Ben stared out Round Trip's windshield. *Wish ya could see me now, Brice. Find it hard to believe myself. Feels like you're ridin' along with me.*

The flight up the Atlantic coast to Brooklyn was uneventful, as Ben and Gordy traded off flying, since their B-17G had no autopilot.

At the morning briefing the following day, Silverman said the 509th would lay over at Bennett for two days, to wait for another B-17 group to join them for the flight to England. The delay was expected to give them favorable tailwinds along the northern route. He instructed navigators to check with base operations for tips on charting the course across Greenland and Iceland.

"New York City is just across the bay," he added. "Get with your squadron commanders and work out a schedule for releasing half of you on twenty-four-hour passes tomorrow and the other half the day after."

Silverman took Ben aside. "Ben, I'd like you to join me for dinner tonight at my favorite New York restaurant."

"Renee's," Ben said. "That'll be swell!" He blinked, remembering his first dinner there with Ted.

They sipped a crisp chardonnay after placing their orders with Renee's headwaiter. Silverman looked steadily at Ben. "We're about to join something bigger than either of us can imagine," he said evenly. "I don't know how much you know about the Eighth Air Force, but let me give you a quick overview—"

"I heard about the Eighth while still flying with the RAF," Ben broke in. "Reggie and I talked about that outfit setting up in England when I was still makin' up my mind to switch to the USAAF."

"Okay, then you know something about their operations," Silverman said. When Ben shook his head, Silverman continued. "Well, they took a hell of a beating in the early phases last year. Heavy losses, especially with the B-17 groups, that were not sustainable. Learned some valuable lessons: the absolute need for long-range escort fighters, the importance of flying close box formations for mutual defense, and improved armament on the B-17, specifically the forward-firing chin turrets we have on our new G models."

"Yeah," Ben muttered, pondering Silverman's "heavy losses" comment. "Where'd the Eighth come from? Who started it?"

"Ah, the Eighth. It was formed in Savannah, Georgia. It's the brainchild of a lot of military strategists, including Gen. Billy Mitchell, who formulated a heavy aerial-bombardment strategy in the 1920s," Silverman said. "Mitchell clashed with a lot of top army and navy brass who didn't believe in airpower. He continued to push his campaign, however, and ended up getting court-martialed for insubordination.

"Our three top generals, Hap Arnold, Carl Spaatz, and Ira Eaker, served under Mitchell. They became strong believers in his strategy. As the war loomed, they pushed development of the concept. When Boeing flew the B-17 prototype in 1935, they finally had the tools to carry out Mitchell's dream. The Consolidated B-24 bomber came along a couple of years later and filled out the USAAF's heavy bomber force to what we see today.

"So when Arnold became chief of the USAAF, he appointed Spaatz commander of the Eighth, and Eaker head of the Eighth's Bombardment Group," Silverman continued. "Spaatz then was promoted to commander of air operations for Europe, and Eaker moved up to commander of the Eighth.

"That's where we are today. Eaker's our overall boss, and we have one helluva job ahead to prove that daylight bombing can be carried out without unacceptable losses. We have to demonstrate we can bomb the Germans by day while the Brits bomb them by night."

The words "unacceptable losses" resounded with Ben.

"But that's enough strategy for now," Silverman said. "You said you'd tell me about your experiences in the RAF and how you ended up in bombers."

Ben sighed and began an abbreviated account of what transpired after he and Silverman parted on the dock at Portsmouth. He became increasingly animated as he led Silverman through his checkout in the Spitfire and launched into a hand-waving description of the swirling dogfights during the Battle of Britain. He talked through the meal, stopping occasionally to savor the French specialties on his plate.

Finally, he said that when the Inter-Allied Personnel Board colonel convinced him to switch to the USAAF, he decided to request assignment to a B-17 unit. This would satisfy his desire to inflict the kind of suffering on Germany that he had seen the Luftwaffe wreak on Spain and England.

When the dessert cart was wheeled to their table, Ben sat back and regarded Silverman. "Now it's your turn, Frank. What happened to you after you got back here?"

Silverman concentrated on his fruit tart for a moment, then cleared his throat. "I went through a bad stretch, Ben. Couldn't shake the feeling that I led you and the other fellas into something I had no right to. Ah, . . . you and Fred were the only two who survived. Dunno what's happened to Fred. We exchanged a couple of letters, then lost touch."

Coffee arrived, and Silverman asked Ben if he'd like a cognac. That ordered, he continued. "I wrapped up final details of the Spanish civil war's volunteer operation and concentrated on writing a lot of letters . . . you know, to the families. Made the mistake of thinking I could drink myself through the hard part. Only made it worse, of course."

Ben stared unblinking, feeling he was looking into Silverman's soul.

"When war broke out in Europe in '39, I considered going to Canada to join the RAF," Silverman continued. "That didn't pan out, but I was able to get work ferrying lend-lease airplanes to the Canadian border. Canadian pilots picked them up and flew them to God knows where. Getting back into flying helped me stop the heavy drinking."

He stirred sugar into his coffee and tapped his spoon on the edge of his cup.

"By the end of 1940, the army was advertising for pilots," he said. "Apparently someone realized America might get into this war, and they saw how pitifully undermanned the USAAF was. They took me in a flash. After Pearl Harbor, all hell broke loose. I ended up in B-25 light bombers and spent a brief combat tour in North Africa. Had some exciting times. Nothing to match yours, by any stretch, but we saw a lot of action."

Silverman signaled the waiter and ordered two more cognacs.

"'bout time I completed my tour in late '42, I could see that the big air war was going to be fought in the European theater," he said. "So I opted for heavy bombers and transitioned to the B-17. I was tasked to form the 509th Group at MacDill, and our paths crossed again."

Both men sat, contemplating the past and speculating on the future. Ben broke the silence. "Ah, Frank, umm, are you bothered by what's happening in Germany? I mean, what the Germans are doin' to, ah, your people?"

Silverman gave him a long look. "I guess by 'your people,' you mean the Jews? Ah, if I'm totally honest, I have to say yes," he said, then paused. "But I'm not going out on a personal vendetta. Everyone's sickened by what the Nazis are doing to the Jews and a lot of other people, of course. As bad as that is, as inhumane as it is, there's a bigger issue. The Nazis and Fascists have to be defeated, Ben. Hell, we saw that in

Spain! That's why we—or at least, I—went there. Too bad more people didn't." He signaled for the check.

"But I'm not going to drop bombs on Germany to get revenge. We have a bigger task, Ben. We're part of a mission to free a lot of oppressed people and protect a lot of others from suffering the same fate . . . Uh, sorry, didn't mean to get up on my soapbox. But I feel a personal responsibility here. I guess that's what's motivating me."

Ben mulled what he had heard. *And what's motivating me?*

Chapter 72

RETURN TO ENGLAND AND THE WAR

Two days later, forty-five B-17s from the 509th and 306th Heavy Bombardment Groups made a streaming takeoff from Floyd Bennett Field at midday. They circled and gathered in loose formation. Once formed, they headed north for Newfoundland, then turned northeast onto the great circle route across Greenland to Iceland. They flew into the night and arrived at Reykjavik the next afternoon.

Gordy proved an excellent copilot, switching off with Ben flying Round Trip every two hours. Ben noted that Gordy held position in the formation well and guided the crew with confidence.

All forty-five airplanes made the first leg. Only two landed with minor mechanical problems. These were repaired overnight. The weather gods smiled, and the two groups took off from Reykjavik at 0730 hours for Prestwick, Scotland. The flight plan included the option of continuing nonstop to Parham, if fuel reserves and crew fatigue permitted. Silverman opted for a stop at Prestwick and radioed the following bombers. It took four hours to refuel the fleet and get it airborne again.

As they approached Parham, the 306th broke off and headed for their assigned base. Ben recognized familiar landmarks around Cambridge and across Suffolk to Framlingham. He'd spent many hours flying Spitfires over this territory.

Parham loomed large as they approached. Its three long runways were laid out in a diamond shape, ringed by a perimeter track with at least fifty dispersed aircraft parking pads. There were two large hangars and several smaller buildings on the main ramp. Nests of Quonset huts, used as crew quarters and service buildings, were scattered around the perimeter.

"Gonna need wheels just to get around the base," Ben said to Gordy. "Probably sleep two to a room in the Quonsets. Wonder where the officers' mess . . . uh, officers' club is?"

The 509th settled in at Parham. They spent the next two weeks flying over Suffolk and the adjoining counties of Cambridgeshire and Norfolk, practicing close formation, and learning local landmarks. Since this was Ben's home turf from RAF days, Silverman asked him to lead the group on the area familiarization sorties. In the last phase of their training, they dropped dummy bombs on a West Country bombing range. The formation practice drills dragged on, with Silverman hammering at the crews, "We're gonna keep doing this until we get it right!"

A week later, Silverman alerted the crews for a briefing at 0630 hours the next morning. They were awakened at 0530 hours, wolfed a quick breakfast, and gathered in the briefing room. While waiting for the colonel to arrive, Ben paced the floor in the front.

"Hey, Ben," someone yelled. "What's up? When's Colonel Silverman gonna let us go to war 'stead a droning around boring holes in the English sky?"

"You heard what he said," Ben responded. "We're gonna keep practicing formation flying until we get it right. Tell the truth, I think we're makin' real progress." Then he shouted, "*Attention!*" as Silverman and Major Patterson entered the rear door.

They marched to the front of the briefing room, and Silverman ordered the men to sit. He answered the question the pilot had shouted at Ben. The 509th was alerted for its first operational mission. Today they would fly a final training mission.

The next day, the flight crews fidgeted at the 0430-hours briefing as Silverman signaled Major Patterson to draw back the curtain covering the mission map. They relaxed when they saw the target was German V-1 weapon launch sites along France's western coast. This was an early phase of the Operation Crossbow attacks against the nearly completed V-1 launch sites in the Pas-de-Calais in occupied France. They weren't going to penetrate Germany's airspace and face the Luftwaffe's first-line air defenses. But, Silverman said, they would encounter significant flak from antiaircraft defenses. Major Patterson provided details of the mission, and Silverman said he would lead the raid. Takeoff time was 0830 hours.

Ben made a final crew check on the intercom as he taxied Round Trip in the line of B-17s and into position on the runway. *Hot dog! First combat mission.*

He grinned at Gordy, who looked a bit pale but gave him a hearty thumbs-up. Ben signaled Gordy to lock the tail wheel in takeoff position, did a quick sweep of the instrument panel, and eased the four large throttle levers forward. Gordy adjusted the turbo-boost on the four engines. Round Trip accelerated quickly, despite her six-thousand-pound bomb load, and lifted off smoothly from the three-point taildragger stance.

"Okay, Gordy, gear and flaps," Ben shouted.

Gordy adjusted the engine and propeller controls, and closed engine nacelle cowl flaps without being told. Ben settled back and felt the big bomber responding to the thunder of its four Curtiss-Wright engines. *This is one swell flyin' machine.*

Twenty-one of the 509th's B-17s circled around a vertical radio navigation beam broadcast from Parham. They eased into a loose formation and rendezvoused with three other heavy bombardment groups. The 509th led the flotilla of one hundred bombers and fifty P-51 escort fighters, and wheeled east to the Channel. Ben ordered his gunners to test-fire their weapons over water. The hammering recoil of thirteen .50 caliber machine guns pounded through the airframe. Pungent cordite fumes swirled into the cockpit. Ben grinned at Gordy, who gave him a thumbs-up.

As they swept over France, Silverman led the combined groups in a wide turn toward the target and hit the initial point (IP) from which they started the final bombing run. Heavy antiaircraft flak burst around them, but no Luftwaffe fighters rose to attack. Keying on Silverman's bomber, Ben called Lieutenant Whitney on the intercom. "Your airplane, Whit."

The bombardier controlled Round Trip through the final bomb run, using knobs on his Norden bombsight to keep the bomber flying straight and level. He opened the bomb bay doors. Squinting through the Norden sight, Whit centered the crosshairs on the target and hit the toggle switch. "Bombs away!" he called and turned control back to Ben, who rolled the bomber into a steep right turn. As they followed Silverman's lead away from the target, Gordy adjusted the throttles.

"Pilot to tail gunner, how'd we do, Archie?" Ben asked on the intercom.

"Tail gunna to pilot. Formation's holdin' tight, as a bull's a . . . Uh, holdin' real tight, skipper. Think we hit the target real good, suh, but I saw bombs just bouncing off those concrete buildings!"

Ben shook his head in disgust. The Round Trip crew responded with excited chatter on the intercom. Ben cut in with a curt, "Knock off the gossip! Keep the intercom clear!"

All the bombers returned to Parham, a few with minor flak damage. Ben's crew gathered under the nose of Round Trip as Sergeant Carter painted a white bomb next to Peaches. One mission down, twenty-four to go.

Ben motioned the crew to close in around him. "Okay, Round Trip got us there and back. Hope that starts a tradition. We had our first taste of combat today, and you all did very well. Only complaint is intercom discipline. Stay off the damn radio unless you got something really important ta say! And don't think all our missions are gonna be like this one. We got some tough ones comin', especially when we go after targets in Germany."

Their next mission was not a milk run. At the morning briefing, several flight crews muttered curses when Patterson pulled back the curtain and revealed the target: Hamburg! They were to bomb the Elbe River harbor and industrial center on the outskirts of the largest city in northern Germany.

"I heard a fella from the 307th say there's a lotta crack Luftwaffe fighter units protectin' Hamburg," one pilot whispered. "And the Krauts put up so much flak you can walk on it."

"We'll rendezvous with five other heavy bombardment groups and four groups of escort fighters," Silverman said. "Once formed up, we'll fly out over the North Sea, then turn southeast to attack Hamburg. Other bombardment groups across England will launch more B-17 and B-24 bomber squadrons to strike alternate targets in Germany. This'll force the Luftwaffe to spread their air defenses across a broad front."

Once airborne, the ten bombers of A Squadron maneuvered into two loose-formation boxes of five airplanes each, to concentrate the fields of fire from their twelve defensive guns. They would tighten the formation as they approached German airspace. Ben shifted the squadron into trailing position to the left and slightly behind Silverman's lead V of three B-17s. Sanderson moved B Squadron into position below, on Silverman's right.

As they climbed through ten thousand feet, en route to their cruise altitude of twenty thousand feet, Ben ordered the crew to don and check oxygen masks. The waist gunners in their aft stations donned electrically heated coveralls and fleece-lined gloves. In addition to enemy fighters, they'd be battling windblasts of minus thirty degrees Fahrenheit that swirled through their open gunner's windows.

"Pilot to gunners," he called on the intercom, "on your toes. We're now showin' on the Kraut radar. Soon as they see us turn toward Hamburg, they'll launch fighters. Expect to see Me 109s and probably the new Fw 190s. Sing out when you spot 'em. Remember, numbers, altitude, and heading. It's gonna get hot once we enter German airspace."

He exulted to Gordy, "Hot damn! First chance to drop bombs on Germany."

"Six . . . no, ten bogeys, two o'clock high!" Gordy shouted on the intercom. "Look like 109s . . . They're gonna make a head-on attack!"

The sky erupted into swirling dogfights as the flotilla's P-51 escort fighters tangled with the German attackers. The ten fighters heading for the 509th sliced through the defensive shield and dived. Gunners in Silverman's formation fired long bursts.

"No!" Ben yelled. "Too early! Pilot to gunners, hold your fire till they're closer. Don't waste ammunition."

The 109s separated and flashed past on both sides of Silverman's V formation.

"Comin' at us on both sides," Ben radioed to the crew. "Andy, watch 'em!" he called to Sergeant Anderson in the powered turret atop the fuselage. "Give heads-up to the other guns."

Ben's gunners poured bursts of .50 caliber rounds at the fighters as they dived through the formation. The 109 pilots rolled inverted as they flashed past firing their guns, presenting their airplanes' armored bellies to the B-17 gunners.

"Pilot to crew, anyone hurt?" Ben yelled over the intercom. "We take any hits?"

"Okay back here, skipper!" Miller called from his right waist gunner position. "I got a piece of that last bastard!"

"Tail to pilot, Ah can confirm. That 'ere Kraut was smokin' real good when he went by."

Waves of Me 109 and Focke-Wulf Fw 190 fighters sliced into the bomber formation. Fighters from both sides tumbled out of control and spun smoking to the ground. Two B-17s on the outer box of Ben's squadron were hit. One lost its number one outboard engine but thundered on, holding formation on three engines. The second, the top portion of its vertical tail blown away, also held position.

"That's Wilkinson's ship!" someone yelled over the intercom. "Looks like they're hangin' on okay!"

The intercom was a babble of voices as Round Trip's gunners shouted warnings to each other.

"Three 190s at nine o'clock! Art, Paddy, watch it! They're going over and under!"

"Whit! Pair comin' in on the nose! Andy, get on 'em!"

"Sonofabitch! He nearly took our tail off!"

Round Trip shuddered as her crewmen fired all guns. Enemy cannon shells slammed into the fuselage. Smoke curled from the bomb bay. Lights and instruments flickered as the electrical system fizzled and switched to backup circuits.

"I'll get the fire!" Weisman shouted as he burst out of the radio compartment and grabbed a fire extinguisher.

The fighters pressed their attacks. Four B-17s spun out of control. Three others bucked under 20 mm shell impacts from German Me 109s. A B-17 off Round Trip's left wing reared its nose into a high-speed stall, smoke and flames pouring from its two inboard engines. It too rolled into a spiraling dive.

"Who was that?" someone yelled. "How many chutes?"

"Dunno. No chutes."

As the bombers turned up the Elbe River to Hamburg, the Luftwaffe fighters broke off.

"Pilot to crew, here comes the flak!" Ben called. Shell bursts blossomed into ugly black clouds along their line of flight. German 88 mm antiaircraft shells boomed and flashed around them. White-hot jagged shrapnel punched through Round Trip's thin skin, snapped and sizzled across the deck, and ricocheted off bulkheads.

"Jesus! That stuff is thick!" someone yelled. "Cover your ass! I'm sittin' on my helmet!"

"Stay the hell off the intercom!" Ben snapped.

At the initial point, Ben turned control over to Whitney, hunched over the Norden bombsight in Round Trip's glass nose. Ben and Gordy tensed as Whit held the bomber straight and level. He finally shouted, "Bombs away! Your airplane, skipper!"

Ben and Gordy both grabbed their control yokes and banked into a left turn, trailing Silverman. The German antiaircraft gunners anticipated the maneuver and peppered their escape route with increasingly accurate flak bursts. Ben saw all three airplanes in Silverman's lead V take hits. A flak shell burst off Round Trip's right wingtip and slammed the bomber into a left roll. He and Gordy wrenched it back level and looked at the right wing. The tip was shredded.

"Number four's on fire!" Gordy yelled. He punched the fire extinguisher button for the right outboard engine. Four hands flew across switches and controls as the pilots shut down number four and feathered its huge propeller.

"Okay!" Ben shouted. "We got her under control."

The flak lessened. Ben's pulse banged in his ears. His body shook. "Pilot to right waist, damage report."

"Waist to pilot, the wingtip's gone, and there's one helluva big hole in the bottom of the wing. Don't see any fuel leaking. We gotta lot of shrapnel holes back here."

"Jasus!" Paddy radioed from the ball turret under the fuselage. "Somethin' come up between me legs and jammed the motor drive. Somebody, hand-crank me turret open!" Ben sent Anderson, the flight engineer, back to help Paddy.

"Tail to pilot," Archie radioed. "Ah ken see lotta daylight through the walls back here, suh. Whole buncha shrapnel hits, but no serious damage."

"How's the formation look, Archie?"

"What's left seems to be comin' along okay. Ah guess they all took some hits, but a good number's still with us."

All the remaining B-17s landed back at Parham with damage. Round Trip and several other B-17s limped in with feathered engines. Red flares, fired to signify wounded onboard, flashed from half the returning planes. The medical teams and maintenance crews faced a long night. The 509th would be lucky to have eighteen serviceable bombers by morning.

The excited babble in the debriefing hall was deafening. Adrenalin surged as the flight crews recounted the air battle that had swirled around the attack on Hamburg. Ben motioned the Round Trip crew aside.

"Got a good taste of what we're gonna face over Germany," he said. "That second bomb painted on Round Trip's nose means a lot. We survived the worst, and she brought us back again. Now you know what we're up against."

Ben continued. "Sergeant Carter tells me the repairs will take a couple of days, so we're off the operational list for at least that long. Ah, Miller, great work today. I'm puttin' you in for a probable kill."

After a five-day respite, they flew two missions back-to-back. Round Trip looked like it had a bad case of chicken pox. Maintenance crews had not had time to paint the numerous patches they'd riveted over the shrapnel holes. The first mission, an attack on the German navy's submarine pens along the French coast, was a milk run. They faced no fighters and encountered minimal flak. Two days later, they penetrated to the heart of Germany's industrial region, to bomb a large ball bearing factory in Schweinfurt.

Ben was relieved that the 509th flew in trail position behind the two lead bomber groups. The leaders were pounded by fighters and then by flak. Five B-17s spun out of control in flames. Four others were damaged, and drifted singly out of the main formation. Fighters swarmed around them and shot them out of the sky. By the time Round Trip reached the target, fire, smoke, and dust obscured it.

"Bombadier to pilot," Whit called. "Can't see the target. Gonna have to salvo 'em into that mess. Bombs away!"

Ben peered down into the maelstrom. *God almighty! Like lookin' into hell. Wonder what we're hittin'?*

As they turned away from the target, Archie radioed from the tail. "Tail to pilot. Awful mess, skipper. Bombs spread all over hell's half acre. Ah saw couple little ole towns get hit real bad."

Ben pushed back in his seat. He signaled Gordy to take control and lifted his oxygen mask to wipe sweat from his face. "Dammit! I didn't come here to bomb little ole towns!" he snarled.

Outbound from the target, they twisted and turned through heavy flak and were met by swarms of Luftwaffe fighters. The attackers again broke through the fighter escort and slashed into the bombers. The lead groups bore the brunt of the attack, but a 509th B-17 on the outside position in B Squadron was hit by fierce cannon fire from two 109s. The bomber faltered and spun out of control.

"Pilot to crew. Who's that?"

"Lieutenant Jefferson."

"How many chutes?"

"Only two."

Back at Parham, the crew silently watched Sergeant Carter paint the fourth bomb on Round Trip's nose. The mission had been a disaster. They shuffled quietly into the debriefing room, gave short reports, and left. Ben's postmission pep talk did little to brighten their mood. Round Trip got them home again. But they hadn't done the enemy any significant damage and probably killed a lot of civilians. Worse, a lot of their buddies hadn't made it back.

Bad weather halted all operations. In late November it cleared, and the 509th was alerted for a mission. Excitement surged through the briefing room as Major Patterson pulled back the curtain. *Berlin*! They were going to bomb the German capital.

Ben punched Gordy on the shoulder. "This is it, Gordy!" he yelled. "The big one. We're gonna hit the Krauts where it really hurts. What I've been lookin' forward to," he added quietly.

"Yeah," Gordy grinned back, pounding his fist on his thigh. "Maybe we can get ole Herr Hitler's ass!"

Their mood quickly sobered as Patterson continued the briefing. The Luftwaffe had pulled fighter squadrons back from the Eastern Front following disastrous defeats the German army suffered in Russia. These units were reinforcing air defenses protecting Berlin. Intelligence sources also reported an unprecedented buildup of antiaircraft batteries around the German capital.

"Expect the heaviest fighter attacks we've ever faced," Patterson said. "It's more important than ever that you fly tight box formations. This'll be your best defense against concentrated fighter attacks."

The pilots stirred uneasily.

"And in close to Berlin, the flak'll be very heavy. You pilots have all been trained how to maneuver to confuse flak gunners. Go over this again with your copilots before takeoff."

The 509th formed up and joined six hundred B-17s. Escorted by one hundred fifty P-51 and P-38 fighters, they headed out over the North Sea. They climbed to eighteen thousand feet and turned southeast toward Berlin. All pilots took Patterson's warnings to heart and closed to tight formation. Round Trip's waist gunners cracked over the intercom that they had somebody else's wingtip sticking in both open windows. Silverman radioed "heads up" as they approached German airspace.

The fighter attacks were ferocious. Luftwaffe pilots hurled their Me 109s and Fw 190s into the B-17 formations with suicidal fervor. The escorting USAAF P-51s and P-38s shot down many attackers, but eventually were overwhelmed. B-17s from nearly every group were hit hard. Several spun smoking out of the formation.

Ben gasped when Patterson's B-17 in the lead three-airplane V was hit by cannon fire from three 109s. The bomber rolled inverted and dived, trailing a long snake of black smoke.

"Pilot to crew!" Ben called on the intercom. "Major Patterson's ship's going down. Watch for chutes."

"None yet, skipper," someone responded. Then, "*Jesus*! She just blew up!"

Ben caught a glimpse of fiery debris streaming earthward. Around them German fighters chopped at other bombers. A B-17 above them exploded, and the bodies of crewmen hurtled past, some without parachutes.

Silverman radioed, "Close the gaps! Tighten it up! Re-form those boxes!"

"Gawdalmighty!" Gordy shouted to Ben. "We gonna get through?"

"Hang in there!" Ben yelled back. Then over the intercom, "Pilot to gunners. Calm down. Take time to aim. Concentrate your fire. Keep 'em at bay."

As if to mock him, two 190s knifed past, raking Round Trip with machine gun and cannon fire. They were met with fierce return fire from gunners in Round Trip and other nearby B-17s. Both enemy fighters were hit; one exploded in a ball of flame, and the other tumbled smoking out of control. All crew members were exhausted, sweat-stained, and trembling by the time the fighters broke off. Berlin loomed, and they slumped back on piles of 50 mm shell casings to await the flak.

The 509th formation maneuvered to confuse the antiaircraft gunners' aim, but black explosion clouds still blocked the approach to Berlin. A direct hit blew the left wing off Dancin' Daisy, the trailing B-17 in Ben's box. The bomber spun out of control and exploded.

"Skipper!" Art called from the left waist gunner's position. "Lieutenant Watkins's ship just got it. No chutes."

Ben, concentrating on holding formation through weaving turns, didn't respond. Watkins had been his pinochle partner since they joined the 509th in Florida.

"How're we doing, Brad?" Ben called to his navigator.

"Approaching IP, skipper. Expect turn onto final in less than two minutes."

As they turned onto the bombing heading, Ben looked over the nose. They were headed for the heart of Berlin. "Paying you back for London and Coventry!" he muttered.

The flak intensified. Ben marveled that they could fly through what appeared to be a solid curtain of hot shrapnel. Round Trip was hit twice but sustained no critical damage. Flames and smoke swirled up from the city as Whit peered into his bombsight.

He called, "Bombs away," and Ben and Gordy banked the airplane away from the roiling inferno below. As they formed for the flight home, Sanderson's bomber was hit hard by flak. The airplane rolled left, then right, and dropped into a tailspin. It disappeared into the smoke and flames below.

Ben gasped. "Oh god! There goes Sandy!"

Three more B-17s from the 509th Group were shot down before the formation beat its way back over the North Sea. The remaining bombers straggled back to Parham. All had sustained damage, and many carried badly wounded and dead crewmen. As if joining in the group's mourning for their lost comrades, the weather turned damp and gray. Heavy rain lashed the airfield. The 509th crew sank into a gloomy funk.

Weather forecasters said a wave of cold fronts was moving through from the west. They'd be grounded for another week. There would be time to lick their wounds, repair damaged bombers, and snatch a few moments of relief from the strain of battle. Ben entered Silverman's office.

"Frank, I want to get together with Reggie," he said. "Been too busy since we got back to England. He's a wing commander now, running a Spitfire wing at RAF Wittering. I can phone him. Wittering's near Stamford, about eighty miles from here—easy drive."

"Good idea. I'd like to see that crazy Englishman again," Silverman said.

Reggie was in rare form. He charged Ben and Silverman, gave each a fierce bear hug, and shouted "*Good show*!" greetings.

"So much for the reserved Englishman," Silverman said dryly.

They adjourned to the officers' mess. Ben noted deep fatigue lines in Reggie's face and gray streaks in his hair. But his red mustache was bristly as ever.

"Damn good to see you two blokes!" Reggie said as they sipped pints of bitter. "Ben, captain, eh? You're looking fit. Flying aerial lorries agree with you?"

Ben nodded.

"And you, Frank. Full colonel yet," Reggie said, turning to Silverman. "You look a hell of a lot better than when I last saw you in, umm, when the hell was it? I say, seems like a lifetime ago."

"Early '39," Silverman said. "Lots happened since then."

Silverman launched into a long account of how he had flown a brief tour in B-25s before being assigned to form the 509th. He saw Ben's name on the graduation list from the Sebring B-17 commander's school and grabbed him for the 509th.

"Bloody hell!" Reggie said. "And here we are again, still having a go at the cursed Jerries."

"What about you?" Ben asked. "When did ya make wing commander?"

"Year ago. RAF weenies ran out of qualified blokes, so promoted me. Had a tour on Hawker Hurricanes, but now back on Spitfires. Suits me to a tee. Flying the Mark VIB variant. Sweet machine."

"How about the rest of the old squadron?" Ben asked. "Where's Stitch? Did he follow you here?"

Reggie's face darkened. "Stitch got it over France . . . six months ago. Bloody cock-up! We were on one of those damned Circus ops. Escorting a flock of Blenheim bombers and various other wallowing turd droppers . . . Umm, sorry, no offense meant. Anyway, got bounced by a flock of 109s. Were hard-pressed to protect our slow-moving friends. Stitch tangled with two 109s. Shot both down before you could say, 'Bob's your uncle.'"

He took a long draught of his bitter. "Jerry swarmed all over us. Like the old days in the Battle of Britain, Ben. Anyway, two other 109s bounced Stitch, and that was that. I was busy trying to save my own arse and couldn't give him any help . . . I really miss that silly sod."

They dined in the mess and nursed brandies into the early evening. They covered all the intervening years since they had met in Spain and fought for the losing Republican cause. They parted with handshakes, embraces, and promises to get together soon. Silverman drove a weaving course back to Parham.

The 509th flew multiple missions against the V-1 buzz bomb targets in occupied France as 1943 drew to a close. Lt. Col. Norman Cole, who had replaced Major Patterson as the 509th executive officer, led the raids, several of which survived heavy flak defenses, albeit with losses.

Reggie telephoned the first week in December and invited Ben and Silverman to join him at Calvert Hall for Christmas. But the 509th remained on alert during the holidays, and they couldn't get away.

On Christmas Day, Ben phoned Calvert Hall to wish Reggie and family a merry Christmas. A familiar voice answered. "Calvert Hall, Bates speaking."

"Bates, Ben Findlay calling! Wanted to wish you all 'Happy Christmas'!"

"Ah, Leftenant Findlay. Thank you, sir. Umm, good . . . good of you to ring . . ." Bates had not heard of Ben's promotions, and Ben didn't correct him.

"Is the ole wing commander there?" Ben asked. "How are Lord and Lady Percy, and Elizabeth?"

"Umm, Leftenant Findlay, ah, could you hold the line, sir? Lady Percy would like a word."

He heard a murmur of voices. His heart sank. *What's happened?*

"Hullo, Benjamin . . ." Her voice sounded weak, strained.

"Hello, Lady Percy. I called to wish you all a happy Christmas, and—" he heard a stifled sob. The phone clattered to the floor. More urgent murmuring. "Hello, hello?" Ben repeated.

"Hullo, Leftenant Findlay. Bates here again, sir. M'lady has, ah, has had a sinking spell. Umm, I'm afraid this isn't a good time."

"*Bates*, what's going on?" Ben yelled. "Let me speak to Wing Commander Percy!"

"Ah, sir, umm, you haven't heard then. So sorry . . ." His voice broke. "Ah, the wing commander was, umm, was shot down two days ago, sir. Umm, his squadron mates reported his aeroplane, umm, they thought, umm, may have crashed into the sea. No one saw him parachute. I am so sorry to bring you the news this way, sir. Lord and Lady Percy are very, umm, well, very broken up, as you might imagine."

Ben's stomach churned, his vision blurred. Reggie killed?

"Ah, Bates, ah, I'll call back later. When, when things settle down . . ." Ben dropped the phone.

Two weeks later, he and Silverman attended a memorial service for Reggie in Calvert Hall's chapel. Ben could hardly bear to look at Lord and Lady Percy, crumpled with grief. Elizabeth stared in blank-eyed shock, wounded beyond feeling.

The two Americans returned to Parham in silence, Ben immobile, devoid of feeling.

Chapter 73

THE AIR WAR OVER GERMANY, 1944

The pace of the air war against Germany slackened early in the new year, partially due to bad weather, but also because the command had lost over three hundred bombers and crews in the waning days of 1943, and was ordered to stand down. American air forces in Europe were reorganized in February. Lt. Gen. Jimmy Doolittle, named commander of the reconstituted Eighth Air Force, reported for duty at headquarters, RAF High Wycombe air station.

The heavy losses suffered by the B-17 and B-24 bomber groups raised new questions about the validity of daylight bombing raids against Germany. But after a full review, USAAF commanders decided to press forward with accelerated daylight missions as long-range P-51 fighters began to arrive. The Eighth Air Force resumed full operations in March, and the 509th averaged two missions a week. The drive to destroy Germany's fighter force and smash its industrial base entered its final phase.

Ben functioned like a zombie, unable to push Reggie's death from his mind. A three-day leave in London with Gordy didn't help. The lovely old city was dark, drab, and somber. The forced levity in the music halls, the haggard prostitutes roaming the streets, and the spiritless feeling of the pubs quickly wore thin. Ben and Gordy returned to the base early.

Ben and Silverman nursed beers at the officers' club bar. "Frank, what's happening? Now we've been put under General Eisenhower's overall command? Don't they think Doolittle and the Eighth can manage the mission?"

"Scuttlebutt says final preparations are under way for the cross-Channel invasion of France," Silverman said. "Eisenhower's been put in command of the whole shooting match. We're part of that."

He stared at Ben over the rim of his beer glass. "Look, American and British armies have scored big victories in North Africa, took Sicily, and are slugging their way up the Italian boot. Channel invasion's next. So pressure's on us to knock out the Luftwaffe, cut the rail and canal systems, and continue to hit Germany's oil and heavy industries. That's a huge undertaking, but it's all needed to pave the way for the invasion."

What neither Silverman nor Ben knew was that Allied commanders had decided to offer Eighth Air Force bombing missions as bait to draw the Luftwaffe into aerial battles of attrition. They reasoned that losses sustained in these aerial slugging matches would break the Luftwaffe's back and ensure Allied air superiority over the landing beaches selected for the cross-Channel invasion. Massive losses of Eighth Air Force aircraft and crews were reckoned as part of the price that had to be paid.

The painted bombs marched across Round Trip's nose. Ben's crew flew several relatively easy missions, but others degenerated into hellish flights through ferocious fighter attacks and intense flak. So far the Round Trip crew had escaped without serious wounds.

Their luck ran out on a mission to Dortmund. German flak gunners zeroed in on the 509th. An 88 mm shell burst off the right side of Round Trip's aft fuselage, slamming the aircraft into a vicious roll to the left. Hot shrapnel punched through the thin fuselage skin. A large piece sliced through Sgt. John Miller's neck as he hunkered below his right waist gunner's position. He crumpled to the deck. Blood spurted from his severed carotid artery and immediately froze on the bulkhead and deck.

"Left waist to pilot!" Stanley screamed into the intercom. "Miller's been hit bad. Bleeding from a neck wound! Need help!"

"I'll go," Weisman called from the radio room. He crawled back to the aft fuselage and gagged when he saw frozen blood icicles hanging from every surface. Stanley knelt over Miller, desperately trying to staunch the flow of blood gushing from his wound. Grabbing a first aid kit, Weisman ripped out a large compress bandage and pushed it against Miller's neck. The stricken gunner's body twitched three times as he died.

Back at Parham, his shaken crewmates watched grim-faced as Miller's body was lifted out of the fuselage and placed in a base ambulance. Stanley sobbed. He and Miller had been bunkmates as well as gunner mates, and had become as close as brothers.

Ben gathered the crew after the ambulance left. "We're all going to miss Johnny. Art, he was a damn fine gunner. You ought to know, fighting back-to-back with him at those waist guns. Uh, Colonel Silverman told me after this morning's briefing they'd reviewed the records, and were crediting him with shooting down that fighter over Hamburg. Wish I'd had time to tell him before takeoff."

He paused. "Now . . . we close ranks. Get on with our missions, and help get this job done."

Silverman ordered their B-17 taken off the active roster until the aft fuselage could be cleaned up and repaired. The maintenance crew also took the opportunity to replace the number four engine, which had been burning excessive amounts of oil. Following

Miller's funeral, Ben arranged four-day passes for the Round Trip crew. All headed for London except Stanley, who moped around the base.

Ben sought out Major Cole and asked for a replacement for Miller.

"Have just the man for you," Cole said, riffling through the personnel files. "Sgt. Lawson, Andrew H. Hails from Ohio. Was a waist gunner on Lieutenant Porter's B-17—uh, Buxom Baby, I think they named it. Lawson was grounded with a head cold when Porter took Buxom Baby to Heidelberg. They didn't make it back. Uh, let me see. Yeah, Lawson has five more missions to fly. Should fit it with your crew just fine."

Lawson knew most of the enlisted members of Round Trip's crew, and was readily accepted. He gained their complete respect by knocking down an Fw 190 on their next mission to strike the synthetic oil-producing facility at Leuna, Germany. All Eighth Air Force groups participating in this raid suffered heavy losses, as they did on subsequent strikes. The number of unoccupied bunks following each mission told the story.

As they tumbled exhausted out of Round Trip one afternoon, Weisman pointed to the nose. "Count 'em, fellas. Carter's gonna paint bomb twenty-three up there today. Two more and we get our tickets punched. Home we go! Round Trip, we love ya, baby!"

The crew was especially tense on mission twenty-four. They were going back to Hamburg and were not happy. But USAAF operational planners again launched multiple strikes against Germany, hoping to stretch the Luftwaffe's fighter defenses to their limits. The 509th got to Hamburg with only two losses, rained bombs on the burned-out remains of the city, and beat a retreat to the safety of England. Round Trip's crew crowded around the nose and cheered as Carter painted the twenty-fourth bomb next to Peaches.

A soggy, slow-moving cold front crept across England, forcing a halt to all operations. One dreary afternoon, Ben wandered into Silverman's office. "Got a minute, Frank?" he asked.

Silverman gestured to a chair. "What's on your mind, Ben?"

Ben cleared his throat. "Ah, Frank, I've been talking with some of the other pilots. An', uh, I also hear what some of our crews are saying. We hit a lot of high-priority military targets on earlier missions. But now we seem to be bombing targets—ah, railroad yards, small factories, and such—that're in city centers. Frank, we gotta be killing a lot of civilians, probably women and children an' old folks. Last week we smashed the hell outta what was left Hamburg, an' it musta been mainly civilians we were hitting. There didn't seem to be any military targets left."

Silverman started to comment, but Ben pressed on.

"Seems to me that the big city raids we've been flying, Berlin especially, are aimed at the German people. An', uh, that's botherin' me. I know RAF Bomber Command's been on a city-busting binge from the beginning, but I thought our mission was to hit military targets."

Silverman raised both hands, cutting off Ben's rambling. "I know what you're saying, Ben. I don't like what we're being asked to do any more than you do. There's a lot of dissension among our top commanders about our mission objectives as we get ready for the cross-Channel invasion. And you're right, the RAF is playing a role in this. The Brits want to destroy German morale and Germany itself, for that matter. Our commanders are discussing what the Eighth's priorities ought to be—aircraft manufacturing, Germany's oil production industry, the rail and canal transportation systems, or, I'm sorry to say, the German people. There're some in the USAAF high command who think we can shorten the war by destroying civilian morale. I, uh, must say I have problems with that.

"But Ben, we knew when we got into this business that we'd be killing a lot of people in the process. That's war. Can't be helped—"

"Yeah, I know that," Ben cut in. "But dammit, Frank, there's a big difference between killing people as part of, whadda ya call it, collateral damage, and purposely targeting people. When I left the RAF, I wanted to get into bombers to pay back Germany for what it did in Spain and especially to England. Now I'm not so sure this is how I want to do it."

He added quietly, "An', an', I think a lot of our pilots and crews are beginning to feel the same way."

Silverman studied Ben in silence, then said, "I hear you, Ben. Are you telling me you want to quit?"

Ben waved his hands angrily. "*No*! I came here to do a job I thought was worth doin'. I still feel that way. But I have some misgivings about how we're doin' it."

"Okay, Ben. We have to leave it at that for now. We have a couple of big missions coming up, and your crew has one more to fly before going home. Let's talk about this another time."

The Round Trip crew was alerted for another strike against the ball bearing plants at Schweinfurt. The Eighth Air Force had suffered horrendous losses trying to destroy what mission planners thought was the Achilles' heel of Germany's aircraft manufacturing industry. Ben would lead the group on Round Trip's twenty-fifth and last mission.

He stared at the briefing map. "Bitch of a trip for our last mission, but gotta keep faith in Round Trip," he muttered to Gordy.

The mission to Schweinfurt was one of those on which everything seemed to go right from the very start. They took off on time, made their rendezvous with several other B-17 groups, and headed for the target. They encountered minimal fighter attacks on the way in.

"Where's the Luftwaffe today?" he yelled to Gordy.

"Dunno. Damn glad they decided to take the day off," Gordy grinned back.

But the flak made up the difference. Even though Schweinfurt had been pummeled by repeated raids, the antiaircraft sites guarding the factories had been repaired. They blasted a curtain of exploding shells into the path of the B-17 formations. The 509th was the second group approaching the target. Ben led the 509th on a weaving path to the IP turn. Two of the group's B-17s were knocked down on the way in, and one on the way out. Round Trip took another beating from flak shrapnel but plowed on.

Once they reached the Channel, the intercom erupted with hoots and cheers. To hell with intercom discipline! They had survived the big two-five and were going home.

Back at Parham, Ben radioed the group that he'd be the last to land. When all the other bombers had rolled off the runway, he turned to Gordy. "Let's give 'em a buzz job."

"Right! A weed cutter!"

Ben told the crew to hang on and rolled Round Trip onto final approach. He asked the tower for a low-level flyby. With the controller's okay, Ben leveled Round Trip at less than fifty feet above the runway, and Gordy advanced the throttles. As they flashed past the tower, the crew waved and yelled. Archie gave a parting single-digit salute from the tail gunner's station.

Ben pulled the B-17 into a swooping-and-climbing turn, rolled out at pattern altitude, and brought Round Trip in for a smooth landing. At the remote parking pad, the crew tumbled out of the bomber, hopped, danced, and kissed the tarmac. They cheered as Sergeant Carter painted the twenty-fifth bomb next to Peaches. A jeep slid to a stop in front of the nose.

"Captain Findlay?" the sergeant driver called out. "Colonel wants to see you ASAP, sir!"

Ben told the crew he'd see them at the postmission briefing and hopped into the jeep. Silverman wore his stone face when Ben entered his office. Expecting a chewing out for the low-level pass, Ben decided to report formally.

Silverman waved off his salute and pointed to a chair. "Ben. I've got some tough news."

Ben stared impassively. *What now?*

"Ben, there's no way to do this but give it to you straight," Silverman said gravely. "Right after you took off, we got a message from High Wycombe. Doolittle has raised the tour requirement to thirty missions. You and your crew have to do five more."

Ben choked back a string of expletives, blinking rapidly.

"Ah, okay, Frank, I, ah . . . ," he croaked. "No! Goddamnit! It's not okay. This is a real kick in the ass! Know it isn't your fault, ah, sorry, umm. But Frank, we kept our end of the bargain! And did a damn fine job of it too!" Remembering he was talking to his commanding officer, Ben started to apologize.

Silverman waved him off. "Up to me to apologize, Ben. I'm sorry we couldn't give you any advance notice, but you'd already taken off. Had to wait until you got back."

Silverman continued, anticipating Ben's question. "Why now, you may ask? Well, dammit, you know we've suffered heavy losses. And Doolittle can't get replacement crews quickly enough. With the big show coming up, we have to put out maximum effort. We can only do that by extending the mission requirements and keeping our experienced crews."

Ben grunted.

"This is going to be tough for your crew," Silverman said. "But you can tell 'em Doolittle is the same fella who brought in the long range P-51s that could stay with us all the way in and back. That's saved a lot of crews. Ah, want me to help break the news to your boys?"

"No! Umm, thanks, Frank. That's my job. Damn! They're probably celebrating at debriefing. I gotta give 'em the news."

Ben rose to leave. Silverman stepped around his desk.

"Two more things, quickly," he said, handing Ben a set of oak leaf insignia to pin on his uniform. "Congratulations, Major, you've really earned this promotion."

Ben choked and muttered thanks.

"With the promotion comes a new job offer. Norm Cole's been promoted. Been given command of a new B-17 group. I'll need an executive officer. I want you to take the job."

"Don't wanna sound ungrateful, Frank, for both of these. But I really gotta get to my crew before they start celebrating too much," Ben said. "Ah, about the new job . . . yes, of course, I'll take it. But if my crew has five more missions to fly, I'm gonna fly with 'em."

"No problem, Ben. Norm doesn't leave for three more weeks. Should be plenty of time to finish the last five with your crew."

Ben found his grinning crew waving their arms in the debriefing hut. He called them outside.

"Fellas . . . ," he faltered. "Look, there's no way to give it to you but straight, like I got it from Colonel Silverman. Doolittle has extended the tour cycle to thirty missions."

"Sonofabitch!" Gordy yelled. "How can they do this?"

"Easy, Gordy. Doolittle signs the order. and that's it. It didn't just come from him. He takes orders too. Won't give you all the bullshit about heavy losses and replacement problems. But there are real reasons for the extension."

Weisman lead the crew protest, kicking the dirt and shouting obscenities. Others joined in. Only Archie took the news passively. "Heard this good ole boy say sometime ago, only way not to go nuts in this crazy business is assume you're already dead," he mumbled. "Guess that's the way ah feel."

Ben let the others vent for another ten minutes. "Okay, okay! You earned the right to be highly pissed-off and disappointed," he snapped. "But that ends it. We have five more missions to fly, and by God, we're gonna fly 'em the best way we can. The only hope we have of surviving is to do the job right. Nobody slacks off! Nobody gives a half-assed effort! Understand?"

The crew nodded sullenly.

"Now how about some three-day passes? Give you a chance to relax, get used to the idea."

"Ben, far as Ah'm concerned, we need to climb back into Round Trip and fly those goddamn missions as quick as we can," Whit said quietly. "Let's get it over with and get outta here before Doolittle and company tack on any more."

"I'm with Whit," Gordy said. "Let's fly!"

Ben looked carefully at each of the nine men. All nodded.

Chapter 74

THE LAST HURRAH

Ben told Silverman of the crew's desire to complete their last five missions as quickly as possible. Silverman moved Round Trip to the top of the operational roster. Their next two missions involved carpet-bombing attacks on railroad marshaling yards and bridges in southern Belgium and the Pas-de-Calais region of France.

"Is this why Doolitle kept us here, ta bomb railroad tracks?" Weisman grumbled as the crew watched Sergeant Carter paint bomb number twenty-seven on Round Trip's nose. "Don't seem like high-priority targets to me."

"Knock it off, Weisman," Ben snapped. "Every target is high priority. We're helping with preparations for the invasion. Keep your focus on doin' your job."

"Yes, sir, . . . Major."

As part of the mounting pressure on the German aircraft industry, the 509th joined with several other B-17 groups on back-to-back attacks against factories near Bernburg and Oschersleben. Gordy was quiet and withdrawn, almost sullen. He performed his copiloting duties with his usual precision but didn't join in any of the crew banter, forced though it was. He showed little interest in watching Sergeant Carter paint bomb twenty-nine next to Peaches.

In the officers' club bar that night, Ben asked him, "What's up?"

Gordy stared at him with bloodshot eyes. "I feel like shit, Ben."

Ben touched his forehead. "Christ, Gordy! You're burning up. Better get to sick call. You've got one helluva fever!"

That evening, the air doc ordered Gordy to bed with a serious sinus infection. Two days later, Silverman called Ben to his office. Ben could see he was disturbed.

"Ben, we have a tough mission tomorrow, and I need you to lead it. I know this'll be your thirtieth mission. This one really earns your crew their tickets back home. Wish I could offer you a milk run, but I can't. Got a tough one to throw at you."

Ben waited.

"I want to lead it, but Doc says I have an infected eardrum. No flying until it's healed," Silverman said. "And Norm's airplane is a mess. Half his crew is still in the hospital, and he's a little beat-up himself." Cole had led an attack on Dortmund four days prior, and they had been badly mauled.

"Okay," Ben said, locking eyes with Silverman. "What's the target?"

"Regensburg," Silverman replied. He averted his eyes. "The Messerschmitt airplane assembly factory, to be precise. Look, Ben, if I—"

"I said okay, Frank," Ben interrupted. "Let's leave it at that. What're the details?"

"Yeah, well, you'll lead the 509th to a rendezvous with twelve other B-17 groups. We're sending four-hundred-plus airplanes on this one, including P-51 cover. There'll be four other mass formations in the air at the same time, some making feints to the north and some heading for central Germany. The plan is to again force the Luftwaffe to split its fighter forces. They won't know which attack is the main one, so they'll have to stretch their defenses. It should take some pressure off you."

"Maybe," Ben grunted. "Last time we went south, we found the Luftwaffe had a helluva lot more 109s and 190s than our intelligence fellas been telling us."

"Maj. George Anderson, executive officer of the 328th Heavy Bomber Group, will lead the formation," Silverman said. "You'll be in second position, with the remaining groups spread out behind. Briefing's at 0530 hours. Keep the target to yourself until then."

Ben nodded. "Okay, I better go and make sure Round Trip is ready."

As he saluted and turned to leave, Silverman said, "Ah, Ben, I want you and your crew seated in the front row tomorrow morning."

"Yessir." *Front row. First lambs to the slaughter?*

"How's your crew doing? Excited about finally going home?"

"Yeah, I guess so, Frank. But they ain't gonna believe it till they see it. All except Gordy, my copilot. Air doc grounded him with a sinus infection. They're sending me a new kid from the copilot reserve pool for this mission. Hope I get someone who can find his ass with either hand."

"Good luck, Ben. Oh, by the way, we'll assign Captain Baker, the group's lead navigator, to your crew for this mission. Need to be sure this one goes off without a hitch."

Ben leveled Silverman with a steady stare. "Don't want to do that, Frank. Lieutenant Jones has been Round Trip's navigator from the very beginning. He's got us there and back twenty-nine times, and I want him leading us again on this final mission."

Silverman pouched his lips and frowned. "You've got a close-knit crew, Ben. If Jones is that important to you, I don't want to do anything to upset your applecart. You sure Jones can do it?"

"Positive, Frank. And I want Jonesy to go home with the rest of Round Trip's crew."

Before the briefing, Ben told his crew they'd been given the honor seats in the front row. They shot him sullen frowns. They knew what the "honor" meant. Ben introduced their substitute copilot, Second Lt. Billy Joe Starkey. The crew eyed him warily.

"Starkey, as soon as the briefing is over, you hightail it out to the airplane and give it a thorough walk-around inspection," Ben said. "This is our last mission, and I don't want anything overlooked. No screwups. Understand?"

Starkey nodded.

The briefing was succinct. A groan rolled through the assembled crews when they saw the target was the airplane plant at Regensburg.

"One of the best-defended targets in Germany," one pilot grumbled. "And we have to fly clear across Germany to get to the damn place."

Silverman silenced the bitching with a wave of his hand. He announced Ben would lead the group on this mission. Colonel Cole presented the mission details: time for manning the airplanes, takeoff time, rendezvous point, headings, altitudes, and the myriad details of the mission plan.

Ben gathered his crew in front of Round Trip. He asked Starkey if he found everything okay during the walk-around inspection.

"Ah, no, sir. Ah actually didn't need to do one. Sergeant Carter said he already done it."

Ben wheeled on him and snarled, "Listen, Lieutenant! I gave you an order. I told *you* to do a thorough walk-around. That did not mean wandering out here and taking somebody's word that one had been done! Now you get your ass moving and give that airplane a *thorough* inspection. You've got fifteen minutes. Do you understand, Lieutenant?"

Starkey slunk off to comply.

Ben motioned the crew closer. He gave them a pep talk, trying to rally their spirits. It fell flat. They knew they had drawn a bitch of a mission for their last sortie over Germany.

After takeoff, Ben shepherded twenty-one heavily loaded B-17s from the 509th Group to their rendezvous with twelve other USAAF groups. They formed a four-hundred-aircraft bomber force. Four groups of P-51 fighters provided escort. Ben looked around at his group's formation and smiled. They hadn't been able to put up this many in a long time. The 509th was lookin' pretty good.

Ben positioned the 509th behind and slightly below Major Anderson's high group, the 328th. At ten thousand feet, Ben ordered the crew on oxygen. The following groups continued in loose formation, ready to close ranks as soon as they reached Germany or spotted the first enemy fighter.

Ben's crew shifted into their accustomed mission alertness, eager to finish their combat tour. Ben was troubled because the Regensburg mission was long and dangerous. He didn't relish bombing runs to the limits of the maximum range of their escort fighters. And Ben was even more uneasy with his replacement copilot. Starkey had performed the routine tasks of engine start and had assisted in the takeoff. But Ben grimaced as he glanced at Starkey, who sat staring vacantly through the windshield, apparently oblivious to what lay ahead. *Helluva time to be saddled with this dummy in the right seat. Not sure I can depend on him for much when things get hot.*

Ben ordered his bombers into close formation with the 328th as they approached German airspace. He knew the Luftwaffe still had some of its best veteran fighter pilots, who would rise to meet them en route to Regensburg. And the final approach to the airplane factory was going to be a bitch. It wasn't known as flak alley for nothing.

Anderson's high group was not holding formation. They'd had one of those days when everything that could go wrong, did. A snag at the bomb depot delayed delivery of their payloads, which made them miss the briefed takeoff time. Two B-17s had engine trouble. One caught fire at engine start. When Anderson got the group moving to the runway, a B-17 taxied off the edge of the tarmac and got mired in the mud. Anderson finally led the remaining sixteen bombers into the air. The 328th pilots appeared distracted by their shaky start. They couldn't hold even a loose formation. Since the 328th was lead group, their floundering sent disorienting ripples through the entire attack fleet.

Ben shook his head in disgust as he jockeyed the four throttles on his B-17, trying to maintain position with the 328th group's trailing bombers.

"Come on, fellas!" he shouted. "Settle down. I can't be horsing this thing around all the way to Regensburg."

Starkey sat silently in the right seat. He obviously didn't understand what was going on and had no idea what had to be done.

"Starkey! Are you formation-trained?" Ben shouted through his oxygen mask. He didn't want to use the intercom and worry the rest of the crew. "Can ya give me a hand here?"

"No, sir!" Starkey shouted. "We didn't get to close formation flyin' before they shipped me over here."

Ben grimaced. *Shit! Hafta hand-fly this thing all the way by myself. My arms already feel like they're gonna fall off!*

No Luftwaffe fighters rose to challenge them until they crossed the German frontier. Ben knew they would arrive soon. Several crack squadrons flying Me 109s and Fw 190 fighters were based around Frankfurt and Nurnberg. He was not surprised by the radio warning, "Fighters . . . ten o'clock high . . . estimate twenty . . . P-51s engaging!"

This seemed to further rattle the 328th Group pilots. Their attempts to tighten their formations were ragged. Ben fought to stay out of the swirling prop wash from the airplanes ahead.

Several German fighters penetrated the P-51 escort screen and attacked the 328th bombers. The enemy fighters slow-rolled and slashed inverted through the bomber formation, firing long bursts from cannons and machine guns. All hell erupted.

Gunners in the lead bombers fired wildly. They were not effective, having never achieved concentrated fields of fire. Two bombers were hit hard; one pitched up and wheeled into a death spiral. The other faltered as both left engines belched fire.

Ben's headphones crackled. "Fighters two o'clock high . . . coming in hot . . . Watch it, starboard gunners! They're goin' for the lead group!"

Starkey shook in the seat next to Ben. "Sweet Jesus!" he yelled over the intercom. "Why aren't the 51s holdin' 'em off?"

"Starkey, get off the intercom!" Ben yelled. *Can't have this sad sonofabitch rattling the rest of the crew!*

The German pilots pressed their attacks. Several fighters spun smoking toward the ground. Ben couldn't tell whose. A B-17 fell out of formation above them, trailing a streamer of smoke and flame. Another drifted out of the formation and started a slow descent. It was attacked by two Fw 190s.

"Who said the Luftwaffe was done for?" Ben hissed through gritted teeth. "They're puttin' up a helluva fight!"

The attacks lessened. The German fighter squadrons broke off and turned back to their bases. The B-17s droned on, but the 328th lead group could not close the gaps left by the four lost bombers. Before they regained their formation, two more bombers drifted out of position. One with two engines feathered turned back. A second followed, trailing black smoke.

Ben watched grim-faced. "Good luck, fellas," he muttered. "Hope ya get past the fighters. Remember Switzerland's just over there to the southwest."

Anderson, now down to ten bombers, could be heard on the radio ordering his pilots to "Close the gaps! Close the goddamn gaps! Tighten the formation, or we're all dead!"

Ben keyed the intercom and called his tail gunner. "Archie, how are the trailing groups doin'?" he asked.

"Hanging in there, skipper!" Archie responded. "They're closing up real tight. How's the lead group doin'?"

"Not so good. They're down to ten bombers, and a couple of them look shaky."

The rest of the crew listened intently.

Paddy in the ball turret asked, "Skipper, if the lead group falls apart, where's that leave us?"

Ben keyed the intercom again to reassure them. "Okay, crew, it looks like what's left of the 328th is getting organized," he said. "Let's settle down. Concentrate on what we have to do. We're closing on Regensburg, so watch for more fighters before we get to the flak nests."

New waves of Luftwaffe fighters flashed into view. The escorting P-51s ripped into them and shot down several. But the German pilots pressed their attacks, and some broke through the protective screen. Again, they went after the 328th lead group. Gunners in the following groups got quick snap shots as the fighters wheeled past. They sent two attackers smoking toward the ground.

But two more 328th bombers were hit. A wing crumpled on one B-17, and it tumbled out of control. A second slid out of the remaining formation. Anderson's group was reduced to an eight-ship flight. He struggled to marshal the remaining bombers into a viable formation. The German fighters broke off and fled. The P-51 escort, short on fuel, turned back.

"Means we're approachin' flak alley," Ben muttered grimly.

Whit keyed the intercom from his bombardier station in the glass nose of Ben's B-17. "Skipper, we're approaching the IP. Hope Anderson is able to lead us in the turn."

"Right, Whit," Ben radioed back. "Keep an eye on Anderson's plane. We're about to enter flak alley."

Shells exploded ahead of them. Ben tensed as they approached the lines of ugly black clouds. "Starkey, stay alert!" he yelled. *Why the hell am I yelling at him? Nothing he can do but sit there and watch this stuff explode around us.*

Flak shells burst on both sides of Ben's bomber. Smoke and cordite fumes clouded the cockpit. The airplane bucked and heaved, and red-hot shrapnel slammed into the fuselage and wings. A piece struck the three-inch-thick windshield in front of Starkey, crazing it into a spiderweb of cracks.

"Sweet Jesus! Sweet Jesus! Save ma miserable ass!" Starkey screamed, flailing his arms.

"Starkey! Shut up!" Ben yelled as he wrestled the control column. "Get on those throttles. Gimme more power!"

"Sweet Jesus!" Starkey moaned, rocking back in forth in his seat.

Ben swung his right arm and hit him on the side of the head. "Dammit! Pull yourself together! Get on those throttles!"

Multiple flashes ahead nearly blinded him. *Christ! Anderson's bought it!*

Anderson's B-17 disintegrated. Flaming pieces streamed back, hitting two B-17s. Both spun out of control. The 328th Group scattered, and Ben's group was in the lead.

"Whit!" Ben yelled into the intercom. "Can we still make the IP turn?"

"Yeah, skipper," Whitney croaked. "Sorry . . . nose is shattered . . . an', an' I caught some shrapnel. Uh, ah, we're still on course. Turn in one minute."

Ben switched to the open channel on the radio, "All bombers, all bombers. This is Findlay leading 509th Group. Anderson's group's gone. I'm now lead. Less than a minute to IP. Prepare to turn on us."

Starkey whimpered, occasionally yelling, "Sweet Jesus!"

Ben hit him again. "Shape up, you sorry bastard!" he yelled. "Help me with this turn!"

The formation wheeled after the 509th, and they swung onto the final run to the target.

"Target dead ahead, skipper!" Whitney yelled over the intercom. "Two minutes to drop."

"Right, Whit," Ben yelled back. "Your airplane."

Ben turned control over to Whitney, who kept the bomber straight and level on the final track to the target. The flak bursts intensified, and the explosions were blinding. Shrapnel hammered the bomber like giant hail.

Ben shifted back in his seat. Hands off the controls, he gasped for breath. Starkey writhed and mumbled next to him. Ben blinked rapidly. *Less than two minutes, and we get the hell outta here!*

"Okay, skipper," Whitney yelled over the intercom. "Steady, steady . . . Bombs away! She's all yours!"

Ben grabbed the wheel and banked into a hard right turn. "Archie!" he radioed to his tail gunner. "How's it look? Is everyone following?"

"I think so, skipper! Two Forts goin' down, but we hit the factory pretty good!"

The German antiaircraft gunners pressed their attack. Flak explosions bracketed their airplane. Hot shrapnel hammered Round Trip; white-hot fragments sizzled and snapped into the flight deck and aft fuselage. Smoke and cordite fumes swirled through the bomber.

"Sweet Jesus! We're gonna die!" Starkey screamed.

Ben wheeled and swung at him. Starkey ducked. As Ben turned back to the controls, his eyes swept the wide horizon ahead. He smiled. "Can see a helluva lot farther up here than from that ole windmill platform back home," he muttered.

A giant fist smashed into Round Trip's nose. A brilliant flash blinded Ben. His mind didn't have time to register the massive explosion that consumed his airplane.

Epilogue

A week later at Parham, Silverman shoved aside the report listing Ben and his crew as "missing in action, presumed dead." He picked up the citation awarding Ben the army's Distinguished Service Cross, and signed his endorsement with a shaking hand.

"Schaffer!" he snapped at his sergeant clerk. "Follow me."

He strode to the Quonset hut barracks. His grim-faced sergeant trailed two steps behind. They stopped at Ben's door, then entered.

"Schaffer, I want all this packed up carefully! And get it on the next logistics flight back to the States," he ordered. "I'll go through his letters and things. Need to make sure there's nothing here that shouldn't go home."

Silverman opened Ben's flimsy wooden locker and found several letters. One was addressed to Ben's mother. The second was to his brother, Joe. The third, addressed to Brice, would have to be forwarded to Al Simpson. The fourth was addressed to Wing Commander Reginald M. Percy, and the fifth to Col. Frank Silverman.

Silverman choked and smashed his fist into the locker door, splintering it. Schaffer jumped and stood uncertainly, eyeing Silverman.

"Get this done ASAP, Schaffer," Silverman rasped, stumbling to the door. "I've got letters to mail."

The End

Edwards Brothers Malloy
Thorofare, NJ USA
November 16, 2012